DIRTY DYLAN

THE OUTLAW CHESS SERIES

HARLEY DIAMOND

Published by House of Books Press

www.harleydiamond.com

Edited by Karen Sanders Editing

https://www.karensandersediting.com/

PA Services by Arcane and Reverie

contact@arcaneandreverie.com

Proofreading Services by Proofreading by Mich

https://www.instagram.com/proofreadingbymichx/

PR Services by Peachy Keen Author Services

https://www.peachykeenauthorservices.com/

Cover Design by Vicious Desires Design

https://www.instagram.com/viciousdesires/

Cover Model is Andrew Biernat via Wander Aguiar Photography

https://www.instagram.com/andrew.biernat/

http://wanderaguiar.com/

Created with Vellum

Blurb

WHATEVER OUR SOULS ARE MADE OF

I'm the gregarious biker with the shiny exterior.
The girl who craves being center of attention.
Who never wants to be forgotten.
Who's perfectly lonely.
He's the Duster introvert
whose name no one remembers.
The brother who craves
the darkness of the shadows.
Who always wants to be forgotten.
Who's perfectly lonely.
Forced proximity. I found the hidden switch that turned this Irish mobster on.
But an arranged marriage means
he can't ever be mine.
Seems we're not opposites after all.
Seems we're the same difference.
And our souls?
His and mine are the same.

Playlist

Wish You Were Here by Pink Floyd

Trigger Warning

This book contains mature content, violence, swearing, and other potentially triggering situations that some readers may find offensive.

Please do not read this story if you are uncomfortable with any of the above.

Thank you.

Author's Note

DYLAN'S story starts from where RAZR's ends (EXCLUDING the epilogue).

DIRTY DYLAN is NOT standalone.
DIRTY DYLAN is BOOK 4 of a SERIES, which contains an ONGOING STORYLINE that CONCLUDES in BOOK 6, DIRTY PADRAIG.

These books contain MULTIPLE POVs from characters across the entire series.

Due to the nature of the CONTINUING STORYLINE, these books MUST be
READ IN ORDER.

ACE
DIRTY CILLIAN
RAZR
DIRTY DYLAN
DIRTY EOIN
DIRTY PADRAIG

CHAPTER ONE

JESSIE

The Hudson Dusters' HQ, Manhattan, New York

BLAH. BLAH. BLAH.

I roll my eyes as I silently mouth the words behind Eoin O'Connell's back. Have I got a death wish? No siree. Only Dylan and Paddy saw me. Cill's face is buried in his phone. I'd yawn exaggeratedly too, but that might be taking things too far. They know I'm only messing, but he's still their big brother.

The future Da Duster.

He who must be obeyed. And listened to, obviously, even if somewhat reluctantly at times. At least by me.

Is blood thicker than water? Not always. At least not in this life. I've got an older brother of my own, and as much as I love Tadgh, I'd have been tempted to kneecap him right about now.

I switched off from the conversation a full ten minutes ago. If you can call it that. See, to me, conversing means holding a meaningful discussion where one or more other receptive parties are allowed to participate.

Eoin talks rather than listens. He doesn't like to be interrupted either. The Irishman loves the sound of his own voice.

If he were chocolate, he'd eat himself.

I'm not saying he's not making complete sense. He is. He's articulate. Intelligent and then some. But dear Lordy Lou, does he go on. I blame economics. It's when he's allowed to go off on a tangent on matters relating to that particular subject. It's the equivalent of me boring people to death talking about balance sheets. I bet he jerks off in the shower every morning while daydreaming about the laws of supply and demand.

He walks to the end of the room and then turns around and stares straight at me. I immediately switch to my poker face. Is he expecting me to look impressed? I smile and nod, trying to appear just that—anything for a quiet life.

Well, he is my boss, sort of, as he is paying handsomely for the privilege of me undertaking contracted work for The Hudson Dusters here in New York City via my company, Jones and Associates Accountancy. Or JAA for short.

For the record, I'm the *Associates* in that title.

Also, for the record, I'm worth every dime.

Eoin is tall, dark, and looks menacingly handsome in his ten-thousand-dollar business suit. And he wears that autocratic leadership style of his pinned to his lapel like a badge of honor.

He's the eldest son at thirty-seven. The heir to this whole shebang. Rumor has it he's under pressure to find himself a suitable mobster wife. That the stopwatch to his nuptials is now silently counting down whether he likes it or not.

It's never been mentioned aloud, but until recently, he had his sights set firmly on my business partner, Jaine Jones.

Unfortunately for Eoin, Jaine recently got married. Fortunately for the rest of us, she kept her own name.

Not that Jaine being wed is any deterrent for him. Eoin won't simply take no for an answer. That word doesn't exist in his vocabulary.

Jaine recently stood him and his parentals up at the 'potential future ma Duster' altar. Why? Because she's not interested in the man, the role, or the title. Brave girl. Not many would dare insult one Duster, let alone three, including the matriarch and patriarch.

No longer under the scrutiny of the eldest brother, I turn my attention to the youngest.

Padraig O'Connell.

At twenty-nine, Paddy is deemed the most handsome of the siblings, with his inky black hair and sparkling blue eyes on a face as perfect as the rest of him. Charm oozes out of every pore, as does cheek. He's the life and soul wherever he goes.

Paddy handles the legal side of things for the Dusters. Internally only. He's the sociable sort, so there's always the risk he may share too much confidential information with someone on the outside. Of course, he'd then have to kill them.

Then again, maybe that's intentional on his part. That it's the method in that madness of his. Rumor has it Paddy likes to purge, and he does so by gutting his victims before carving them into visual works of art Hannibal Lecter-style.

Paddy's been entered into an arranged marriage with Sophia Ruocco. Sophia's a high-ranker in the Sicilian mafia, or at least her brother, Luc, is. In our world, theirs is deemed a good match.

Keep your friends close and your enemies closer. You can't get much closer than taking the vows with them then sleeping in the same bed every night.

I switch my attention to Cillian, the second eldest at thirty-five. Cill's handsome, if angular-featured, short-tempered redheads do it for you. There's always something going down in Dusterland that requires his attention hence why he's always got his face in his phone. No rest for the wicked, and he's definitely that.

Cillian works the streets. He and his army of toy soldiers handle the day-to-day, making sure this big old Duster ship runs with military precision at the customer-facing end. An undertaking indeed when your clients represent the upper echelons of New York's high society. Cill's the only brother who's married. His wife, Sarah, is the sister of Paul Delaney. Razr, as he's more affectionately known, is dating my baby sister, Bailey.

Ours is a small world. What can I say?

My attention switches to the last remaining brother.

Dylan O'Connell.

The second youngest at thirty. Same age as me. Delectable Dylan hides his extreme male hotness under a dodgy haircut, professor-style grey suit, and old man spectacles. He's weird in a nerdy kind of way. He's also eye candy.

Totally. Fucking. Delicious

In fact, I'd give anything to be able to unwrap that outer layer of his and see what tasty delights lay hidden behind that dowdy exterior. It's my guess it would be the equivalent of revealing a Willy Wonka golden ticket.

I watch as his cheeks turn red. He's realized I'm looking at him. I then watch as he pushes his prim and proper glasses further up his nose.

Fuck prim. Fuck proper. Fuck me.

I wish.

He shifts in his seat, his expression one of discomfort, likely because of my blatant ogling. Lifting his glass, he takes a sip of water, and I watch as his tongue flicks out to lick a stray droplet from his bottom lip. My gaze is automatically drawn to their now glistening fullness.

Tongue. Teeth. Lips.

I wonder what he can do with all three of them. Separately. Together. I then watch as his fingers tighten around his Mont Blanc pen like his very life depends on it.

"Jessie!"

"Eoin, I heard you the first time." Going by his irritated tone, he's been trying to catch my attention for some time.

I told a white lie. I didn't hear him. Neither the first time nor the second.

I give myself a mental slap to remove the infatuated expression I'm no doubt still wearing. I'm sure Eoin deliberately spoiled my daydream just when it was getting to the good part. It's like he could read my mind. Conscious I'm sucking on the end of my pen like a mini dick, I pull it from my mouth with a loud pop and smirk at him. He responds with one of his own.

Yup. He knows exactly where my thoughts have just been and who the star was in my very own smut show for one. Big brother has just witnessed me lusting over little brother.

I wipe my chin. I'm pretty sure I haven't been drooling, but it's better to be safe than sorry. I then shift as discretely as I can in my chair in an attempt to stop my center from throbbing.

Fuck, I need to get laid. And soon.

See, my fantasizing over Dylan won't get me anywhere. The reclusive O'Connell is never going to be able to scratch that itch. Dylan apparently has a cliché blonde he's pining over. Who is she? No one knows. Do I want to stand on any invisible toes regardless? Nope. That's something I do know.

If a man is rumored to be attached to any female aside from nuns, ones he's related to, or ones that fall into the category of gay best friends, then that's enough for me. He's strictly off-limits. My whole life, I've been on the receiving end of glares and barbs from angry females when their men have shown an uninvited interest in me, even though I've done nothing to entice their unwelcome attention.

Could I kill the females in question if I wanted to? I guess. But it's too much effort. And way too messy. Who wants blood on their shoes? Or, worse still, other bodily fluids?

I really should have been born into a family whose folks wanted their offspring to live the all-American Dream. I was a head cheerleader, after all, and I dated the quarterback. That's a number one best-selling teen fiction novel right there.

Instead, I was born the daughter of a murderous biker. Go figure. Maybe I was switched at birth.

I glance around the ostentatious, white-walled room with its priceless artwork hanging from the walls, and its marble flooring. Placing my pen on the leather-topped circular table, I lean back in my chair, cross my legs, and straighten the skirt of my dark grey pinstriped suit before placing my hands on the armrests.

"The IRS, Jessie." He's borderline hissy now because I've kept him waiting.

"It stands for the Internal Revenue Service." I just can't help myself. I have boundary-pushing down to a fine art, and I like to hone my craft on old Eoin here as often as possible.

"I know that!"

"Oh. Do you want to know where things currently stand? Is that it?"

"Well, that would be helpful. Before we have to go into our meeting with Da." He's inwardly rolling his eyes at me. I get on his last nerve. I know I do. I stretch that bad boy to full capacity.

Story of my life. I have a lot of them. Stories, that is. Not lives.

I don't get to attend their meetings because I'm a woman. Also, my surname isn't O'Connell.

I smile politely. I don't need notes or a pen. Instead, I store the important stuff in my head. It's safer that way.

"As you know, we started with several businesses that our IRS friends were sniffing around. I'm pleased to advise that's now been reduced to just one. Play. It seems your previous accountant, for reasons known only to themselves, was using the newly established gentleman's club as a vessel for writing off the Dusters' entire petty cash expenditure and then coding it all to various general expenses. Interim accounts have been published. The balances are recorded in black and white. The ink is now dry, making their manipulation extremely difficult."

"General expenses."

"You know, the nominal codes incompetent accountants the world over journal things to in an attempt to hide wrongdoings. These are always the first codes organizations like the IRS look at. There's currently a throughput on Play's ledger of several million dollars. Unfortunately, that figure doesn't correlate with the length of time the business has been trading, nor its turnover."

"Surely we can just declare it as profit and pay the relevant taxes."

I snort at his naivety. "Oh, right. And you think the IRS will be happy with that? 'Sorry, boys. Just reallocate these millions, will you? Then if you pay your taxes, we'll be merrily on our way.' These people are not stupid. Never treat them as such. Trust me, they know they're potentially scratching at the surface of something way more lucrative with Play. They'll be wanting a far larger slice of this big old Duster pie of yours. They'll also be hoping they can slap one of you on the wrists, maybe even all four of you, then send you on a family holiday to Rikers Island for not complying with due diligence. I hear it's lovely there this time of year."

"So, what do we do about it?"

"Well, now we've got it down to one business, we need to review every general expense transaction and recode it to a believable account."

"And we're doing that?"

"Yes, but there's one small problem."

"Which is?"

"Volume. If they decide to investigate, they'll want that information yesterday. They'll pretend to offer, but will then, in fact, insist on sending in their people to help us out. You know, being the kind and considerate organization they are. They call it an audit. Sounds innocent enough, right? Wrong. It's an opportunity for them to dig up every piece of dirt and stick it to you personally."

"We can't have that."

"Nope. We can't. So, we need to buy ourselves some time while I work my magic."

"Legally?"

"Yup."

"Our Paddy?"

"Sorry, no offense 'our Paddy.'" I use air quotes as I smile at him, and he smirks and holds his hands up in mock surrender. I turn my attention back to Eoin. "But no. As far as I'm aware Paddy has zero experience when it comes to dealing with the IRS."

"Jaine?"

I nod. "Help us, Obi-wan Jones. You're our only hope."

CHAPTER TWO

DYLAN

The Hudson Dusters' HQ, Manhattan, New York

I grimace in discomfort. My dick's only just stopped twitching. Jessie O'Brien will be the death of me, she really will. She just can't seem to help herself. Constantly toying with me when we're in meetings together. She strolls in at almost six feet with the face and figure of a goddess. All long blonde hair and beautifully carved features. And all the time Eoin is talking, she stares at me like she wants to eat me up with a spoon while sucking suggestively on the end of her pen. My face heats at the blatant attention. The thought of that mouth of hers on a certain part of my anatomy… well, I dare any red-blooded male not to get a hard-on at that thought.

Is she just playing mind games because she can, or is she genuinely interested? I'll never know because Jessie thinks I'm infatuated with another woman, so she avoids me at all costs. How do I explain there is no cliché blonde without making myself out to be some sort of serial liar in front of Jaine, or without revealing Paddy's dirty secret?

I can't. So, I avoid her too.

As discreetly as possible, I move my erection to a more comfortable resting position. The only positive about that meeting rolling into this one is I don't need to leave my seat. And as soon as my da opens his mouth, my hard-on will disappear.

I zone back into the conversation.

"Is there no one else we can instruct on this, son?" Da directs his question at Eoin. We all watch as he then stands to pull back the ball on the Newton's Cradle before retaking his seat. It swings into life.

Its purpose is to reduce his blood pressure. And it would appear he's stressed right now as he's not receptive to using Jaine for the legal aspects of the potential money laundering investigation we're facing. I'm not sure why, as JAL's sister company, JAA, is already handling the accountancy requirements. The reason behind his reluctance is anyone's guess. It'll be something else that will have gone down the rest of us weren't party to. It'll also undoubtedly be tied to why Eoin gets annoyed and fidgety whenever Jaine's name gets mentioned these days.

"According to Jessie, it would appear not, Da."

"But why can't our Paddy run with it? What was the point in spending good money for him to go to that fancy pants college if we can't put our highly qualified legal guru here to good use?"

He peers at Paddy over the top of his glasses like this is all his fault somehow, while absent-mindedly waving his pointer finger at him. Paddy lets Eoin answer on his behalf.

Wise decision.

"Paddy has enough to do with all the internal goings-on, Da. Plus, he's never had any dealings with the IRS before...."

"Surely there has to be a first time for everything?" Da interjects.

"I don't think now is the time for him to be diving headfirst into unchartered waters to deal with those sharks. Not with the potentially catastrophic consequences if it all goes wrong."

"But Jaine Jones is in California. How can she help when she's currently living on the opposite coast? She also has a husband to care for now and a child. Another wee one on the way."

My curiosity is piqued. Da never makes it his business to know anyone's background unless he has good reason. Now I know something has gone down. How come he knows so much about Jaine? Mind you, Ma did ask for a copy of all the intel we held on her. Are the two related? And why is he telling us something we already know?

Is it an audible reminder to all of us? Or to one person in particular?

"Jaine's a businesswoman, Da. She has several clients in Manhattan she's still hands-on with. I'm sure she can easily add one more to the mix." Eoin is determined to get his way. Da's the same. Peas in a pod, the pair of them. We'll be here all day at this rate.

"And who will she deal with at our end?"

Everyone shifts their attention to Paddy. He's the obvious choice. Lawyer to lawyer. It makes the most sense. He looks hopeful. He'll take any scraps he can get where Jaine's concerned.

Eoin glances at Paddy then turns his attention back to the old man. "She'll have to deal with me, Da."

He's not deliberately trying to burst our Paddy's bubble. He's just trying to ensure he's the one who gets to interact with Jaine personally.

Da frowns down at his empty pad. He's not happy with that response. His blood pressure will have spiked further. And that means heads are now at risk. My gaze shifts from the Newton's

Cradle to the paperweight, then back to my da. If I had to choose, I'd pick the paperweight. I already wear a scar from when one hit its intended target previously. It's still the smaller of the two, though, so surely to God it's easier to avoid.

"Jaine's already handling the accountancy side of things, Da. Surely it would make most business sense for her to deal with the legal aspects of the same matter. Avoid any repetition?" Cillian drags his face from his phone long enough to voice his opinion. He must be feeling brave today. Da glares at him. He reaches towards the paperweight, running his fingers across the smooth glass dome.

Silence fills the space. And not a comfortable one.

"It's not Jaine that's handling the accountancy aspects, Cill. It's Jessie O'Brien." Da's borderline hissing.

Eoin frowns at him but says nothing. It's safer that way. Da's coiled now and ready to chuck. We all remain quiet and wait for him to speak.

Time passes. The only sound is the Newton's Cradle that's potentially going to put one of us in an early grave.

Click. Click. Click.

"Fine. I agree we need to look at the bigger picture, at least for now," he answers eventually, his tone reluctant. "If Jaine Jones is the only workable solution to the IRS problem, then so be it. But on this occasion only. We can't be relying on her moving forward. She already knows too much and has her finger in way too many pies."

"Jaine is totally trustworthy, Da." Paddy raises his head above the parapet to defend his lady love. We're all now in danger of having our heads caved in.

"That woman is currently looking at the inner financial workings of this organization. Now we'll be welcoming her with open arms to analyze the inner workings of the legal side of the business too. She's being allowed to infiltrate and learn too much. She's not an O'Connell, and she never will be." He stares at my eldest brother like that comment is directed solely at him.

Is this to do with Paddy still? Or is it now to do with Eoin?

"Anyway, enough. I don't want to hear any more about it. Eoin, you deal with the biker woman. Instruct her if we have to, but on this matter alone."

"Da, we've already agreed we would have her firm handle our side of the alliance with the MCs and La eMe. The Mexicans have insisted she represent them on the matter, and I think we should do the same. We can't have a repeat of what happened in Nevada. A situation that arose due to all of us taking our eye off the ball combined with a lapse in communication."

"Fine. But no more." Da slams his hand down on the table. His mind is obviously made up. Given the anger in his tone, no one with a sane mind will dare cross him. Right now, I'm not sure even mentioning Jaine's name would be a good idea.

What the hell is going on?

It's my guess only Eoin and Da know that answer.

No one speaks as Da continues to stare at his blank pad. He's got something else on his mind. Going by the way all of us are now glancing at each other, I'm not sure it's anything he's shared in advance with anyone sitting around this table. Maybe that's why he's in such a foul mood. He has at least one unpopular announcement to make. Maybe more.

"Now, I want to touch on two things today, boys."

Here we go. I look at Eoin, and he returns it. His expression confirms he's not aware of what either is. Maybe now he'll appreciate how the rest of us feel most of the time.

"Firstly. Our Cillian…" He waggles his finger in my brother's direction. "…has already provided us with little Caoimhe whom we all love the bones of, and I know he and Sarah are keen to grow their family. With that in mind, your ma and I think it's unreasonable to expect him to go traipsing all over the country looking after the day-to-day as he's always done. More so when we're now dealing with alliances on the west coast. Our Cill's a family man now. He needs to be allowed to enjoy that. Wee ones grow up quickly. Me and your ma know that only too well."

Cillian's jaw almost hits the table. My da's being thoughtful. Has he banged his head or something? I guess there's a first time for everything. I wonder what he's got up his sleeve. I mean, I can understand what he's getting at. Aside from our Cill, the rest of us are typically office or home-based unless Paddy's on wet work.

"So, with that in mind, we've decided to add to the O'Connells stateside. I've been speaking to your Uncle Mick and your Uncle Ruairi, and they, in turn, have been speaking to their boys. We'll be expecting your cousins Aidan, Shay, and Donal to be joining the Duster ranks here in New York to lend us all a much-needed hand. Arrangements are already underway."

My da's parents moved to Hell's Kitchen from Dublin when he was twelve years old. It was his da's destiny to take over the Duster reins as it was his and as it will be Eoin's. When his folks passed, his siblings, Mick and Ruairi, moved back to Ireland along with their wives, my plethora of cousins, and a multitude of grandkids. Aidan, Shay, and Donal are the same age as our Paddy. Shay and Donal are two of Uncle Ruairi's boys and are identical twins.

None of us speak. We're all just digesting this first announcement. On the surface, it's a good result for the rest of us. Bolstering our ranks with trustworthy blood relations as the organization grows.

"Secondly." Da looks at me and then at my eldest brother. I know that look, and I now know exactly what's coming next. I'm guessing Eoin does too. It was only ever a matter of time.

"Your ma and I have found Eoin and Dylan two young women

who we think will be perfect for them to court then take the vows with."

I don't have to look at Paddy to know he'll be gloating. That we're being made to suffer the same fate as him.

I glance at Eoin, and he looks furious. My big brother doesn't like being told what to do. Never has. Never will. I'm guessing he'll have something to say about that.

A lot to say, in fact.

CHAPTER THREE

EOIN

The Hudson Dusters' HQ, Manhattan, New York

"I WILL NOT BE ENTERED INTO AN ARRANGED MARRIAGE, DA."

My brothers have left the room at my request. I've also asked Candice to leave this floor. Not that it's dangerous for her. I just don't want her over-hearing anything she shouldn't. I fuck her. She knows nothing of my life apart from what's common knowledge and what I expect from her in bed. It's safer for her that way.

My gaze is directed out the window. Our HQ overlooks one of the finest views in Manhattan. It's quite breathtaking. The visual is, of course, reflected in the value of this building. It's one of several properties we own in the immediate vicinity. I'm immensely proud of what the Dusters have achieved. Of what we continue to achieve despite the masses who continually pray to one God or another for our failure. Vultures who wish to instigate and witness our downfall so they can then pick through the bones of our demise.

We have many adversaries, each one loathing us for their own unique reason. Most warranted, I'm sure.

Do I want someone to share all of this with? To stand by my side and orchestrate all of this power with me. Of course I do. I want a wife. I want children. I want my own family.

But I want it with *her*—no one else.

It's like my da can read my thoughts. With each day that passes, we become more and more alike.

"She's married now, Eoin. She has a child. Another on the way. It's time to move on, son. Your ma and I have been more than patient, but this *thing* with Jaine Jones? It's done. It's over."

I glance over my shoulder at him and watch as he opens the back of his unused writing pad, pulling free a plain brown A4 envelope. He throws it on the middle of the table, and it smacks against the surface.

"The girl is from good stock. Your Uncle Mick has had her thoroughly checked out. Her family is a good fit for the Dusters. She's lived our ways all her life. Multiple killings under her belt. Good with a variety of weapons. She's not afraid to roll her sleeves up and get stuck in. They're a Dublin family. Extremely wealthy and practicing Irish Catholics. The girl, Molly McGrath, is twenty-eight years old."

I pick up the envelope which has been left unsealed, pulling out the images of the girl my parents want me to wed. I flick through them. She's beautiful. Stunning, in fact. Slim, tall with long black hair, pale skin, and clear blue eyes. She even looks Irish.

I may have been tempted once. Once when she was exactly my type. But not now. Not now my thoughts are forever plagued by a blonde-haired, green-eyed biker with the mouth of a sailor. Someone I look forward to having heated exchanges with more and more each day. I push the photos back inside the envelope and throw them on the table.

Da snorts as he reads my mind once more.

"I agree Jaine Jones's credentials as an outlaw lawyer are beyond compare, Eoin. I will grant both you and her that. But has she now lost that hands-on rapport she had with the people who matter? Let's be honest, son. She's been out of the loop for the past eighteen months or so. That's a long time in this life. Plus, how many lives has she actually taken? One, maybe two at most? Molly, on the other hand, has taken many. Ending a life is like water off a duck's back to her now, and let's face it, we have to end plenty. And what can Jaine offer the Dusters by way of an alliance? We already have the bikers in our back pocket. Molly will bring with her a host of new connections and all from the old country. I'm sorry, son, but it's our opinion she's far more suited to being the next Ma Duster."

"You need to meet Jaine."

I watch as he shakes his head, immediately turning down my request. I can't blame him. What Jaine did was disrespectful. Unforgivable in my parents' eyes.

"We offered to meet her once before, and she didn't show, Eoin. She should thank her lucky stars we didn't task The Exterminator with planting a bullet in that skull of hers for the blatant show of disrespect she showed me and your ma. And as I've already pointed out, she's taken the vows with this other biker. So, what are you going to do? Send him to meet his maker so you can claim her as your own? No. I'm sorry, son, but mine and your ma's minds are made up. Young Molly is flying into New York next week. You'll meet with her, and we'll take things from there."

I nod at my father. There's no point arguing with him, so for now, I outwardly pretend I will accept his decision knowing full well I have no intention of ever doing so.

CHAPTER FOUR

JESSIE

The Hudson Dusters' HQ, Manhattan, New York

"HOWDY, PARTNER."

I take in my reflection in the restroom mirror as I call Jaine to update her on the outcome of the recent meeting.

"Are you sure you're not from Texas?"

"Definitely Nevada. I triple-checked. With him being present at my birth, I also asked my daddy, just to be one hundred percent certain."

There's a pause. I get the distinct impression Jaine doesn't like my daddy after what went down in Nevada when he intimated she might not be doing things by that professional legal handbook of hers. Offense was definitely taken. Then again, I also think she's still coming to terms with my whole family situation. The fact that Bailey and I are sisters. That her ex-boyfriend is now shacked up with my youngest sibling.

"Any update?"

She changes the subject. Yup. She's not prepared to give my daddy the time of day.

"On?"

"Tell me about Dylan first. And I refuse to call him delectable."

"Spoilsport." I snicker immaturely. "Well, there's no change on that front. I continue to stay out of his way. It's only when I have to attend Duster meetings that we're ever in the same space. You know, those times I've told you about when I catch myself drooling. Eoin caught me blatantly ogling him today."

"He was probably pissed off because you weren't admiring him."

"Trust me, it's not me he wants to admire him."

She ignores that comment completely.

"Anyway, enough about the O'Connell brothers, what's happening with the IRS?"

I exhale loud and slow. "It's not good news, Jaine."

"Don't keep me in suspense then. Just tell me how it is."

"Apparently, the wheels are now in motion. I'm reliably informed they want to conduct an audit into Play with a view to calculating the tax avoidance they believe has taken place there. If any related party transactions are discovered, it could then create a domino effect with any other Duster companies Play has traded with being next in line. The resultant ripple could see audits rolled out through the entire group."

"Audits that will lead to criminal investigations in due course."

"Yes. So I need to provide all the necessary supporting evidence to substantiate the transactions under suspicion. Interim financial statements have already been published. The balances cannot be altered."

"We'll be able to do that?"

"We have no choice."

"And then?"

"We have to offer the information up willingly when they ask to audit, which will be imminent, going by the buzz of excitement inside the organization."

"Best case?"

"We nip it in the bud at Play, get hit with a large fine, and life goes on as we know it."

"Worst case?"

"They audit Play then move on to a criminal investigation when they're not happy with their findings. They then use this as the catalyst to roll it out across the other Duster companies potentially unearthing a plethora of wrongdoings as they go. Over and above the substantial fines each company will be served, they may also try to make an example of the Dusters by attempting to incarcerate our boys."

"That's a death sentence right there."

"Exactly. Now I can do what needs to be done from my side. There's just one itty bitty problem."

"I'm not sure I like the sound of that. Go on."

"We need access to a tax lawyer."

"Nope." Her tone is firm.

"Paddy doesn't have any experience dealing with the IRS, Jaine." I realize I'm whining like a child that's just been refused a shitty one-dollar toy at Walmart.

"JAL's not getting involved."

"I don't think you have much choice. Paddy's as much at risk as the others. Perhaps more so as he's the Duster's lawyer. They'll cite he should have made sure the holding company adhered to its full legal obligations." I realize I'm being underhanded, but needs must.

"For fuck's sake."

"Indeed."

"Listen, Jessie. Let me think about it."

"We need an answer like yesterday."

'*I said* I'll think about it."

"I hear you."

I pause before moving on to the next sensitive subject.

"Now, about my identity."

"What, the revelation that you're Lucifer's daughter, Bailey's sister, and Paul Delaney's future sister-in-law?"

"Yes, that little tidbit of information right there."

She lets out a long sigh. "Let's allow the dust to settle on the Nevada shitshow, get this IRS situation put to bed, and then I can drop that bombshell on the O'Connells. It's then up to them what they do with it. Sarah's agreed not to mention anything. At the end of the day, you're contracted to them through JAA. You're not employed. It's not for you to divulge any sensitive information. It's for JAA to do that."

"It could be deemed a blatant conflict of interest by the Dusters. Details that should have been declared as soon as the connections became known. The fact that my daddy's MC now forms part of the alliance through La eMe."

"I realize that, Jessie. But JAA was already too heavily involved. If we'd pulled out or been pulled out it could have spelled disaster. They're Irish. They're prone to making rash decisions. I don't think those boys grasp just how serious this IRS situation is. How easy it would be for each of them to face jail time."

"I'm sorry."

"It's not your fault. Shit happens. I made the call, not you."

"I'm also sorry about Little Bee. About what she did. I should have locked my systems down better. I guess I never thought she was paying attention when she looked over my shoulder all those times. Still, JAL is now as secure as Fort Knox as a result. History will never be repeated."

"Good to know. It still doesn't excuse what Bailey did."

"Nope, it doesn't. But she's learned her lesson."

"Let's hope so."

"On a positive, there's one other piece of news. Well, it's gossip, really. I overhead the employee with benefits, Candice, having a heated exchange with Eoin about it. I'm not sure if it was before or after they had desk sex."

"This had better be good."

"It is."

"Well?"

"Rumor has it Prince Eoin is to be entered into an arranged marriage."

She lets out a long whistle. "Well. Goddamn. That is good news. Karma. Finally."

"Thought that would make you smile, partner."

"Make me smile, Jessie? It's made my day."

CHAPTER FIVE

JAINE

Jaine's House, Rising, California

I let the phone ring out. Sitting on the old cream leather sofa, I mentally prepare myself to take his call. I already have the reasons why I can't assist them with the IRS matter listed firmly in my head.

"Eoin."

"Jaine."

"I hear congratulations are in order." I sound smug. I know I do.

There's a pause.

"News travels fast. Not that anything's been decided yet, Miss Jones."

Good news or bad from where he's standing, I wonder?

"So, we're already back to Miss Jones. What's wrong? Are you not happy with Ma and Da Duster's selection for you? Such a shame. Karma can be a real bitch."

Another pause. A lengthier one.

"On the contrary. Molly is from the old country, is extremely beautiful, and has a wealth of experience under her belt."

"Really. And what is this wealth of experience she has? Or maybe I should just ask for a number. I'm guessing that's what's important. How many times she's had to roll up her sleeves and muck in?"

"A lot more than you."

"And you'd know that how?"

"You're a lawyer."

"I'm a biker first and foremost." I'm also a sniper.

"Are you saying your number is higher?"

His tone is mocking, but I don't rise to it. Maybe one day this asshole will find out exactly how high my number is just before he adds to it by one.

"I'm saying never judge a book and never underestimate. We both know you're guilty of doing both where I'm concerned. So aside from you believing she has more notches on her weaponry belt than I do, what else does Molly do?"

"She's studying law."

"Ah, a noble career choice. Good for her."

"Speaking of which, this IRS business."

"Yes, Jessie's already broached the subject with me. And I've now got an idea of how best to proceed.

"And that is?"

I know exactly what I'm going to say. He's just given me the perfect excuse and saved me from having to use a flimsy one of my own.

"Ask Molly."

I put the phone down and smile to myself.

He rings back less than a minute later. I guess he doesn't fully appreciate my recommendation.

"Jaine. That wasn't at all helpful."

I roll my eyes even though he can't see me. He was never going to let me walk away that easily. "Listen, Eoin. I'm sure Irish can handle the IRS matter, and I'm sure Molly can assist. I *was* actually being serious."

"Paddy has no experience in dealing with the IRS, and given Molly has lived in Dublin her whole life, she won't have any relevant experience either."

I take on board what he's saying, and he does have a valid point, but there's another reason I don't want to get embroiled in this potential investigation.

"From what I hear, the current Da Duster doesn't want me getting involved."

"Jessie really does have a big mouth," he mutters under his breath.

"She's my business partner, Eoin. We talk. You forget JAL holds the controlling interest in the company that's currently heading the Dusters' accountancy function."

"I understand all of that. For the record, Da has backed down. He's now happy for you to assist."

"He's now happy for me to assist. Does he think he's doing me a goddamn favor?"

"I'm sure it will be extremely lucrative."

"You're making it sound like I'm desperate for money, and we both know that's not the case."

"Unfortunately, he's not your biggest fan."

"Because of what happened, or should I say didn't happen, in Manhattan?

"Yes."

It's my turn to pause. So, I've well and truly pissed off Fergal O'Connell over this standing-up matter. I naively thought it would be forgotten over time, but it seems time is only exacerbating his and, no doubt, Roisin's bitterness towards me.

"Then, unfortunately, I do feel it's best for all parties concerned that you find someone else. I don't need to be antagonizing your da. The IRS may also insist on a face-to-face. I won't be able to do that. I'm not local. I won't be returning to New York for some considerable time as you know."

"I'm sure we can cross that bridge if we come to it. The Dusters need access to your expertise. I'm personally asking for your help. Are you going to provide it or not?"

"I have no owing."

"I beg to differ. We're owed as much over the Nevada incident as La eMe. Speaking of which, you also agreed to represent us on the alliance."

"I did no such goddamn thing. I agreed to nothing."

"Are you saying there's no owing?"

"I defused the situation."

"Yes, you did. And quite admirably too. But we need to ensure it doesn't happen again. So, if you undertake that function, if we have to sign with JAL on that matter, then where's the harm in you undertaking two roles for us?"

"I'll think about it."

"It's urgent, Jaine."

"Oh, because you want something we're back to Jaine now, are we? I *said* I'll think about it."

"That's exactly what you told Jessie."

"Because that's exactly what I'm doing. Goodbye, Eoin."

NOT FIVE MINUTES LATER MY PHONE VIBRATES.

Padraig: *Can you do me a huge favor, darlin?*
Jaine: *Depends on what it is. Dyl.*

I know fine well what it is. Eoin has immediately called for backup. Manipulative asshole.

Padraig: *Will you represent us legally on this IRS matter?*
Jaine: *Has Eoin asked you to ask me?*
Padraig: *Yes and no.*
Jaine: *Meaning?*
Padraig: *He's told everyone you've said you'll think about it.*
Jaine: *And I am.*
Padraig: *Jessie and Eoin are worried about it.*
Jaine: *I realize that.*
Padraig: *I'm worried about it too, darlin'.*
Jaine: *That's a low blow, Dyl. Listen, aside from the reasons I've already given your big brother, I do have another reason for wanting to refuse. My IRS knowledge is limited. I'm in no way an expert on these matters. I'd like to try to source someone who has more experience under their belt if I can.*
Padraig: *The Dusters won't use a third party they don't already know.*
Jaine: *I understand that, but by all accounts, your da's also not enthused at the thought of having to utilize my services.*
Padraig: *No, he's not. I'm not going to lie to you. I'm not sure what's going on there, but I know he thinks you're already too heavily involved in our business.*
Jaine: *Hence the reason I'm trying to source a more well-rounded alternative.*

Padraig: *While that's very kind of you, I'm not sure we have the time for that, plus, as I've said, Da won't use an unknown.*

Padraig: *Jaine?*

Padraig: *Jaine! Have I upset you?*

Padraig: *Listen, I'm not trying to back you into a corner.*

Jaine: *Aren't you? Because from where I'm standing that's precisely what you are doing, Dylan. And what your big brother is doing. Who knew you two were so alike? Anyway, I'm not upset. I'm just thinking it all through in my head and trying to reach a decision.*

Padraig: *And what have you decided?*

Jaine: *I haven't decided anything because the way I see it, I have no goddamn choice, do I?*

Padraig: *You'll be handsomely rewarded.*

Jaine: *What is it with you O'Connells and money? I've already explained to your manipulative asshole of a brother that I don't need the money. My services will be given freely.*

Padraig: *Does that mean you'll do it?"*

Jaine: *Yes. To repay yet another owing that Eoin has fabricated in that big fat head of his. I'm also doing it for you, Dyl. I don't want you to be worried. But for the record, this is strictly a one-off. Next time, you can use Molly.*

Padraig: *What about the alliance with La eMe?*

Jaine: *A two-off then.*

Padraig: *So, you've heard about her? Molly?*

Jaine: *Yes. Jessie mentioned Eoin's to be entered into an arranged marriage with her if she ticks all your mobster boxes.*

Padraig: *How do you feel about it?*

Jaine: *I don't feel anything about it. Maybe if big brother*

Eoin is busy with his new legal eagle fiancée, he'll stop pestering me for attention.
Padraig: *LOL. So, I'm okay letting the family know you've agreed to help us out?*
Jaine: *Yes.*

CHAPTER SIX

JESSIE

Jessie's Apartment, Hudson Yards, New York

Bailey: *Dress shopping?*
Jessie: *The TV show lied. You'll never say yes. Not to any dress.*
Bailey: *I haven't tried on that many.*
Jessie: *Liar.*
Bailey: *I never lie.*
Jessie: *Oh, really? That right there's a lie, Bee.*
Bailey: *Touché.*
Jessie: *What you did was almost a career-changing moment for me. And not a positive one. I scored the perfect opportunity, and you almost blew it.*
Bailey: *How many times have I apologized to you? How many times have I apologized to Jaine?*
Jessie: *Listen, I have some documents I need to drop off*

for Razr. Let me know what day works best and I'll pick you up from the clubhouse at the same time. Love you, Little Bee.

Bailey: *Love you too, Jay.*

I SMILE AT THE MESSAGE EXCHANGE WITH MY TWENTY-TWO-YEAR-old baby sister before placing my phone in my jeans pocket and filling the coffee press with boiling water.

Bee's eight years my junior and is currently living love's young dream. Well, I say young. Her boyfriend, Paul Delaney, is eleven years older than her. So, I guess it's love's young/old dream or something like that.

Still, they deserve their shot at happiness after everything they went through to be together. Bee losing her almost-fiancé, Raf Flores in a shoot-out and Razr being pretty much declared insane by high-rankers in the medical profession. Not that we all weren't already aware of that or at least suspected it.

My daddy took a lot of convincing before he reluctantly agreed to part with the hand of his youngest on account of just how mentally unstable Razr is.

Or was.

In his defense, even I can see a marked improvement in him these days. Down to sheer determination on his part? Rehab? My baby sister? Likely a combination of all three. He will forever be a work in progress, though.

I push down the filter and gaze around my open-plan living area. The kitchen is white high gloss with all the latest mod-cons. Everything in the apartment is white, glass, or mirrored.

Simple. Minimalistic. Clean.

My brain is so active most of the time I need this oasis of tranquility to be able to switch off. To balance. To breathe. To unwind.

To just be me.

I inhale. I've been here months, and it still smells like fresh paint. It's a clean smell. A new-start smell.

New start of what, though? My life? When nothing fundamental has changed? When nothing ever does or likely ever will? It's the same life I was leading in Vegas.

Just a different location. A different view.

Perfectly lonely.

Am I envious of my baby sister's newfound happiness? Is it wrong of me to admit that I am?

I mean, who do I have aside from a handful of close friends and my family? At the ripe old age of thirty I've never once had a serious significant other.

The smile fades from my face as my good mood evaporates, and I let out a long sigh.

From the outside looking in, most could be forgiven for thinking I have it all. All anyone ever sees is the over-confident, outspoken, and gregarious Jessie O'Brien with her successful career, own company, and own apartment.

They see what's on the surface. Nothing more. It's all anyone has ever seen. In fairness, I accept that's in part because it's all I've ever allowed anyone to see. But then no one's ever shown any interest in getting to know the person underneath the shiny, exuberant exterior.

If they did, maybe they'd realize that the girl who claims she wants to be the center of attention doesn't always crave the spotlight. That maybe all she really wants is the one thing she's never had. The attention of that one special person.

Because what does all the success and material stuff matter when you have no one to share it with?

Still, I shouldn't complain or throw myself a pity party. I'm sure if it's in God's big old masterplan it will happen for me, same as it did for Bee.

My thoughts then drift to him. My complete opposite in pretty much every way. Well, apart from in the looks department, even though he tries his darndest to hide his male hotness underneath clothes he looks like he borrowed from his daddy.

Dylan O'Connell.

All those months ago. An instant connection of whatever the fuck it was. Whatever the fuck it still is, at least on my part. Given he's hankering over some blonde, it's obviously no longer the case for him. Then again, it likely never was. It was just wishful thinking.

For me, he's he who must be avoided at all costs, which is no mean feat given he lives in the penthouse above. Still, I've managed to stay out of his way since moving here. I've turned it into quite the art form too. Spying around corners and creeping around like a ninja. Is he also avoiding me? Is that the reason it's been relatively easy to achieve?

Most likely. I mean, who needs an awkward confrontation?

No good would ever come of our paths crossing. If he is in love with someone from his past, which Jaine assures me he is, I'd only ever be a sidepiece if we ever did hook up. And I'm better than that. Way better. I have too much respect for myself.

I'd far rather be alone.

Maybe his love for his cliché blonde is unrequited. Not that it's any of my business. And not that it matters anyway. Because even if it is, it still means his heart belongs to someone else.

Anyway, let's be honest, he barely ever glances in my direction. This attraction is definitely one-sided.

Jaine: *You there?*

Jessie: *Where else would I be?*

Jaine: *Borrowing coffee? Cream? Sugar?*

Jessie: *We've already been through this. If there's even a*

hint of another woman, I'm not going there. Not. Ever. No man is worth it. Not even the Delectable Dylan O'Connell.
Jaine: *I know, I know.*
Jessie: *Sometimes dreams don't come true, you know? Sometimes there is no happily ever after to be had. I won't say that out loud. I don't want to break the hopeful hearts of little girls the world over. It's the equivalent of saying I don't believe in fairies.*

Jaine understands. She explained all about what went down with her, Paddy, and Ace. And what the O'Connells' decision was in the end. An arranged marriage for Paddy. It's one of the reasons she's currently residing in California. She refuses to tempt fate when it may lead to a bullet in Padraig O'Connell's head.

Jaine: *Yup. I get that. Anyway, you'll be pleased to know I've signed on the dotted line with the Dusters today. I've reluctantly agreed that JAL will represent them should the issue with the IRS require legal representation.*
Jessie: *Well, I can't say I'm not relieved. Eoin will be delighted for sure.*
Jaine: *That makes one of us. I've told him next time he can use Molly to do his legal work. If she's going to be Ma Duster, she'll need to get her hands dirty at some point. No point delaying the inevitable.*
Jessie: *Apparently, she still has to finish her on-the-job training. Maybe she could do that at JAL?*
Jaine: *She'll be a Duster, Jessie. She'd report everything back to her future Irish king husband. I already have to put up with him sticking his unwelcome nose in my business affairs every opportunity he gets, so I'll take a hard pass. Anyway, I just wanted to let you know.*

"Jaine? It's the middle of the night. Is everything okay?" I'm lying in bed, wide awake and staring at the ceiling.

"Nope. Word is the IRS will be with us sooner rather than later. Eoin and I have a conference call with them tomorrow at nine a.m. your time. I'm preparing for it now. I only found out an hour ago. The email went into Candice's clutter folder. That work you need to do? It needs doing now."

"Holy shit."

"Exactly. We can't have them infiltrating any of the information before it's ready to be forensically examined, so you're going into lockdown before the conversation with them even takes place. There's a delivery being made in thirty minutes, hence the call. Fresh foodstuffs and produce, that sort of thing. Enough to last a couple of weeks. Beyond that, you'll have enough canned and dried food to last years."

"Years?"

"Well, you're in charge of the timeframe, not me."

"So, I'm staying here on my own until it's concluded?"

"Nope. Dylan is staying with you. He'll make sure no one tries to hack into any of the systems while you concentrate your efforts on finalizing what needs doing."

I sit bolt upright in bed. "Jaine, I really don't think that's a good idea."

"Well, I'm sorry about that, Jessie, but it's not like we have any choice."

CHAPTER SEVEN

DYLAN

Dylan's Apartment, Hudson Yards, New York

LOCKDOWN.

Through no fault of our own, Jessie O'Brien and I have been flung headfirst into a lockdown situation. Some might argue it won't make any noticeable difference—I can still hide out in the penthouse above while she can still live her life in the apartment below.

But it is different. Before, even if we chose not to go anywhere, we still had the option. And if we didn't want to go out, we could at least keep ourselves to ourselves and mind our own business in our own separate space. No communication required. No interaction required. She'd stay in hers. I'd stay in mine.

But now we're in a forced proximity situation. Now we're stuck here with no way in or out. Together. Alone. For the foreseeable future.

And we can't continue to ignore each other. Avoid each other. Deliberately stay out of each other's way. Because right now, I need to go downstairs and run a check on her systems. Something our Eoin's tasked me with doing at regular intervals throughout the day, and even the night if needs be.

I mean, would he know if I did his bidding or not? Probably. When it comes to him, I reckon big brother is always watching. It's the reason I just do as I'm told. It's easier that way—anything for a quiet life. I've never rocked the boat. Not once. The only problem is it means I'm going to have to speak to Jessie.

And I don't know how to.

What if she asks questions about the make-believe blonde? Does she know my da's considering entering me into an arranged marriage with an as-yet-unknown female? What if she asks about her? What exactly has Paddy told Jaine? All these lies and untruths will catch up with him, and me, one of these days.

Then again, would Jessie even care? Is she just toying with me on the rare occasions we meet? Like a cat with a mouse. Is she pretending to like me just to pass the time of day? For entertainment value because she's bored.

I realize I'm not like my brothers. That I'm quieter and more withdrawn. I know I'm thought of as a bit weird for preferring to spend time either in my own company or with my immediate family. There's no untoward reason for it. I wasn't abused or mistreated or any horror story like that. Growing up with our Paddy and with him being loud and craving attention, I guess I was just happy to let him take center stage. I was content living my life in the shadows.

Hiding or unseen? I'm not too sure which. Regardless, now I just prefer it there. I can be myself there. I can't make small talk with strangers for the life of me, and in truth, I don't really want to. I don't really want to socialize or go out either.

I'm content living in my own bubble and doing my own thing.

Of course, I get lonely at times. Of course, I'd like to meet that one special person. But any girl I've met has just used me as a stepping-stone to gain access to one of my way more popular and way better-looking brothers. I'm not interesting like our Eoin. I don't tell funny stories or jokes like Paddy. And unlike Cillian, I'm socially awkward. And I'm okay with all of the above. I accepted myself a long time ago.

Could I change? Would I for the right person? As long as they accepted me for who I am and that my change was to improve our relationship, then I would consider it. Of course I would. But I've never met the right person. Then again, I've never met the wrong person either.

When I first met Jessie, I was blown away. It's a cliché, I know, but sparks flew. Or at least I thought they had. She walked into the room, commanding all our attention, and she's had mine ever since.

They say opposites attract. I can hand on heart vouch for that.

Because Jessie's everything I'm not. Outgoing. Vibrant. Stunning. A real people person. She's the female version of Paddy. At least in terms of personality and looks. Would someone like her ever notice someone like me?

Don't be daft.

This attraction is definitely one-sided.

Jessie's Apartment, Hudson Yards, New York

"Door's open," Jessie singsongs from inside.

The top two floors of the building are currently sealed off and pretty much everything-proof. No one can get in. No one can get out. My apartment houses all the Duster's surveillance and security systems for every property and business we own, including our private apartments and homes. It also houses a database containing every piece of intel we hold on all of the people who matter.

Everything has been written, coded, and set up by me. It's impenetrable.

Jessie's apartment houses the hardware and software systems she's personally developed. It allows her to view every single transaction of every Duster business, enabling her to drill right down.

Who. Where. When.

I'm told she can manipulate everything, including altering time and date stamps if need be.

Impressive.

Her hacking software is currently viewing the same level of detail within some of the key organizations throughout the world.

Or so I've heard.

I can't deny I've got a geeky hard-on at the thought of seeing it all in action. But it might also be because I'm about to see *her* in action.

I push the door open and step inside her apartment. I had to take the stairs as the elevator was out of service due to the lockdown. I tell myself that's the reason my heart is pounding in my chest.

I swallow thickly as I look around the space. Her space. Everything is white and mirrored. It's pristine and stunning. Just like her. Months later and it still smells newly painted. I like the smell. It's clean and fresh with just a hint of Jessie.

Springtime.

"I'm through here, Dylan."

After wiping my sweaty hands down the front of my jeans, I run one down my face. We could be locked down for a week. Maybe more. I need to get used to being in her company.

I follow her voice to the back of the apartment. As part of the fit-out, she specified that one room be large and windowless. I'm guessing that's where she keeps her equipment, away from prying eyes. Even airborne ones.

Her subtle scent gets even more enticing as I approach the door. I can hear her now. She's humming along to *Comfortably Numb.*

I take her in as I push the room door open. She's a vision in tight white jeans and a tank top, finished off with a pair of sneakers that have seen far better days. Her white-blonde hair is piled on top of her head in a messy bun. She has her back to me, her attention focused on three giant wall-mounted screens, her hands gliding across them effortlessly. It's like something from that old *Minority Report* movie.

"This isn't the sort of music I thought you'd be in to."

She smirks at me over her shoulder. I feel my cheeks redden when I realize I've spoken my thoughts aloud.

She turns to fully face me, resting her backside against the narrow white table that's been positioned directly below the middle display.

"And what did you expect me to listen to, Dylan?"

Jessie's accent is like Jaine's, but with a sprinkling of Irish mixed in, the soft lilt undoubtedly inherited from her daddy. I swear to The Almighty it's the best thing I've ever heard. I stare at her, lost for words.

Enraptured. Captivated. Dumbstruck.

Not that it takes much for me to be the latter. I see a flicker of something cross her eyes. It's understanding. She realizes how difficult this is for me. How uncomfortably numb I am right now trying to hold a conversation with a stranger which, in truth, is what she is. She continues when I don't respond, so there's no pressure on me to reply.

"I bet you've got me down as listening to heavy rock or thrash metal. Am I right? That you reckon I like to headbang in my spare time just because I'm a biker."

I nod, my face reddening further when I realize I've assumed her music choices because of her background.

She smiles gently, but it's forced, I can tell. I'm not too sure why. She then turns back towards her screens.

"See, that's where you're wrong. Just because I'm from an MC life doesn't mean I ride a hog and wear leather pants. I don't. Or at least, not often."

I watch, hypnotized, as she flicks across thousands of numbers on the screen, drilling down when she spots something of interest. Meanwhile, the other two displays are rolling with real-time data. I have no clue what or where from. For a nerd like me, it's fascinating. I want to know more. I want to know how it all works. What makes it tick.

What makes her tick.

"I like classical music," she continues to fill the silence. "Or anything I can have on in the background that doesn't disturb my concentration. As you can see, I like to focus on what I'm doing with my hands at all times."

She winks over her shoulder, her real smile returning when she takes in my worsening cheek situation. She probably knows I'm now thinking about her hands and what she could do with them.

To me.

"And then I like bands like *Pink Floyd*, Dyl."

She called me Dyl. She's never called me that before. She glances at me over her shoulder once more. "You're okay with me calling you Dyl?" She arches one sleek eyebrow on that beautiful face of hers with its elegant nose, pointed chin, and high cheekbones. She can call me whatever the fuck she likes, and I'll answer. Any fucking thing at all. I'm not fussed.

I don't say that aloud, though. I simply nod once more.

"Well, let's be clear. You don't get to shorten my name. You don't get to call me Jess. And you definitely don't get to call me Jay. Only my baby sister and people from my hometown call me Jay."

CHAPTER EIGHT

JESSIE

Jessie's Apartment, Hudson Yards, New York

"YOU HAVE SIBLINGS?"

He finally speaks. His voice is deep, but soft at the same time. He sounds different from the rare occasions he talks in meetings. Is that the real him, or is this? His accent is New York mixed with Irish. It's the best sound I've ever heard. I want to record it then play it aloud when I'm alone in my bed so I can get off to that soft lilt of his over and over again.

Dylan O'Connell and I are having a conversation. Just me and him. It may be like pulling teeth because he's so far out of his comfort zone, but he's communicating with me all the same. He's asked a question I don't really want to answer, though. Jaine doesn't want me to spill any details on my background until we've concluded this IRS matter. Given how reserved Dylan is it's unlikely he'll interrogate me though, so I do answer.

“I have one sister and two brothers.”

He nods, pushing his glasses further up his nose before dropping his attention to the floor, no doubt to avoid any eye contact. I use the opportunity to give him the once-over. It’s the first time I’ve seen him out of a business suit. A fitted long-sleeved white tee clings to his tall, lean frame, and dark blue jeans fit snugly on his slim hips.

He’s fucking beautiful. Ridiculously so.

I shift my gaze upwards to admire inky black hair that’s grown untidily out of a buzzcut to a face that’s impressively pale with a strong chin and nose and cheekbones any woman would kill for, all perfectly set of by neatly trimmed facial hair.

His lips, though. He has a fucking pout. I mean, what does a man need with one of those? How is that even fair? I only realize I’m staring and that he’s caught me doing so when I raise my eyes further and our gazes connect.

Blue on blue.

Sapphire to be exact. My heart skips a beat. For the first time in my life, I find myself at a total loss for words because there are none worthy. None that can adequately describe the emotions running through me right now as I stare straight into Dylan O’Connell’s beautiful soul.

I want to laugh and cry at the same time. And both for the same reason. At the pantie-wetting perfection standing in front of me that will never be mine. The unfairness of it all. This connection. This attraction. It can’t be all one-sided, surely?

I lick my lips, and his gaze drops to my mouth. He licks his own in silent response, and I’m held captive by their glistening fullness. Does he want to kiss me?

I say a silent prayer that he crosses the floor and does just that. He doesn’t, though. He just blushes, rocks back and forth on his feet, and clams up once more.

It's obvious forcing a conversation just won't work so I decide to try a different approach. He needs to be in his comfort zone.

Well, we're in a lockdown situation so I've got all the time in the world to prize Dylan O'Connell out of that shell of his.

I wheel over the white leather executive chair from the desk on the other side of the room.

"Take a seat and I'll explain how all this works." I decide to speak in his language instead. From one geeky expert to another.

CHAPTER NINE

DYLAN

Jessie's Apartment, Hudson Yards, New York

SHE WHEELS A CHAIR ACROSS AND PATS THE SURFACE FOR ME TO SIT down.

"Take a seat and I'll explain how all this works."

The nerdy side of me is curious to witness the inner workings of all these systems she's created from scratch, but the neanderthal male side of me that I didn't even realize I possessed until now suddenly wants to kiss her. Because he's managed to convince himself that's exactly what it is that she's chasing.

Is this attraction one-sided? Or have both of us been in denial as we danced around each other for months skirting whatever *this* is.

Because when Jessie looked at me, I swear to God, I felt something.

Then again, did I.

Let's face it, it's more likely the case that, underneath it all, I really am just a caveman like my brothers. That all it took was the right woman and the right set of circumstances to unleash the uncouth O'Connell side in me that they all possess and bring it to the surface.

Physical urges. That's all this is.

I sit down. Mistake. The subtle notes in her perfume wash over me, and my dick twitches. Fuck. I can't sit here with a hard-on.

"Shall I make us a drink first?" I quickly stand while blurting out the words, and she arches a sleek eyebrow at me, no doubt surprised by the offer, but also at my speaking without being prompted.

"Coffee, black. In fact, I should come with you. You won't know where anything is."

"I'm sure I can…."

She ignores me and walks past, making her way to the kitchen. I follow, my traitorous eyes trained on her arse the entire time. It's as perfect as the rest of her, as are her two endless legs. My dick situation worsens. This is not good. Not good at all. I pray to the Holy Father that she doesn't notice.

"You okay if I make it using the press? I'm not a huge fan of coffee machines, although I have both."

"Yes, that's fine," I mutter. Right now, I couldn't care less. I'm no longer paying attention to anything apart from her backside in those tight white jeans.

See, having these alien feelings is one thing, but I could never act on them, and definitely not uninvited. But I'm not ashamed to admit that, right now, I wish I were more like my brothers because I know they'd just go for it. I know they'd have flicked the bird at said alien feelings and kissed her senseless by now.

Lost in my thoughts, I follow, then, like the eejit I am, I bang into her when she stops dead in the kitchen.

She immediately spins around and smirks at my clumsiness, and my eyes drop to her cupid's bow lips. Fucking perfect they are. I stare at them, watching as she flicks her tongue out to lick their surface.

Hot. Wet. Pink.

Yup, I'll take some of that. All of that, in fact. And anywhere at all. I'm not fussy.

Jesus Christ, Dylan. Get a grip.

Tilting her head up, she stares at me, our faces mere inches apart.

Kiss her. Kiss her. Kiss her. Do it.

I can feel her breath on my face. Against my mouth. My dick's now rock fucking hard. Closing my eyes, I quickly turn away, hearing an escape of breath as I do. Was that me or her? She must know that was an almost-kiss moment. Is she disappointed? Relieved? Or did she not realize what was going through my one-track mind? What I almost did. What I was so fucking tempted to do.

"Cream or sugar?"

The moment has passed. She's still her chirpy self, so I guess she never picked up on any of it.

I don't get a chance to reply as she answers her phone on hands-free while continuing to make the drinks.

"Howdy, partner. A word of warning. Dyl's here, so keep it clean. We don't want to be labeled as bad influences by the rest of the O'Connell clan, although I think we already fall under their heading of sacrilegious."

"Dyl."

"Jaine," I answer with a smile in my voice.

"Sacrilegious? Do you mean I'm that alongside the other colorful names they call me? Big brother Eoin in particular."

"Well, he does have the hots for you." Jessie smirks at me and winks.

So, Eoin's infatuation is obvious even to her and Jaine.

"Eoin only has the hots for himself. He'll be the type that kisses his reflection in the mirror every morning while whispering a prayer of thanks to The Lord for making him so good-looking. Anyway, enough about him. Is everything going according to plan?"

"We're on with it. I'm just making a coffee, and then I'll be showing Dyl my systems. It's important he understands their synergy, so he knows which areas to focus on."

"Good idea. Listen, I'm just about to go on a conference call with Eoin and the IRS. I'll let you know the outcome."

Jaine hangs up. She seldom, if ever, uses the words hello or goodbye. I find myself wondering if Jessie knows about her out-of-hours role, quickly realizing that it's doubtful.

Jaine wouldn't put her in danger by burdening her with that heavily guarded secret.

Dylan's Apartment, Hudson Yards, New York

"Paddy."

"Jesus Christ, who stole your scone, Dyl? Or should I say pancake as you sound as flat as one. Is it this thing with Jessie?"

I glance around my apartment with its contrasting black and white theme before sitting down and leaning back on one of the black leather sectionals. I don't even need to reply. He already knows the answer.

See, me and Paddy have a different relationship from our other siblings. It's like we have a telepathic bond. Maybe it's because we were born so close in age. We grew up doing everything together. Always with him front and center and me lurking in the background. It was never done maliciously. Paddy was just being himself. He's not the type to trample over others to get what he wants. The rest of us leave that up to our Eoin.

"Listen, Dyl, if you want Jessie, then go for it."

"Were you not at the same meeting as me, Paddy? I'm to be entered into an arranged marriage. Same as you and Eoin."

"Does Jessie know that?"

"No."

"So, ignore it for now. Anyway, it might never happen. If the wheels were already turning, I'm sure Da would have pulled you aside and stuffed an A4 brown envelope brimming with air-brushed photos in your hand same as he did our big brother."

"It still doesn't mean I can back out if it is on the cards. You weren't able to."

"My situation is different. My marriage is a signed in blood contract with Luciano. Plus, what happened to me was partly my own fault. I never mentioned Jaine to anyone. Not even to you. If I had, things might have worked out differently for us. Then again, she never loved me anyway, so it all turned out for the best. It saved me from making an even bigger fool of myself than I already had."

If only you knew, brother.

One day he will. And then Eoin will be toast.

"Arranged marriage aside, Jessie still thinks I'm in love with a ghost from my past."

"Then maybe it's time I told the truth."

"What? Reveal that it's you who messages Jaine? The first thing she'll do is spill her guts. She's her business partner."

"What will be will be. It was always going to come out at some point."

"I can't let you do that."

"And I can't sit back and watch you give up on what may well be your one shot at happiness because of me."

"Jaine would never speak to you again."

He laughs dryly. "She doesn't want to talk to me again anyway, so I'm losing nothing. Meanwhile, you're potentially giving up everything. Anyway, I'll be married soon, so maybe it's for the best that I let her go sooner rather than later. Let's face it, I'll have to at some point. Even if I don't love Sophia, I'll need to show her respect. She'll still be my wife."

Hearing Paddy refer to Sophia as his wife sounds all kinds of wrong. He should be with Jaine. Then again, who witnessed the unconditional love they shared before the Duster Sword of Damocles landed on their doomed relationship? None of the rest of the family did. Only me. Is he finally accepting of his fate? Showing forgiveness to the others for the life-altering decision they made on his behalf because they didn't possess all the facts?

While he may, Jaine never will. Especially not Eoin for the callous and indifferent way he handled the whole sorry affair.

"Look, Dyl. If you pair can't see what's in front of your nose, some of us can. You've been making eyes at each other for months. You're in lockdown together. Get to know her. Spend some quality time with her. Right now, you both have a captive audience. If it turns out you don't like each other as much as you first thought, then I get to hold onto my secret a while longer. If you do, then maybe it's time for the truth to come out. I won't see you suffer the same fate I did because of my lies and deceit. Agreed?"

"Agreed."

But I know I don't agree. I will never agree. My brother already faces a bleak future. I refuse to take away from him the only thing in his life he feels is worth living for, even if, by his own admission and acceptance, he only has Jaine for the short term.

CHAPTER TEN

DYLAN

Jessie's Apartment, Hudson Yards, New York

"Jaine's good people. Right?"

"The best." I immediately agree.

Jessie and I have been working side by side for several days now, and from pretty much nine to five.

It turns out, my stomping ground is similar to hers, so we have a lot more in common than either of us first realized. From talking about systems, our conversations just seemed to flow organically. Before I knew it, we were chatting about everything and anything.

Right now, we're extremely busy. Thankfully, that stops the Neanderthalic brain I now seem to possess going down paths it shouldn't. Whilst it still takes the one-track mind route any chance it can get, I've learned to control it by leaving the room and calling our Paddy. Talking to him about mundane family matters takes my mind off the increasingly inappropriate thoughts I'm having about

Jessie O'Brien. Turns out it's also much easier to hold an adult conversation with her when I'm thinking with the right head.

"It's a shame, you know?"

"About?" I ask the question, but I know exactly where this is going.

"Jaine and Paddy."

I glance at her then frown. Not over what she said per se. More because I'm worried about her. She looks like she hasn't slept properly in days, and it's likely because she hasn't. She's always working when I get here and still doing her thing when I leave.

Apparently, time really is of the essence.

I'm not sure my family fully appreciates the effort she's going to. To save us from what I don't fully know. While I realize she's being handsomely rewarded, she's still going above and beyond to the extent where it's clearly becoming detrimental to her health.

She's staring at her screen, rapidly manipulating data, and wearing an ancient pair of blue jeans, a tatty old grey tank top and the same 'seen better days' sneakers. Worryingly, she mumbled something about her outfit being what she wears when she needs good luck.

"I know," I eventually reply.

"I mean, this arranged marriage business. It shouldn't be allowed in this day and age."

I exhale. This really isn't a path I want our conversation to go down for obvious reasons. The main one being I don't want to tempt fate.

"It's fairly common in influential families. My own parents' marriage was arranged." This is the perfect opportunity for me to admit to my own situation.

I don't use it.

Paddy assures me nothing's been mentioned about my following suit with Eoin, so for now, I'll stick my head in the sand and pretend it's not going to happen. He doesn't think it will. Maybe he's right. Maybe it won't.

"And are they happy?"

I shrug. "I've never met two people more so."

"And that's what's on the cards for Eoin?"

"It is."

"I can't imagine he'll be over the moon at being told what to do and who to wed."

"He isn't, but he'll come around to my parents' way of thinking, I'm sure."

"And what about you?"

"What about me?"

My heart sinks in my chest. If she's asking me outright, I'll have no choice but to tell her. I can't blatantly lie. It will change our relationship. I know it will.

And I don't want it to change.

Because it might only be fleeting and due to the unusual circumstances we've both found ourselves in, but these past few days I've seen the other side of Jessie. Not the loud, in your face, gregarious girl everyone else sees. The quiet one she turns into when the cameras are off and the world's not watching.

The girl I'm falling for.

The girl that, underneath it all, is just the same as me.

JESSIE

If someone were to tell me that by prizing Dylan O'Connell out of that shell of his, he'd do a full one-eighty, I'd have straight up called them a liar.

Is it because we've been talking geek speak most of the time? Probably.

We've been working together for well over a week now. We

didn't discuss or plan it. It just sort of happened. We drifted together, one computer nerd to another, and now here we are sitting side by side drinking coffee, talking systems, and swapping hacking and security tips.

At times I catch him staring. I know he's as surprised by the changes in me as I am by the ones in him. Changes that are surfacing because neither of us have anywhere to hide.

The contrast.

That due to complete exhaustion on my part, I've allowed my exuberant persona to temporarily slip and shown him the me that's only allowed to surface when I'm on my own. The quiet and contained me I wear like a comfy old pair of slippers when I don't need to be the center of attention, or when I don't want to be loud or quick-witted. Was letting my guard down in front of him a mistake? Who knows. Right now, I'm way too busy and way too tired to care.

Meanwhile, Dylan has gone from being a classic introvert to someone who can not only hold a meaningful conversation but can quite easily start one.

The tables have turned. Who'd have thought it?

I've worked out that his reluctance or inability to speak is when he's having to converse with strangers, and it would appear he no longer considers me one of those.

From talking systems we then digressed to other subjects. It turns out Dyl is also a Pink Floyd fan, although he much prefers *Wish You Were Here* to my choice of *Comfortably Numb.*

We're now talking arranged marriages. It's a hot topic in the O'Connell household given Eoin's situation. I mean, it almost happened to me and my sister, so I'm not sure why I'm so surprised that Ma and Da Duster want to make sure the Duster heir marries the right mobster girl.

"And what about you?" I ask, my gaze remaining focused on the data I'm working on.

I realize I'm asking a question I don't really want the answer to. What am I thinking? Who even does that?

But do they have the same plans for Dyl?

My heart sinks at the thought. Then again what difference does it make when there's his cliché blonde to contend with?

Actually. Nope. Best to stick to being geeky friends. There's less chance of my heart being broken that way.

"What about me?"

I'm now wishing I hadn't asked. Thankfully, he doesn't get a chance to answer as his phone vibrates to let us know big brother, as regular as clockwork, is calling at the pre-arranged daily time.

Dylan accepts the call and puts it on hands-free.

"How's progress?"

Eoin gets straight to the point. He's all business. He ignores niceties and human interaction as much as possible. He won't care that this tall order of theirs is starting to take its toll on me both mentally and physically.

I exhale then rub my hand slowly over my face, only grateful that he can't see me and vice versa before switching on my happy-go-lucky persona.

"It's coming along slowly but surely, Eoin."

There's a pause. I can tell he's not happy with that answer and with how long all of this is taking, but right now I'm surviving on a couple of hours sleep a night.

"Isn't there anything we can do to speed matters up? Jaine's coping admirably keeping the IRS at bay by asking them to document everything before responding with a plethora of questions of her own, but time is running out, Jessie. Eventually, they'll see our delaying tactics for what they are. That's if they haven't cottoned on to it already."

I open my mouth to respond, but I don't get the chance as Dylan interjects.

"Jessie's working flat out, Eoin. I won't allow you to ask any more of her. She's already exhausting herself on our behalf." His tone is firm.

I swing my attention to him, mouth agape, as he defends me while sitting there barefoot in a pair of ancient blue jeans and a black tee.

Little brother has just told big brother to get off my case.

Would the real Dylan O'Connell please stand up because surely this can't be the same introvert who couldn't make eye contact with me until fairly recently.

Then I grimace.

I didn't realize that he'd noticed how tired I am. I guess I must look as shit as I feel.

Great.

"I understand that, Dylan, and I appreciate we're asking a lot, but there's also a lot at stake. Jessie, is there anything Dylan can assist you with to help speed up the process? Anything at all?"

Dyl turns to face me with so much understanding in those sapphire eyes of his that I immediately feel tears of self-pity prick my own. He wants to help. But, like him, I'm used to working on my own. Doing everything on my own.

Being on my own.

Perfectly lonely.

I don't want to relinquish any control. I don't want to let him in. I can't. The consequences if it doesn't work out don't bear thinking about.

He reaches out his hand and gently squeezes mine, causing more tears to prick my eyes.

My daddy would be so fucking proud.

"I'd need to give him full access to all my systems. I've never given anyone those sorts of privileges before." I'm answering Eoin but staring at Dyl.

It's a double meaning. Does he realize that?

"Do you trust me, Jessie?" he asks softly while smiling gently at me, and I can't help but return it with a nervous one of my own.

I nod slowly.

"Then show me what it is you need me to do."

And right there was the moment I let him in, knowing there was no way back.

CHAPTER ELEVEN

JAINE

Jaine's House, Rising, California

Padraig: *What would you do if you found out someone had been misleading you, darlin'?*
Jaine: *Is that an admission of guilt? Is there anything you'd like to get off your chest, Dylan?*
Padraig: *No.*
Jaine: *Good to know. So, are we talking a twisting of the truth or a blatant lie?*
Padraig: *Let's just say it's a combination of both.*
Jaine: *Well, an outright lie in this life would typically come with a compulsory death sentence attached.*
Padraig: *True. But I want to know what* you *would do. How* you *would react.*
Jaine: *Shoot the asshole in the goddamn head.*

Padraig: *Well, that's a given, but aside from that, darlin'. Say, if you were feeling generous.*
Jaine: *Well, I've had someone lie to me recently, and I was able to see my way past it, but only because they did something in return, and the positives far outweighed the negatives.*
Padraig: *Naming any names?*
Jaine: *Nope.*
Padraig: *So, what if the deceit was long-term? If the person had been lying for quite some time.*
Jaine: *I guess whether I'd want to end their life would depend on who it was and what the betrayal was over. On how big of a deal it was. It's not a one cap fits all answer, Dyl. Would I be able to forgive them? Trust them again after lying to me long-term? Nope.*
Padraig: *Right.*

THERE'S A PAUSE AND IT HAS ME WONDERING WHERE THE FUCK THIS is going.

Padraig: *And are you guilty of it?*
Jaine: *Of what?*
Padraig: *Lying.*

Yes. Yes. Yes.

I'm as guilty as sin. My mind immediately drifts to my little boy and the secret that will one day unfurl. The clock is counting down to the revelation of the biggest secret the O'Connells will ever have witnessed. The existence of a beautiful child with hair as black as coal and eyes of sparkling blue. The little boy that, with each passing day, looks more and more like his Irish daddy. Fin's parentage is undeniable. He has the same cocky nature and the same matching smirk. If he has any of my traits, I don't see them. All I see is my Irish shining out of him. His son is him in miniature form.

But then, is that all I'm choosing to see? Because with each passing day, I miss him more and more. They say time heals.

Bullshit.

All it does is fill you with regret and make you forget things you never wanted to let go of. I don't want to forget. I'm trying to preserve the memories, but more and more drip away each day like they're being held in a bucket with a hole in the bottom. And there's nothing to replenish them with. So soon it will be empty. Nothing left of a relationship that spanned nine years of my life. Both anger and guilt flow through me, and the tears that go hand in hand these days prick my eyes.

Yes, the clock is ticking rapidly now. I'm almost four months gone. Not much longer.

Jaine: *Yes.*
Padraig: *Is the lie you're telling forgivable?*
Jaine: *No, Dylan. It's not. So, I can only hope the person, when they eventually do find out, will understand my reasons for doing so.*
Padraig: *Same.*

WITH AN EYE ROLL I ANSWER MY PHONE TO HIM.

"Thank you, Jaine."

"For?

"Keeping the situation contained as much as you have done. I had no idea the IRS could be so quite so forensic."

"They're only doing their job, Eoin. Same as I'm only doing mine."

"You've been magnificent."

I laugh dryly. "I wouldn't go that far. But then I guess not all of us spend all day sitting around our ivory tower."

"Meaning?"

"Meaning I built my company from the ground up with my own two hands. I earned my success the hard way. You simply inherited yours."

"None of us get to choose the lives we're born into, Jaine."

He's tetchy now. And I'm actually not trying to be demeaning. I'm merely highlighting the truth. He was handed this life of his on a silver platter. He has an army of yes-people he delegates to over and above his siblings. Don't get me wrong, I do the same these days, but I made sure I learned the ropes inside out beforehand. There isn't one role in my firm I can't undertake and fulfill personally.

It's unlikely Eoin O'Connell can say the same.

"I fully appreciate that. It's not a criticism, so there's no need to get defensive about it. It's more an explanation. I've had to learn my craft inside out from the bottom up. Then perfect and hone it. Dealing with the IRS isn't something I'm experienced in, but I am very skilled when it comes to tying people in knots and causing delays where the situation demands it."

"And it's that experience we're paying for."

"You're not paying me."

"What do you mean?" He sounds surprised. I'm not sure why.

"You insisted I had created an owing."

"I didn't say we wouldn't pay."

"If I owe, I owe. It's not like I need the money, Eoin, as well you know."

"So, if there hadn't been an owing?"

"In my opinion, there wasn't one. That aside, in the end, I did it for Dyl. He was worried about the IRS situation. About the possible consequences. As was Jessie."

"What about me?"

"What about you?"

"Wasn't there a small part that saw you do it as a favor for me?"

"Let me think about that for a second.... no."

"So, you really do hate me that much."

"Jesus Christ, not this again There's an age-old expression, Mr. O'Connell. You reap what you sow."

"You'll be back in Manhattan soon enough."

"Yes. I will. And your point is?"

"You can then resume your friendship with Paddy."

I laugh in disbelief. Is this asshole for real? "And do you honestly think Sophia will allow that?"

"She won't be able to stop you."

"And do you not know your brother at all?"

"Meaning?"

"He would never disrespect her in that way. And I wouldn't either, for that matter. Or expect or ask him to. She'll be his wife. What he and I shared we can't ever get back. It's gone. I can't believe you're only just realizing that now. That you really thought Irish and I could just pick back up where we left off. After two years of not speaking and after he's wed."

Tears spring to my eyes. Tears of self-pity, which I'm not proud of. Tears for Finian. Tears for Irish. None of us deserved this fate. Especially not my little boy. Having to be kept a dirty secret.

"Jaine...."

I disconnect the call.

CHAPTER TWELVE

DYLAN

Jessie's Apartment, Hudson Yards, New York

"Thank you."

I turn to look at her. It's been a few hours since our conversation with Eoin. As soon as I hung up, I insisted she take me through the searches she needed me to run. The crucial data she had to urgently pinpoint. I know she was reluctant to allow me access to her systems, just as she was reluctant to go back to bed, but I insisted on both. I think she was surprised when I put my foot down and when she realized I wasn't going to take no for an answer.

The roles have well and truly reversed.

"For? Oh, and you have bedhead, by the way." I chuckle.

With a small smile, she rolls her eyes exaggeratedly and pats down her hair before retaking the seat beside me.

"For putting Eoin in his place." She was emotional earlier and, despite her best efforts to appear the opposite, she's still emotional now. We've been living in each other's shadow for over a week. I can read her. And what I'm currently seeing is a raw and exposed Jessie O'Brien.

And I don't like it. I don't like seeing her upset. I'd happily commit cold-blooded murder with no family coercion necessary because I'd willingly kill anyone who ever upset her.

More alien feelings.

I turn my attention back to the data manipulation because I don't want to make her feel uncomfortable by staring at her in her moment of weakness.

"You're working your fingers to the bone, Jessie. It's not sustainable. Unfortunately, our Eoin never sees these things. It's not his fault. He has a lot to orchestrate heading an organization as large as ours. I was merely highlighting it to him. To make him aware. Because I do see these things."

Because I see her. Every day. And I don't want that to end anytime soon.

If ever.

She's silent for a moment. Fidgety. It's clear she wants to say something and she's thinking how best to word it. She starts flicking through her screens to give her hands something to do, and I know why.

Because she feels vulnerable.

She exhales before she speaks. "This is me, Dyl. Or at least the other me. No one ever gets to see this Jessie. They see what I want them to. The loud, opinionated girl that always wants to be in the spotlight. But I don't need to be the center of attention when I'm on my own, and that's when this Jessie is allowed to surface. Unfortunately, this… our having to spend all this time together…. well, I don't normally spend this amount of time with another person. In fact, I don't spend time with anyone at all."

Silence.

I know I have to respond. To acknowledge what she's said. I guess this situation is a bit like being held in captivity. When you say things you wouldn't normally. Behave in ways you wouldn't usually. Show a side you much rather wouldn't.

Bare truths.

Then I just say it how I see it. "I guess we're more alike than we both realized, Jessie."

JESSIE

His response hit the nail on the head.

He's right. But then, wasn't that always going to be the case? Being an O'Connell, it was a given that Dyl would have an assertive alter-ego behind that passive exterior of his.

In so many ways, we're the same. The only difference is I choose to display my strength whereas Dyl chooses to hide behind his weakness. It's just the role each of us performs best. The skin we're most comfortable wearing on the outside world.

"Whatever our souls are made of, his and mine are the same." I chuckle as I say the cliché words aloud.

He laughs loudly. It's a nice sound because it's heartfelt and genuine. "Are you quoting Emily Bronte at me now?"

"You read?" I raise my head in surprise, immediately disappointed in myself as I do. Because the very thing I hate happening to me, I've just done to him. I've pre-judged him.

Did he realize?

He laughs again so probably not. "When you're as reclusive as I am, there's not much else to do but look at screens, work out, or read. I enjoy the classics." There's a pause. "I don't really spend time with anyone else either so I'm on my own a lot of the time too. But I'm fine with that. You know…being alone."

His voice fades away. I know why. Because like me, he can say it's fine, but it's not. Not really. Not that either of us will ever admit as much.

Perfectly lonely too.

Another pause.

We both realize Pandora's box has been well and truly opened during this lockdown. Truths have come out that we won't be able to simply hide away again, at least not from each other.

I shrug as I glance at him. "I just thought it sounded fitting."

He grins back. "You do know many would argue that Heathcliff and Cathy's relationship was toxic and incestuous, and that there was nothing romantic about it."

"I wasn't trying to be romantic." My response is immediate to the point of sounding clipped.

Was I sub-consciously trying to be romantic?

His smile disappears as his eyes search my face. I bite my bottom lip, feeling guilty at how dismissive my reply came across.

He turns his attention back to the data.

"I didn't think you were, Jessie," he answers eventually, his tone quiet, the atmosphere now noticeably cooler. Have I hurt his feelings?

I quickly discount that thought. How could I have? He's in love with his cliché blonde. Why would he have romantic feelings for me?

If we do hook up, at best all I'll ever be is next in a long line of O'Connell fuck buddies.

CHAPTER THIRTEEN

DYLAN

Jessie's Apartment, Hudson Yards, New York

"*PULP FICTION* IS ON NETFLIX."

We've been working together for weeks now. The data manipulation is all but concluded. Jessie's just finalizing and consolidating the last remaining items. I'm sitting in her screen room, scanning her set-up for any signs of external interference.

There is none.

Or at least none that can crack her coding. Her software is impenetrable, like mine. She's a techie perfectionist like me.

I don't need to check her systems as often as I do. I don't have to sit here day after day either, but it's become a habit. She's become a habit.

It's gone full circle. I'm aware of that. I now look forward to spending my time with her.

She's like a breath of fresh air. She's also certifiably insane most of the time. When the opportunity arises not to take life too seriously, Jessie O'Brien seizes it with both hands.

With every day that passes, I'm becoming more and more addicted to her.

I'm doomed.

"Is it?" I'm not sure what else there is to say.

Was it a question or just a general observation? We don't spend our evenings together, only our working hours. And in the unlikely event it's been offered as an invitation, there can't be any romantic innuendo attached. Jessie shot any chance of a relationship of that nature down in flames a few days ago during the Emily Bronte conversation.

My cheeks burn at the thought. How could I have been stupid enough to think that someone like Jessie O'Brien would ever be interested in someone like me?

Eejit.

She has her back to me. She's scrolling through her screens and adjusting things here and there. I could watch her doing this all day, every day. Then again, I could just stare at her doing nothing twenty-four seven. My gaze drops to her arse. It's perfection, wrapped today in a pair of ridiculously short pale blue jean shorts, her long, tanned legs on very welcome display.

"Since we're almost done, and we're stuck here, just the two of us, I thought we could watch it together. You know, maybe recreate that famous dancing scene. I could be the Uma Thurman to your John Travolta. Uma is my ultimate heroine, just so you know."

She pretends to swing a katana over her head, causing me to snicker. It's good to see her back to her old self, her brief moment of weakness well and truly over now the pressure's eased off. Will I ever see the other side of Jessie again? Who knows? It's my gut feeling likely not. I reckon she likes to keep her well and truly hidden. Still, I feel privileged that she felt comfortable enough to let her guard down around me, even if it was a one-off.

I watch as she starts dancing around the room while humming along to *Never Can Tell.*

"You're nuts," I mutter, pretending to concentrate on what I'm doing, the corners of my mouth twitching upwards as I take in her antics out of the corner of my eye.

"So, what do you say, Vincent Vega? You up for it?" She places her hands on my shoulders and whispers the question in my ear.

My blood immediately starts to travel south at the physical connection combined with the warmth of her breath. Even if I'm not up for it, my dick's telling me he sure as hell is.

"I…" I stutter.

I silently curse myself for sounding hesitant because I know it's the reason she quickly moves her hands away. I immediately miss them. I want them back on me more than I want anything else in the world.

"It was just a suggestion, Dyl. It's what friends do, you know? Catch a movie together."

Friends?

I don't want to be her fucking friend.

"I'd like that," I mumble, knowing I probably sound less than enthusiastic, but now with good reason.

Jessie O'Brien just friend-zoned me. Not that I should have expected anything else.

"I DIDN'T KNOW WHAT ELSE TO BRING." SHE ANSWERED THE DOOR the instant I knocked. It was strange seeing it fully closed as during the day it's wide open.

"Just yourself was enough, Dyl, but for the record, I'll never say no to potato chips. I'm a savory girl. And any flavor. I'm not fussy." She grins as she takes the pack from my hands while motioning her head for me to come in.

I stand just inside the entrance after she closes the door. Why am I acting awkward when we've spent so much time together? I guess it's because it feels a bit like a date, even though I know it's not. Jessie doesn't want to date me. Why would she when she could have anyone she wants? She's also made it clear she wants us to be just friends.

"You can come all the way in. Even after hours, I don't bite. Well, not unless you ask nicely." She smirks.

Cue red cheeks.

Even if she didn't mean it sexually, she now knows I've interpreted it as such.

Jessie, you can bite me anywhere and anytime you like.

I take a seat on the white leather sofa. It's only a two-seater, which means we'll be sitting close together—touching almost. My dick twitches at the thought. I swear to God he's reacted more these past weeks than he has in all the years preceding.

I run my hands through my hair. I need to shave it off again. It's messy, unkempt, and hanging past my ears, and not in a fashionable way like our Paddy's used to.

"I can sort that for you if you like."

I stare up at her as she places popcorn, chips, and dip on the glass table in front of us.

"Your hair. I'm not a professional by any means, but I used to cut my baby brother's until he reached driving age. We didn't have a hair salon in my hometown. You got any scissors?"

I nod.

"Bring them tomorrow?" She raises an eyebrow, and I nod again.

I DON'T REALLY PAY ANY ATTENTION TO THE FILM. THANKFULLY, I've seen it before, so I can answer any questions if quizzed.

My attention has been focused as discreetly as possible on Jessie the entire time. From the get-go, she's been a tease. With popcorn in hand, she immediately sat on the sofa, then stretched out her long limbs so her bare feet rested on my lap. She then preceded to part her legs before placing the bowl at the juncture of her thighs. It took me a full ten minutes before I reached for a piece. When I did, she snickered immaturely, causing me to snicker back.

I watched as she laughed, sang, danced in her seat, and became engrossed in the classic movie.

It captivated her. She captivated me.

Dance like nobody's watching. Sing like nobody's listening. Live like it's Heaven on Earth.

That right there sums up Jessie O'Brien.

Love as though you've never been hurt. I pray she never has been. Adrenaline surges through me at the thought of anyone ever hurting her. Of anyone trying to control, tame, or rein in that free spirit of hers. For the first time in my life, I feel murderous about something. About someone.

More alien feelings.

I'm not daft. I know the root cause is protectiveness and possessiveness. That I want to care for her, look after her. That I want her to be mine even though she doesn't want me.

Lost in my own thoughts, I don't realize she's fallen asleep. Her long blonde eyelashes lay on her golden cheeks, her lips parted just slightly as she breathes slowly in and then out.

I watch her. Is that weird? Maybe it is. My excuse is I'd never get the chance otherwise. Not unobserved like this. Not without her noticing and making some smart-mouthed comment.

I frown as my gaze graces her face. She looks exhausted still. Her eyes have the tell-tale dark circles. She's been working flat out, doing all she can to sort this worrying situation for my family. Yes, she's being paid handsomely for her efforts, but it's clear Jessie takes pride in her work. She also has a vested interest in my family because Jaine does.

I have no doubt she'll pull it off.

But when it's over, then what? Yes, she'll still live in the apartment below, but we both know how easy it is to avoid each other. We'd been doing it successfully for months.

I don't want to avoid her. I want to see her every day. I want her feet in my lap. I want to deal with her off-kilter moments. I want to laugh at her wild antics and her, at times, toilet sense of humor.

I want all of that.

For me.

Not for anyone else.

Lifting her legs slightly, I stand before placing them gently back down. Deciding not to wake her, I cover her with the throw that's resting over the back of the sofa.

I want her in my life. But she's friend-zoned me. And the question is, can I be happy with just that?

CHAPTER FOURTEEN

DYLAN

Jessie's Apartment, Hudson Yards, New York

"Stay still and stop fidgeting. In fact, it might be best if you took your shirt off. That way, it won't get any hair on it."

We're in her kitchen. I'm sitting on the leather executive chair, staring at her like she's finally gone round the bend.

"I'd much rather keep it on."

She steps back and smirks cockily at me, her hands on her blue jean-covered hips. "You do know you've not got anything I haven't seen before, right, Dyl?"

Jealousy courses through me. I don't want to think of her with other men. Looking at them. Touching them. I realize my Neanderthalic brain has taken over once more, and I'm thinking like my cavemen brothers. It must the O'Connell blood. I'll be dragging her around by the hair next.

Jessie is her own person. I have no right to lay claim over her. Especially when someone might be about to lay claim over me.

Standing, I remove my Henley, so I'm left in only a pair of black jeans. I'm tall at around six-three. While slim built, I'm toned and defined. I have a gym in my apartment. In the absence of having much else to do, I work out most days, so my body is in pretty good shape.

I feel the heat of Jessie's gaze as she takes in my half-naked form. I wait for her to speak. She doesn't.

"Cat got your tongue, Jessie?"

Another alien feeling.

Confidence.

Given the way she's admiring my body, I feel bold enough to use one of our Paddy's expressions. I like the attention. I want her to look at me and like what she sees. And she does. I can tell.

"I think it's best we don't talk about pussies, Dyl. Or tongues, either, for that matter."

Jesus Christ. My one-track mind doesn't need any more encouragement, but her saying that means it's now all I *can* think about. Her pussy. Her taste. Her smell. Her wetness. Her heat.

And my tongue.

"Dear Lordy Lou. You sure as hell are rocking that eight-pack." She exhales long and slow, then exaggeratedly fans her face in an attempt to inject some light-hearted humor into an atmosphere that's suddenly gotten very heavy and very heated.

As a result, that's not the only thing I'm now rocking.

I run my hand slowly down my abs, resting it at the top of my jeans. I watch as Jessie tracks the movement then clears her throat. When she finally drags her gaze upward, our eyes connect. For the first time ever it's *her* cheeks that are flushed.

I retake my seat, and she stands behind me, running her fingers through my hair before gripping its length. There's a growl. I realize the sound came from me. That I like the feel of her small hands fisting my hair.

Now would be a really good time to call our Paddy to talk mundane family matters, but I know I'm not going to be allowed that opportunity.

Fuck.

"You like that, Dyl?" she asks teasingly and deliberately does it again.

I don't reply. She knows I do. The animalistic response I made was all the affirmation she needed.

We eventually lapse into a comfortable silence as she precedes to cut my hair using the small pair of scissors.

"Would you…" She nudges against my knees, motioning for me to part my legs so she can step in between. I do so, and her tits are then inches from my face. From my lips. From my tongue. From my teeth.

Two. Perfect. Fucking. Handfuls.

Her springtime scent envelopes me like an aphrodisiac, and my fingers are suddenly itching to grip her waist, and pull her down onto my lap so I can kiss her. Is she as affected by our close proximity as I am? Because I can see her heartbeat in her throat. It's pounding, just like mine. I'm sure of it.

Fast. Furious. Erratic. Synchronized.

I close my eyes and lose myself in everything Jessie while gritting my teeth for control as she pulls on my hair.

I want time to stand still. I pray for this torture never to end.

"Tada," she announces way too soon.

I open my eyes and take in her proud as Punch grin. Putting down the scissors, she places her hands on her hips once more and my gaze instantly drops to the bare skin of her tanned, flat stomach displayed by her little crop top. She then holds one out, motioning for me to take it in mine before yanking me to my feet.

"Come see my handiwork, Dylan."

I don't let go of her hand when I stand, and she doesn't remove it either. It feels right. Perfect. Like hers belongs inside mine.

She chuckles when I pretend to drag my heels as she pulls me across the apartment. I'm guessing it's her bedroom we end up in as it smells of her. It's all glass and mirrors. Reflections everywhere.

My already provoked brain immediately thinks of us fucking. Seeing ourselves from every angle possible. How many men has she had in here? The thought of even one makes me feel murderous.

We stand in front of the mirrored wardrobes, and I stare at our reflection. Her blonde to my dark. Her tanned to my pale. Her softness to my ridged. We look good together.

So fucking good.

"Well, what do you think?" She nibbles on her bottom lip as she awaits my response. It's the first time I've ever seen her look unsure of herself.

I take in my haircut. Long on top, short on the sides, and falling into my eyes. I look normal instead of resembling a Rikers Island inmate with an almost shaved head. I look a lot like our Paddy. I never realized how much until now.

"Handsome?" Smiling, she elbows me in the ribs as she asks the question of my reflection in the mirror, her hand still held firmly in mine.

"I don't really think that's for me to say, is it, Jessie?" I turn around to face her, and she does the same. "What do you think?"

There's a pause. Is she struggling to find her words?

"Well, I think you're very handsome. In fact, I quite often refer to you as Delectable Dylan." Her voice has gone quiet.

"Delectable?" Is Pandora revealing even more of her secrets? The corners of my mouth twitch upwards as my confidence soars.

"Alliteration. It sounds good. You know. The two Ds together," she mumbles, her gaze now fixed on mine. She's waiting for my reaction.

"There are other words that start with a D." I smile gently.

"Well, I was going to use dickhead." She snickers quietly.

"But you didn't." My voice is low and teasing.

"No. I didn't." It's whisper-like. Is she embarrassed by her admission? That she finds me physically attractive? I think she is.

All I can hear is her breathing and mine. I'm sure if I listened closely enough, I'd be able to hear our hearts pounding too.

Kiss her. Kiss her. Kiss her. Do it.

My gaze drops to her mouth, and hers sinks to mine. My attention flits back and forth. Mouth. Eyes. Mouth. Eyes. She's hypnotizing me without even trying.

How it happens, I don't know, but suddenly our breaths are mingling. Did I move? Did she? Did we both? Or is it something neither of us had any control over?

Our mouths are so close. Our noses are touching. She breathes out. I breathe her in. I breathe out. She breathes me in.

Our lips brush. Sparks fire through me, and my dick is immediately rock hard because I reckon they fired through her too.

The moment is gone when her phone rings in the other room.

We both step back.

"*The Notebook* is playing on Netflix tonight."

"I'll bring the chips," I reply quietly, before reluctantly releasing her hand as she walks off to take the call.

Dylan's Apartment, Hudson Yards, New York

"What do you mean you almost kissed Jessie?"

I put him on handsfree to continue the conversation, then lie back on the sectional, running my frustrated hand down my face.

When I left Jessie on the phone, I silently prayed to God our moment hadn't passed and that He grants us another.

Because I demand a do over.

"Just what I said, Paddy. She cut my hair, and then things just sort of happened."

"You let her cut your hair?"

"Yes, and now I look like you."

"Well, that's no bad thing, brother." He laughs.

"I don't know what to do, Paddy."

"Well, you put your mouth against hers…."

"Very funny."

He chuckles again. I'm glad he's finding this situation amusing. I'm not.

"I don't know what to do about this arranged marriage thing. If she is interested, I don't want to lead her on only for history to repeat, and for me to wind up in the same situation as you."

"Who's to say you will? Personally, I'm still of the opinion Da was just spouting hot air where you're concerned. And even if he wasn't, maybe Jessie's just chasing sex. Maybe she's not wanting any sort of formal commitment."

"What do you mean? She doesn't strike me as the promiscuous sort."

"I'm not saying she is, Dyl. What I am saying is that people take what they want from relationships these days. Whether that be casual sex or something else. Just because she wants to fuck you doesn't mean she's looking to marry you or carry your offspring. Both men and women have fuck buddies these days. A handful of partners they rotate. You know. Like our Cill had before Sarah, and like Eoin does now. Everyone using everyone else for their own selfish needs."

"And you think that's all she might be chasing?"

"What I'm saying is don't read too much into it just yet. Jessie's a grown woman. I'm sure she'll make her wants and expectations known in due course, and then you can decide if what she's after is something you're able to give her. And vice versa."

"And what if she asks questions about the family?"

"As pillow talk?" He laughs. "It's not likely. Given the amount of time you've spent together I'm pretty sure she won't ask anything she hasn't already. If she does, just change the subject. Simple. Da would turn even more insane if we were to spill our guts to any female about what it is we actually do. Women may suspect, but we can never admit to anything unless we commit to them first."

"Jaine knows."

"She's the only one who's ever been allowed to live, and that's strictly on the basis that she never tell the tale, and you know it. Plus, you and I know the secret we hold over her is far greater."

He pauses momentarily.

"Listen, Dyl, for what it's worth, my advice is this. If you decide you want Jessie for keeps, find out about her, and then run her credentials past Da. From what I can gather, Jaine thinks she's a good match, which means she's further up the rankings than you and I know or suspect."

"You're right."

"And I know it's probably been a while, but fucking's like riding a bike. You never forget how to do it."

Should I pretend or should I just tell him the truth? I decide to opt for the latter.

"I've never ridden that particular bike before, Paddy."

There's a long pause.

"Jesus Christ. Not ever?"

"No."

I'd never have admitted that to anyone. Only him. And he knows it's because I trust him. I know he won't take the mickey or breathe a word. He probably can't believe it. I'm not sure I can either. I mean, opportunities arose, but I'm just not the type to have meaningless sex.

"Well, you've watched the Discovery Channel, Dyl. All I can say is hop on and try not to fall off."

"Helpful." I laugh dryly.

"Listen, you're an O'Connell. It's in our blood to be the best at everything we do. Trust me. Jessie O'Brien will have no complaints."

CHAPTER FIFTEEN

JESSIE

Jessie's Apartment, Hudson Yards, New York

"What do you mean you almost kissed Dyl?"

Jaine's on handsfree. I grin at her shocked tone as I press the filter down on the coffee press then wait for it to do its thing. "Well, truthfully, partner, it wasn't the first time we almost kissed."

"Jesus Christ, Jessie."

"I know. I know. There's a Disney princess lurking under his bed, waiting to jump out and yell 'surprise'! But there's been no sign of her. Not one single blonde hair. There hasn't been the entire time I've lived here. I know it's a gamble. That one day she may magically re-appear. But then, maybe she won't. Is it a risk I'm willing to take? I think it is. Because underneath that professor exterior of his there's a rock-hard body just going to waste. A body that's been designed for the sole purpose of committing lots of dirty sin."

"How the hell did you see his body?"

"I cut his hair. I asked him to take his top off, and he obliged. Did you know he looks just like Padraig with his hair cut in a similar style?"

"I didn't need to know that."

"Anyway, the attraction is definitely not one-sided. So what have I got to lose by giving in to temptation?"

"Your heart?"

Valid point. I quickly change the subject, so I don't have to dwell on that thought or answer any more questions. I don't want common sense to prevail. It's too late for that. If all we're destined to be is fuck buddies, then so be it. It's not ideal but I've come round to the idea now. Beggars can't be choosers.

Can I be that and not let myself get any more attached? Sure I can. It's just casual sex with no emotional entanglement, right?

"Anyway, O'Connell brothers aside, what's happening with the Undertakers? I just spoke to my daddy. He mentioned them briefly but didn't give much away. It was all one-word answers. He sounded worried, though."

She lets out a frustrated sigh.

"Rumor has it their ex-VP, Ghost, is in talks with their former backers—the suspected traffickers. Rumor also has it he's been trying to entice some of the brothers to form a new club by offering more money. When that's not worked, seemingly, he's threatened to harm their families. Ace is helping mediate, but I'm not sure what good it's doing."

"That doesn't sound like Ghost to me." I frown.

"You know him?"

"Since I was a young girl. He may be ruthless and ambitious, but he'd never turn on a brother, not unless having worked with Reaper for so long he's changed for the worse."

"Maybe he has."

"Maybe. Do you think we should involve the Irish or the Scorpions?"

"I've been holding back on both. What kicked off last time was an alliance issue, so it involved all of us. This time, it's more of an MC problem. I'm not sure it's appropriate to drag the Dusters into this mess. And Delaney's still healing. I don't want to set him back."

"He's the prez of an MC, Jaine. It comes with the territory." My tone is firm.

I appreciate she cares for him, as does my baby sister, but the prez role comes with responsibilities that can't be shirked.

"I realize that. Look, let's play it by ear. You keep checking in with your daddy, and I'll do the same with Ace. If things start to spiral, then we may have no choice but to ask the others for assistance."

"You may create another owing."

"It's what I'm trying to avoid."

"But if the Dusters can help?"

"I don't want to owe Eoin anything, Jessie. The pound of flesh he claws back every time far outweighs the purchase price of the initial loan."

"ARE YOU WEARING COLOGNE, DYLAN O'CONNELL?"

I inhale the citrus notes exaggeratedly as he stands in the doorway of my apartment.

"It's body wash. I've just showered." He's looking at me like I've finally gone insane. Given what's on my mind, maybe he's right.

"You been working on that eight-pack of yours?" I grin as I raise one eyebrow, rejoicing inwardly as his cheeks redden. It happens so rarely these days, as we're so familiar with each other. I don't think I'll ever tire of finding ways to make this Duster blush.

It's way too cute.

My eyes graze over him as he stands there in navy jogging pants that are hanging low on his slim hips and a white tee that clings to his toned upper body.

Did I just use the word cute? Scratch that. The word I'm looking for is hot. He's so fucking hot he's smoking. His black hair is still wet and messy from the shower. I desperately want to run my fingers through it and yank hard on the inky strands. I want to hear him growl.

Again. And again. And again.

I realize I'm staring. "Where the hell are my manners? Come on in."

I step aside and let him enter, my eyes immediately dropping to feast on the most perfect of visuals while his back's to me. His ass. I raise my gaze just as he turns. Given the small smile tugging on his lips I figure he knows exactly where I was looking.

"I brought these." He passes me the bag of potato chips he's holding, and I watch as his gaze drops to my tits. I know why. I'm braless and wearing a tight white tank top. My nipples feel painful, so they're probably making their presence well and truly known. Shouting silently for his undivided attention.

Lick me. Bite me. Suck me. Fuck me. In any order. Please. And thank you.

"Popcorn's ready. I'll bowl both up and be right with you. Why don't you go make yourself comfortable." I smile sweetly then walk towards the kitchen. I'm fully aware his eyes are trained on my ass, which is barely covered in a pair of tiny cotton shorts.

"It turns me into an emotional wreck every time I watch it. I don't know why I do it to myself. I'm such an idiot." I sniff loudly before blowing my nose.

As usual, my feet are resting on Dylan's lap. I watch as he traces small circles on the inside of my ankle with his finger. He's being tactile. He's trying to comfort me.

"Why does the movie make you cry, Jessie?"

He looks at me and I suddenly feel self-conscious as he takes in my no doubt red-rimmed eyes and color-matching nose. I lean my head back on the arm of the sofa, sighing loudly before replying.

"Noah and Allie's perfect, imperfect relationship, you know? The meaning behind it. That we shouldn't settle and that we should all try to find that unconditional kind of love. That once-in-a-lifetime love. A love that's just yours."

He turns away and frowns slightly before looking at me again. "And do you think there's someone like that for all of us?"

I nod. "I'm sure of it. But whether we're fortunate enough to ever meet that person in our lifetime." I shrug. "Well, that's a different story."

I sigh loudly once more, then reluctantly remove my feet from his lap and stand. I feel emotionally drained.

Damn movie.

Closing my eyes, I stretch upwards, my hands grabbing at the air.

My body immediately starts to tingle. I know it's because his eyes are drinking me in. Feasting on me because they can, and because I'm not witnessing them doing so. My nipples react, which I'm sure won't go unnoticed.

I know. He knows. My body knows. It has his full, undivided attention.

Opening my eyes, I look down, and our gazes connect. Eye contact no longer makes him uncomfortable. Having me as his captive audience doesn't either. He no longer looks away. He holds his own. And he's gotten even more confident since I called him delectable to his face.

Unbelievably so.

It also hasn't gone unnoticed that he's making more of an effort with his appearance these days. I realize it's because he wants my eyes on him. And truthfully, there's nowhere else they'd rather be.

Dylan O'Connell is beautiful. Both inside and out.

"Well, I should get going." He stands, breaking our brief moment of silent mutual appreciation, and in doing so, we end up mere inches apart. I can feel the heat from his body. Smell the citrus notes from his skin. I lift my face to look at him. His pale, chiseled features, his full mouth, his eyes of sapphire blue. I part my lips in silent invitation, and his gaze drops to them.

Will he? Won't he?

Kiss me. Kiss me. Kiss me. Do it.

I close my eyes, leaving the decision in his hands.

Is he going to? I breathe in through my mouth, suddenly filled with the overwhelming need to capture him in my lungs. To oxygenate my heart with his expelled air.

His breath is hot against my lips. Is he stealing my oxygen, as I suddenly can't breathe. Every part of me is just anticipating.

Wishes. Waits. Wants. Seconds. Minutes. Hours.

His lips brush mine. At first, I think it's just my imagination as the touch is nothing more than an almost non-existent caress. They brush mine a second time, and it's followed by a soft moan that I know came from me.

He. Kissed. Me.

He made the first move. It proves he wants this as much as I do.

Snaking my arms around his neck, I close my eyes and press my nose against his throat, inhaling his masculine scent. He swallows thickly. Is he as nervous over this moment as I am? The one that's been building between us for weeks. For months.

Since forever.

Slowly lowering my hands, I press both against his chest. I can feel his heart beating. Its rhythm matches my own.

Fast. Furious. Erratic. Synchronized.

I push him gently, and he lands back on the sofa. As I straddle him, his hands instinctively move to cup my ass. It feels right. He feels right. Everything about this feels right.

It's like his slim hips were made to fit perfectly between my thighs.

He lifts his face to look at me. His cocky smile still lingers on his lips, but his eyes are dark now. He's watching and waiting for me to make the final decision.

Lifting my hands, I run them through his still damp hair before tugging on it. Hard. He growls, and I silence him by pressing my mouth against his, running my tongue along his full bottom lip before pulling it down with my teeth and dipping in to taste him.

His unique flavor explodes on the tip of my tongue. Salt from the chips mixed with adrenaline and everything else that makes up Dylan O'Connell. An instantly addictive taste. One I know I'll never get enough of, and one I know I don't ever want to share.

My tongue asks his to dance with mine. I groan in response when he immediately accepts by filling my mouth.

Claiming the space. Claiming me.

His mouth is firm, his breath is hot, and when his teeth bite down hard on my bottom lip, it causes a gush of wetness between my legs. Sensing my arousal, the wild animal in him is instantly unleashed. Fisting my hair, he bites and sucks on my neck before his mouth devours mine once more. I can't breathe. I'm not sure I want to. What a perfect way to fucking die.

Lips. Tongue. Teeth. I want them all.

His hips thrust upwards instinctively. Hard. Huge. Throbbing. I'd heard a rumor about the O'Connell boys, and given what I can feel beneath me right now, I'd say those rumors are both accurate and well-deserved.

I grind against him in silent invitation, and his hands grip my hips, holding me in place so he can thrust back his acceptance over and over, his dick pressing deliciously against my clit each and every time.

"I need you to fuck me, Dyl." My breath is hot against his ear.

"I realize that's what you're chasing, Jessie, but I haven't got a condom." The words are spaced out, his mouth sucking hard on my neck in between each one.

"I'm on the pill. Are you clean?"

"What do you mean?" His mouth stops. I'm not sure what part of that is difficult to understand. My hands fist his hair, yanking his head back.

I frown down at him. His lips are swollen, and his eyes are drunk with desire. "I mean, have you been checked out recently? Since you were last with someone else?"

He tenses. "There's never been anyone else."

I'm not sure how long it takes for that reply to filter through my lust-addled brain and finally sink in. Is he saying what I think he is?

"Dylan, are you telling me you're a virgin?"

That tenseness he was emanating is superseded by a full-on shutdown on both our parts as I scramble off his lap. My thoughts and feelings are all over the place. Given he doesn't get out much by personal choice, I fully expected a lack of experience. What I never expected was for him to have none.

Being his first carries way too many emotional risks for me.

We sit side by side in silence. I'm not sure how long passes.

"I think I should go," he finally mutters.

"I think that's best."

CHAPTER SIXTEEN

JESSIE

The Hudson Dusters' HQ, Manhattan, New York

"Expertly handled. Thank you, Jessie girl."

"No thanks necessary, Fergal. I was just doing my job." I smile warmly at him.

I've been invited to attend their meeting today. I figure it's for two reasons.

The first is the IRS has now concluded its audit on Play. The result? The Duster boys earned themselves a slap on the wrist and a ten million dollar fine.

They got off lightly in my opinion, and all because, on my advice, they held their hands up, admitted the error of their ways, reassured the revenue service that valuable lessons had been learned, and vowed it would never happen again.

JAL then subsequently picked up the baton and pled the Duster's case by insisting the inaccuracies were a result of professional negligence. JAL then successfully managed to negotiate the fine down from ten mil to two by convincing the IRS to go after the named and shamed former accountant for the other eight mil.

Jaine cited this route may be more financially rewarding as, having done a background check on the accountancy firm in question, it turns out several other wealthy clients employed the use of their incompetent professional services. In other words, plenty of other lucrative avenues for the IRS to venture down that wouldn't see them or their family members having to be fitted for concrete shoes. Obviously, any threats of the mobster variety would have been veiled, made off the record and worded far more eloquently as in I don't think the word concrete would have been used, merely implied. Then again, it may all be hearsay. Although I suspect not.

"Nonsense. You've gone above and beyond."

"Well, I couldn't have done it without Jaine. It would have been a far different outcome had she not tied them up in legal knots."

"Yes, our thanks to the biker too." It's said grudgingly. We can all hear it. He makes no attempt to disguise his loathing these days. He hates her guts. It must be over the standing up matter. The wound of disrespect is festering as time goes on as opposed to healing.

"I'm also a biker, Fergal," I casually remind him.

He nods in acceptance. "Yes, you are, Jessie girl. Please accept my apologies for being dismissive of your colleague's contribution. I appreciate we needed access to her expertise on this matter. Us O'Connells are grateful for everything you've both done for the Dusters. That aside, now we have young Molly working alongside our Paddy, we'll no longer be requiring Jaine's services, although we will still be needing access to your skillset."

"Of course, Fergal. It goes without saying I'm here for as long as you need me." I smile at him once more, and he returns it with a fatherly one of his own.

For whatever reasons, I've been blessed with being able to wrap Da Duster around my little finger. Not sure how it happened. It wasn't intentional or planned. We just developed a soft spot for each other from the get-go.

I'm not complaining about our daddy-daughter instabond. I'm not about to look a gift horse in the mouth. Let's be honest, it's better to have Fergal O'Connell on side than off.

"Will you still be requiring Jaine to represent the Duster's part in the alliance with La eMe, or do you want me to let her know Molly will now be undertaking that commitment? I'm sure she'll be more than happy to hand the reins over to someone as competent. She'll still be actively involved, of course, as JAL represents all the other interested parties. I'm sure she won't mind lending Molly a professional hand if it's needed."

"Is Jaine now representing the Sons? If I recall, her relationship with Lucifer didn't start on the best of footings," Eoin asks.

I look at him. He was present at the Nevada meeting, so he'll be aware of what was said by my daddy, and of Jaine's less-than-receptive reaction and subsequent response.

I smile as I tell a little white lie. "No, you're right. It didn't. But that's all water under the bridge. JAL will indeed be representing Sons of Satan on this matter moving forward."

"Noted."

The second reason my presence has been requested here today?

It's my guess it's to enable a certain introduction to be made. I look across the table and my eyes meet with the ice-cold barb of who I suspect to be Molly McGrath. Twenty-eight years old, from a well-to-do Dublin family and currently earmarked as the future Ma Duster. She's extremely beautiful I have to say.

She'll be here on a trial basis for sure. Given the importance of the role in question, this won't be a done deal. She'll be put through her Duster paces before being crowned big bad Ma, and likely by the reigning matriarch herself.

Molly sits to the right-hand side of Eoin. I switch my attention back to him briefly and she tracks my gaze, then glances at him possessively. They're fucking. I can always tell. Not that it's any of my business, but that sure didn't take long. She's only been stateside for five minutes. I suppose they have to make sure they're compatible in *all* ways.

The frigid look she cast in my direction is because she's prejudged me and now thinks I'm competition. The reason I know is because I've been on the receiving end of the same look a million times before. It's a look that irks me every time because it's undeserved every time. It's tiresome. I'm only interested in one O'Connell, and that one currently refuses to even glance in my direction.

"And this must be the lady herself." I initiate the introduction in the absence of any of the O'Connells appearing willing to do so.

"Yes, this is Molly." Eoin doesn't add anything to that, and definitely not that she may be his future fiancée.

"Molly, this is Jessie O'Brien. Jessie handles our accountancy function."

I smile warmly at her. She may have judged the book by the cover, but I'll give her the benefit of the doubt and let her earn her three strikes.

"It's good to meet you at long last, Molly. I hear you're a lawyer in the making but you've still to finish your studies, is that right?"

She narrows her eyes briefly. Does she not like that question? I thought it a pretty tame icebreaker.

She flicks her long jet-black hair around her shoulders. "I've concluded my studies. It's the relevant work experience I still need to acquire."

Her accent is thick Irish. She sounds like my daddy, although his has softened over the years. I immediately note the absence of any niceties or pleasantries. Maybe it's a lawyer thing. Or does she think I'm intentionally highlighting what she feels is a flaw?

"Perhaps you could acquire the necessary on-the-job experience working for JAL. Jaine's looking to expand operations as soon as she returns to Manhattan, and I know they're currently hiring in preparation."

It's true. Both JAL and JAA have been full-on head-hunting, leaving no stone unturned in recruiting the very cream of the outlaw crop, both in terms of legal and financial.

"Jaine's expanding her business?"

I smile warmly at Paddy.

"She is. With her new commitments to La eMe among many others, she was given no choice. It's all or nothing with Jaine, as you know. She's going all out to ensure her clients' needs are met by implementing plans to operate coast to coast. Moving forward, our kind will want to be dealing with JAL and JAA. You'll definitely want us working with you, not against you." I chuckle.

I expect Molly's already aware of all this. That she'll have done her digging and asked pertinent questions on the legal grapevine in advance.

She waits until she's sure I've finished speaking before she replies. "As a lawyer, Padraig will be able to sign me off."

Is she for real?

We've just had to dig the Dusters out of a great big hole as a result of their using financial services that were woefully lacking. You don't use nepotism to sign off on professional qualifications like ours.

I lean back in my chair and frown at her. "Surely, you're not just looking for a signature in a box, Molly? That's a bit of a risky strategy given who you'll be representing. Is your aim not to be the best at what you do?"

I know mine always was. And I am the best. Or at least in my own humble opinion I am. That's why I'm working for the Dusters.

"Of course my aim is to be the best, but rumor has it Jaine Jones has slept her way to the top of the legal profession. That it had nothing to do with professional competence. As I'm sure you'll appreciate, I'm not sure that's the sort of experience I wish to add to my own repertoire. Most women would rather achieve success without having to resort to lying on their backs."

My poker face is now firmly in place to hide my surprise at her lowering the tone and at this very personal attack on Jaine.

"I can assure you those accusations are unfounded. Jaine *is* the best at what she does, and from my experience, to be as good as the best, you need to learn from the best. As I've already offered, let me know if you wish me to have a word with her on your behalf. I'm more than happy to do so."

I leave it there. I know I've made an extremely valid point, and everyone sitting around this circular table knows it. In all walks of this life, more so ours, even a professional qualification is no substitute for cold, hard, murderous experience.

In this outlaw world of ours, Molly here has none, whereas Jaine Jones has it in spades.

CHAPTER SEVENTEEN

JESSIE

Dylan's Apartment, Hudson Yards, New York

"Can I have a word, please?" I'm standing in the doorway of Dyl's apartment. I've never been up here before, but he's avoided me long enough.

Today's meeting saw him not look in my direction once. Pretty soon, it will be noticeable to others, that's if it isn't already.

He's dressed down in grey jogging pants and a black crew neck tee. His feet are bare, and his black hair is wet from the shower, so he's obviously been working on those mouth-watering abs of his.

Meanwhile, I'm still dressed in my office finery, having just left a meeting with Paddy and a very grumpy Eoin. It's my guess, despite outward appearances, that the eldest brother's arranged marriage contract is chaffing him somewhat.

Dyl's face is impassive as he motions for me to step inside. I walk straight across to the window to take in the visual it affords, but also to distance myself.

Well, there's no point asking for trouble.

The view from my apartment is exceptional, but from his penthouse, it's truly breathtaking. Only the best for a Duster. I glance around his monochrome living space. It's immaculate and minimalistic like mine. Something else we share in common.

My gaze finally lands back on him. The man who's been haunting my every waking and sleeping thought since I first laid eyes on him all those months ago.

The man I almost fucked.

The man who's a bonafide virgin.

I still can't wrap my head around it, but he wouldn't lie about something like that. I doubt he'd lie about anything, but then, what do I know?

He could be lying about absolutely everything.

The truth is, I thought we were on the same page. We weren't. We never have been.

It should have been casual sex. Nothing more. A fuck for a fuck. An exchange of no-strings pleasure. A simple case of wham-bam-thank-you-ma'am.

Yes please to all of the above and with no emotional entanglement, thank you.

But that's not possible, is it? Because I'd be his first. And firsts are always messy. Because firsts trigger something emotionally. And that right there? Well, that's dangerous territory.

But not for him, for me.

Because it's not him that's in danger. I'm the one at risk of falling even further than I already have. Because, unlike him, I'm not pining over anyone else. Unlike him, I have no male secret who could appear at any given moment and whisk me off my feet.

So I can't be his first. Because Jaine's right.

Unlike him I could lose my heart.

"How long has this cold shoulder treatment to go on, Dylan? I'm sorry I didn't sleep with you. Is that what you want me to say?"

"I don't appreciate being led on, Jessie." He remains expressionless as he stands with his hands stuffed in his pockets. There's a dark confidence emanates from him these days. I realize it's his Duster mode. Let's face it, it was always going to be there. He just needed someone to activate his dark side.

Lucky me, I found the hidden switch that turned this bad boy on.

"I didn't lead you on, or at least not intentionally. You should have told me."

"What difference would it have made? What difference *does* it make?"

I get why he's asking the question. I really do. He's a man. From his point of view, sex is nothing more than a physical act.

A form of release.

And if he hadn't mentioned it, would I have realized it was his first time? No, I wouldn't have. Because despite him having zero practical experience, from what I could tell he's way more than capable of carrying out the act without any guidance or tips from me.

But he did say, so emotionally, for me, it's a disaster waiting to happen.

I just know it is.

"Your first time should be… I don't know. A momentous occasion. A fireworks display. A big deal." I'm clutching at straws.

"Was yours?"

My thoughts drift to the old pick-up truck I lost my V-card on the back seat of while parked behind the diner on Colton main street. I had just turned sixteen, and he was eighteen. He was a brand-new prospect with the Undertakers. A man of the world, or so

I thought. All the girls were chasing him, but I caught his eye. After several weeks of dating and him promising me the world, I caved in and let him fuck me. He did so exceptionally well and set an extremely high benchmark. But then he dumped me the very next day.

At least he did the decent thing by letting me go before he moved straight on to the next in a long line of eager-to-be-filled holes.

It hurt.

Both physically as well as emotionally.

Thankfully I didn't see much of him after that, what with me going to school in Vegas and then heading straight to college.

Then again, I was a Son and he was an Undertaker. That right there was a sure-fire sign we were ill-fated right from the start.

"You're different from me."

He laughs dryly. "Stop lying to yourself, Jessie. You and I both know that's not the case. We're the same. We just express ourselves differently, that's all."

He folds his arms across his chest, causing his pecs and biceps to bulge indecently. I don't need any more temptation, thank you, God. I drag my eyes back up to his now smirking face.

"You're way more sensitive than I am." I toss in another flimsy excuse, and one we both know is definitely not true.

"You cried over a movie."

"I dare anyone not to cry over *The Notebook*." I laugh, too exaggeratedly

"I didn't."

"No. You're right. You didn't," I answer quietly, my laugh evaporating. Seems he's not in a jokey kind of a mood.

We stare at each other. The atmosphere is changing. I need to get out of here. There's only so much willpower a girl can be expected to have in any given period of time, and the little I do have is rapidly dwindling.

"I should go." I quickly make my way towards the door, slowing when I realize I need to walk past him in order to leave. Shit. Did he position himself there on purpose? "If we can go back to being friends and being civil to one another, that would be great."

He grabs my arm when I reach him, much like I anticipated he would.

Much like you hoped he would you mean.

"And what if I don't want to be friends?" He pulls me flush against his hard body, his arm snaking around my waist giving me no choice but to place my hands against his chest.

Jesus Christ, he feels so fucking good beneath my fingertips and doesn't he just know it.

Smug sapphire blue eyes bore into mine.

Lust. Desire. Determination. It's all going on in there. They're also letting me know there's no escape for me this time.

His gaze drops to my mouth. He's going to kiss me. And I won't stop him.

"With benefits."

I stare at him, momentarily confused by his words. Then I understand precisely what he's suggesting.

"Are you okay with that, Jessie? That you and I are friends with benefits." He raises one eyebrow. It's not a question. It's more a case of him being polite and letting me know how it's going to be from here on in.

"I…." I don't even get the chance to respond before his lips capture mine, his tongue pushing past to fill my mouth. The familiar taste of undiluted adrenaline and everything Dylan O'Connell floods my senses, drowning every inch of common sense in its path.

His hand fists my hair as he devours my mouth and I snake both arms around his neck in silent acceptance.

Green light given his other hand yanks my front against his. He's hard. Rock hard. I can feel his dick throbbing against me.

Picking me up, he starts walking. Our mouths only disconnecting when he stops to set me down. I glance around. It's his bedroom. It smells of him. Citrus. A huge black metal framed bed takes center stage.

I push him back onto the grey-sheeted surface. Resting on his elbows, he watches as I remove my clothes. His nostrils flaring when all that remain are my black lace panties.

"Off." He growls, motioning his head toward them.

Easing them slowly down my thighs, I step out, then stand there naked. I have a good body. I know I do.

"Come over here." His voice is low as he stares at me.

I'd love to know what's going on inside that head of his. Does he like what he sees? Am I the first woman he's seen naked? I mean, just because he's never fucked anyone doesn't mean he's not done a whole host of other downright dirty things.

I walk to the edge of the bed, and he grabs my hand and yanks me down beside him. I shiver as the coolness of the sheets touches my warm skin. We lie there on our backs, side by side, staring at each other.

Him dressed. Me naked.

Figures.

I don't care what he says. This *is* a big deal for him. There's only one first time for any of us. It can't ever be repeated. There are no do-overs. And it's something none of us ever forget. No matter how under or overwhelming it turns out to be.

He stands and pulls his tee over his head, giving me the perfect visual of his gym-honed torso. He then deliberately toys with the waistband of his jogging pants, that cocky smirk of his playing on his lips once more.

Will I be the first female to ever see him naked?

He yanks them down his legs to display his body in all its glory. He is *the* single most spectacular sight I have ever seen in my life.

No exceptions.

And the rumors are true. Those O'Connell boys really are packing. His dick is massive, all throbbing veins and leaking pre-cum.

My mouth waters just looking at him.

He stands there letting me admire him. He knows I like what I see. It's not difficult when there's nothing not to like.

His body covers mine as he rejoins me on the bed. Skin on skin. Hot. Smooth. I groan as his weight pins me down, appreciating the sensation of feeling trapped and unable to move.

His mouth covers mine, his tongue sweeping deep as his hand drops to cup my pussy. I'm soaked. He growls his approval before thrusting two fingers inside me.

"Fuck, Dyl." I whine.

Even his fingers are perfect. He pumps them slowly in and out as his thumb circles my clit, all the while watching my face to gauge my reaction to what he's doing to me.

"You like that, don't you." It's not a question. He already knows I do.

"Are you sure you've never done this before?"

He chuckles against my lips. "Just because it's my first fuck doesn't mean I don't know what I want and what you need, Jessie."

I nod. I can no longer speak. To do that, you need to be able to breathe. I can't. Raising my hips, I silently beg for more, and his fingers oblige by fucking me faster. Harder. The sound of just how aroused I am filling the room.

His mouth drops to my nipple, and as he bites on the sensitive tip, I reach my high, crying out as the orgasm takes hold and my walls clench around his fingers.

It's not enough.

"Dyl." I whine.

He moves, positioning his slim hips between my thighs, and I groan when the blunt, slick head of his cock touches my bare pussy.

He looks at me, his blue eyes almost black. Then we both watch as, inch by perfect inch, he sinks into me until he's fully sheathed and buried.

Our eyes meet. I smirk, deliberately clenching around him, causing him to curse before pulling out and pushing straight back in with one single punishing thrust.

I groan as the friction of his dick embraces every pleasure point all at once.

Perfect. Fucking. Fit.

"Dylan, please," I beg shamelessly, needing more.

Moving my hands above my head, he pins them down with one of his own. Then he gives me exactly what I begged for.

More. Way more.

Those O'Connell boys? Well, they must be born masters of their craft as all I can do is anchor my legs around his hips as he drives into me with deep, ruthless thrusts. I try to pull my hands free, but he holds fast, and I sink my nails into his skin as I come again.

"Fuck." He curses as my walls grip his thick shaft, pulling him over the edge with me, his hips jerking as he fills me with his cum in short steady thrusts.

We lay there afterward, his sweat-sheened body still pinning mine down, his heart thudding in time with my own.

I'm fucked. I know I am.

I've caught the feels and then some.

As I lie here, tasting him, smelling him, breathing him into my lungs, I realize every fuck will just be another nail in the coffin that already contains my doomed heart.

CHAPTER EIGHTEEN

DYLAN

Dylan's Apartment, Hudson Yards, New York

MIND-FUCKING-BLOWING.

It's the type of word our Paddy would use, but it's the only one I can think of that adequately sums up what just happened between Jessie and me.

My whole body weight lies across her, and she loves it. I know she does. It seems she likes to be pinned down. If she could purr with contentment right now, she would. If I could, I'd be doing the same.

My deflated dick is still nestled in her pussy. He doesn't want to leave the paradise he's found, and I can't say I blame him. I lift my face from the crook of her neck and look down at her. Her lips are swollen and bruised, and she's glowing. Orgasms suit her complexion. I need to make sure she has plenty. Every day. Several times a day.

I can't quite believe it. Right here. Right now. Jessie O'Brien is all mine.

Her two endless legs are wrapped around my hips, her perfect tits are smashed against my chest, and her fingers are stroking gently up and down my bare back.

I've died and landed in heaven with a brainiac blonde supermodel angel.

My mind drifts unwittingly to the recent conversation with Da about this arranged marriage malarkey. Nothing's been said since, so maybe it's not happening. I mean, the girl ear-marked to be our Eoin's future wife is now living in New York, working for the company, and he's fucking her on a daily basis. Meanwhile, I've still not been told anything nor shown any air-brushed photos of my proposed intended.

I reckon our Paddy's right. I reckon it was all a false alarm.

Da likes Jessie. Would he and Ma deem her suitable if I were to ask to court her? It's not like I can accidentally get her pregnant like what happened with Cill and Sarah. It's just my luck that Jessie's on birth control. Would she let me fuck her bareback if she wasn't? Probably not. And I'm not sure my dick would want to give that up.

Da would want to know how high up the rankings she is, although as our accountant, maybe that could be bypassed. She's already proven herself invaluable to our organization.

But would Jessie want to date me? Our relationship has changed from strangers to working colleagues to friends with benefits. Is that all she'd ever want from me? Or would she want more? Our Paddy says most people have fuck buddies these days.

Is that all I am to her? All I ever will be?

I should ask her. But we've just taken a huge step. Maybe it's too much too soon to start talking about relationships and commitment. Perhaps she'd run a mile at the mere mention of anything more permanent. She knows in this life, combined with the fact we're both Irish Catholic, what courting leads to.

You don't court without intention. Marriage at the end is almost a given.

I realize I'm staring down at her, and that she's frowning back. I can only imagine it's because I'm wearing some deadpan expression on my face as I'm lost in my own thoughts.

"Well?" She smiles almost shyly. A rare sight from someone usually so gregarious and confident.

"Well?" I raise a questioning eyebrow at her, even though I know exactly what she's asking.

"Oh, playing games are we, Dylan O'Connell? You think because you've fucked me you can turn into an even cockier asshole."

I grin at her, then groan when she clenches her pussy around my dick, immediately perking his interest.

"I've got no complaints, Jessie."

"High praise indeed. Then again, you have nothing to compare me to." She smiles, but she knows what I'm saying. She can read between the lines. That it was out of this world.

"Well?" It's my turn to ask.

"Well, Jaine did mention you O'Connells have huge cocks and you know exactly what to do with them. Let's just say she wasn't lying."

"That's maybe too much information about our Paddy."

"Sharing's caring." She chuckles at my grimace.

I push her blonde hair behind her ear. Its soft, silky length slips between my fingers. Our gazes lock, and I feel my soul connecting with hers as it's done several times before now. Smiling eyes of baby blue gaze up at me. Warm. Caring.

Loving?

"Which MC do you belong to, Jessie?"

"And that question came from out of nowhere." She laughs out loud. "I could tell you, but then I'd have to kill you."

I frown at her. "Why? Is it a secret?"

She shrugs. "It's no secret, but our relationship's a business one so I'm not sure why it's important."

"Our relationship *was* business."

"Friends with benefits including business. How's that?"

"Better." I grin at her.

"Why do you want to know?"

"Just curious, I guess. You know a lot about my family, and all we know about you is that you're from an MC on the west coast."

"I only know about your business ventures. I don't know what you boys get up to the rest of the time. It bet there aren't many you'd admit that to, even though most will suspect."

"Let's just say my other commitments are way less than those of my brothers."

"And mine are way less than those of my siblings."

We both know we're talking about killing and the like, but neither of us will admit that aloud. I'm glad we're similar. That if she has taken lives, there haven't been many.

"And have you always been so outgoing on the surface?"

She nods. "It was just easier to show a personality that fit the overall visual. To be who everyone expected me to be. I was head cheerleader, dated the quarterback, and lived the high school dream." She smiles, but it doesn't reach her eyes.

"Not so much of a dream, then?"

She lets out a long sigh, then pauses before she carries on. "Listen, Dyl, I'm not vain, but I'm not blind either. But being easy on the eye isn't all it's cracked up to be. My school days weren't the best days of my life because of how I looked. No one saw what was underneath, as no one bothered to search below the shiny surface. I wish I had a dime for every girl who said they envied me. The truth is, if they'd known the reality of what it was like being me, maybe they wouldn't have been quite so keen to trade places."

Her mood has changed. I'm seeing glimpses now of the other Jessie. The one she wears when she lets her guard down. I'm glad she feels comfortable enough to share her with me again.

I'm surprised by her admission though. I would have thought she'd have been popular because of her looks. Turns out, she wasn't. It seems being close to physically perfect doesn't make you happy.

"It's the thing I hate most." She speaks quietly.

I look at her and wait for her to continue.

"Being judged for the way I look or for my background."

I think back on her reaction to when I commented on her music choices, cursing inwardly when I realize I'm no better than most she's encountered in her life.

"I judged you, didn't I?" The fingers stroking my back stop then slowly restart.

"You did, but then I judged you too, I'm ashamed to say. When you said you were a reader, I was…taken aback."

I think back to that conversation. I hadn't picked up on the fact she'd judged me. But then, how many times have we both been silently judged by others?

Too many to count.

"And have you always been so quiet and reserved?"

I smile as my thoughts drift to my brother. "I have, but I have an excuse. I grew up with Paddy. Us two have always been thick as thieves. There was no way I could ever compete with him, so I stopped trying. Well, not that I tried very hard in the first place as I never wanted to be center of attention."

She laughs. She knows what I'm saying. I love my baby brother, but God help anyone who drags the focus and conversation away from him.

Nuzzling my face back into her neck, we lie there in comfortable silence, each of us lost in our own thoughts. All our lives others have made assumptions about us because of how we act or how we look. I think we've both come to realize that with each other, we can just be ourselves, warts and all.

No pretense. No hiding. Just Dylan. Just Jessie.

She clenches that pussy of hers around me once more, and my dick twitches into life, more than ready for round two.

I lift my head and raise a questioning eyebrow. I know exactly what she's going to ask.

"Will you fuck me, Dylan O'Connell?"

"Gladly, Jessie O'Brien." I smile against her lips as my mouth devours hers once more.

CHAPTER NINETEEN

JAINE

Jaine's House, Rising, California

"So, you're fucking him."

It's a statement more than a question. Reading between the lines, it's obvious. She's been AWOL for days. No doubt all of them spent in bed with Dylan. Surprisingly, he's been as responsive as always with his messages, which is strange considering he must surely be preoccupied with other things.

My heart sinks in my chest when I realize I'll have no choice but to lessen my reliance on him. That Jessie's growing needs and demands for his time and attention will, quite rightly, now take precedence over my own. I can't be selfish. I've used him as my crutch for long enough.

"I'm saying nothing, your honor."

"You don't have to. It's obvious given you've been pretty much uncontactable."

"Yes. Sorry about that."

She sounds guilty. She shouldn't.

"Don't apologize for taking time out given the hours you had to commit to the IRS matter. And for the record, there's only one reason he's asking to know more about you."

"And that is?"

"I could be wrong, but it's my guessing, he wants to, as they call it, court you, but he wants to get Da Duster's approval to do so beforehand. So, he needs to make sure you're a match."

"Dear Lordy Lou. It's all so old-fashioned."

"Despite their murderous tendencies, these boys have been raised the old-fashioned way. They take these matters extremely seriously. Marriage. Kids. Family. It's a lifetime commitment for them."

"Speaking of marriage, I've met Molly McGrath now."

"And? What was she like?"

"Well, she's young, beautiful, and she even looks Irish, so pretty much what you'd expect. Disappointingly, she took one look at me, judged that book cover, decided I was competition, and immediately got all possessive over Eoin."

"And did you set the record straight by telling her you're not interested in the arrogant asshole?"

"Nope. If she wants to believe I am, then let her." She huffs.

"Bitchy?"

"I disagree. I wasn't the one who made the assumptions. She also didn't have anything complimentary to say about you."

My back is immediately up. Normally I don't pay any mind to nasty comments. Let's face it, I've had to tolerate them most of my life. But I'm already fucked off at being a regular talking point at the O'Connell meetings without the future Ma Duster throwing in her two cents' worth.

"What's her goddamn problem with me?"

She pauses before responding. "I'm not sure I should tell you this."

"Jessie." I say warningly.

"She suggested your business successes have only been achieved because you have a professional mattress attached to your back."

I pause. Is she joking? When she doesn't continue, I realize she isn't.

"She actually said that?" I hiss.

"She did, but maybe it's just a simple case of sour grapes, partner. Maybe she's done her homework and she knows who her *real* competition is when it comes to Eoin."

"But I'm not competing. I have no interest in Eoin or in being the next Ma Duster."

"I realize that. Hopefully, Eoin will do the decent thing and bring her up to speed. It's not like he doesn't know how you *actually* feel about him."

"That's not likely now, is it? He'll want to make himself look like he's Mr. Popular with the ladies."

"On a positive note, Da Duster is anxious for her to fill your legal shoes."

"Figures. He hates my guts. Well, she can be my guest."

"I did mention it may not be in the Dusters' best interests to make any rash decisions given she has very little practical experience, but Fergal seems hell-bent."

"Does he now? Well, do you know what, Jessie? I may take that decision out of their hands. I've had enough of Da Duster looking down his nose at me. Of the O'Connells thinking they're doing me a favor. And let me break the news to the future Irish king that you're fucking his baby brother before you go mentioning anything to Dyl, please."

"Of course, there's no rush. Or at least none that I'm aware of. Just keep me posted. Oh, and one other thing."

"Jesus Christ. I'm not liking the sound of this."

"The Sons of Satan."

"What about them?"

"Eoin asked if JAL would be representing them. I said yes and…."

"You did what?" I snap.

"Let me finish. He asked the question. I didn't want to say no and for him to put Molly forward."

"Why not?"

"It's my daddy's business, Jaine. He's worked hard to make the club a success and she has zero experience when it comes to our MC ways."

"But Lucifer thinks I'm a bent lawyer."

"He doesn't."

"Those words came out of his mouth. I watched them do so with my own eyes."

"It was tongue-in-cheek. A joke."

"It wasn't funny from where I was sitting."

"Please will you represent the Sons?"

I sigh. I can't really say no to her. It's not her fault her daddy's an asshole.

"A three-month trial period once he's out of contract with his current legal representation. And I'll need that confirming in writing. If he pisses me off one more time, then we're done, and it will never be revisited. Agreed?"

"Agreed. And thank you. I'll let my daddy know."

"I'm doing this for you, not him."

"I appreciate that, partner."

"Eoin." I call him the moment I come off the phone to Jessie.

"Jaine, how are you?"

"Are you sure you don't already know the answer to that question? My ears are constantly burning because I seem to be the main topic of conversation at Duster HQ these days. It's starting to piss me the fuck off."

"Jessie and that big mouth of hers," he grumbles under his breath. "We were discussing how well you handled the IRS situation."

"Well, thank you for the unnecessary recognition for the small part I played and the eight million dollars in petty cash I saved you, but there really was no need. I was merely satisfying an owing that didn't exist. And what else was said about me?"

"From your tone, I suspect you already know."

"Too goddamn right I already know. And why would Molly say such a thing? Call my professionalism into question with such blatant, unfounded lies? I suspect a bitter Ma Duster is behind this, filling her head. Am I right?"

There's a pause. It tells me all I need to know.

"If by your silence you're trying to suggest you're in any way unsure then allow me to call bullshit. That aside, even if your ma had made unsavory comments about me to Molly, they should never have been aired. Who else is Molly bad-mouthing me to? The Dusters need to rein her in."

I'm aware I'm hissing but I'm pissed off.

"She's Irish. She's headstrong and opinionated."

"What's being Irish got to do with it? I know a lot of Irish people, and The Almighty appears to have bestowed manners on the majority of them. It was uncalled for and rude. She needs to keep her thoughts about me to herself. She doesn't even know me. She hasn't even met me. *They* haven't even met me, so who are they to judge?"

"They tried to."

"Jesus Christ. Listen, I didn't want to meet them. Why is that being turned into such a big deal? I'm a biker. I'm a lawyer. I have no need to interact with your folks as either, so there was no reason for me to meet them. If they now dislike me due to my not turning up to a meeting I hadn't agreed to attend in the first place. If they feel insulted or disrespected in some way as a result, then that's your fault, Eoin. Not mine. And I don't give a damn if Molly is earmarked to be the next Mrs. Claus. You need to rein her in. I will not tolerate my professional reputation being slandered."

He attempts to speak, but I don't allow him to. Because enough is enough. It's time to draw a line under this fiasco.

"Let me just finish what it is I have to say, please. Now Jessie also mentioned that your da is keen for Molly to take over any legals currently handled by JAL. Given how strained things have become I believe that would be the best course of action for all parties concerned. As per the terms of our contract, therefore, I'm verbally advising that JAL is withdrawing all professional services from the Dusters with immediate effect due to the working relationship becoming untenable. To adhere to the terms of notice contained within said contract, I shall write to you formally this evening."

"So, you're withdrawing your services?"

"Yes."

"So, if the IRS comes back?"

"Then I'm confident that between them, Irish and Molly can handle any legal aspects that arise."

"And if there's an issue with the alliance?"

"Then I'm also confident Molly can deal with that. If she's currently ear-marked to be the next Ma Duster then she'll have to roll her sleeves up and get stuck in sooner rather than later. There's no time like the present."

"You still have an owing."

Here we fucking go. Same shit, different day.

"The owing you fabricated in relation to the Nevada incident has been repaid. The IRS matter was addressed free of charge in full and final settlement of said owing."

"So, you're choosing to make an enemy of the Dusters."

"On the contrary, Mr. O'Connell, I'm not choosing to do anything. It would appear the Dusters are choosing to make an enemy of me."

There's a pause. He won't take this lying down, so I know he'll come back with something to try to rein *me* in. Good luck with that, asshole.

"Then we may have to consider which MCs we use as part of the alliance."

I laugh dryly. "I'm guessing this is aimed at the Scorpions and the Angels, right? Obviously, you can't make any decisions when it comes to the Sons as they operate via La eMe themselves."

"Correct."

"So that's the best you can come up with? Do you honestly think I couldn't secure a plethora of new alliances and transport opportunities for both MCs given the rate my business is expanding and who it's expanding to incorporate? Finally, you're showing your true goddamn colors. The colors I first witnessed when you came to my apartment that day. Well, if you want to resort to underhand tactics and blackmail, Eoin, then, please, be my guest. I may then have to consider whether to also terminate JAA's contract with the Dusters."

"You're making a mistake, Jaine." It's his turn to hiss. I can't help but smile at his pissed off tone.

"On the contrary. I'm making a stance—something I should have done a long time ago. Don't call me, I'll call you, which translates to goodbye. Forever."

I disconnect the call.

CHAPTER TWENTY

JAINE

Jaine's House, Rising, California

"ACE, WHAT THE HELL IS GOING ON? IT'S BEEN THREE DAYS." I'M home alone again. It's happening way too often. I pick absentmindedly at the ancient cream leather sofa as I sit on its cold surface. It's as old as me. It's slowly falling apart, but I'll be damned if I'm ever letting it go. The memories it holds of Pop. Of Ace. They're irreplaceable. Those memories are also likely the only things still holding the thing together.

"I'll be back tomorrow, PJ."

"You're doing too much. You're spreading yourself too thin. You sound exhausted." Tears prick my eyes. It's not tears of self-pity for me. It's tears of concern for him. Ace is on the road way too often. He's running himself into the ground.

"It's only for a little longer, sweetheart. Just until we get things tied up with Ghost."

"But why are you having to get so involved in what the Sons and the Undertakers are doing? Surely Lucifer and Tadgh can handle things their end? Conor too? They're three grown men. It's not right they expect the Angels' council to be operating without their prez."

"Clay can handle it."

"But he shouldn't be expected to."

"*I said* Clay can handle it."

There's a pause. Something's wrong. Or if it's not wrong yet, it soon will be. I can feel that shit in my goddamn bones.

"I'm sorry for snapping, PJ. Anyway, how's Fin? And how's my other son cooking?"

"Fin's caught a cold. He's snotting everywhere and being all melodramatic, just like his biological daddy would be. And your other son is causing me to visit the restroom every five minutes. Apart from that, everything's the same. Nothing ever changes in Rising. You know that, Ace."

"You should make the most of it. You'll be back in Manhattan soon enough."

"And what if I don't want to go back?"

He exhales in frustration, and I know he's running his hands through that beautiful long black hair of his. "You have to go back, PJ. We've been through this already. Fin needs to have a relationship with his daddy."

"Yeah, I know." I exhale loudly. "Anyway, speaking of the O'Connells, I had a long talk with Jessie today followed by a run-in with Eoin. The end result is I pulled JAL's services."

"Shit."

"Well, he's an asshole and the girl earmarked to be the future Mrs. Eoin O'Connell has taken an instant dislike to me, most likely no thanks to Roisin. She said the only reason I'm successful in business is because I have a mattress attached to my back."

He lets out a low whistle. "She actually said that? Has she got a death wish or something?"

"That's what she insinuated according to Jessie. Anyway, I've just about had enough of them."

"They're your family, PJ. Whether you like it or not."

"Correction. They're Fin's family. And they don't even know that yet."

"You're five months gone. They'll find out soon enough."

"I just needed a break from Eoin, Ace." I hate myself for sounding whiny. "He's too demanding. Always asking for my help. Saying I owe him. I'm not asking him for any more favors. He always wants way more in return."

"I know exactly what it is he's chasing." His voice is low.

"What do you mean?"

I know I must sound surprised, but Ace has never even seen me in the same room as Eoin, so how would he know the eldest brother looks at me like he wants to fuck me every time we meet?

"When he and I met for the first time in Nevada. If looks could kill. And then when he sang your praises during the meeting? Well, his infatuation with you was pretty obvious. Even Razr picked up on it."

"Ace…"

"I know you won't have led him on, PJ. I just pray for his sake that Padraig never finds out."

"Why would Irish care? He's getting married soon."

"An event he's still not happy about. Cill and I were talking about it earlier today. Padraig is just accepting of his fate."

"But I thought…."

"He's marrying the Sicilian because he has to, not because he wants to. Because it's his Duster duty. I thought you'd have known that given how often you speak to Dylan."

"We don't talk about Irish. We agreed from the outset it would be best for everyone that way. I guess I just assumed as he'd never reached out in all this time that he was happy."

"Nope. And my concern is he'll be even less so if he finds out his big brother wants you for himself."

"Well, the asshole can't have me. I'm already taken."

"I figure I'll keep watching my back all the same. I hear the eldest O'Connell stops at nothing to get what he wants." He laughs, but I think he's being serious.

"Eoin's been entered into an arranged marriage now anyway. And he sounds accepting of it. Hopefully, they'll wed sooner rather than later."

"I wouldn't hold your breath, sweetheart. Eoin O'Connell isn't a man who likes to be told what to do. Not even by his own folks. He won't be rushed into anything. This girl will be on trial for sure. There's no way it's a done deal. Not considering the importance of the position that needs fill…."

"Enough about him, Ace." I interject. The asshole's not worth the oxygen. "I'll see you tomorrow. I love you." Tears prick my eyes again, and this time they are ones of self-pity.

Fucking hormones.

"I love you too, PJ. I'll show you just how much the minute I get home."

"Promises, promises."

"You know I always deliver on them, sweetheart."

WITH THE PHONE STILL CLUTCHED IN MY HAND, I MAKE MY WAY into the bedroom, thinking about what Ace said about Irish.

Does he miss me? Does he think about me? Is it wrong of me to want that? Selfish? To want him to love me still, even after all this time?

I lie back on the bed and stare across the room, taking in its tones of greys and creams. It's Pop's old room—a grown-up space. It's nothing like my pink childhood bedroom with all its sparkly, feathery, and glittery things going on.

From time to time, I still lie on my white metal princess-style four-poster bed in that little pink room. It's when I want to recapitulate on certain parts of my past. The parts from ages seven to eighteen and from ages twenty-eight to now almost thirty.

When I want to think about Pop. About Ace. About my life here in Rising.

In a way, I've lived two lives. In two separate places. And as two different people. One life here in Rising with Ace as plain Jaine Jones. And one in Manhattan as Jaine Jones the businesswoman.

Ace has never been part of my New York life. Irish has never been part of my life in California. I've spent almost equal amounts of my past in each. Is that the reason I need Ace and Irish? Why I feel so incomplete without them both? Same as I feel incomplete without Rising and Manhattan?

My gaze drifts to the crib at the side of the bed, my eyes now fixed on the pale chubby cheeks of my baby boy. He's nine months old now, and he's his daddy's double in every way. Fin would have a great childhood growing up in Rising, but I know he'll never get to experience that because of his parentage.

Could I continue to live a lie? Of course I could. I'm thousands of miles away. No one would ever know. And I'd be lying if I said the thought hadn't crossed my mind.

But if I did, it would be for selfish reasons. Not wanting to face reality. Not wanting to deal with the consequences of the secret I've carried since Fin was born.

I could never do that to Irish. I could never do that to Finian. And Ace would never allow me to do that even if I wanted to, same as he won't allow me to give up my career.

As if he knows he's in my thoughts, Fin stretches his chubby little arms in the air and my eyes are instantly drawn to the horseshoe on his wrist. The birthmark that all the O'Connell males carry.

Will Irish love him as much as I do?

I hope so.

Wiping the tears from my eyes, tears I didn't even realize had started falling, I scroll through my phone and stare at his number. The one that used to light up the little screen on my phone at least a million times a day, maybe even more. Not that I need to search for it to remember the digits as they'll forever be imprinted on my heart.

Would he answer if I called? Would I answer if he did?

I guess we'll never know.

CHAPTER TWENTY-ONE

DYLAN

Dylan's Apartment, Hudson Yards, New York

"Fuck me, Dyl."

Magical fucking words indeed, and who am I to refuse? I don't think my dick has ever been harder as I take in the perfect vision in front of me. Jessie is on her hands and knees with her pert little backside in the air, begging for my cock.

Her legs are parted in silent invitation, her perfect pink folds wet with her arousal. She wants me. No one else. And that's a god-like feeling right there.

I run my fingers up and down her soaking wet heat, and she arches her back, raising her hips higher.

"You want my dick, Jessie?"

"Yes." She's hissing now. She's desperate. I'm taking too long, and she's pissed off at not getting what she so desperately wants. I sink two fingers into her, and she groans her pleasure. She tries to press back to take more, but she can't as her wrists have been bound to the bed frame with my tie, so she's restricted.

Positioning myself behind her, I rub the head of my rock-hard shaft up and down her entrance, lubricating the blunt tip with her slickness. I press inside her—just an inch. Then pull back out. I do it over and over.

"Dylan!"

"Beg for my cock, Jessie."

"I will not beg." She hisses as she yanks on her bindings. It's a half-hearted attempt at best. There's no escape. In truth, she doesn't want to.

In direct contrast to her professional self, Jessie likes to be told what to do in bed. Held down. Tied up. We've not gone beyond that yet.

Where's the rush.

I don't know where her boundaries lie. I'm not even sure she does. But hopefully, we've got a whole lifetime together to discover that.

I rub my hands over the smooth skin of her arse, then slap one cheek hard, leaving a beautiful red handprint.

Right now, it's mine. She's mine.

"Fucking asshole." She swears at me, but it's clear she loves it as her arousal is now coating her thighs.

"Beg."

"No."

"Beg."

"No!"

"Then you're not getting my dick."

"Please."

"I didn't hear you, Jessie. What was that?"

"I said please, you asshole!"

"No need to shout."

Gripping her hip tightly with one hand, I use the other to rub my dick up and down her slickness once more, and then I thrust in to the hilt. I grunt, my eyes immediately rolling to the back of my head as her hot walls clench around my cock. Embracing me. Welcoming me home. Sheathing my dick just fucking right.

"I need more, Dyl. Please," she whines, her face now flat on the surface of the bed, her eyes closed.

"You're a greedy girl. But because you said please, you're going to get more. Way more."

I pull out, then push back in. Slowly. Over and over. Her little pussy tightens around me perfectly every time.

I shift us forward so the bindings aren't pulling so much, and then I fuck her hard, fast, and deep, her hips pushing back to take more of me each time. Sweat sheens my body and drips down onto her back to mingle with hers. She arches further, taking me deeper. I look down as I drill into her, and the sight I behold is fucking beautiful. There is not one inch of my thick cock that's not glistening with her slickness.

Her legs start to shake, and I know she's close.

"Are you going to come all over my dick, Jessie? Tell me what you need."

"Harder!"

The rest of her words are garbled now that the blood carrying oxygen to her brain has traveled south. With one hand, I press her top half firmly against the bed so she can't move, then, lifting her hips further with the other, I slam into her. She shatters around my cock, strangling me with that little pussy of hers as her wetness coats my shaft. I feel my own release clawing at the base of my spine as I continue to hammer into her. She knows I'm close as she spreads her legs farther and then clenches. And with that move, I'm royally fucked, and she knows it. My balls explode as I thrust as deep as I can, coating every bit of her inner walls with my cum before collapsing on top of her. She groans her approval, appreciating my weight pinning her down.

We lie there for a time in comfortable silence, my body covering hers. I know neither of us wants the other to move. Neither wants to end this perfect moment. Nothing else matters. I know deep down that no-one else will ever matter. Not to me. There's never going to be anyone quite like Jessie O'Brien.

Fuck buddy. Fuck buddy. Fuck buddy.

The niggle is back. Annoyance that he is. When we're in the moment, I'm confident that she wants this as much as I do. Wants us as much as I do. But the afterglow? He has me questioning everything. Turning me into a doubting Thomas.

Is this a premonition of what's to come? Is this magical world we've created just an illusion?

Is me and her forever just wishful thinking on my part?

"So, you can't tell me anything."

We're naked. Catching our breaths between rounds two and three. Our legs are tangled, the grey bedsheets are twisted around us, her head is resting on my chest, and her hand is stroking lazily across my skin. Even after two rounds of pretty intense sex, she still smells fresh as a daisy. Like springtime.

"I agreed with Jaine."

"I know, but surely that agreement's been superseded by everything that's gone on recently between her and the Dusters."

"Between her and Eoin, you mean, and because of what Molly insinuated."

"She's his future wife."

"Potential."

"Potential." I correct myself. "Jaine put him in a difficult position."

"Are you for real?" She raises her head and frowns down at me. "She accused Jaine of sleeping her way to the top of her profession."

"I know what she said. I was there, remember?"

"And you think that's acceptable?"

"It's not my place to say anything, Jessie."

She rolls her eyes at me before lowering her head back to my chest. "Jaine won't back down. You do know that."

"I know. We're only grateful she's not pulled the accountancy services."

"Yet."

"Has she intimated that she might?"

"No, but if the Dusters, or more so your big brother, puts one more foot wrong, then she will. Jaine's just looking for an excuse. She wants nothing to do with him. No contact. No anything. He's been manipulating her for months, and she's had enough. I can't say I blame her."

I breathe out slowly. I know what he's been doing. I also know the secret he's been keeping from Paddy. A secret that's not mine to spill. And the one Paddy's keeping from Jaine. Again, another one that's not mine to spill. At some point soon, there's going to be the equivalent of the big bang Hudson Duster-style.

"I know. Anyway, he's been warned to stay away from her now."

"By?"

"Ma."

"Why?"

"Because she's aware of his fondness for her. I'm sure Molly also suspects who her competition is."

"Jaine's not competing, I can assure you. On the contrary. She hates your eldest brother with a passion. I don't understand how Paddy can't see this obsession of his when it's visible to everyone else."

I shrug. "I think even if he suspected, he'd immediately rubbish it. He'd never believe his own brother could do that to him."

She snorts. "Does he not realize that the resident king of the hill only ever looks after numero uno?"

"Yes, he does, but I don't think he realizes he'd walk over everything and anyone to get what he wants. Even his own family. I don't think any of us realized that."

"Well, now he's dating Molly, hopefully he'll back off from Jaine."

"Hopefully, but that still doesn't help my situation. About wanting to know more about you."

"Where's the rush?"

Her hand drifts lower, her fingers circling my cock, which instantly hardens. She's such an insatiable little thing, but I'm not complaining.

Where's the rush, indeed? No mention's been made of my arranged marriage, so I guess I'm off the hook.

CHAPTER TWENTY-TWO

DYLAN

The O'Connell Home, Darling, New York

I STEP OUT OF THE SUV AND TAKE IN MY FAMILY HOME. IT'S A bordering-on-vulgar mini-mansion with numerous bedrooms and way too many other living spaces. I'm not sure why my parents never downsized once we'd all flown the nest. They could live here and avoid each other for days if they wanted to.

To hold on to memories maybe. Then again, underneath and covering the entire footprint of the property is a safe space laden with everything the family could ever possibly need to survive an apocalypse.

As Da would say, you can never be too careful. He's right, of course.

In this life, you can't.

The building's ostentatious appearance is finished with water fountains and landscaped gardens. The only real blight is the security system—cameras at every turn and electrified everything, all coordinated and monitored by yours truly. Unfortunately, there's only so much you can do to beautify such things.

It's Sunday. The day of the week when the Duster masses descend on St. Peter's Church to confess our multiple sins and take our well-deserved penance on the chin from old Father O'Reilly.

Before he settles himself in that confession booth for the day, he rattles the donation plate in your ear as he walks around with it personally. There's a method in his madness. That way, he can see who puts in what. God forbid your offering isn't enough. If he thinks it's on the light side, your penance will be doubled, maybe even tripled.

Short arms. Deep pockets.

He's been heard to mumble that more often than not when he deems your tip to The Almighty himself to be insufficient in his eyes. You'll pay for being stingy when you're inside that booth.

Valuable lesson learned for next time in more ways than one.

I'm just grateful it's not the last Sunday of the month. That's when the family has to stop at home for lunch. When our ma makes full use of the kitchen and produces enough meals to feed an army. Most remains un-eaten. All are crammed full of potatoes, so we can cling to our Irish roots by filling our guts with starchy carbs before spending the following days detoxing.

I open the front door to the smell of home-cooking and the sight of the familiar gold flock-papered wall heavily laden with photos of my brothers and me. The opposite surface is a shrine to the rest of the family and holds a plethora of images of my uncles, and their families.

Given our recent expansions to the west coast, our cousins, Aidan, Shay, and Donal have been signed up to join the Duster ranks here in New York. They could be due to land next year. It could even be tomorrow. Da doesn't tend to furnish the rest of us with the finer details. He prefers the element of surprise.

"Is that you, Dylan?" he shouts from his office, which is just off the front door. He spends most of his time in there. I don't know what he does within its four walls, but I do know an arsenal of weapons surrounds him. It makes sense. We have a plethora of enemies. He's even more careful now wee Caoimhe comes visiting most days.

"Aye, Da. I'm here to look at that intermittent fault you're experiencing with the CCTV. I can't see anything wrong at my end, so I thought I'd best come and take a look at it from yours."

I make my way into the most used of the family rooms. It's a comfy space, all neutral colors, with a massive TV hanging from the wall and two large black leather sectionals to lounge on. It's where me, my da, and my brothers hang out when we're at home to play poker or watch sports.

Not a minute later, he appears. He's dressed down from church now in a pair of grey slacks, a cream button-down, and with his glasses perched on the end of his nose. All of this topped off with a pair of tan sheepskin slippers. New York's biggest serial killer is wearing fluffy mules.

He looks like any typical almost seventy-year-old. He's not. His death toll will be three figures minimum, and he won't regret a single one. He commits his atrocities and then thinks that by confessing his sins and taking his penance on the chin that he'll still get a heavenly pass. He won't. No one with an ounce of sense would ever tell him that, mind you. Definitely not me. I keep my opinions to myself. I quite like my head attached to my body.

"Dylan."

My attention switches to my ma, Roisin O'Connell, who's come to join us. I'm sure she gets smaller every time I see her. At sixty-six, she's now barely five feet. She's a redhead like our Cill, but only the most stubborn streaks can now be seen through the several shades of grey. She's a beautiful woman. Always has been. Elegant is probably the best way to describe her—all twinsets and pearls on the outside. On the inside, it's a different matter. I try not to dwell on the things I've heard she's taken part in. Of the horrific endings she's inflicted on some of our enemies—the females in the main.

To me, she's just my ma.

They stand side by side in their matching slippers—a perfect show of solidarity, just staring at me. Why? Then it dawns on me. My heart sinks.

I look from face to face. "There's no issue with the CCTV, is there." It's a statement rather than a question. My throat suddenly feels dry, and my heart is thudding in my chest.

No. No. No.

Ma shakes her head. I know her voice is about to go that soothing way of hers. It's when she pretends to have a conscience for some godforsaken sin or act of betrayal, she's either committed or is about to commit.

This time, it's one that involves me.

"No, Dyl. The CCTV is working fine, son. Me and your da…" She links her arm through his for moral support, and in return, he pats her hand reassuringly. "Well, we wanted to do this away from the office. We know you hate being the center of attention and there's someone we'd like you to meet."

Ma leaves the room, and I stare at my da. Please, God, tell me this isn't happening. Not now. Not when I thought I was off the hook.

I watch as my ma brings in the girl. She's pretty enough with her shoulder-length straight blonde hair and large green eyes framed by glasses of a style similar to mine. Beautiful, some might say, in a geeky sort of way. She's dressed sensibly in black pants and a cream blouse, and even though she's wearing flat shoes, she's still tall. Does she not like to be the center of attention either? Is that another reason we're being introduced here, away from the others?

"Dylan, this is Grace. Grace, this is our Dyl." Ma introduces us.

She walks forward and holds out her hand, and I shake it. We take each other in. She doesn't speak. I don't either. Why bother? The handshake signified precisely what this is. A business arrangement.

"Dyl."

I look at my da.

"We'd like you to court young Grace here."

Jessie's Apartment, Hudson Yards, New York

"I've missed your cock." I've only just walked into her apartment, and her lips are already caressing mine. She tastes like coffee. She drinks way too much of that stuff. It'll be the reason she's always so hyperactive. Then again, that's just Jessie. The proverbial blue-arsed fly.

I wouldn't change anything about her for the world.

I growl against her lips as her hand drops down to rub my hardening dick through my suit pants. Moving her mouth to my neck, she bites down, causing me to curse, as she pushes me back against the wall before sinking to her knees.

"Fuck, Jessie."

I watch as she unzips my pants and they drop to my ankles, then she yanks down my shorts to join them on the floor. I kick both aside.

I wrap her hair around my hand as she wraps those cupid's bow lips of hers around my cock before licking the entire length and then sucking hard on the nerve-endings right under the tip. My legs almost buckle as my orgasm immediately grips my balls.

I look down at her kneeling on the floor in a white tank top and the tiniest of Daisy Dukes, her little pink tongue lapping up my pre-cum. Closing my eyes, I rest the back of my head against the wall as I give in to the sinful delights of that hot, wet vacuum of a mouth of hers.

I grunt as she sucks on both my balls at once, looking back down to take in the perfect visual. Fisting my shaft with one hand and with the other still gripping her hair, I rub the blunt head of my leaking dick across her lips.

"I want to come in your mouth, Jessie."

"Oh, is that right?" She smirks up at me, my pre-cum now glossing her lips.

I curse as she takes my cock deep. Fisting her hair tighter, I immediately start to fuck her mouth.

Hard. Fast. Wet.

I know she enjoys it like that. We both do. Her eyes never leave mine as she takes every inch of my dick over and over, causing a mixed trail of pre-cum and saliva to drip down her chin.

It doesn't take long. My balls tighten, and I nod to let her know I'm about to blow.

The first wave of pleasure has me almost doubling over with its intensity, and I watch as she nearly chokes on my release before greedily swallowing it down. I continue to fuck her mouth, gentler now, giving her time to drink every last fucking drop. And she does. She then licks my cock clean before finishing off with a satisfying smack of her lips, causing us both to laugh out loud.

I want to reach down and pull her up to me, but her mouth has sucked all the strength out my legs. When she eventually stands, I briefly lose myself in those baby blues of hers before grabbing the back of her head, pulling her in, and devouring her mouth.

I can taste the musky tang of my cum on her tongue. I don't want her sucking any other man's dick. Not fucking ever. I feel violent at the thought of it.

But she's not mine. And she never will be. My fate was sealed earlier today.

Grace Ryan. Thirty years old. A computer expert with a background in hacking and with the best mobster parents Dublin has to offer. Her folks are friends with my Uncle Mick and his wife. We're a match made in heaven, according to my parents and hers.

My idea of hell now all I crave is the woman in front of me.

Fuck buddy. Fuck buddy. Fuck buddy.

Maybe it's for the best. Maybe Jessie's lack of urgency about furnishing me with personal details is her way of saying that's all she wants. Because that's all I'll ever be able to give her now, and even then, only for the short term.

They've given me a week to make up my mind, but I know the decision's already been made on my behalf. Saying no would just fall on deaf ears. It's not an option. It wasn't for Paddy. The contracts will have been drawn up and signed.

The ink on the story of my life is now dry.

I've always done my parents' bidding. Done what was expected. Done what was asked. Why would this time be any different?

In one week they'll announce to the rest of the family that I've begun the courting process. Then my cards will be well and truly marked.

Grace Ryan will be my wife, whether I like it or not.

CHAPTER TWENTY-THREE

ROISIN

Private Dining Room, Palace Hotel, Manhattan

I sip on my Bloody Mary as I wait for my guests to arrive. My phone vibrates. I take it from my handbag, which has been set on a gilded side table. As I expected, it's a photo of my grandbaby, Caoimhe, sent by my daughter-in-law, Sarah. I smile at the image of the red-haired wee one. She's the double of our Cillian at that age and my pride and joy.

I love the very bones of her. I'd do anything for her.

One grandchild. I want more. Lots more. I know Sarah and Cillian are trying for number two, but the onus can't just be on them. Paddy will be married soon enough. Eoin and Dylan… well, their da and I have found them good Irish girls. Sensible girls. Girls from the right background, with the correct breeding and mobster credentials. I know our Dyl will do as he's told. He always has done. He's a good boy. Dylan's not my concern.

Paddy and Eoin are. I'm not sure if they're not going to try to delay matters because *she's* due back in Manhattan soon.

Jaine Jones.

The girl that's turned the head of not just one but two of my sons. The girl that insulted me and Fergal by not turning up to a pre-arranged meeting. They say revenge is a dish best served cold. I'm a firm believer in that. What goes around comes around. She should have chosen more carefully who she so blatantly insulted that day. I've not forgotten. I never will And I've made sure my Fergal hasn't either. She will never get her heathen hands on either of my two boys.

Hell will freeze over first. And hopefully with her in it.

I watch as Molly McGrath enters the room. The future Ma Duster if she plays her cards right. She's dressed in a pinstriped business suit. Ever the professional is Molly. She's now working alongside our Paddy learning the legal ropes of our organization.

I have to grudgingly admire Jaine for what she's achieved in her career. But I will make it one of my own life goals to ensure Molly achieves just as much success, if not more. I don't care how much it costs or who we have to employ to guide her.

I'm backing this horse. I will not lose.

I stand and air kiss her on both cheeks, as is the perfunctory method of greeting in places such as this. Her perfume is subtle. Jasmine. Her presentation immaculate. Her hair is as black as coal, and her eyes are so pale they're almost the color of ice. She's tall, slim, and extremely beautiful with her Celtic complexion. She'll make a good wife for our Eoin. Out of a long list of potentials, she was head and shoulders above the others, both as a professional wife for our eldest and as the future Ma Duster. They'll also make beautiful children together, I'm sure.

From what I can gather, Molly's already working on tying our

Eoin down in that way, so there's no escape for him. Rumor has it they're sleeping together. That they have been since the moment she landed stateside. Well, good for her. You have to think ahead in this life.

My thoughts drift briefly to poor Cara. God rest her soul. That girl never did think ahead. If she had, things might have ended differently for her. She never used her initiative and look what happened. Another woman entered the fray and caught our Cillian's eye. Cara got desperate and sloppy because of it. She paid the price with her throat.

Molly, on the other hand, seems to have pre-planned everything. She'll be carrying a future Duster soon if she has her way. She may even be pregnant now. This girl knows you have to be one step ahead of the competition at all times. And mark my words, Jaine Jones *is* competition. Married mother or not.

I know my Eoin. I know my Paddy. They're half me, half Fergal, which makes them both determined and deadly.

Determined to get what they want. Deadly when they don't.

Their obsession with this biker woman could see my two boys going head-to-head. And it would be a toss-up over who would win.

But there can only ever be one winner.

If I have my way, it's a battle that will never take place, hence why I've called this meeting here today.

"Roisin, it's lovely to see you. You're looking well."

Molly's accent is thick Dublin. In a way, it makes me feel homesick. She was allowed to live in the old country for twenty-eight years, whereas I only got eight.

Still, I can't complain. I've lived a good life. New York is home for me. And it's home for her too now. Molly is just taking her seat when my other guest walks in.

"Sophia, it's good to see you."

Air kisses all around again. Such a waste of time and effort when nothing is meant or gained by it. It's all fake niceties. All for show. I smile at my Paddy's seventeen-year-old fiancée. Like Molly, her hair is long and dark, and like Molly, she's extremely beautiful, probably even more so, but everything else about her is in direct contrast with the Irish girl. Sophia is petite with flawless olive skin and dark eyes. Everything about her screams money. It's just as well we have more than we know what to do with as, from what I hear, this girl has expensive tastes, and she likes to shop. Still, her brother is the current Sicilian mafia don, so she has the right connections.

Both girls smile politely at each other. They're not friends. They likely never will be. Do you ever truly have friends in this life? I think not. You'd be a fool to believe you do. As I see it, every so-called friend is just a potential Judas offering you the air kiss of death before stabbing you in the back the moment you turn around. They'll both do well to remember that. Going by how they're eyeing each other, that lack of trust is already there. It comes with being born in the life. From the moment you take your first breath, you have a wealth of enemies, praying it'll be your last.

I wait until they've ordered their drinks, and the waiter returns with them before I speak. Sparkling water for Molly. Still for Sophia.

"Jaine Jones."

I have their immediate attention at the mere mention of the biker woman's name.

"I don't know what rumors you've heard about her, so I brought you here today to give you the facts, so there's no speculation. You girls will hopefully be O'Connells soon. It's what you both want, and it's what my Fergal and I want."

I look at Sophia.

"Our Paddy is in love with her. He has been his whole adult life. Since he was nineteen years old."

I'm sure she'll have suspected it but hearing it aloud will reinforce any suspicions. They say hate can turn a beautiful person ugly. It's true. That's precisely what it's doing to Sophia right now. It's the reaction I wanted to see. Molly glances at her sympathetically. Sophia glares at her. It's clear she doesn't want the other girl's pity. She needn't worry. Molly's gloating will be short-lived.

I turn my attention to her.

"Our Eoin also fancies himself in love with her. He has for the last year or so." Molly's expression remains unchanged. The only thing that gives her annoyance away is a slight narrowing of the eyes. She'll need to work on that. As the future Ma Duster and external legal representation for our organization, nothing must ever give her away.

Molly takes a sip of water. "I already suspected Eoin had a fondness for the biker, Roisin, but thank you for clarifying. I'm working on getting him to forget all about her, but I'm happy to be guided by you on this matter. You know your son. Tell me what I need to do and then consider it done."

Politely, she's asking me if I want her to end Jaine Jones's life.

I don't. Or at least, not yet.

"I last saw Jaine at Leoluca's function," Sophia interjects. "She gloated when she announced that Padraig was in love with her and not me. Thankfully, it was only said in front of Luc and Sarah. Luc was not happy that she disrespected me in that way. That she disrespected the Ruoccos. I was not either. It was rude. She is a detestable human being and one who is beside herself with jealousy because Padraig will be my husband and not hers."

I heard all about that confrontation. The one and only time Jaine Jones publicly let her professional image slip and it was over my youngest.

Sophia looks smug. It shows immaturity, but she is only seventeen, after all. I have to make allowances for that.

My Paddy is a good catch. In some ways, a better one than Eoin. He is, after all, the most handsome of my boys and has the most charismatic personality. He also won't have the same level of responsibility as Eoin, so neither will his wife.

"Jaine will be returning to Manhattan in the not-too-distant future. Some say she'll be back within the next six months. Some say it will be as long as twelve. But she will be back. When she returns, she'll be throwing herself at my boys, and both will be receptive to her advances." I speak plainly. There's no point in beating about the bush.

"But she's a married woman. By then, she'll have two children." Molly frowns.

"She's also a biker, and as I've already explained, bikers are typically women of loose morals. She'll already have a harem of men at her beck and call. Probably most of the influential men on her client list. They'll have signed up because of the add-on services she offers. Both my boys are so enraptured by her, they'd follow suit."

The girls look at each other. They might never be friends. But they will be sisters-in-law. They will be family. And that shared look tells me that, from this day forward, they will form a united front, close ranks on Jaine Jones, and have each other's backs.

"Sophia. Your relationship with Paddy?"

"What about it?" She knows exactly what I'm asking. And her pink cheeks give me all the answer I need. I know right then it's not gone anywhere. At best, a kiss and a cuddle.

"Has it progressed?"

She shakes her head.

"Then you must do something about that. You're at the age of consent now. Our Paddy is the loyal sort. I'm sorry for my vulgar mouth, but as a virgin, if he fucks you, he will keep you. There's no question. You need to encourage him to do just that."

She nods again. She knows I'm right. But she'll have her work cut out for her. As beautiful as she is, if Paddy's not been chomping at the bit, it likely means he doesn't find her sexually attractive, the twelve-year age gap most likely the problem. If she's not careful, she could end up in a loveless, sexless marriage. Worse still, Jaine Jones could get her hooks back into him and jeopardize the whole thing.

"And you, Molly?"

Molly smiles politely. "Eoin and I are fucking like rabbits."

Inwardly, I breathe a sigh of relief. It's what I suspected. But then, our Eoin has his own harem. Has he just added Molly to keep us quiet? Time will tell. I know I'll need to keep an eye on him. He's a game player. And a very successful one.

"Good." I take a sip of my Bloody Mary.

"So, what is it you want us to do, Roisin? Aside from keep your sons' attention away from her."

I stare at Molly. She's the only one capable of undertaking what I'm about to ask. The other is too young. She'll still be at the name-calling and hair-pulling stage.

"As the potential future Ma Duster, I want you to have a word with this Jaine Jones and tell her to back off."

"Do I make a threat?"

"A veiled one. But still loud. Still clear."

"Gladly." Molly smiles politely, drinks the rest of her water, and then with a slight nod of her head, she stands and leaves.

"And what do you want me to do?"

I look at Sophia. "I need you to hold on to your man."

She nods, stands, then walks off before suddenly stopping and turning around. "If my man is lost to me, then I will make sure Jaine Jones's is lost to her too."

She turns and resumes walking, and I watch as she leaves. Her back is proud and rigid. Clearly it's not wise for anyone to try to take away one of Sophia's possessions. Or to make an enemy of her.

I file that information away. I need to be careful not to underestimate the teenager. She's Sicilian, and from my experience, every single one of them is untrustworthy.

CHAPTER TWENTY-FOUR

JESSIE

Dylan's Apartment, Hudson Yards, New York

"Have you told anyone?" My head's resting on his chest. It's my favorite place to be. Listening to the steady thrum of his heart, a heart that I want to belong to me. A heart that, for some reason, I don't think ever will.

"About?"

"Us."

"No."

I lift my head and look at him. We haven't left his bed for days. Well, only to eat junk food, have a quick wash, and take care of any necessary bodily functions. It's like he's cramming for sex exams or something. Making sure he's got enough practical experience. In a matter of weeks, he's mastered the encyclopedia of fucking.

"Don't people wonder where you are?"

He chuckles as he looks up at me, his fingers combing through my tangled hair. "No. They're used to me not making contact for days on end. Paddy suspects, but I've never confirmed or denied anything. Have you told anyone?"

"Jaine. But she won't breathe a word."

I then ask the question that's been bugging me for days. "You've stopped asking about my background."

I watch as a blush creeps up his neck all the way to his cheeks. I know his ways now. It means he's hiding something. Can I ask? Then again, what gives me the right when I'm hiding things too?

"Is..."

He flips me over and pins me under him.

"A little less conversation, a little more action, please." He whispers the words against my lips. It's a blatant distraction tactic.

"Okay, Elvis." I chuckle, then groan as he sucks on my nipple.

The feeling of dread won't leave me though. Something's about to go down, and I'm not going to like it. No siree. Not at all.

The Hudson Dusters' HQ, Manhattan, New York

"She's not taking my calls." He doesn't sound best pleased as he directs the statement at me.

It's the weekly meeting, so all of us are sitting in our business glad rags. I've been invited into the inner sanctum once more, but only because Fergal is notably absent.

Why have two meetings when one will suffice?

Apparently, he's on childcare duty. It's my guess we'll see less and less of him as he starts to wind down now the future Ma Duster is in place. Spend his time on grandparental duties. Spend his money buying little Caoimhe full-sized *Chucky* dolls complete with realistic plastic knives.

Everyone else in the room remains silent. It may as well be just Eoin and me here today for the amount of effort the others have contributed in their da's absence. Maybe they're keeping their heads down. Perhaps they think there's more chance the eldest will throw a paperweight. Let's face it, the apple doesn't fall far from the tree. The rumors are true regarding the similarities between Da and his eldest son.

Barefoot, I walk over and pull on the silver ball of the Newton's Cradle, letting it go before returning to my seat.

Click. Click. Click.

I shrug. "And what do you expect me to do about it, Eoin? Jaine's a big girl. She makes her own decisions. Why do you need to speak to her anyway? The IRS matter is concluded. For now, at least. Unless you know something I don't. And she doesn't owe you for anything as far as I'm aware. You don't have any pound of her flesh to claw back in exchange for outstanding debts."

I watch as Molly's hand reaches under the table. It's clear she wants his attention off Jaine and back on her. Is she squeezing his thigh? Rubbing his dick? Whatever she's doing, it's highly inappropriate while he's mid-conversation. He knows it too.

He reaches under the table, no doubt to remove her exploring fingers. He glances at her and then looks away.

"I wanted to speak with Jaine about the alliance. We need her to be involved. She's personal friends with Rodolfo, so it makes most…."

I interject. "Jaine is personal friends with a lot of outlaw aristocracy. What are you going to do? Call on her services every time you have dealings with one? I'm sorry, but I thought that's what Molly was brought in to do. You know, interact with the other factions and win them all over with that charming Irish personality of hers." I nod in her direction.

"We can't just throw Molly in at the deep end, Jessie."

"Why not? Have you asked Molly what she wants? What she feels she's capable of? Or are you just being your usual chauvinistic self about it all?" I raise an eyebrow at her. "Molly?"

I know what she's going to say. He does too. It's the answer he doesn't want to hear because it will prove that Molly is currently not Ma Duster material. Not if she's incapable of putting the organization's needs ahead of her own. In the best interests of the company, she should insist they use Jaine, at least while she finishes her training and gains the necessary practical experience.

Instead, she'll put herself first. Because for the moment at least, it's more about her own personal vendetta. I hear the warning bells ringing loud and clear.

And Eoin does too.

I consider what he said. And he does have a valid point. Eoin will have been forensic when it comes to doing his homework this time around after what happened in the past. I've known Rodolfo Flores my whole life. Jaine's known him most of hers too. He doesn't suffer fools, and in my opinion, if Molly makes the wrong business decision on behalf of the Dusters, she is one.

Because if she then drops the ball, there's every likelihood La eMe, after the fiasco that went down in Nevada, will hit that fucker so far out the park it will spectacularly mark the end of the alliance with the Mexicans altogether. The end of La eMe's tether has pretty much been reached. I know that. Eoin knows that. He's fully aware of the multi-million-dollar risk to the Dusters if he pisses Rod off further.

"If Jaine Jones can handle it, then I'm confident I can." Molly answers confidently and with no hesitation whatsoever.

Whoops! Red buzzer. Wrong answer.

Eoin frowns briefly before resuming his impassive expression once more. Is it wrong that I can't wait to see Molly with egg all over that perfect face of hers? For her, it'll no doubt make a nice change from Eoin's cum.

"Well, I do believe the future Ma Duster has spoken." I grin at Eoin before turning my attention to his potential wife. "You should touch base with Jaine. I'm sure she'll be more than happy to fill you in and update you on whatever it is that's required from you legal eagles."

"Don't worry. I fully intend on speaking with her." There's an underlying threat of something there. Silly girl. I do hope she realizes who she's messing with.

"I'll be sure to let her know to expect your call." I smile politely before standing and leaving the room.

Jessie's Apartment, Hudson Yards, New York

"Eoin's crying into the crook of his elbow because you won't talk to him, partner." I smile as I lean against the kitchen worktop waiting for the coffee press to do its thing and waiting for her to blow up.

"I don't give a damn. I have nothing to say to him. He's an asshole!"

"He has plenty he wants to say to you."

"He should have thought about that before he pissed me off."

"His other half."

"What about her? What have you done now, Jessie, Jesus Christ."

"I perhaps told her she should touch base with you over the alliance. So you can debrief or whatever it is you legal types do."

She exhales. "Surely, Eoin can do the honors. He knows what's entailed. She can then introduce herself to the other parties involved. She doesn't need her hand holding to do that. She's a big girl. If she needs guidance at this stage, she won't last five minutes."

"Ah, you see. That's where you're giving her way too much credit. She's not the big girl she's making herself out to be. I reckon I'll be able to hold my breath longer than she'll last in that arena."

"She's only a year younger than me." She snorts. "If she's going to be the next Ma Duster, she needs to learn the ropes the hard way and quickly."

I take a sip of my coffee. "Rodolfo will eat her alive. You know what he's like."

"Not my problem."

"She said she was fully intending on speaking to you anyway?"

"About?"

"I have no clue."

"I'm not sure what's worse. The prospect of speaking to him or the prospect of speaking to her. Maybe I'll change my number."

I laugh out loud. "He'll show up on your doorstep. Say he was just passing by."

"I live in California in the middle of nowhere. There's no way he can ever be just passing by."

"I'm not sure that would stop him. Anyway, if you take his call, you'll be back at square one. I doubt you'd be able to shake him off so easily next time. You pulled the rug out from under his arrogant feet. He's vain. He likely thought you looked forward to your tete-a-tetes as much as he did, so he won't have seen that coming. He'll be prepared for that moving forward. He'll have learned his lesson."

There's a pause while she no doubt weighs out the lesser of the two evils.

"True. Give her my number then. Ask her to call."

"Will do. Oh, and I saw Bailey yesterday. She mentioned Cillian and Sarah are coming to see you next week? Some west coast mini tour while he touches base with the Angels and the Sons? Maybe then would be a good time to mention the unrest with the Undertakers?"

"I'd rather not involve the Dusters now I've shaken Eoin off, but I'll leave that decision up to Ace. It's his call. Anyway, things seem to have calmed down. Ghost is denying he's setting up with the previous backers. I guess we'll just have to take his word on that. He's managed to coerce a handful of brothers to join him so seems content for now."

"Do you think he's definitely going to set up a new MC?"

"Seems that way."

"Three in the same town?"

"Yup. That is unless we can encourage them back into the fold."

"Achievable you think?"

"Anything is achievable, Jessie. Money talks. If the backers are involved and offering large sums of cash, we need to consider our position and maybe increase our own offer."

"Or?"

"Or, who knows? Things could remain amicable, or they could turn nasty. It could go either way. Anyway, how are things with Dyl? You still fucking him?"

"Might be."

"Either he's sticking his dick in you or he isn't. There's no might be about it."

"Yes, he's definitely doing that. But listen, I'm pretty sure something's going on. He's stopped asking questions about my background, and he's fucking me so hard and so often it feels like his cock's taken up permanent residency in my pussy."

"He hasn't said anything?"

"I don't like to pry. It's not like I'm not keeping my own secrets, Jaine."

There's a pause. I've got a feeling she suspects what's going on, but she wants clarification before she furnishes me with her suspicions.

"Leave it with me. I'll see what I can find out."

I frown at that response as I pour myself another coffee. I don't like the sound of that. I'm sure I can already hear the sound of the shit hitting the fan.

And I'm pretty sure the outcome will stink.

CHAPTER TWENTY-FIVE

JAINE

Jaine's Home, Rising, California

Padraig: *Jaine?*
Jaine: *Dylan.*
Padraig: *Won't you just speak to him?*
Jaine: *No.*
Padraig: *He's making everyone's life a misery, darlin'.*
Jaine: *Tell him to go hibernate himself away. Not just for the winter. Permanently.*
Padraig: *What did he do this time?*
Jaine: *The asshole tried to blackmail me. That aside, my ears are burning every time you have your meetings. So much so I can smell smoke. Your da doesn't want to use my services, and according to Molly, I have a mattress attached to my back. Trust me. It was a no brainer to walk away and*

to kick your brother into touch. I don't have to put up with that shit. I won't put up with it.

Padraig: *I know her remark was out of order, but she's been hand-picked.*

Jaine: *Well, I'm sorry, but her character assassination of me shows a certain level of immaturity. Maybe they shouldn't rush into things. It's not like the decision can be reversed if it turns out to be the wrong one.*

Padraig: *It's far from being set in stone, Jaine. But my brother is thirty-seven. He needs to get wed. Produce heirs. My parents want grandchildren. They've only got Caoimhe. Our Eoin's spent way too long dilly-dallying.*

I exhale slowly. My secret will be earth-shattering for them. They'll hate me more than they do already for keeping Finian away all this time, but what choice did I have? What choice *do* I have?

Jaine: *So, you're messaging to ask me to take pity on your big brother.*

Padraig: *Yes. For some reason, he seems to like your heated exchanges. I can't for the life of me figure out why.*

Jaine: *Well, I don't enjoy them. All he does is look for ways to manipulate me into doing his bidding. Anyway, he's a big boy. He can do his own dirty work. Why can't his lordship ask me himself?*

Padraig: *You won't answer your phone to him, darlin'.*

Jaine: *Touché. Listen, I'll think about it.*

Padraig: *Thank you. The rest of us O'Connells will be forever in your debt if you would put him out of his misery.*

Jaine: *Enough about him. What's going on with you? Jessie* *says you've been acting weird and like something's about to go down.*

Padraig: *You could say that.*

Jaine: *Well?*

Padraig: *It's not been broadcast yet so I'm not sure if I should say anything.*

Jaine: *Since when has that ever stopped you spilling your guts to me?*

Padraig: *True, and I guess I can tell you since it's expected to be announced this afternoon. I'm to be entered into an arranged marriage.*

I almost drop my phone in disbelief then stare at the handset, stunned into silence. What the fuck? He's said that so matter-of-factly when he's currently sleeping with my business partner. I know she's developed feelings for him. I'd hoped it was a two-way street.

Padraig: *I expected a different response from you. One of shock and outrage on my behalf. Not radio silence and tumbleweed.*

Jaine: *The only outrage I feel right now is on Jessie's behalf.*

Padraig: *Why?*

Jaine: *Well, since you've been sleeping with her, I'm surprised you're being so casual about this whole thing. The fact this arranged marriage is a done deal tells me you've known about it for quite some time. I guess what surprises me most is you've still been fucking Jessie while not bothering to mention any of this to her. Who even does that?*

Padraig: *Shit.*

Jaine: *Shit? Well, that's the understatement of the century.*

I'm disappointed in you, Dyl. I never thought I'd hear myself say that. After what happened in the past, you go and pull a stunt like this.
Padraig: *What happened in the past?*

I stare at my phone screen again. Is he for real?

Jaine: *Has that lobotomy you appear to have had made you lose your memory as well as your conscience? I don't want to talk about it.*
Padraig: *Tell me.*
Jaine: I said *I don't want to talk about it. We agreed not to remember?*
Padraig: *I should never have said anything.*
Jaine: *No, you should have. It's better late than never. But you should have told Jessie, not me. If you even suspected this was on the cards for you, you owed it to her to say something before she became involved. Who is this girl anyway?*
Padraig: *A friend of the family. Someone already known to us.*
Jaine: *And what about your cliché blonde?*
Padraig: *It's her. That's exactly who is it.*
Jaine: *Seriously? I'm not sure if that makes things better or worse.*
Padraig: *Listen, Jaine, darlin'…*
Jaine: *Don't 'listen, Jaine, darlin' me. I'm sorry, Dyl. I have to go. Someone has to do the right thing and tell Jessie.*
Padraig. *You can't.*
Jaine: *What? And you think it's fair she finds out after it's been announced today? I can tell her. And I goddamn will.*
Padraig: *Jaine!*

I ignore him and toss the phone to the side.

My other phone rings the instant I stop messaging. I lean my head back on the old leather sofa and roll my eyes. Does he think by calling me he can get me to change my mind?

"Listen, Dyl…"

"Is that Jaine Jones?" It's not Dylan. The accent is broad Irish, and the owner of the voice is female. I know exactly who this is.

"Molly McGrath."

"That's correct." She sounds smug. She's no doubt up herself because I recognized who she was without introduction, but it's not like I know any other females with an accent like hers, more so any who have my direct number.

"Jessie told me to expect your call." I take the wind out of her sails. "It's about the alliance with La eMe, am I correct?"

"Yes. I want you to tell me what's involved and where things stand."

My back is immediately up at her commanding tone.

"I'm sure Eoin can explain the terms of the agreement to you."

I'm well aware I'm coming across as unaccommodating, but she really isn't enticing me to be anything else.

"I'd much prefer it if you did."

"Communication problems this early on? That doesn't bode well for your future relationship."

"We have no problems communicating."

"So, I'm not sure why you can't ask him what forms the basis of the alliance and where things currently stand."

"That's not in any way helpful."

"Well, I'm sorry you feel that way, Molly, but you're a lawyer. It's part of the job to find out whatever's necessary. Our interpretations may vary. We all also interact with others differently. I've known the people involved for a long time. You haven't. You need to form your own connections with them, and not just rely on my opinions."

"I'm reliably informed that the likelihood is you've slept with them all. As I won't be stooping so low to build *my* professional relationships and to further *my* career, I thought I'd just ask you."

I laugh dryly. "Reliably informed? By Roisin, I take it."

Her lack of response is all the answer I need.

"Whether I've fucked them or not is irrelevant. I suggest you speak with the individuals concerned and introduce yourself. And make sure you do your homework first."

"That's why I'm calling you."

Is she actually for real?

"Do your own research. It's part of the job. Find out about these people. About these factions that form part of our life and this alliance. But, before you do any of that, I suggest you know exactly what the Dusters' expectations are. You're representing them, after all."

"I already know what Eoin wants."

I think I've just been a little sick in my mouth.

"Good to know, but I'd focus more on what Fergal and Roisin want for their business as opposed to what Eoin wants in the bedroom."

"Are you jealous?"

"Are you insane?"

"Stay away from him. And from Padraig."

"Are The Hudson Dusters threatening me?"

"It's a warning I'm allowed to pass on with Roisin's blessing. We're aware you're coming back to New York. She wants you to keep away from her sons."

"Do you want to add the 'or else' or shall I?"

"You can add it if you like. You heard what I said. Stop sniffing around Eoin."

I laugh out loud at the audacity of this girl. "I'm married with one child and another on the way."

"Stay. Away."

"Or what, Molly?"

"I'm told the O'Connells have access to the infamous sniper. The Exterminator."

"You know him?"

"I spoke to him this morning."

"Oh, you did, did you? And what did the marksman have to say for himself?"

"That he's happy to consider working exclusively for the Dusters moving forward."

"Exclusively. He said that did he? The Exterminator?"

"Yes."

Well, the Dusters deserve everything that's coming to them if they do make her ma.

Lies? In this life?

"Well, see, here's the thing, Molly. And make sure you share this message with Roisin.

"One, all my calls are monitored, recorded, and instantly backed up to a remote server."

Thank you, Jessie, for insisting I do that.

"Two. I don't take kindly to being threatened. When I am, I go out of my way to do the opposite of what's being asked of me. As you know, I haven't been speaking to Eoin, but rest assured, I will be resuming all contact with him after this conversation.

"Three. Please give The Exterminator my regards. I look forward to his engraved bullet connecting with my skull.

"And lastly, never forget, that in this life, a threat should always be veiled and never blatant. You'd do well to remember that."

I disconnect the call. Leaning my head back against the sofa, I let out a long sigh as I run my hand down my face.

I know that won't be the end of it. Roisin and Fergal are gunning for me, that much is obvious. They see me as a threat, which means I need to watch my back and also the backs of those closest to me. I'm not the only sniper they have access to. And it's not like our kind hold weekly conference calls so we can discuss who's on each of our hit lists for the coming week.

Should I warn Ace? Speak to Eoin?

I know there's one thing I need to do. And I need to do it urgently.

I need to speak to Jessie.

CHAPTER TWENTY-SIX

JESSIE

Jessie's Apartment, Hudson Yards, New York

Did you know you can actually hear the sound of a heart breaking. I think it must be made of glass as I'm sure I just heard mine shatter into a thousand tiny pieces.

You can feel it too.

First, the overwhelming breathlessness you experience when your feelings implode in your chest cavity all at once in an attempt to halt the torture the relentless beating of your heart brings. Then the physical ache from the vice-like grip that tightens around the very thing that's trying so hard to keep you alive.

Constricting it. Suffocating it. Fracturing it into fragments.

If it's not beating, then there's no more pain. And right now, I'd welcome that stillness in my chest more than anything because all I'm experiencing is a myriad of every kind of pain imaginable.

I've fallen in love with Dylan O'Connell.

Not that I'll ever admit that to anyone but myself. It's just another one of those short straws I just keep right on pulling in life. Good old Jessie. The life and soul. The modelesque girl who, on the surface, appears to have everything. When in fact, she has nothing at all. Now fated to always having no one at all as no one will ever compare.

Perfectly lonely.

Having just spoken with Jaine, I'm left to process the unwanted yet not entirely unexpected news in my head. To sift through my thoughts, feelings, and regrets one by one and file them away. Pouring myself another coffee, I wrap my hands around it. Its heat offers no comfort today. Its taste more bitter than usual. I stare around my home and inhale the paint smell, which still clings determinedly to the air. I didn't even get to live here long enough for it to disappear.

Figures.

The apartment I've just bought, I'll now need to leave. I can't stay here. Not with him living upstairs. *Them* living upstairs. Living *their* happily ever after.

Tears prick my eyes. What a wuss. My daddy would be so proud of me right now.

The warning signs were there from day one, and I ignored them. It's my own fault. No promises were made from either side. And now I know why. His wanting to know about me was obviously just pillow talk.

Was this always on the cards for him?

I guess Dyl did well. He's luckier than his siblings. He's getting to wed his cliché blonde.

The true love of his life.

Fuck buddy. Fuck buddy. Fuck buddy.

That's all I ever was to Dylan. Friends with benefits. Still, I knew that; accepted it. It's no wonder he was practicing so much.

He wants to impress his new fiancée. His new wife. Show off his sexual prowess. A craft that's now been honed to perfection.

As far as he knows, I'm still an ignorant fool. The idiot who's blissfully unaware he's about to enter the courting process with someone else. That big announcement is expected to take place this afternoon, I'm told.

Guess it's time for one last hurrah.

Dylan's Apartment, Hudson Yards, New York

"Jessie."

My name's a whisper on his lips. It's the best thing I've ever heard in my life. I don't want him to whisper any other woman's name like that. Like a caress. Not ever.

But he will. Hers.

His girlfriend. His fiancée. His wife.

He's obviously just showered as beads of water still kiss that pale Irish skin of his. I have to fight the almost overwhelming urge to walk over and lick them off.

One. By. One.

A pair of grey jogging pants hang low on his slim hips. He's wearing nothing else. I let my eyes trail slowly up his lean muscled torso until our gazes connect.

Deep wells of sapphire blue. I want to drown myself in the very depths of the soul they currently expose.

He licks his lips, and my gaze drops to his mouth. I want to bite down on that full bottom lip of his. I want to feel it on my fucking skin. Along with his hands. His teeth. His tongue. My eyes rise to his face once more. He's fucking breath-taking.

Delectable. Delicious. Divine.

Walking forward, I place one hand against his chest. I push him backwards before closing the door behind me. I'm only wearing a slip. Nothing underneath. That much will be evident, as my nipples are now waving at him. Demanding attention from his mouth. His hands. His anything.

"Fuck me."

Two words. All that's needed to unleash that Duster monster in him. Yanking my slip over my head, I stand naked. His eyes roam over me, lust blazing in their depths with such an intensity it feels like they're scorching my skin. He slowly drinks me in. Taking his time. He's imprinting me to memory. I know he is.

And now I know fucking why.

Spinning me, he pushes my back against the wall. I shiver at the coldness of the surface, or is it at what's about to happen this one last time?

His hand fists my hair as his lips cover mine, his tongue thrusting deep, possessing my mouth, claiming it as his. It *is* his. It will always be his.

Tasting. Tangling. Torture.

I can taste his desperation. His craving. His desire. All sprinkled with the carnal sin that is lust. He wants this as much as I do. Maybe even more.

Pushing his sweatpants down, he lifts and thrusts into me in one movement. I whine as I anchor my legs around his hips. I lean my head back against the wall, waiting while my body adjusts to accommodate the physical intrusion that's taken my fucking breath away. His dick feels different.

Harder. Longer. Thicker.

I can feel it pulse inside me as we stand there, not moving. He pulls out and thrusts straight back in. And then? Then he's fucking me for real.

Hard. Fast. Deep.

There's no kissing. No encouraging words. This is just sex in its simplest form.

Raw. Pure. Forni-fucking-cation.

Both of us are taking what we need from this. I'm hoping it's enough to last a lifetime. It has to be. For my sake.

He angles my hips and pistons into me, and I cry out as I shatter all over his cock. Still, he continues.

Forceful. Relentless. Determined.

He's showing me what I'm going to be missing from this day forth. What she's going to be getting from here on in.

His girlfriend. His fiancée. His wife.

His fingertips dig painfully into my skin. Bruising it. Burning my flesh and searing my memory with what's taking place. Right here. Right now. He doesn't want me to forget this moment.

I never will. Not ever.

His skin is hot and damp with sweat, and my mouth immediately connects, my tongue licking the saltiness off, the raw taste of him turning me on even more. The sound of flesh slapping against flesh and our mutual groans of appreciation fill the room as he fucks me into oblivion.

I don't want to see. I don't want to hear. I just want to feel. My body is singing for his, as he orchestrates it perfectly.

Tears prick my eyes as I come again, this time taking him with me. His hand fists my hair as he sucks hard on my neck. Marking me. Claiming me. He roars as he embraces his release, his hips jerking erratically as he empties deep inside me.

We stay there. Seconds. Minutes. Hours. Panting. Just holding on to one another. Even though it remains unspoken, we both know this is the last time.

Pressing my nose against his damp skin, I inhale his familiar citrus scent once more before lifting my face from his neck. My eyes meet his sapphire ones, but they're now closed off. The connection we shared gone. Lost forever. I can no longer see into his soul. I understand why. It no longer belongs to me. It belongs to her now.

Hasn't it always?

What little remains of my heart shatters at the realization.

I was just allowed to borrow Dylan O'Connell for a short while. Now it's over, and it's time to give him back. To her. To his cliché blonde. To the girl he's been pining over for so long. Placing my feet on the floor, I step away before pulling my slip back over my head.

"I need to go." It's barely audible. I have no voice. I have nothing right now. My lips find his. A brief touch. A memory more than a kiss. As all of this will be now.

Then?

I walk away.

CHAPTER TWENTY-SEVEN

JESSIE

The Hudson Dusters' HQ, Manhattan, New York

"So, you're going to gatecrash their meeting?"

I'm in a cubicle in the ladies' restroom, where I'm mentally preparing myself for what's about to go down. I'm chipper. I will remain chipper. If you look Jessie O'Brien up in the dictionary, it says precisely that.

Chipper.

After I left his apartment, I cried a boatload of tears into the crook of my elbow while wallowing in a bathtub full of self-pity. I then washed off all visible traces of Dylan from my person, aside from a few stubborn bruises and hickeys, then got out and dried myself off.

After staying put to watch the last of the water drain away, I exaggeratedly dusted my hands.

Life goes on. It has to. That Duster ship has sailed.

"Yes, siree."

"And do what?"

"I don't know. Maybe I'll confront Despicable Dylan on being the spineless piece of shit he is. Maybe I'll tell the Dusters who I am. Maybe I'll go into the meeting and pull the cliché blonde's hair. I haven't decided yet. I'll play it by ear when I'm in there. I'll likely end up flicking them the professional bird by quitting on the spot. Can I do that? Legally? If I want to?"

"JAA can terminate the contract if that's what you choose to do, yes. I'd find a loophole, don't worry. I'm not sure about the notice period, but you can always work from home unless you have to undertake a formal handover procedure to a third party. That said, we can always offer up a suitable JAA alternative from one of our new recruits. We can decide once you've done whatever it is you feel you need to do, Jessie."

"Move on with my life, Jaine That's what I need to do."

"You resigning will go down like a lead balloon. You do know that?"

"Yes. I also understand the predicament I'll be leaving them in, but I can't continue to work here. As you've said, Dylan must have known this was on the cards for some time. The fact he didn't bother saying anything shows how little regard he had for my feelings. While I appreciate we were just fuck buddies, he still should have made that fact known. Shit like that's disrespectful. In fact, it's unforgivable."

"You have feelings for him?"

"Yes. But when I distance myself, they'll soon disappear."

"Coming from someone who's been there, I wouldn't be too sure about that."

"What else can I do, Jaine? He's one half of an arranged marriage!" I sound frustrated and pissed off. I never get short-tempered. I pride myself on the fact I always remain unruffled. It's the first time I've let my guard down and my true feelings show in front of anyone since him.

"Nothing. All you can do is chalk it down to experience." She ignores my outburst because she gets it.

"You warned me this would happen."

"I warned myself it would happen to me too. It didn't stop me from making the same mistake."

"Fools."

"That's exactly what we are."

"Maybe Dyl's new woman is an accountant."

"That's unlikely. Accountants versed in our life are way more difficult to source than lawyers. That's the reason Eoin approached me in the first place. Still, we've gotten them through the IRS issue relatively unscathed, which is all we ever agreed to do. JAA never signed up as a long-term solution to their problems. And your services were only ever contracted. Never employed."

"Will you still speak to him after all this? Dylan?"

"Would you want me to?"

"I'm not sure."

"I'll go with whatever you decide, Jessie. I've used him as my personal crutch for long enough. Maybe it's time for both of us to let go. Keep me posted. I'm only sorry I can't be a fly on the wall."

"Fergal would probably chuck his paperweight at you."

She laughs out loud. "True."

CANDICE IS SITTING IN HER USUAL SPOT OUTSIDE THE MEETING room, looking her tall, willowy self and dressed in a pale grey suit. I take in her creamy complexion, dark hair, and large hazel eyes. She looks beautiful. Immaculate as always. She also looks miserable. Because like me, she's lost her O'Connell fuck buddy.

Unlike me, though, she'll sit there and take whatever Eoin dishes out on the chin. Whereas Jessie? Now that I'm clean out of self-pity? I'm not taking anything on the chin. Not from anyone.

"Jessie. You can't go in there."

"No? Just you watch me."

The heels of my stilettos click on the marble floor as I storm past and open the door before she can stop me. Not that she tried very hard. She barely rose from her seat. Maybe, deep down, she wants me to confront these assholes too, on behalf of us both.

I know Cillian's absent as he's on his way to the west coast on a family trip but there are still seven of them sitting around the table, mouths agape, eyes staring at yours truly.

The hum of discussion I could hear before I opened the door has stopped. I've stunned them into silence.

Yup. I've still got it.

Jessie O'Brien broken? Never. At times I may be down, but I'm never out.

"Jessie, what are you doing here? We rescheduled our meeting until next week." If looks could kill, I'd be toast. Fortunately for me, they can't.

Fuck Eoin. Fuck Dylan. In fact, fuck them all.

No more Mrs. Nice Person. That shit doesn't get you anywhere.

I smirk at Eoin because I know he hates it when I do. If he hates me, he'll never forget me. My goal in life to never be forgotten? Well, that applies more than ever to everyone present here today. If I'm going out, I'm doing so with a bang.

Just hopefully not literally.

"I appreciate that, Eoin, but what I have to say can't wait."

"Jessie girl." Even Da Duster looks miffed at my interruption. I'm dicing with death. Still, today's as good a day as any to die.

"Fergal. Give me a few minutes, and then I'll be on my way."

He stares at me as he considers what I've asked. We've connected over the months. We understand each other way more than the others realize. We also share a mutual respect. He'll let me speak. That respect is way too much for him to stop me. He nods, and I smile.

I take in the faces of the people sitting around the table. Three of the four O'Connell brothers I met on that very first day. And their daddy.

Today, there are three girls present in place of the beautiful inside and out Sarah O'Connell. Two with jet black hair and one blonde.

There's only one I've met before.

"Molly." I nod at her. Jaine filled me in on their little tete-a-tete. The threat Molly made with Roisin O'Connell's blessing. The conversation that's now being held securely under lock and key. She nods in response, her face as impassive as her fiancé's.

As I did the first time, I place my briefcase on the leather-covered circular tabletop then lean against it briefly. This time, I'm letting the women have their fill—two in particular. I'm guessing the petite dark-haired girl with olive skin is Sophia. Padraig's fiancée. It's my thinking the other, the blonde, is the future Mrs. Dylan O'Connell.

A cliché blonde Disney princess? She's sure not what I expected.

Aside from being blonde, looks-wise, she and I couldn't be more different. I'm guessing personality-wise, it'll be much the same story. Then again, given the façade each of us portray to the outside world, no one would ever suspect Dyl and I would be so similar and have so much in common.

That he and I could ever be the perfect match.

"You must be Sophia." The petite dark-haired girl stares at me but doesn't respond. "Well, the cat's got someone's tongue," I mumble loud enough for everyone to hear. No one laughs at my poor attempt at humor. Not even Paddy. Well, he can't, I guess.

"And you are?" I ask the blonde.

She stands, reaches across the table, and offers her hand. "Grace Ryan."

I smile at her as I shake her hand, and she smiles back. "A good, strong Irish name. Mine is Jessie O'Brien. I like to think of it as also being a good, strong Irish name."

Her smiles widens. An act or not? That remains to be seen.

"Well, Sophia, Grace. If you don't know who I am, I'm the financial representation for the Dusters. Or at least, I was."

I drop that bombshell.

Kaboom.

Might as well get that right out there. There's a sea of mumbles, which is what I fully expected. Having recently promised Fergal I was here for the long haul, here I am not five minutes later packing my bags and reneging on that deal.

"Unfortunately, a personal situation has arisen, making my current position untenable." My eyes connect with Dylan's briefly. I watch as his neck slowly goes red, followed by his cheeks.

Sorry, but if you can't stand the heat, stay out of Jessie O'Brien's kitchen.

"Jessie?"

I turn and take in Fergal's furrowed forehead. He shifts his gaze between Dyl and me.

Maybe he suspects. Perhaps he doesn't. Maybe they all do. Frankly, I don't give a damn. I don't want to upset the senior O'Connell, though. I know Jaine doesn't like Da Duster much, but I do.

"Let me finish what I have to say, please, Fergal." I smile at him, and he nods slowly.

"As mentioned, unfortunately, I have to withdraw my services for personal reasons. Now, I would like that to be with immediate effect if at all possible. Jaine is currently looking into the contractual side of matters. Rest assured, I will abide by whatever clauses and conditions it contains. All will, of course, be confirmed in writing by JAL before the close of business today, and a sensible exit strategy put in place."

"Can I ask why, Jessie? You seemed happy with us here. Have we done something to upset or offend you?" Fergal's frown deepens. He flicks through his blank pad like that somehow holds the answer.

I suddenly feel overwhelmed with guilt. He's almost seventy. He's already in the winter of his life, and he's only just being allowed to wind down. He's finally getting to spend some quality time with his little granddaughter. And here I am throwing a spanner in his retirement works. I walk across to stand behind him, squeezing his shoulder when I do.

"Let's not delve into the reasons behind my withdrawal of services right now, Fergal. You and I can discuss that afterward in private if you wish. I just wanted to let you know my contract, or should I say JAA's contract with the Dusters is to terminate. I also want to make it clear this is at my request, not Jaine's."

Molly smirks. She looks like all her Christmases have come at once. First, Jaine departs. Now me. I ignore her. She's not worthy of a reaction.

I walk back around the table, my eyes making contact with Eoin's.

"Jaine told me to let you know she'll call to discuss the matter before she documents anything in writing."

He nods. My gaze switches briefly back to Molly. I take in her pursed lips. Is it wrong that it gives me satisfaction to announce

Jaine will be conversing with her potential fiancé once more? It's something I know she didn't want to happen. If she were a decent person, I'd feel guilty. But she's not, so I don't.

I walk to the window to take in the view. It's still one of the best Manhattan has to offer. I'll miss it.

But not as much as I'll miss *him*.

Still, it's too late for any of that now.

I turn back to face them and watch as they look around each other. They're waiting for me to close. To get to the point of why I interrupted their family get-together. I guess it's time for me to do just that.

"Moving forward, I will continue to deal with the Dusters as JAA will be representing the Scorpions, the Angels, and La eMe on the alliance. We'll also be representing the newest member, the Sons of Satan.

I pause.

"You're already aware that my background is MC. Well, just so you know Lucifer, aka Liam O'Brien, is my daddy."

My announcement is greeted with a wall of silence. I deliberately don't make eye contact with Dylan. He can go fuck himself.

"So, Bailey? Paul Delaney's fiancée?"

I turn to look at Eoin as he finally puts two and two together. He likely now sees the strong family resemblance.

"Bailey is my baby sister."

He nods. "So, you know Rodolfo personally. The same as Jaine."

"Rod is one of my closest friends. We grew up together." I smile at him. I walk back to the table. "Now, the alliance is on shaky ground after what happened to Raf as you know." A melancholy silence fills the room as those who remember do. It's hard not to be affected by the memory of the vibrant twenty-three-year-old who lost his life in the Nevada shoot-out. I lift my briefcase, realizing I've stood the entire time. "As neither JAL nor JAA will be representing the Dusters, I just wanted to assure you all that I shall do my best to ensure things progress smoothly for all parties concerned, at least from a financial perspective."

"Jessie girl, would you please reconsider?" Fergal stands abruptly, his hands fisting at his sides.

I don't want to turn him down. To walk away and leave him in the lurch. It's not his fault. It's not anyone's fault, really. It's just timing, circumstance, and the unfortunate fallout from this contract relationship game our kind keeps insisting on playing.

A game where there are seldom winners. Only losers.

The only person guilty of any wrongdoing in all of this is Dylan. He should have told me. He shouldn't have allowed me to sink deeper and deeper into the quicksand of whatever the fuck this is.

Was.

I walk across and squeeze Fergal's shoulder once more to let him know I won't reconsider. It's my silent refusal.

"For old time's sake." I smile as I then pull back the silver ball on the Newton's Cradle and let it swing before turning to leave.

"Good riddance."

Two words spoken to my back cause me to stop dead in my tracks. Slowly, I turn around. I'm aware my familiar annoying smirk is now crossing my face as my eyes connect with hers.

"What the fuck did you just say?"

"*I said* 'good riddance." A matching smirk crosses her face.

I seldom have murderous thoughts, but after the day from hell I've had, I sure am having them now.

I nod slowly. "Fergal. All of what I said? Forget I opened my mouth." I glance at him, and he smiles. I don't miss the flicker of relief that crosses his face.

"And what are you saying now, Jessie?"

"I'm going nowhere." My eyes reconnect with those of Grace Ryan. Good riddance? The cliché blonde has thrown down the gauntlet. If she wants war, then who am I to refuse?

I'll give her exactly that.

CHAPTER TWENTY-EIGHT

DYLAN

The Hudson Dusters' HQ, Manhattan, New York

"You did what?"

"I told Jaine that Grace was the cliché blonde."

We're sitting in Paddy's office. Everything is either polished silver, white, or black. It's an impersonal space, unlike his home. His desk is some sort of shiny metal, and the top is finished in leather. He's not a fan of traditional wooden furniture. The walls are white, and the floor is the same marble flooring that runs throughout the place.

There are no images on display simply because there's no space. It's crammed floor to ceiling with legal tomes and contract documents, all neatly organized and alphabetically displayed for ease of access and reference on tall metal shelving units. Our Paddy may come across as not taking things seriously, but he does. It's all a smokescreen.

When it comes to business, Paddy's meticulous and focused. I'm a geek when it comes to computers and the like. He's the same when it comes to the law. He knows his craft inside out. It's a shame he can't represent the Dusters in the outside world. He'd wipe the floor with most business and legal professionals. I'm sure he'd even give Jaine a run for her money. But he's way too bloodthirsty. If someone disagreed with him or said something he may take offense to, he'd start carving them up before the meeting ended. And if they're too amiable? Then he'd probably say something he shouldn't. Spill a dark Duster secret or something without thinking. Then he'd still have to carve them up.

Some might say that's the method in his madness. That either way it winds up the same outcome for the unfortunate third party, and our Paddy still gets to have his fun. It's way too much mess for the family to clean up, though. That's why he's kept behind closed professional doors at all times.

"And why the hell would you spin an even bigger web of deceit, Paddy?"

"It seemed like a good idea at the time to tie up that loose end. Jaine put me on the spot. I didn't know what else to say. You forgot to mention you and Jessie were fucking."

"Because it was none of your business. Jesus Christ, what must Jaine think of me?"

"Does it matter?"

"Yes!" I hiss back at him. "Jaine's opinion of me matters a lot. And you do know she'll have spouted that pack of lies to Jessie."

"Well, you were already lying to her, brother."

"On your advice and recommendation! You were the one who told me to go for it. That Da was just spouting hot air when it came to an arranged marriage for me. That it would never happen."

"I'm not denying what I said, Dyl, but that was superseded, and you know it. You've known for a week that's no longer the case. You've known all that time it was actually on the cards."

He's right. That part's not his fault, so I shouldn't be trying to pin the blame on him. It's mine, and I need to own it. As soon as I was introduced to Grace, I should have done the right thing and come clean to Jessie.

I didn't. I couldn't. And I'd do the same all over again if it meant I could have her just that bit longer.

"That's beside the point. An arranged marriage is one thing. I could have tried to unravel myself. There was still a chance I could have convinced Da. You know how much he likes Jessie."

"But you were still lying to her."

"It was unintentional in the beginning, Paddy, and you know it. Like you, I assumed the marriage was shelved. Aside from that one time, nothing had been said. I was only told the week before you lot it was on and that I was to be married off."

He leans back in his chair as he observes me. I was unreasonable on the first part. I take the entire blame for that firmly on the chin. But he must realize he's made things worse. And the second fuck up is all his doing, not mine.

"You've made matters ten times worse because Jessie now thinks I'm to be married to the love of my life. To a woman I've been pining over for years. She'll never forgive me for that act of betrayal because she'll never believe I didn't know about all this well in advance."

"And that you fucked her regardless."

"Yes!"

"Do you love her?"

"Aye, Paddy. I really do." I'm admitting it to myself as much as to him.

More alien feelings.

"Shit." He runs both hands down his face as it dawns on him my future is now as bleak as his.

"Yes, shit. And your lies have exacerbated an already complex situation. She'll think it's game over. That I've found my happily ever after with Grace Ryan. Not that I had much of a chance beforehand where Jessie's concerned, but I've zero now."

"What do you mean you never had much of a chance?" He frowns.

"Have you seen her? She's way out of my league."

"Obviously she doesn't think so, or she wouldn't have fucked you. So, do you reckon she doesn't love you back?"

I shrug. "I've never asked her, and she's never mentioned it, so we'll never know now, will we? She probably assumed, like me, that there was no rush for such a heart-to-heart conversation. I was going to speak to Da once I had found out who she was. I thought it would be a done deal since they get on so well and she was already making an impression doing what she does for our organization."

"Why didn't she tell you who she was?"

I run my hand through my hair in frustration. It's getting too long again but I don't want anyone else to cut it. Only her.

"She was leaving it up to Jaine. It's what they'd agreed between them. Apparently, Jaine wanted to speak to Eoin first. I guess because there was the potential for a conflict of interest. Jessie is part of the Sons, who are now part of the La eMe alliance. She's also going to be Razr's sister-in-law."

"It's all quite incestuous." Paddy laughs.

"Isn't that the norm in this life when we typically wed our own kind?"

"I guess. And with Jessie's background, she's the perfect match."

"Jessie's the perfect everything. Shit, Paddy. My life is over."

"It's not over. It will all work itself out."

"You mean like your situation did with Jaine?"

The moment the words leave my mouth, I instantly regret them. Guilt flows through me as I watch his mouth turn down. I remember it like it was yesterday. Jaine breaking her heart over the phone. Our Paddy turning to the drink. Neither has ever recovered. I usually back the decisions we make as a family, but we really did drop the ball that day.

We ripped apart a fated pair.

Now I know exactly how he feels. I've only experienced it for five minutes, but Paddy's been living it for years. How the hell does he cope?

Day by day, I guess. Same as I'll have to learn to.

I know he didn't mean any harm when he said what he did. I realize it was a spur-of-the-moment decision, but it hasn't helped.

"I'm sorry, Paddy. I shouldn't have said that."

"No, I'm the one who should be sorry, Dyl. I'll do my best to sort it." He smiles, but it's forced. I know he's just been reliving the same moment I was.

"How?"

"Let me worry about that."

CHAPTER TWENTY-NINE

DYLAN

The Hudson Dusters' HQ, Manhattan, New York

"Take a seat, Dyl." I've been summoned. It's the equivalent of Daniel heading into the lion's den.

The opposite of Paddy's, Eoin's office is dark wood furniture which contrasts against the same white background the rest of the offices are finished in. Images of our ancestors line the walls.

Past Dusters. People he admires and aspires to be like.

In the absence of a mirror in here, he's likely itching to add his own mugshot to the line-up of serial killers and murderers so he can look at himself every day. He's managed to abstain, for now at least. It would make him appear totally vain as opposed to only partially.

There's a wooden case filled with books on finance and economics. The areas he studied. Personally, I'd rather pull my fingernails out one by one than be forced to read any of that guff. Still, each to their own.

The other piece of furniture in the room takes pride of place. It's a huge antique walnut desk. An ugly monstrosity if you ask me. It would look better on a bonfire. It's finished in a clear shiny coating, so it's easily wipeable, which is just as well given he fucks Candice over it most days.

Or at least he did until Molly came along.

I sit on the tan-colored executive chair that faces him. His is almost identical. The only difference is his has a higher back and it also has armrests. See, even when it comes to office furniture, no one can have exactly what he has. He always has to have something that bit bigger or better than everyone else.

It's easy to see why my folks believed he and Molly to be the perfect match. They both have a constant need for one-upmanship.

He paces slowly back and forth behind his desk, his contemplative face turned towards the floor, his hands clasped behind his back. He walks slightly farther, then stops at the window, lifting his head to take in the impressive skyline.

Yup. You've guessed it. Eoin also has the best view.

I look at him. He's formidable is my big brother.

Impressive. Commanding. Authoritative. Deadly.

He was born to lead. Born to rule. He's not someone you'd want to make an enemy of. Even with the same blood running through our veins, his own siblings have enough sense to avoid doing that.

Eoin gets more like our da with every passing day. Even lookswise, his once jet-black hair is slowly turning silver at the sides. A constant reminder for him and for all of us that time is ticking. In truth, I'm surprised he's not started dyeing it. Maybe he's not as vain as we first thought.

"So, you've been fucking, Jessie O'Brien."

The silence is broken. I don't speak. There's no point. He already knows the answer. The way she looked at me during the meeting. The way my face colored in silent response. Everyone knows the answer to that question—even Grace Ryan.

He turns around and faces me, his hands still behind his back. "I have to say, I'm impressed. I never thought you had it in you. She's a strong character. One of those untamable sorts like…."

There's a pause.

"Jaine," I finish the sentence on his behalf.

He frowns. I feel a flicker of sympathy for him. He misses her something rotten. I know he does. Sadly, for him, the feeling's not mutual and it never will be. Still, she's agreed to start speaking to him again. Hopefully, her tolerating him once more will make life that bit more bearable for the rest of us.

"Yes."

Sitting down, he leans his forearms on the desk, links his fingers in front of him then looks at me. He's waiting. He's letting me speak. Typically, Eoin's the one who does all the talking, and the rest of us have to listen whether we want to or not.

"I was trying to find out about her, but Jaine wanted to speak to you first. I'm guessing over any potential conflict of interest about what Jessie revealed today and her role with us. But then you and Jaine had the falling out, I'm guessing in part over what Molly insinuated, and it sort of got waylaid."

My brother frowns. He won't say anything, but I suspect he's thinking the same thing I am. That Molly isn't right for the Ma Duster role. Not yet at least. Maybe not ever. She'd need to focus on the bigger picture and what's strategically best for the company. There would be a lot of people relying on her as one of the top two in our organization. There's no time for personal vendettas. Then again, our ma has it in for Jaine, so maybe she and Molly are more alike than the rest of us would care to admit.

"I love her, Eoin,"

I say it how it is. I only wish I'd had the guts to tell Jessie.

Maybe she would have said the same back. Maybe she wouldn't. But at least I would have known either way. I wouldn't be facing the prospect of living a life filled with regret and what ifs.

Like poor Paddy.

He frowns. I know what he's going to say. What he has to say.

"Unfortunately, Dylan…."

I interject. "I know, I know. I have to accept my fate like a good little Duster, the same as our Paddy's had to." The same as Eoin's had to do, too, I reckon.

"Do you love her?" I throw the question out there. He knows fine well who I'm referring to and it's not Molly. I'm not expecting him to answer. And definitely not truthfully.

"I honestly think I might."

And there you have it. I thought my situation was bad. His is even worse. He's being forced to marry someone he doesn't love. Double whammy? The woman he does fancy himself in love with has taken the vows with another man and carried their offspring. Triple whammy? She's in love with our baby brother.

"But Paddy."

He stands and walks to the window once more. Eoin seldom talks about anything personal. I think he's only doing so because my situation is highlighting and perhaps magnifying his own.

"You think I don't know? How much he loves her? How much she loves him? But Paddy's bed was made. The Ruoccos would have had a bullet put in his brain if he so much as thought about pulling out of that signed-in-blood arrangement. What I did, I had to do. I had no choice but to say what I did to her. Both Paddy *and* Jaine would have been at risk otherwise.

"If the Sicilians had thought they were crossing the line in any way, it would have been game over for them both. Jaine understood that. She left town to keep Paddy safe. She said what she had to because she had no choice either. He would never have let her go otherwise. That marriage *must* take place, or war will break out and people will perish as a result. Our Paddy would be first in that queue."

I nod. I understand how it happened. I also realize it can't be changed, and that there's no way back for them. "But even married to Sophia, he would still never be accepting of you with Jaine."

He keeps his gaze directed out the window. "I thought maybe in time." It's the sound of wishful thinking. I know it only too well.

"He would never be accepting of it, Eoin, and you know it. It would be like me watching you with Jessie. Or you watching me with Jaine. Right in front of you. Right under your nose. Having to witness that day in day out would destroy Paddy."

He doesn't reply, but he must know it's true. And it could destroy our family. Paddy could end up killing him or vice versa. There would only be one man standing after a come-to-Jesus moment like that, blood or not.

"And I'm sorry to say, but Jaine…."

"…. hates my guts." He butts in. "I'm well aware of how she feels about me. Jaine's not backward in coming forward when speaking her mind."

I snicker. I can't help myself. "No, she tends to just say it how it is and as colorfully as possible."

There's a pause.

"I know about the messaging. That it's Paddy and not you who messages Jaine."

Fuck. My bowels feel like they've turned to liquid.

"How?"

"I've known for some time. Paddy told me himself. He was worried about her when she was driving to Nevada the night Rafael Flores lost his life. It's why I went in the end. Because he couldn't. We agreed he could continue to message her provided no other contact was ever made. He can't speak to her. He can't see her. She can't know it's him. No one must know. Jesus Christ, if Sophia ever found out…"

"Sophia won't. We've been careful all this time. But Jaine will find out at some point. You do know that."

"I know. But hopefully, by the time she does, Paddy will be wed, and we won't have to worry about an attack by the Sicilians. Jaine's married now anyway. She has a family of her own. A life of her own. She's moved on."

There's another pause. We're both lost in our thoughts—both of us wanting someone we can't ever have.

"Why do Ma and Da hate her so much, Eoin?"

"Jaine?"

"Yes, Jaine."

"I asked her to meet with them."

"You did what?" I'm taken aback by that response. Did our Eoin want to court Jaine so badly he approached our folks and told them of his intentions?

"I asked her to meet with them, and she agreed in principle."

"So, they know? How you feel about her?"

"I told them I had feelings for her, yes.. I also told them I thought she'd make the best Ma Duster. I wasn't lying. I still believe that."

"And what happened?"

"We went to the Palace to meet with her. I naively thought it was all arranged. Jaine stood us up. She said she never agreed to anything. It turns out she had no intention of showing up. She was telling me what I wanted to hear simply to buy herself time. She was already back in California when I messaged to find out where she was."

"Shit, she's lucky…."

"They never had The Exterminator end her life? I'm aware of that."

My face remains impassive when he mentions the sniper. That's one secret that's not mine to ever share or reveal. I gave my word. And I will honor it. But if our Eoin thinks Jaine is perfect Ma Duster material now, if he ever finds out she's the infamous hit person, he'll immediately be calling her his queen, whether anyone likes it or not.

Even Jaine. Even Paddy.

"So, what now?"

"We're Dusters, Dylan. We can't delay our fate forever. At some point, we must be accepting of it."

"And pray for a miracle in the meantime?"

He laughs softly. "And that too."

"Cill was granted one."

"He was. So maybe there's still hope for the rest of us."

He turns and looks at me, his expression subdued. He's my eldest brother by seven years. For some reason, I always assumed life was easier for him. But as heir, he probably takes the full brunt of what comes our way and deflects most of it from the rest of us like big brothers do. He'll have had it tough I reckon. It's just, he's never complained, so us lot have just assumed he was always getting what he wanted. That he was happy with the decisions being made on his behalf because he was party to them.

It turns out not to be the case.

I stand, walk across, and then I hug my brother. He's tense and not receptive initially, but then eventually he hugs me back.

It's only taken almost thirty-one years for me to catch a glimpse of the man behind the mask of the future Irish king.

And I realize now. He's not all bad.

CHAPTER THIRTY

JAINE

Jaine's House, Rising, California

"Good riddance? The future Mrs. Dylan O'Connell said those exact words?"

"She sure did, partner. And just as I was about to leave the room, so she could use them to full effect."

"And so let me get this straight. As a result, you're now staying."

"For now, at least. Well, I couldn't leave after that, could I? She deliberately said them to get a reaction from me in front of the O'Connells. If I'd just left, I would have look like I wasn't prepared to stand my ground. And my daddy didn't raise no yellow-bellied quitter."

"No, I can imagine," I say dryly. Her daddy's an asshole. "And have you spoken with Dyl since?"

"Nope. Candice said he went into a meeting with Paddy, came

out, and went straight into another with Eoin. Anyway, I have nothing to say to him. Apart from offering my congratulations that he's going to get hitched to his happily ever after, what's there to say?"

"What's she like? This cliché blonde Disney princess of his."

"The only word accurate in that description is blonde. And that's not me being in any way unkind or disrespectful. But *Disney*? And princess? I get the impression if you described Grace Ryan as either of those two things to her face, she might just hit you with something. It was all a bit bizarre. She seemed perfectly agreeable at first. I couldn't believe it was her mouth those words came out of. I was totally taken aback."

"So, what's next?"

"For me to take things one day at a time, I guess. Meanwhile, I'll speak to Bailey. See if Razr has any suitable properties I can move into while I sort out my place and get it moved on."

"Maybe the Dusters will repurchase it."

"Maybe. I'll get it independently valued, and we can take it from there."

"You sure you can't stay? After all the time and effort you put in to creating the perfect living space?"

"I'm not sure I could cope with colliding with the newlyweds. It's not like I could avoid them forever. It wouldn't be fair on either them or me. They shouldn't have to hide the fact that they're together and happy."

"And how are you coping with it all?"

"To be honest, I don't think it's sunk in yet. That what we had is actually over. I mean, I only fucked him earlier today."

"Jesus Christ. Only you would do something like that, Jessie."

"I'm pretty sure you would have done the same thing."

I smile to myself. She's right, and we both know it.

"I'll be on a sex hiatus once more and probably for the long term. And a girl has needs, you know? So, you have to take it where you can get it, especially if it's the good stuff, and let me tell you, Dylan O'Connell is in the 99th percentile when it comes to the art of fucking."

"That's way too much information." I grimace.

She laughs out loud.

"Anyway, enough about him. I also announced in the meeting that you would be resuming all communications with Eoin."

"Thanks for that." I exhale loudly.

"You're welcome. But you did agree."

"I know I did."

"Will you call him today?"

"As soon as I get off the phone to you."

"Are you going to tell him about Molly's threatening call?"

"I'm not sure. The girl's inexperienced, but she's also a liar. That's a dangerous combination right there. Maybe I'll let the Dusters find both out the hard way. I mean, it's not really my problem, nor is it any of my business."

"I think you should mention it. Just in case anything kicks off. Maybe Eoin can have a quiet word with Roisin."

"What, and create another owing in his eyes? No, thank you. Anyway, I can fight my own battles."

"Speaking of battles, what's happening with Ghost?"

"We've offered him and his brothers more money. But they still maintain they want to remain independent. They're sticking to their guns. Last I heard, they want in on the alliance but as a separate MC."

"Will that work?"

I shrug. "We can make anything work within reason. Between us, we make the rules."

"Still nothing on who this silent backer is?"

"Nope. I reckon only Ghost knows but that's pure speculation on my part. If indeed he does, it's my guess if he breathes a word, he'll be a dead man walking. Much like Reaper would have been if he had lived to spill his guts."

"So, how can they join the alliance if they're already involved with this backer?"

"Who knows? Maybe they can walk away with the guarantee they're sworn to secrecy forevermore. The truth is we all just need the unrest to disappear so we can get on with our lives. It's not good for business. We're focusing on the wrong things. In fact, I may have a quiet word with Rod about it."

"Do we need to involve the Irish?"

"I'm not sure. Maybe not at this stage. Cillian and Sarah will be here in a couple of days, so no doubt Ace will mention it to Cill. There'll be stuff I've not been party to knowing him."

"You're pregnant, Jaine. He won't want you getting stressed."

"I am pregnant. But that doesn't mean I need to be handled with kid gloves. Plus, it's the not knowing that's giving me the stress."

"I hear you. You'll keep me posted?"

"I will. I'll probably know more after Cill and Sarah's visit."

"Well, enjoy your conversation with big brother Duster."

"I can hardly goddamn wait. And Jessie?"

"Yeah?"

"I'm here. You know. If you need to talk."

There's a pause. She's putting on a brave face, I know she is. I think with Jessie, there's a lot hidden beneath that attention-seeking surface of hers that she doesn't want anyone to see. I want her to know I'm here for her. That I will always be here for her. But as a friend, not just as her business partner.

"Thanks." She tries her best to hide it, but I can hear how broken she is in just that one word. I know the sound because I'm the same most days. Having had years of practice, I'm just much better at hiding it.

"Eoin."

"It's good to hear from you, Jaine."

"Well, I did say I'd call."

There's a silence—an unusually awkward one. I can sense things have changed between us. Is it the fact he's now in a serious relationship? Or over the Dyl and Jessie situation? Then again, maybe it's because we haven't spoken in a while. The atmosphere just feels different. I can't pinpoint why. I speak again.

"So. This Jessie shitshow."

He chuckles, and I find myself doing the same, grateful the awkwardness evaporates with it.

"Have you missed me turning the air blue, Eoin?"

"I've missed everything about you, Jaine."

He sounds sincere. He means it. There's another pause. Not awkward this time. More because I'm taken aback over his admission. Am I glad he missed me?

"Right." I mean, what else is there to say?

He clears his throat. Does he regret thinking out loud?

"I'm not sure whether that description is an understatement or an overstatement." He speaks.

"It's Jessie O'Brien we're talking about. It's definitely an understatement." I laugh again, but it's more forced as I'm now considering how to phrase what I have to say.

"True."

"Eoin, I need to apologize."

"For?"

I exhale. "Normally I would advise a client immediately I became aware of any potential conflict of interest. Jessie's sister is Delaney's fiancée. Her father is prez of the Sons of Satan. I know several clients who might not be receptive to contracting with someone with Jessie's connections. In my defense, I acted at all times in what I believed to be the Dusters' best interests. I have complete confidence in Jessie. Both in terms of her loyalty and commitment and in terms of her work ethic and confidentiality. When I weighed up the potential risk, I believed the IRS matter presented far more of a threat to the Duster organization, which is why I decided to withhold the information on Jessie until that was resolved in its entirety.

"For the record, I went against my own business ethics. I always believe in complete transparency. In this situation, however, works had been committed to and were underway. It was also a time-critical matter. With both in mind, I did not believe the revelation would have been in my client's best interests at that time, so I made the call."

There, I've said it. If I made the wrong decision, then so be it. But I acted with the best of intentions. I put the well-being of the Dusters above all else, even my own principles and professional integrity.

"Thank you, Jaine."

"For?'

"For being honest. For keeping the focus on the most important matter at hand. For doing what was best for the Dusters."

I sigh loudly. "Yes, but it's since transpired it was to the detriment of something just as important."

"How do you mean?"

"I mean, if I had come clear about Jessie as soon as I found out. If I had mentioned who she was. They would have stood a chance, wouldn't they?"

"You're talking in riddles, Jaine."

"Jessie and Dylan."

There's a pause. We both know it's a case of non-disclosure resulting in history repeating.

"We'll never know."

"Don't skirt the question, Eoin."

He hesitates before he responds. Because he knows he's going to say something I don't want to hear. Even though I already know the answer.

"Most likely, yes." And there it is. We both know if I'd come clean about this sooner rather than later, the outcome could have been entirely different for them. Guilt floods me. Jessie will suffer and it's all my fault.

"Is Dylan in love with her?"

"Yes. He came to me himself and told me so."

I frown as something suddenly niggles away at me. See, none of this is stacking up.

"But what about this cliché blonde of his? This Grace Ryan girl? I thought he was besotted with her and had been for some time. Several years, in fact."

There's a lengthy pause before he responds. "I'm not sure how he feels about Grace. It's not really for me to say." For the first time ever, the eldest Duster sounds unsure of himself. What the fuck is going on? Because something clearly is.

"Maybe I should just ask Dylan."

He responds quickly. Too quickly. "And maybe it's best you don't. He's upset enough. Maybe it's simply the case that his love for Jessie has superseded his besottedness with Grace."

He could be correct, I guess. I try to push the niggle to the back of my mind, but it won't go.

"Yes, you're probably right. So, is there nothing that can be done?" I know what he's going to say before he says it. I know I'm clutching at straws.

"As in all cases such as this, not without the risk of causing insult and potentially starting a war."

"So, all we can do is pray for a miracle."

"You believe in the power of prayer, Jaine?"

"No. I put my faith in the power of love."

"It's failed you in the past, has it not?"

"If you're looking for an instantaneous result, then I guess you could say that. But there's no time limit on love. At some point, the stars will align."

"Very poetic."

I laugh out loud. "You see? I'm not just a pretty face."

"It's beautiful."

"What is?"

"Your face. It's not pretty. It's beautiful."

"Thank you." I pause. The compliment has thrown me. In fact, the whole conversation has. For once, he's not being a pompous prick. Is he's trying to lull me into a false sense of security? Convince me he's a decent human being when I have first-hand experience assuring me he's not?

"I should go."

"Yes."

"Goodbye, then."

"You never say goodbye, Jaine. You just hang up."

It's not a complaint. He's just saying it how it is. Does it bother him? I frown at the handset. Am I bothered if it does? I disconnect the call without another word, feeling guilty as soon as I do.

CHAPTER THIRTY-ONE

JESSIE

The Hudson Dusters' HQ, Manhattan, New York

I'M IN A CUBICLE IN THE LADIES' RESTROOM. I'M NOT DOING anything as such. I'm just sitting on the closed toilet seat, gathering my thoughts and minding my own business.

No one can disturb you when you're in the john. Well, not unless they're a seriously fucked-up individual with no sense of personal space. It's the only real place of refuge in any office environment—a sanctuary where you can breathe for five minutes.

Well, depending on what's gone on in there beforehand.

Despicable Dylan is in the office today, and I'm trying my best to avoid him. Same as I've been doing when I'm at home.

So far, I've managed to succeed. I don't want to hear anything he has to say. Reasons. Excuses. Lies. It won't change anything. The outcome will still be the same.

He'll still be getting wed to Grace Ryan.

I've excused myself from today's meeting, and I'll sit in here all day if I have to to continue my avoidance quest. It's for the best. I've been reliably informed by my new kindred spirit, Candice, that all of their female partners will be in attendance today. It's my guess they'll be discussing where the organization is headed and what each individual's expected contribution will be.

Business aside, they'll then likely move on to engagement dates, wedding dates, how many kids each of them will have, which former Dusters they'll be named after, and so on.

Trust me. There is no one better than Jessie O'Brien at maintaining a poker face. But today? I just can't stomach it. It's only been forty-eight hours since the shit hit the fan. And I'm not ashamed to admit I'm struggling.

I stayed. I stood my ground. But at what cost?

Quit whining, Jessie. I'm sure it will get easier.

Once I move apartments, then at least I'll only have to avoid awkward office confrontations.

I can do that. I can cope.

Just not today.

"So, how have you been getting on with Roisin's task?"

I recognize Molly's voice immediately. I quickly lift my feet off the floor so they can't be seen under the cubicle door.

"I've tried everything, but I can't get him to kiss me, let alone anything else. I've pretty much thrown myself at him. It's humiliating."

The voice of frustration has an Italian accent. Sophia.

"What do you mean he won't kiss you? Padraig's not gay, is he?"

"Of course he's not gay. He managed to get it up for *her,* didn't he?" she hisses in disgust.

She's obviously referring to Jaine.

"Why then? I mean, it's not like you're not beautiful."

"It never concerned me before or even crossed my mind. When we were first betrothed, I was under the age of consent. Then, when I turned seventeen, I assumed Padraig was being gentlemanly. Perhaps choosing to wait until we were wed. But it's not that. He's not interested. He doesn't find me physically attractive."

I can almost visualize the pout.

"But why?"

"It's obvious, isn't it? It's because he's still in love with her!"

"You can't be serious? Are you telling me Padraig O'Connell hasn't slept with anyone else in all this time?"

"That's exactly what I am telling you. You heard what Roisin said. He's been in love with her since he was nineteen. What other reason can there be that he won't take what I'm pretty much throwing in his face?"

"Roisin won't be pleased with this update."

"And what can I do about that, Molly? I can't force him to have sex with me. And don't think because Eoin is sleeping with you it makes your position any safer. From what I hear, he has a host of individually hand-picked women at his beck and call, including his PA. He may just have added you to his extensive harem so he appears interested. Has he asked your father for your hand yet?"

"No."

"You see? He's using you and keeping you quiet while looking for any excuse to declare you an unsuitable match. He's still in love with her too. I think Roisin is correct on both counts. They're both waiting for her to return to Manhattan."

"But you'll be married before then."

"Yes. Trapped in a loveless marriage having to watch as my husband pines over another woman."

There's a silence.

"Maybe we have to take matters into our own hands, Sophia."

"Yes, maybe we do. Because if Jaine Jones is offering me a lifetime of solitude and misery, then maybe I should afford her the same courtesy."

I stay where I am until the restroom door opens then closes.

You know what? Maybe I'll attend today's little soiree after all, because things sure are starting to get interesting around here.

"It's good to see you, Jessie girl. I thought something had come up."

I smile at him. "Well, I moved things around just for you, Fergal. Nothing is more important than seeing my favorite O'Connell." Taking off my shoes, I walk barefoot to where he's sitting, squeeze his shoulder as I always do, then swing the Newton's Cradle into action.

He chuckles. Da Duster actually chuckles. Not making eye contact with any of the others, I smile at him once more as I walk back to my chair.

Fuck. Them. All.

Apart from Fergal, that is. I'm sure he'll be aware of what's gone on between Despicable Dylan and me now. Not that it matters. He can't change anything as it's a done deal.

I don't even glance at Dylan before I immediately command the floor. Let's get this show on the road—no more hiding out in toilet cubicles. No siree.

"I spoke with Mick yesterday."

"Mick?" Eoin's looking at me like I'm speaking in a foreign language.

"You know. That man in Dublin who calls himself your uncle."

He raises an eyebrow at me. "And how is he…. Uncle Mick."

"Well, he's very flirtatious and likes to tell a joke at every turn. I can tell who Padraig has inherited that gift of the gab of his from."

Paddy laughs heartily in response, while Sophia just glares.

"And why did you have to contact Uncle Mick?"

"I noticed the payment going to their usual Irish account was higher than normal. I wanted to know why. I figured he was the best person to tell me. Was it a one-off increase? Something that would be ongoing? It turns out it's the latter. It's apparently due to a rise in transport costs."

"Go on."

"So, armed with that answer and having calculated the total increase including an apportionment of overhead for the additional workload it will create, I then spoke to Rod."

"So, you've also spoken to La eMe?"

I nod and frown simultaneously. "You make it sound like it's a big deal. I'm just doing my job, Eoin."

"Not at all. I'm just surprised you picked up the phone to Rodolfo Flores."

I frown again. "And why wouldn't I call Rod? As I told you before I've known him all my life. I mean, if my daddy had had his way, I would have been married to him by now."

Cue the mic drop moment right there as they all stare at each other.

"And why didn't you marry him?"

I lean back in my chair. Do I fabricate an outlandish story, or do I tell the simple truth? I'll go with the latter. Honesty is always the best policy.

I shrug. "Rod doesn't like blondes. He told me I'd need to dye my hair. I refused. Too much upkeep involved. I mean, gentlemen are meant to prefer blondes, right? Well, someone forgot to mention that to Rod. Then again, being a mafioso, some might argue that he's not actually a gentleman. I mean, who on earth would want to marry the billionaire who's rumored to be the next silent boss of La eMe anyway?"

I shrug again.

"In the end, the idea was vetoed by all parties concerned due to my reluctance to change hair color. So, I got to stay blonde. And Rod went off in search of a dark-haired Plan B. Maybe I should have agreed. Rod's still searching as far as I'm aware so the vacancy's still open. And Jessie Flores has a nice ring to it, don't you think?"

I watch as Eoin frowns in Dylan's direction. I'd give anything to see the expression on his face, but I can't do that without turning my head.

Then again, there probably isn't one. Or at least not one that shows he's in any way bothered by my admission. He's got Grace now, after all.

"Anyway, all that aside, I spoke to Rod and told him there needed to be an uplift. He's agreed. He'll be paying double what the Dusters' costs are."

"And you handled all this without Jaine?"

Again, I nod and frown. "Have I missed something? Is this 'insult your accountant' day or what? We do have to study contract law as part of our qualification, you know? We're not just hopeless number crunchers who can't survive in the real world without having a calculator on hand at all times to act as some sort of professional soother."

I turn my attention to Molly. "As the external legal representation for the Dusters and as the next alliance shipment is due to land imminently, I've told Rod you'll also speak to him today. I do hope that's okay." I smile at her.

"Well, it's not really convenient." She glances at Eoin and then Fergal as though looking for backup. Does she think I've deliberately dropped her professional self in it? On the contrary, I thought I was doing her a favor. That I'd broken the ice in advance so it's no longer just a cold call.

I frown again. "Rod has a busy schedule doing all those mafia-type things he does, but he's agreed to take your call at extremely short notice as a favor. Shall I let him know you're too busy to speak to him?"

"I'm sure Molly can squeeze in a conversation with your good friend and our ally today, Jessie." Da Duster has spoken. Now she'll have no choice.

"Is there anything else we need to be made aware of, Jessie?"

I look at Eoin. Do I say something or not?

"Well, there is still a bit of unrest in Colton that I think you boys should be made aware of."

I know Jaine will kill me. But I figure it's better that than risking a repeat of what happened last time. We don't need another bloodbath on our hands because of another lapse in communication.

"Go on."

CHAPTER THIRTY-TWO

DYLAN

The Hudson Dusters' HQ, Manhattan, New York

"YOU HAVE TO WORK BETTER AT CONTROLLING YOURSELF, DYLAN."

We're in my big brother's office again. This time, two tan-colored chairs face him. One for me. It's my guess the other is for our Paddy. No doubt there would be a third pulled up for Cill, but he's off galivanting and is currently sunning himself in California.

"What if she marries him, Eoin? What if she decides to wed Rodolfo Flores?"

"And what if she does? You're pretty much spoken for, or have you forgotten? And Grace and everyone else in the room just witnessed your adverse expression over what Jessie said. What if Grace decides to tell her parents you're mooning over another girl?"

"I don't care," I hiss. I'd never have dared speak to him the way I am doing. I definitely would never have raised my voice. But right now, I want to thump someone, and his arrogant self would do quite nicely.

It's another alien feeling for me, but then, so is murderous jealousy.

He leans back in his chair and gazes at me contemplatively. "She really has changed you. You'll be asking to go on wet work with our Paddy next."

"She has. And for the better. And I don't want her to move back to fucking Nevada."

"You don't have any say in the matter. Have you spoken with her?"

I laugh dryly. "I've tried but unsuccessfully. We managed to keep out of each other's way for months, Eoin. Trust me. Jessie's got the ability to avoid me down to an art form."

"Can't you speak to her in the office?"

I shake my head. "Even here she manages to disappear. It's as if she's left the building even when she hasn't."

Eoin looks between us both. One of us has dropped the ball. I'm not sure which of us it is, but I do know that it'll be to do with Jaine.

"The cliché blonde."

Fuck.

"What about her?" Paddy answers.

I'm relieved. It's his woman after all. He can sort out the mess we're in because of him, his big mouth, and this expanding web of deceit.

"Jaine mentioned her. Would you care to explain who she is?"

I don't make eye contact with Paddy. If I do, he'll silently ask for my help. It's his mess. He can dig us out of this hole he's flung us both in. I've got enough drama of my own to deal with.

"She's been around for a while, Eoin. Me and Jaine were talking about love. I told her I had been in love once and it was with a tall, slim, beautiful blonde. In fact, the most perfect woman the world has ever fucking seen. I told her I was still in love with the girl and always would be."

I don't need to look at Paddy to know he'll be on the verge of breaking down just talking about it. About her. He'll be married soon. His life will be over if it isn't already. I don't want to show any empathy. It's not because I'm not sympathetic to his situation. I am. But I know from experience it won't help him offering that. That he'll just withdraw into a melancholy mood.

There's a sniff. I have to fight to hold back my own tears. It makes me want to cry with him. My poor baby brother. A ruthless, sadistic killer who wears his heart on his sleeve when it comes to Jaine Jones.

I stare at Eoin. How conflicted must he be feeling? Witnessing our Paddy fall apart once more over the loss of the love of his life. Potentially the love of both their lives since Eoin's confessed to having feelings for the same woman.

We wait for Paddy to gather himself and continue.

"Jaine joked that as the girl sounded cliche, she must surely be a figment of my imagination, hence a make-believe Disney Princess. So, that's how the cliché blonde came about," he finally finishes.

Eoin nods, now understanding. "So, this cliché blonde is Jaine. And you had this conversation on a message exchange while pretending to be Dylan. Is that right?"

Paddy must nod as he doesn't verbally respond.

"So, correct me if I'm wrong, but this is the reason Jessie kept away from Dyl all those months. Because Jaine mentioned this blonde to her, and Jessie thought Dylan was pining over someone else."

He's looking at me. It seems it's my turn to add my two cents worth.

Great.

I nod. "I can only assume that as Jessie had seen neither hide nor hair of this girl, she guessed she was no longer in the picture. When Grace appeared on the scene, Paddy, having been put on the spot by Jaine, told Jaine that Grace was the cliché blonde."

"Grace? A Disney princess? It's a bit far-fetched."

"Maybe so, but it seemed a good idea at the time. I was clutching at straws for what to say, and it was an existing loose end." Paddy sighs. He thought he'd tied it up, but all he's done is make the situation far worse.

Eoin is sitting with his attention fixed out the window. It would be safer for us if he moved farther away as he probably wants to wring both our necks right about now.

"So, Jessie will think this arranged marriage has been on the cards for some time given how long Dylan has apparently been pining."

"Exactly," I reply. "And that's why she'll be beyond pissed. She'll think I've been having a dalliance with her, all the while knowing I'm to be married off to the supposed great love of my life. She probably thinks I'm a swine for messing both her and Grace around."

"Oh, what a tangled web we weave." Eoin exhales. "Well, she now suspects something, Paddy."

"Who?"

"Jaine!" he hisses, turning to face us.

"Why? How?"

"Because, not knowing the whole fabricated story, I told her that Dylan had come to me professing his undying love for Jessie, which he did. Jaine countered that with this cliché blonde revelation. That Dyl had apparently been besotted with Grace Ryan for some considerable time."

"And what did you say back?" Paddy starts to fidget. He's worried now. That loose end he thought he tied up in a pretty little bow? Well, it seems it's about to unravel the whole sorry mess.

"That I wasn't sure how he felt about Grace. That it wasn't for me to speculate. But this is her business partner who's being messed around. She threatened to approach Dylan direct on the matter, but I suggested perhaps it was simply the case that his besottedness with Grace has been superseded by his love for Jessie."

"Did she buy it?"

"Temporarily maybe, but she won't leave it there. She's a lawyer. She's got a bee in her bonnet over it now. Plus, she won't let it rest if she thinks something can be done to achieve the happily ever after she did for Cill and Sarah. Is there anything else that can come to light from this fiasco? Undermine the web of lies we're all now tangled up in?"

"I told her I fucked her," Paddy mumbles.

"Told who you fucked who?"

"I told Jaine I fucked the blonde. I think my exact words were that I'd slept with her but nowhere near enough times. That even if I slept with her every day until the day I died, it would never be enough. Or should I say those were our Dyl's exact words."

"Very poetic. And?"

Eoin stares at me, and I feel my cheeks going red for the first time in days. Fucking great.

"Seriously?"

I nod.

He turns back to the window and exhales. "Well, considering how most girls like to gossip, I don't imagine it will be long before Jessie reveals that little nugget. So." He looks back at us. "Prepare yourself for the fallout because Jaine will take no prisoners when she finds out it's her Irish she's been communicating with all this time."

"What do we do in the meantime?" I ask, but Paddy and I already know the unwelcome answer. And we both know it's not what Jaine needs right now. She's already struggling emotionally. Then again, it's not what Paddy needs either. Not when he has so very little time left with her.

"You pair communicate with her as little as possible. Let's hope it's a simple case of out of sight out of mind and she forgets all about this cliché blonde. It's unlikely, but we can live in hope."

"I don't want to do that. I can't do that. We message every day. She'll know something is wrong." Paddy's hopeful face flicks between me and Eoin.

Back and forth. Back and forth.

But there is no hope. It's all about damage limitation now. I realize I'll have to handhold him through this if we're not to lose him to the demon drink once more.

He can't function without Jaine in his life.

"We can't afford for Jaine to find out and say something, Paddy. If Sophia finds out, if she tells Luc, war will kick-off, and Jaine will have a target on her back. As will you. Anyway, Jaine won't suspect anything is wrong. She'll think Dylan is simply spending more time with Grace and so he, understandably, has less for her."

"But she'll find out eventually."

"Of course she will, Paddy. But that's an explosion I can handle far easier when I'm standing in front of her and when she's back in Manhattan."

CHAPTER THIRTY-THREE

JESSIE

The Hudson Dusters' HQ, Manhattan, New York

"ARE YOU CALLING ME FROM THE RESTROOM CUBICLE AGAIN?"

"I am indeed, partner. How can you tell?"

"There's an echo. Maybe you should set your desk up in there."

I snicker. "Not a chance. I'm in here because I don't want to be found. When anyone comes in, I just do that thing they do in the movies. I lift my feet off the floor."

"Is it the same cubicle every time? Do you ever lock it?"

"Yup and nope."

"What if someone opens the door?"

"Then they'll see me perched on top of the closed toilet seat. It's no big deal. They already think I'm all wired up wrong."

I smile as she laughs out loud. It's a welcome sound as neither of us have been laughing much these days.

"So how are things going?"

"Same. I just keep out of his way. I'm not interested in hearing anything he has to say. We were fuck buddies and now we're not so let's just leave it at that. Anyway, how did things go with Cillian and Sarah?"

There's a pause. "So so."

"So so. That good, huh?"

"Let's just say something came out that needed to and that I had planned to tell Sarah, but I still wasn't prepared for it being in the open."

"This just gets vaguer and vaguer. Can you tell me what that something is?"

"Nope."

"All righty then. Well, is there anything you can tell me?"

"Something else came up. But it wasn't anything to do with Cill and Sarah."

"Which was?"

"My father-in-law stopped by not long after they left. And, well, strictly between you and me, he announced my pop wasn't my biological daddy."

"Holy shit."

"I know. I'm not sure what to do with that. Or even how I feel about it. My real father is demanding to meet me. He's threatening to reveal himself if Duke and Ace don't make the necessary introductions."

"Did you suspect your pop wasn't your real daddy?"

"Nope. I had no goddamn clue. He never mentioned anything."

"What about your mom?"

"I don't remember too much about her. I'm not sure if I didn't just blank most of those memories out. Many were unpleasant because she was in and out of the hospital so much. She was diagnosed with terminal cancer when I was three and passed just before I turned seven."

"I'm so sorry to hear that, Jaine. Have you got any images of her?"

"A few, but not many. As far as I know, my pop was her second husband. When she left her first, she left most of her personal belongings behind. She was blonde, that much I do know. Pop packed what we had of her away because he couldn't bear to look at it. He never went near another woman after she passed because he loved her so much. No one could ever compare."

"Jaine, that's so sad. I lost my mom too, but my daddy remarried. I'm so glad he did because Tadgh and I wouldn't have Conor and little Bee if he hadn't. So, what are you going to do?"

"I've told Ace to let him know I won't even consider meeting him until this baby is out of me."

"Three months to go. Will he wait that long?"

"He'll have to. I mean, let's face it, he's waited almost thirty years to look me up, so surely, he can wait another few months."

"Do you have any siblings?"

"I have no idea, Jessie. Your guess is as good as mine."

"I hope you have a sister just like me."

"Jesus Christ. Well, if there's a fate worse than death, that's it right there."

I can't help but laugh out loud. I know she doesn't mean that. Well at least I sure hope she doesn't.

"I thought being ma Duster was the fate worse than death."

"That too."

"Equal billing?"

She chuckles. "Exactly that."

"So, did Sarah ask when you'd be back? It's all she ever talks about these days."

"I need to be back inside the next six months."

"Wow. So specific. Need? Or want."

"Need."

YOU KNOW FATE HIMSELF HAS GOT IT IN FOR YOU WHEN YOU LEAVE the safety of the restroom and collide with the person you've managed to successfully avoid for days.

Dylan immediately steps back like a scalded cat, and I do the same, but it's way too late. The citrus notes of his body wash have already wrapped themselves around me like an aphrodisiac, and my panties are wet as a result.

Great. Just fucking great.

Don't speak to me. Do. Not. Open. Your. Deceitful. Mouth.

"Jessie."

That New York accent right there, with just the perfect lilt of Irish.

Well, fuck me. Why yes, please do. Right here. Right now. In fact, wherever you like. However you like. I'll even make do with a wall bang in front of Candice. You know the woman who's standing in front of the copy machine with her arms folded, wearing a massive grin on her face as she takes in this laughable visual going on right in front of her.

Kindred spirit? My ass. Bitch.

I fully realize my gaze will be lust-filled, and my nipples will be standing to attention as I admire the complete snack that is Dylan O'Connell. I'll bet I'm even drooling.

"Can we talk?"

To do that, you need to be able to breathe. I can't. I count to ten slowly in my head as I try to recall how to inhale and exhale.

"There's nothing to talk about. Unless you want to discuss the fact that you're a piece of shit." I look behind him exaggeratedly. "Where's your cliché blonde lady friend? Is she off wedding dress shopping with the other two arranged fiancées?"

He closes his eyes. If he was trying to use the Lord God's name in vain silently, he failed miserably. I heard the blasphemous usage of 'Jesus Christ' quite clearly.

He runs his frustrated fingers through his hair. Inky black strands that I've fisted a million times in my hands as he's fucked me to within an inch of my life.

I want that. Right here. Right now. This fucking instant. I'll worry about the implications of it all later.

"We haven't started the courting process. We're not engaged. I haven't kissed her. I haven't fucked her. Happy now?"

"Yet."

I get that in there. Because it's true. He will court her. He will kiss her. He will get engaged to her. He will marry her. He will fuck her.

He's staring at me. I know I've flicked that switch of his, and he's now entering Duster mode.

"You've been avoiding me for days, Jessie. We need to talk." His voice is firm as he grabs me by the wrist and starts dragging me towards his office.

My useless four-inch stilettos are no match for the marble floor. I might as well be fucking ice skating the way he's dragging me along. The sound of my cursing is met with snickering from the delightful Candice.

Did I already say bitch? Well, let me reiterate that.

Bitch.

CHAPTER THIRTY-FOUR

JESSIE

The Hudson Dusters' HQ, Manhattan, New York

"Quit man-handling me."

He pulls me inside his office, closes the door behind us, then deliberately stands between me and the exit. I roll my eyes and turn away as I take in his workspace. It's sparsely furnished. A black desk and not much else.

"Oh, look. There's only one chair. Shall we share while we have this important conversation of yours?" I say sarcastically as I rub my wrist, which will no doubt bruise up nicely.

"If you like you can sit on my lap, and we can talk about the first thing that comes up." He smirks.

Mature. Really mature.

"I'm going for lunch. This level's empty, so you can make as much noise as you like." Candice announces her departure through the closed door. I can't see her, but I know she's wearing a matching smirk. Yup. Another comedian right there.

I stare at Dyl. He's dressed professionally but his tie is missing, and his messy hair has gotten way too long again.

He looks fucking perfect.

"Jessie, I…." His smirk is replaced by a frown, his tone now borderline apologetic.

I interrupt. "I'm not interested in anything you have to say, Dylan."

Excuses. Lies. Reasons. Apologies. They're all a waste of breath when they won't change anything.

We stare at each other. Not speaking. Because what's there to say?

"So why aren't you courting her?" I break the prolonged silence.

He runs his hand through his hair messing it even more. "There's some contractual paperwork Grace's da wants in place beforehand. Our Paddy's looking into it."

Arranged marriages equal legal contracts. How romantic.

"How long will it take to resolve?"

"It should be sorted tomorrow."

Manana. Tomorrow. The day that never comes. The world could have ended before then. I know we're both now thinking the same thing. Has it suddenly gotten hot in here? There's no sound apart from heavy breathing.

We can't go there. Can we?

Since he's staring at me like he wants to eat me alive, it's obvious he seems to think we can. He reaches me in two strides, spins me around, and pushes me back against the wall.

"Get your hands off me." I try to prize strong fingers from my hips. When I can't, I stick my nails into his skin until I'm sure I can feel blood. He curses but holds fast.

I make eye contact. His are black with lust. I lick my lips. Big mistake. I watch as his gaze drops to my mouth.

"Don't you dare."

Oh, but he does dare. He's taking. Because he knows I'm giving without me uttering a word.

His hand fists my hair before yanking my head back. I whine at the pain, then moan as he sucks on my neck. I know I'm done for the moment his mouth covers mine. His lips are hard and demanding, his tongue pushing past to claim ownership of my mouth. The taste of adrenaline and all things Dylan O'Connell drown my senses. My legs buckle, and he grips my hip tighter to stop me from collapsing to the floor.

His fingers dig in. Burning. Branding. Marking.

I can't breathe. I can't think. All I can do is feel.

"You want my tongue on your pussy, Jessie?"

I raise an eyebrow at him. "Best get on your knees, then."

His eyes never leave mine as he drops to the floor. Yanking my skirt up to my waist, he pulls down my panties and puts them in his pocket.

He then runs his fingers through my soaked folds and smirks.

"You're such a needy, greedy little girl aren't you, Jessie O'Brien."

Using my slickness to lubricate them, he thrusts two inside, before curling them to connect with my sweet spot. Damn, I taught him well. I'm immediately on edge. Like a bitch in heat, I press my pussy against his face, my hands fisting his hair.

Mouth. Tongue. Teeth. Suck. Lick. Bite. I want all of that. Now.

I hiss my thanks as he sucks hard on my clit. Scissoring his fingers, he finger fucks me to get me ready for that massive cock of his.

Harder. Faster. Deeper.

I want more.

Nothing has ever felt so good. I should be embarrassed by the sound of how wet I am, but I don't even care.

"Fuck." The orgasm destroys me with its intensity. Pulling on his hair, I press myself against his face as my release drenches his fingers. He doesn't stop. He keeps right on going until it becomes unbearable. I try to squeeze my thighs together, but he has other ideas. Lifting my leg over his shoulder, he devours me until I come again.

Standing, he kisses me hard, my cum now covering both our faces as his tongue sweeps deep. Sucking his fingers into his mouth, he cleans them off before spinning me around and walking me backward towards the empty desk.

"Bend over."

I almost come on the spot as he utters those two fucking words.

"What was that? I didn't quite hear you."

"*I said.* Bend. Over."

I'm naked from the waist down and going by the hard-on rocking the front of his suit pants, he's extremely appreciative of the view. Rubbing my hand over his erection, I whisper two words back.

"Make. Me."

Spinning me around, he pushes my torso down against the desk, his hand pinning me face down by the neck. I can't move. And I fucking love it.

Belt. Zip. Pants hitting the floor.

The only sounds.

The blunt head of his dick grazes my pussy as he lubricates himself before he takes my breath away by thrusting in to the hilt. I whine at the intrusion. He responds by pulling back out and driving straight back in.

"You want more, Jessie?" His smug snicker is hot against my ear

"Yes." I pant.

Both hands grip my hips as he fucks me hard and fast, the desk banging noisily against the marble floor.

"I want you to come all over my cock. Can you do that for me, Jessie?"

One hand moves to fist my hair. Then, pulling my head back, his tongue pushes into my mouth as he claims my answering scream as his reward for fucking me into oblivion.

"More." I whine.

Releasing my hair, he moves both hands back to my hips, tilting them so he can go even deeper. "Push against me, Jessie."

I do, causing him to bottom out. He roars then with his own release, his cock pulsing inside me as he fills me with so much cum it immediately starts to coat my inner thighs.

We stay there, hot and panting, his head resting on the back of my neck. Eventually, he releases me from his grip and steps back. Walking silently to the restroom connected to his office, I clean myself up and then straighten my suit as best I can.

I stare at my reflection in the over sink mirror. I look like I've just been fucked. My hair's kinked. My lips are swollen. I'm sporting a hickey.

Thanks for that, willpower. Great friend you are.

I leave the restroom.

"Panties." I hold my hand out and wiggle my fingers.

"Not a chance." He shakes his head, a smile playing on his lips.

"Perv," I mutter.

"Don't you just love it."

He tries to kiss me, but I pull back before turning away.

"Jessie." His voice sounds pleading as I walk towards the door. I ignore him because that right there should never have happened. And it must never be allowed to happen again.

I throw open the office door to be confronted by Eoin, who's leaning against the copier with his arms folded in much the same spot his PA was, wearing an almost identical smirk.

"Having fun?" He raises one eyebrow.

Candice, you lying bitch.

For the first time ever, I want to be forgotten. I also want this marble floor to open up and swallow me whole.

CHAPTER THIRTY-FIVE

DYLAN

The Hudson Dusters' HQ, Manhattan, New York

"You fucked her over your desk."

"You fuck Candice over yours all the time," I argue. We're in his office again. We're in here more often than not these days.

"I did. I don't anymore. I'm courting Molly. You're meant to be courting Grace."

"Only after the official paperwork's been signed off. Right now, I'm not dating anyone so I can do what I like. And anyway, I won't be fucking Grace. She's not my type."

"Well, you need to make her your type."

"Jessie's my type."

"Jesus Christ. That ship has sailed, Dylan."

"The ship hasn't sailed. It's just I'm not allowed to board it."

"When you two are quite finished," Paddy interjects from where he's sitting on the chair beside me.

He's got his own arranged marriage problems. He thought he had it all mapped out. He'd managed to convince the Sicilian mafia princess he was being old-fashioned and gentlemanly. That he was waiting until they were wed before he consummated their marriage and took her virginity. I'm not sure if it's because she knows Molly is being serviced several times a day by Eoin, but Sophia's been working hard to get our Paddy to do the same. And he's having none of it. Apparently, she's not handling the rejection well.

Sophia wants some of what Molly's having. And what Sophia wants, Sophia gets. She wants Paddy. She's always wanted him. And I think the teen has only just realized the feeling's not mutual. He doesn't want her.

He wasn't not sleeping with her because he was practicing abstinence like a good Irish Catholic boy. It's because he doesn't fancy her.

At all.

I genuinely believe our Paddy will abstain from sex for life as Jaine's is the only pussy he's prepared to dick.

"What if I can't… you know… get it up?"

"You have no choice, Dylan. Neither of you has." Eoin's looking between Paddy and me. "Ma and Da want grandchildren. I'm not sure any of us can rely on the immaculate conception, which means you'll have to get your dick wet."

"Fuck me," I mutter and roll my eyes.

"No, fuck your soon-to-be arranged marriage wife and produce some heirs. That way, you get our parents off your back, and then you can do what you like."

"What do you mean do what we like? Like, have an affair?"

Eoin shrugs. "It's not common in our religion, and it's definitely not condoned, but it does happen from time to time. If the couple entered into the arranged marriage aren't compatible in that way, they simply produce an heir and a spare then do their own thing. I would suggest you get your wife's blessing before doing your own thing to avoid a blood bath, however. Divorce, as we know, is out of the question once we take the vows, and the rest of your life can be a long time without intimacy."

"I won't be taking Sophia to my bed." Paddy is adamant.

"Not even if Luc holds a gun to your head?" Eoin raises an eyebrow.

"Not even then. There's only one woman for me. I will touch no other."

Eoin frowns at him. "An heir and a spare, Paddy. That will be the minimum required from you, same as the rest of us."

"Let's leave it there, fellas," I interject as I quickly dial Cill's number. I know Paddy will never agree but I also know Eoin will never stop pushing.

It'll just go round in circles.

"Cill, how's it hanging, brother?"

We've agreed to call him for an update. Putting the phone on handsfree, I place it on the middle of Eoin's desk.

"It's hanging all right, Paddy."

"Not all right enough if you still haven't managed to get Sarah pregnant. You're putting pressure on the rest of us. Especially now you've been allowed to play the 'out of sight, out of mind card' and go gallivanting across the country. Ma and Da are paying closer attention to us lot now. Maybe it's those tighty-whities you insist on wearing restricting the flow."

"There's nothing wrong with my flow, you eejit. I've filled one pram. I'm sure I can fill another."

"Talking of kids, what was the wee man like? Young Finlay."

"He's a handsome lad. He's definitely going to break a few hearts when he's older. He looks like Ace, but then, he doesn't."

"What do you mean but then he doesn't?" Paddy frowns.

"He's pale. He'll suffer with that Californian sun of theirs, that's for sure."

"And is he as much of a handful as Jaine makes out?"

"Even more so. He's the opposite of Jaine and Ace. They're so laidback, whereas Finlay is on the go nonstop. And he never stops talking. Not that you can understand a word, mind you. He just loves the sound of his own voice and likes to share his unintelligible words with anyone who will listen. I'm not sure how Jaine will cope having two wee ones under two, especially if the other is as much of a handful as young Fin."

"And how's Ace?"

"The same. I caught Sarah drooling over him once or twice, even though she tried to deny it."

We all laugh. I've never met Ace, but Eoin and Paddy have, and by all accounts, he could be another O'Connell brother.

"And how is Jaine?"

Eoin and I look at Paddy as he asks the burning question. A smile crosses his face as he thinks of her and speaks her name aloud.

"She much bigger this time around, but it's all baby. She still looks like she could do with a good feed. It's a shame she's not going to be an O'Connell. Ma would soon get some meat on those skinny bones of hers by filling her guts with starchy carbs."

There's a pause. Cillian's no doubt realized what he just said. Eejit. Thankfully, Paddy ignores it, and so Cill just carries on.

"She's looking well, though, Paddy. She has the pregnancy glow. The climate in California obviously suits her complexion, but she's not the same girl she once was. It's like she's lost her spark. It's like part of her soul is missing. Sarah says it's because, deep down, she belongs in New York, but truthfully, I think she needs both in her life. She needs California as much as she needs Manhattan."

I can read between the lines, even if the others can't. Cillian's right. Jaine does need both. But it's not Manhattan she's missing. It's my little brother.

"Maybe she's off-kilter due to all the unrest in Nevada." Eoin changes the subject. He's worked out what Cill meant. He won't want to hear that Jaine's pining over Paddy and not him.

"It could be that, I guess. Apparently, this new MC, the Ghost Whisperers I think they're calling themselves, want to have a meeting with both La eMe and the Dusters to see if they can be brought in on the alliance. Maybe by transporting into currently untapped areas."

"I'm sure that could be arranged if all parties are willing to consider it." Eoin leans back on his chair, a smile on his face. More money. More power. Talk of either is right up his street. "What about the trafficking?"

"They're still insisting they're not involved, but who knows? The gun business is pin money compared to what can be made trading women and children."

Eoin frowns and nods. "Let's wait until you get back, Cill, and then we can make the necessary arrangements and set up a meeting. Please don't mention anything to Jaine. There's no need to worry her unnecessarily. At least not until after the baby's born."

"Agreed. Well, we'll be back within the month, and Jaine will be back in six."

"What do you mean?" Eoin sits upright in his chair.

"She'll be returning to Manhattan within six months. It's what she told Sarah."

"That soon?" Paddy is beaming from ear to ear. I'm not sure why. He'll be married by then, and there's no way Sophia will let him speak to Jaine, let alone see her.

"Aye. You know what women are like. There was a lot of hushed whispers going on between her and Sarah. Heated at times.

But Sarah insists it's time now. That she's been gone long enough. Anyway, what's this about Jessie being Bailey's older sister."

"Ah, yes." Eoin smirks at me.

"I have to say, I wasn't happy with my wife for keeping that from me. We've always agreed to have no secrets. But I can understand her reasoning. She'll be wanting to have a word with you, though, Dyl, over your treatment of her soon-to-be sister-in-law."

"I can hardly wait." I huff, running my hand down my face.

"I'm sure you can't. Anyway, I need to head off, fellas. Sarah and wee Caoimhe will be waking soon."

"We'll see you when you get back, brother, unless we hear from you beforehand. And mind you keep practicing for baby number two. Might I suggest you go commando for a few days to see if that helps your firing blanks situation any."

"Fuck off, Paddy, you eejit. Anyway, later."

With the call ended, Eoin unfortunately turns his attention back to my situation.

"The paperwork for Grace's da, Paddy?"

Out of the corner of my eye, I can see my younger brother shuffling uncomfortably in his seat. My heart sinks. I know exactly what that means.

That it's official. That my life is over.

"It's in place," he replies hesitantly.

Eoin nods at him then turns his attention back to me.

"I meant what I said, Dylan. You're a Duster. You do what you have to do the same as the rest of us. You can't continue to appear disinterested in the girl. Now that everything is in place, you tell Grace you need some help setting up something or other at your apartment tonight, and you move things forward with her."

He's right. I can't change anything with Jessie without divine intervention, and for that, I need a miracle.

CHAPTER THIRTY-SIX

JAINE

Jaine's House, Rising, California

Jaine: *Dyl?*

Nothing. No response. It's the middle of the afternoon in New York. He must be around. He hasn't messaged me for almost twenty-four hours. What the fuck is going on?

Because something sure as hell is. That much is obvious.

Tears of self-pity run down my cheeks, and I wipe them away with the back of my hand, cursing my weakness as I do.

I'm struggling. At having to reveal the truth about Finian to Sarah. At finding out my pop wasn't my biological father. At all the shit going down in Nevada. And then, to top it all off, I have Ma and Da Duster gunning for me.

I'm sitting on the old cream sofa. The house is perfectly silent. Totally still. Duke's been and gone. He didn't stay. He knows when he's not welcome. He and Darla called around to take Fin out for the day. He's proving a handful now I'm reaching the final stages of my pregnancy, so I welcome any respite I can get. My father-in-law looked like he'd aged ten years since announcing the breaking news of my paternity.

As for Ace? Me and him are barely on speaking terms. He's kept a secret. A life-changing one. And who knows how long for. He knows that sort of shit doesn't fly with me.

He knows who my real pop is. I don't. And I don't want to know. Not yet. Maybe not ever. But every time he looks at me, I feel like he's comparing me to him. That he's searching for physical and other similarities.

Are there any? Does he see him? Speak to him?

Well, screw him. Screw them both.

This pregnancy has floored me emotionally. I know I'm surrounded by people who care. I know they all want to help. That they're all willing to listen. But it's Dyl who's been there. Dyl who's been my replacement confidant. My sounding board.

And now I'm reduced to getting a message once maybe twice a day because he's no longer alone.

Whereas me?

I've never felt more alone in my goddamn life.

It's history repeating. I'll keep right on staring at the screen on my phone, waiting for a message. They'll continue to get fewer until they eventually stop. Then what will I do? He's my only link.

My only way of knowing how *he's* getting on.

I sniff before taking the call, wiping the remaining tears from my cheeks. A pity party for one won't solve shit. I know that better than most, but it doesn't stop me from throwing those useless fuckers on a daily basis.

"Jessie."

"Jaine, I've gone and done something really stupid," she whines.

I laugh and sniff at the same time.

"Is everything okay, partner?" Even though her own life's a shit-show, she's more worried about me.

"It's just hormones," I lie as I bite back tears. "Anyway, what the fuck have you done now?"

"I had desk sex."

"Please tell me you didn't, Jessie." I close my eyes and exhale loudly.

"I did. With Dirty Dylan."

"So, we've gone from delectable to despicable, and now we've reached dirty?"

I run my hand down my face in frustration, but then I know only too well how difficult it is letting these Irishmen go once they've infected your blood.

"Well, it's kind of a progressive thing. You know? Tomorrow it could be something else. Provided it starts with a D, that is."

"Alliteration."

"Bless you."

"You're hilarious." I can't help but chuckle.

"Thank you. I do try."

"Anyway, I don't want to know what the dirty stands for. So, I'll pretend it's because he needs to wash his hands."

"Oh, he needs to wash way more than those. I mean, these days, he needs to wash out that filthy mouth of his."

"Jesus Christ, Jessie. I really don't need to know that." I grimace.

"It happened during our lockdown, Jaine. Every day he became more and more like his brothers. He's changed."

And don't I just know it. I'm feeling the effects of that only too well.

"He's courting another woman, Jessie."

"Well, he's not dating her just yet. Apparently, there's still some legal wrangle to address. Something his fiancée's daddy wants in place beforehand."

I roll my eyes. "Jessie, even if the process hasn't started it's imminent. You're playing with fire."

"But…"

"There are no buts. Take it from someone who knows. From someone who's been there."

"So, what do I do?"

"I can't tell you that."

"But…"

"You love him. I know you do. And I'm sorry, Jessie." I whisper.

"Sorry for what?"

"If I'd told Eoin who you were sooner, things might have been different. Things *would* have been different."

Her reply is instant.

"You can't blame yourself, Jaine. We just have to leave it in the hands of fate."

Tears of guilt prick my eyes at how understanding she's being given how badly I dropped the ball on her behalf.

"Still. You wanted me to tell them. I never did. And for that, I'm sorry because what I suffer on a daily basis, I would never wish on anyone. I only hope your outcome is better, Jessie. I really do."

Padraig: *I'm here, darlin.*

Jaine: *Listen, if you don't want to speak to me anymore, Dyl. If you're too busy, then just say the word, and I'll be gone.*

Padraig: *I will never be too busy for you.*

Jaine: *You sure about that? Because you could have fooled me.*

Padraig: *I've just got a lot on.*

Jaine: *With Grace?*

Padraig: *Yes, among other things.*

Jaine: *I spoke to Jessie earlier.*

Padraig: *How is she?*

Jaine: *You could have asked her yourself.*

Padraig: *Now, now, Jaine.*

Jaine: *Well, you're meant to be dating the love of your life, and yet you fucked my business partner over your desk earlier today. Jessie's confused. And do you know what? I'm confused for her.*

Padraig: *Are we only ever going to talk about Jessie and me?*

Jaine: *I'm sorry. It's just this situation is dragging the past up. I can see where all of this is headed.*

Padraig: *And where is that?*

Jaine: *What do you mean 'and where is that'? You know exactly where.*

Padraig: *Nope. I don't, darlin'. So, why don't you remind me?*

Jaine: *I think Jessie's got a point.*

Padraig: *What do you mean?*

Jaine: *You've changed. And not for the better either. You've turned into an asshole. Listen, I need to go.*

Padraig: *Jaine.*

Padraig: *Jaine!*

I STARE AT THE CEILING. WELL, THAT DIDN'T GO WELL.

Lowering my head, I stare around the place. This is what my

life's been reduced to. A successful lawyer, a vigilante sniper, and here I am.

Stagnating.

Day after day, I sit on this old leather sofa on my own with way too much time on my hands, being haunted by memories of the past.

Sometimes I wish I could just be absorbed into this piece of furniture. At times, I feel I already have.

I've got a husband who keeps secrets from me and who spends most of his time in another state. A so-called friend asking me to reminisce about one of the worst moments of my life. Maybe he's forgotten. If he has, lucky him. I sure as hell never will.

On top of that, I've got a host of people who don't want to cause me any upset. The end result is everyone's keeping secrets from me.

Is there anyone who treats me like a fully functioning adult these days? Someone who doesn't feel the need to wrap me in cotton wool and handle me with kid gloves?

Even Jessie's hiding something. I know she is.

Isn't there anyone who'll tell me what the fuck is going on?

No. *Yes.*

I dial his number. It finally connects.

"Hello, Jaine."

"Molly." Great.

"If you're looking for Eoin, he can't come to the phone right now. He's in the shower. We've been a bit…. busy. Shall I ask him to call you back?" She laughs smugly.

I disconnect the call.

It looks like I'm definitely on my own if I can't even speak to the eldest Duster. So be it. The solution to my problem? I need to get this baby born and then get the shit show that is my life back on goddamn track.

I refuse to be molly-coddled any longer. I'm taking my life back. Then, hell mend anyone who gets in Jaine Jones's way.

CHAPTER THIRTY-SEVEN

MOLLY

The Hudson Dusters' HQ, Manhattan, New York

I SMIRK AS SHE HANGS UP, THEN DELETE ALL TRACES OF HER CALL before placing his phone back on the desk.

Eoin enters his office space. "Was that anyone important?"

"A wrong number." I smile innocently.

He nods. He believes me. And why wouldn't he?

And Jaine Jones is of no importance.

He's been to collect the La eMe file from Paddy's office. We're going to call Rodolfo Flores together. I told him I tried but couldn't get hold of him.

I lied.

There's a reason for that. If I want Eoin and me to be viewed as the next Manhattan power couple, then we have to be seen to be making decisions together and working side by side. More so in front of influential peers. We're going to be the future king and queen of The Hudson Dusters if I have my way.

Which I will.

I watch as he flicks through the notes at the front of the file, then dials one of the handwritten numbers on handsfree. It's answered immediately.

"Eoin, it's good to hear from you."

"Rodolfo, it's been way too long."

"Yes, it has. Listen, I spoke to Jessie not so long ago. I was expecting a call from someone at your end. A Molly, if I recall. Did something come up as I never heard from her?"

I interject. "I tried to call, Rodolfo, but I couldn't get through for reasons known only to the lousy telephone exchange."

"Right." He doesn't sound convinced, but he can't prove anything either way.

"My name's Molly McGrath." I continue before he can ask any probing questions. "I'm going to be representing the Dusters in the alliance moving forward."

"And may I ask what your role is within the organization, Molly?"

"I'm their external legal representation."

There's a pause as he digests what I've said.

"I thought consideration was being given to Jaine handling that side of things. At least when it came to the La eMe alliance. To ensure all matters, including the lines of communication, remain open and streamlined at all times. We know what happened when links failed last time, and Jaine does represent the other parties concerned."

I narrow my eyes at the mention of her name.

"Rest assured, I am just as competent as Jaine Jones."

"Right." There's a pause. "So, you'll be representing the Dusters legally in all external matters moving forward."

“That’s correct. As Eoin’s fiancée and the future Ma Duster, we thought it important I start to make my presence known both within and outside of our family organization.”

I glance at Eoin. If looks could kill. Fortunately for me, they can’t. I’m sure I can get him to forgive my deliberate slip of the tongue by using it in far more satisfying ways later.

“I had no idea another Duster wedding was on the horizon. My congratulations to you both.”

“Thank you. That’s very kind of you.” I smile.

If Eoin’s not going to make things official between us, then I’ll force his hand. He will be mine.

And then I’ll remove all traces of Jaine Jones not just from his phone, but from his life.

CHAPTER THIRTY-EIGHT

JESSIE

Jessie's Apartment, Hudson Yards, New York

"Do it, Jessie."

I'm standing outside Dirty Dylan's apartment, trying to work up the courage to knock on the door. Why? Because I want to know what the hell's going on.

We fucked. This morning. Over his desk.

No niceties. No wining and dining. It was pure, unadulterated sex. The kind the Bible warns you about. The kind you participate in at your own risk as partaking will see you sent to the bowels of hell, condemned to live in the house of Satan forevermore. Well, I'm already the spawn of the Devil as my daddy is Lucifer. Trust me, I'm used to living in those fiery depths.

And now I know what all the fuss is about with desk sex. Why Eoin and Candice favor it so much.

Hot. Impulsive. Raw.

I'd like to sign up for some more of that, please. Lots more.

Pushed around. Pinned down. I'll be wearing those beautiful bruises he inflicted on my skin for days.

But before I do, I need to know where this is going. My daddy raised me to have pride in myself. And I do. Jessie O'Brien is no-one's sidepiece.

The wi-fi is also down. So, aside from wanting that answer, there's another reason I'm standing here. I know the wi-fi is dedicated to his apartment and mine, so either Dyl's been fucking around with it, or there's a legitimate outage. Right now, I can't work. That's causing me another problem.

I knock. My heart pounds in my chest in a matching fucked-up rhythm.

Bang. Bang. Bang.

The door opens moments later, and he's standing there in all his glory in a white fitted tee, those slim hips of his wrapped invitingly in a pair of dark blue jeans. Hips that earlier today were thrusting between my very receptive thighs as I was bent face down over his desk.

His hair is wet from the shower, so he's obviously been working out. Having looked surprised initially, his expression has switched to the impassive one he seems to favor these days. I guess he's not quite so pleased to see me as he was earlier today.

Great.

I'm no longer sure how to play this. It's all well and good me trying to portray the confident and sassy Jessie. But he's seen both sides so there's no fooling him. And with that less than welcoming response, I suddenly have no clue what to say.

"The wi-fi," I stutter.

"Sorry. We were messing around with the setup then we had an issue with the reboot."

We.

Did he just say what I think he did? He must have. He used the word 'we' twice in the same sentence.

"Jessie."

I immediately recognize the voice. Grace Ryan.

She appears behind him in nothing but a dressing gown. White. Fluffy. Over-sized. The type they provide in posh hotels. Like the establishments the Dusters own a plethora of in Manhattan.

Her legs and feet are bare, so she's clearly naked underneath. And his hair's still wet from the shower.

A number cruncher like me knows two plus two always makes four. It doesn't take a rocket scientist to figure out what's been going on. What they've been doing.

We haven't even started the courting process. We're not engaged. I haven't kissed her. I haven't fucked her.

Did he lie to me? Because it's clear they've done the latter. Was today a case of him simply wanting his own last hurrah with me?

I make eye contact with her. Her expression is as impassive as his. She's also giving nothing away. I'm only grateful she's not smirking. Molly would be. She'd be gloating that she'd won and rejoicing she was allowed to witness firsthand my complete and utter humiliation by doing an Irish jig in my honor. Because that's precisely what this is.

A humiliating defeat.

It's game over.

"Grace. Is it you I have to blame for the wi-fi outage?" I smile at her. It's forced. I know it. Embarrassingly, so do they.

But what else is there to say? What else is there to do? Because I have to do and say something. I have to turn this mortifying situation around so I can walk away with some shred of dignity intact by at least pretending my world hasn't just caved in on itself.

Say something amusing, Jessie. Make everyone laugh, Jessie.

Too late. They're already laughing, but it's at you, not with you, Jessie.

"We'll have it back up and running within half an hour," Dylan replies dismissively.

Go away, Jessie. Fuck off, Jessie. Can't you see I want to get back to impressing my future wife with all those moves you taught me so very well, Jessie?

I force another smile before turning and walking away. I want to run. I don't. I do take the stairs rather than wait for the elevator, though. I'll be out of sight quicker that way.

My guess is, as soon as they close the door, I'll already be out of mind.

"I'll be home in half an hour."

"Jessie, what's…."

"Tadgh. I don't want to talk about it. The Spanish Inquisition can wait."

He exhales slowly. "You girls go to Manhattan. Bee comes back bringing a whole load of trouble with her, and I'm guessing you're about to do the same damn thing."

"If I recall, Bee never brought the trouble. Razr turned up under his own insane steam. Anyway, I've always been the good girl. The one who never gets into any bother."

"That's my concern right there, Jay. It'll be ten times worse if you do bring home any problems as you've been saving that shit up for over thirty years."

I snicker before turning serious. "From what Jaine tells me, trouble's never left Colton the whole time I've been gone."

He sighs. I know he's running his fingers through that long blonde hair of his.

"Anyway, I figured I'd just give you the heads-up to let you know your favorite sister will be home soon. If you could let Daddy know, I'd much appreciate that."

"What do you want me to tell him?"

"That you've known I was coming home for a few weeks, and you clean forgot to mention it. I'll explain everything in my own time. But I'd be grateful if you could just buy me a little breathing space. I don't want to be subjected to Daddy's interrogation while he scans me with eyes that see everything and miss nothing. Not the moment I pull into the drive. You know I can't pull off lies quite like Little Bee can."

"I thought you said you had nothing to hide."

"I don't. But you and I both know he'll have questions about the Irish. And there are things he'll ask I won't be able to discuss. We both know rather than say no to him, sometimes it's just easier to circumnavigate the question. I can't breach client confidentiality. I'll answer what I can. Nothing more. Twenty-five minutes."

"Excuse me?"

"I'll be home in twenty-five minutes."

"Coffee?"

"You know me so well, big brother."

CHAPTER THIRTY-NINE

JESSIE

Jessie's Family Home, Colton, Nevada

COLTON.

Home sweet home.

The place I grew up. The place I never truly felt I belonged.

I park up the hired black SUV, opening the window to inhale the Nevada air deep into my lungs.

There's no smell. Desert air doesn't have a scent. It's just hot and unbelievably dry. Both are currently magnified because it's late afternoon. The sun's riding the sky high.

It's been twenty-four hours since the confrontation. Twenty-four hours since I returned to my apartment and disconnected all my software. I carried out a sweep of my systems, packed the important parts in a suitcase, and then, with a few essentials thrown on top, I chartered a big ass airplane and set off for home.

I left New York without a word. I didn't tell the Dusters. I haven't even told Jaine. I couldn't stay there. Not after witnessing what I did.

I can't even bring myself to think about what went down. I will, though. In time. And I'll dissect it. I'm an accountant, after all. It's in my nature to analyze. But I'll only do so when I'm safe within the confines of my childhood bedroom, and when I get a chance to stop and catch my breath.

Humiliation flows through me once more that he fucked us both on the same day. Me in the morning. Her in the evening. What makes it even worse is that I allowed it to happen knowing he'd already made his choices.

In the end I ignored my own principles and in turn let myself down.

He picked her. He wants her. He loves her. *Jesus Christ, Jessie. What the hell were you thinking? Were you hoping he'd change his mind?*

Still, I'll survive. And that big old outlaw world of ours will keep right on turning.

Us O'Briens are as tough as old boots. I may be the weakest link in our family. I may be the one least deserving of wearing that one percent badge. But I know I've got it in me to do what needs doing should the need ever arise.

Have I killed before? Nope. Never had to. I've never seen the need to without good reason. It doesn't mean I can't. Or won't. That I haven't thought about it or been tempted on more than one occasion. I'm a biker. It's in my blood to spill someone else's blood.

Has Grace killed? It's unlikely. Their love of systems is what brought them together way back when. It's that shared background that made her and Dylan the perfect match in the eyes of both sets of proud mobster parents.

Stepping out of the vehicle, I stare at the cloudless blue sky. Sweat immediately starts to prickle my skin.

My eyes drift over our family home. It's a white-painted property with a cream-tiled roof. It's custom-built, single-story with ten bedrooms, all ensuite, and loads of other living spaces. There are no gardens. Nothing grows in Nevada. Nothing ever changes much either.

The driveway is gravel, and the landscaping is made up of rocks so perfectly oval in shape they look almost fake. The views are to die for. On one side, it's nothing but open space. On the other, mountains. Breathtaking, beautiful mountains.

I lean against the vehicle, close my eyes, and welcome the sound of absolute silence. It's a far cry from the constant hum of honking horns, wailing sirens, and obscenity-yelling yellow cab drivers I've come to associate with the stench-ridden streets of New York.

"And how is my sister?"

"I'm fine. Thank you for asking, Conor."

My heart swells with affection. I smile while keeping my eyes closed as I acknowledge my half-sibling and Bee's full brother. Their mom ran out on Daddy when Bee was just six months old. An addict was the line daddy fed us. But she wasn't. Tadgh and I were old enough to know better. You see true addiction when you grow up just sixty miles outside of Sin City. I think the poor woman was just fed-up fighting for love and affection from a man who gave her neither because he never really wanted her. Because he never really loved her. So, in the end, he couldn't and didn't give her what she needed emotionally.

Who knows, maybe one day she'll return. What I do know is she left in order to survive.

The same reason I left Manhattan.

My daddy's heart broke when my own momma left him. Tadgh and I were just babies at the time, so no one really knows what went on. In the end, she divorced him and married someone else. Something that doesn't happen either in this life or in our religion. Marriage is a lifetime commitment. No exceptions.

Usually.

When she left, none of us ever saw her again. Daddy boasts she got her just desserts when she died some years later. He boasts, but on the inside, it destroyed him, as with her died the only woman he ever loved.

I open one eye and take in my twenty-four-year-old sibling. Unlike me, Tadgh, and Bee, who are all blue-eyed and blonde-haired, Conor's coloring is exactly like his mom's. Unruly black hair teamed with eyes the color of chocolate molasses. He's handsome, being all tall and lean, with his tanned, inked skin. He'll be breaking the hearts of young girls all the way across the state, that's for sure.

My smile fades slightly. He used to get up to those sorts of shenanigans with Rafael. His best friend. It's hard to believe it's been almost a year since he lost his life when my baby sister staged a rescue attempt to save Paul Delaney.

"Jay."

Well, if it isn't the devil himself. I open both eyes and take in all three male O'Briens.

"Daddy. Tadgh."

I stare at my daddy with his long, light blonde hair and pale blue eyes. He's going grey now. He's getting older. My daddy's handsome in his own unique way with his angular features and a well-kept beard to finish off the look. He's a Dubliner. He was born on the Emerald Isle and moved to Nevada when he was sixteen. I never met my grandparents. Both died in a car wreck when my daddy was eighteen. He was embraced by the local MC, then made his way through the ranks to become prez at the age of twenty-two. He's held that position ever since, so almost thirty-four years now.

His real name is Liam. His road name is Lucifer. It's fitting. He's the devil, alright.

He walks over to me, pulling me to him and wrapping his arms around me. His familiar woodsy cologne embraces me almost like a second fatherly hug. He's a mountain of a man. Not fat. Every inch is toned, deadly muscle. He's never let himself go.

"You had a falling out with those Irish boys you been working for?" His voice is dark and deadly. It's a voice you don't disobey. Not if you know what's good for you. Not many do, and those who do seldom live to tell the tale.

"Nope."

"You sure about that, Jay?"

"As sure as eggs are eggs, Daddy-O. And please don't talk to me like I'm Little Bee. I'm a grown-ass woman. I've looked after myself since I was eighteen years old. If there was anything you needed to be made aware of, I'd tell you. You know that."

I walk away from the SUV and head for the house, winking at Tadgh on the way past. He's the carbon copy of my daddy, just some twenty-plus years younger.

For some reason, neither of my brothers ever took a road name. Or at least I don't think they did. Not that I ever associated myself with the MC or frequented the clubhouse, so I don't know for sure.

"Not found yourself an old lady yet?"

"Nope."

"Been looking?"

"Nope."

"You put the coffee on?"

"Yup."

"Nice to know you still have the ability to prioritize, big brother. Oh, and can you bring my bags in for me?"

"What did your last servant die of?"

"Same thing you will if you don't hurry along." I snicker.

"Welcome back, Jay."

"Thank you, Tadgh. It's mighty good to be back."

CHAPTER FORTY

ROISIN

The O'Connell Home, Darling, New York

"But, Da."

Our Dylan turned up at the crack of dawn and is currently pacing the floor. Our second youngest never gets ruffled. But that's exactly what he is.

"Dylan, there's nothing that can be done now, son. We gave you a week to get your head around it, and you never said no to the girl."

"You mean I had a choice?" He stops and stares at Fergal, wearing a look of dismay.

"Yes. Unlike Paddy, you had a choice."

"I didn't know that, Da," he whispers in disbelief.

"We told you at the time."

"I assumed…."

"We all know what happens when you assume, Dyl. Look, I'm

sorry, son. You know I hold young Jessie in high regard. You know how much we appreciate the work she's doing for our organization. If you had enlightened the rest of us to the fact you were fucking her then…."

I elbow Fergal in the ribs. Well. There's no need for such vulgarity.

"Sorry, Roisin." He looks at me sheepishly before turning his attention back to our boy. "If you had mentioned you were seeing her, then we could have considered her."

I listen to their back and forth as I pour myself a cup of tea from the white bone china teapot that's resting on the coffee table. I glance around the sitting room. It's barely used. But it's the last Sunday of the month, so the rest of the family will be joining us later to enjoy a traditional Irish lunch.

I take in the antique walnut furniture covered in countless framed photos of my boys over the years. I'm a proud mother. My lads are my pride and joy, and I want the world to know it.

Tasteful art hangs from the walls, and everything's finished in green and gold, down to the heavy tapestry curtains and other accents.

Dylan's resumed his pacing. He's agitated. Emotional. It's not like him. It's not like him at all. He obviously cares a great deal for this Jessie O'Brien. And I feel for him. I do. But I'm glad it didn't work out. If we added another biker to our family, we'd soon be referring to ourselves as The Hudson Dusters MC.

And who's to say this girl would want to take the vows with him anyway. Most of those Neanderthalic heathens are unwed and choose to remain so. The men just pick a woman from a line-up and then refer to her as their 'old lady.' They then take them to bed, procreate and produce even more of their atheistic sort. Even if they do wed, the men continue to sleep with the loose women that hang around their clubs like it's all some big disease-ridden orgy, and all while their 'old women' stay home raising their offspring.

That's not a life I want my Dylan to be part of. I mean, I love Sarah even if she is a biker. She's a good Catholic girl, and she's rightfully earned her place in this family. She's also given us little Caoimhe and, God willing, she'll bless us with many more grandbabies. But unlike Cillian, our Dylan is a sensitive sort. He's always been happiest at home or just doing his own thing. He doesn't need to be mixing with their type. Getting himself involved in that hedonistic biker lifestyle where they likely practice paganism and engage in BDSM morning, noon, and night.

No. That sort of life is not for my sensitive boy. So neither is this Jessie O'Brien.

Grace is a good girl. She has the right background and comes from a wealthy Irish family that runs in the same circles as our kin in Ireland.

She'll do quite nicely, thank you.

We need to bring this nonsense to a close and quickly. Draw a line under it and put Dylan out of his misery. I can see Fergal is wavering, sitting on the fence and getting splinters. He likes Jessie, and from what I can gather, she excels at the job she undertakes on our behalf. But aside from the fact she's a biker, she also works with that Jaine Jones. I'm already trying to extract that poisonous woman from our lives using whatever means necessary. To welcome Jessie with open arms means opening the door to her business partner once more.

Fergal's not thinking of the bigger picture. But I am. I may be breaking our Dylan's heart, but he'll thank me one day. All of my boys will.

Their future wives have been hand-picked by me, and it's my opinion there's no one more suited to each of them.

And a mother always knows best.

I interject. "I'm sorry, Dylan, but the decision's been made and it's final."

Private Dining Room, Palace Hotel, Manhattan

I sip on my Bloody Mary as I watch two of my future daughters-in-law get themselves settled after getting the air-kissing nonsense out of the way.

I didn't invite Grace along. It's not that she's not welcome, but she and our Dylan will do what's required of them now, so I don't want to scare the girl off by involving her in conversations such as these. At least not until she and Dyl are safely wed.

Molly's looking pleased with herself today. Sophia quite the opposite. Things are obviously not progressing as well as we'd hoped with her and our Paddy. Maybe I'll need to intervene and have a quiet word. It was never going to be straightforward with him. He's the one *she's* got her claws sunk into deepest.

Still, he has a duty to fulfill. A Duster obligation. And perform it he will.

Both girls are immaculate as always—one dressed like the consummate business professional, the other dripping in expensive designer wear.

On the outside, they appear total opposites. On the inside, that's a different matter. Having now spent time with both, I know they're a lot more alike than either realize.

They eye each other as warily as they did before, but there's a recognition and acceptance there now. An unspoken sense of camaraderie that wasn't present last time. They're now working together for the Duster greater good, which is how it should be. How it needs to be. We Duster women need to be on the same page at all times and supporting our men.

"It's good to see you, girls. I thought it best we have a catch-up to discuss how things are progressing and to see if I'm needed to intervene in any way."

They look at each other, but neither shows a willingness to speak first, both of them choosing to play their cards close to their chest.

"Molly." I pause while the waiter places a glass of sparkling water in front of her and a glass of still in front of Sophia. As much as this establishment is expensive because of the levels of discretion it affords, one can never be too careful. "An update, please," I continue after he's out of earshot.

She takes a sip, then smooths down the skirt on her navy suit. "Things are progressing as before. We're having sex. A lot of sex. So, there are no issues whatsoever in the bedroom department." She hesitates before continuing. "I've been tampering with the condoms."

Silence follows as she waits for my reaction.

So, she's devious, this one. In my experience, that can either be a good or bad thing. If she's trustworthy, good. If she's a liar, quite the opposite.

I smile at her and nod, choosing to remain silent to encourage her to continue.

"I've also introduced myself to the leader of La eMe as Eoin's fiancée. I'm hoping the more of our peers I can present myself to using that title, the quicker the rumor mills will start, and the sooner Eoin will have no choice but to get down on bended knee."

I frown at her. "So, he hasn't mentioned the engagement at all?"

She shakes her head. Again, I think back to poor Cara with our Cillian. She waited too long, and in the end, his head was turned by Sarah. Let's hope Molly doesn't make the same mistake. Eoin is fickle. He's been able to pick and choose women his whole life. She needs to nail down his commitment during the honeymoon period of their relationship and before that Dublin novelty of hers wears off. It's very naïve of her to think she can back someone like him into a corner.

"Then that's where you need to focus your energies, Molly. Messing with the condoms will speed up the process if successful, but you can't afford to rest on your laurels. Our Eoin is a man of the world. He's spent time with countless women over the years. You need to keep his interest and quickly create the conversion from courting to matrimony. Bear in mind your legal nemesis will be back in Manhattan in less than six months."

"That soon?" She glances at Sophia.

"Yes. I spoke with Sarah, and that's what I'm told. She didn't go into any other detail, and I didn't pry. They're close, Sarah and Jaine."

"Biker bitches." Sophia smirks, but it's not because she's in any way amused.

I turn my attention to the teenager. "So, Sophia. An update, please."

"He won't touch me. I've tried everything. I even lowered myself to walking into his bedroom naked, but he covered me back up and made an excuse about wanting to wait until we're married."

This is not good. Not good at all. Our Paddy is hook, line, and sinker in love with this biker. If he doesn't perform his marital duties with Sophia and she complains to her brother, all hell could break loose with the Sicilians.

"He's still in love with her. That's why he won't touch me."

Both Molly and I look at her, but neither of us replies. What's there to say? We all know it's true. But it won't do anyone any favors to wallow in self-pity or focus on things we can't change. All we can do is concentrate our efforts on things we can. I understand, though. At seventeen, Sophia's facing a loveless, sexless marriage, and not because the relationship has run its course but because, from the outset, her husband's heart belongs to another woman.

If, or should I say when, our Paddy takes that precious virginity of hers, he'll never walk away. He's too loyal for that. He'll be hers for life then. She just has to find a way to make it happen.

"She'll pay for this." It's spoken quietly like she's speaking to herself.

I'm not sure I'd want to be in Jaine Jones's shoes right now.

CHAPTER FORTY-ONE

DYLAN

The Hudson Dusters' HQ, Manhattan, New York

"It's been four weeks," I mutter

"Same." Paddy.

Eoin glances at us over his laptop but doesn't respond. It's my guess it's the same duration for him.

We're spending more time in his office than anywhere else these days. It's because our intendeds are always around, so the meeting room has become more of a free-for-all. Even more so now Da is working fewer hours.

It would appear all three of us are being ignored by Jaine and Jessie. For the past month, from a business point of view, everything's been conducted with Candice as the go-between. Who would have thought the three of them would find an ally in each other?

The process seems to be working fine, so it's difficult to argue with their justification that we continue as we are.

Jaine is no longer replying to Paddy's messages, and neither is she taking calls. We're all getting the silent treatment.

Reading between the lines, I reckon it's a combination of things for Jaine.

She's had enough of what she sees as me messing her business partner around. She thinks history's repeating itself. That what happened to her is now happening to Jessie. It's dragging up too many painful memories when she's already emotionally strung out.

She's also had enough of Paddy asking questions about what went on in the past when, since he's pretending to be me, he should already know the answers. It's frustrated her no end. She'll either be thinking I've banged my head and am now experiencing some sort of memory loss or I'm deliberately being inconsiderate by bringing up history we agreed from the outset was never to be discussed.

Not that I could tell our Paddy the answers even if I wanted to, as it would open up a Duster can of worms, with our Eoin being exposed as the biggest snake.

To be honest, in a roundabout way, Jaine not speaking should be a blessing in disguise. She's due back in New York in around five months anyway, and with her having thrown her toys out of the pram and pressed the mute button on us all, there's less chance of the cliché blonde secret being revealed. The only way it could be unearthed is if Jessie blabs about the fact she was my first.

And what could go wrong if it did come out?

Well, Jaine would throw a hissy fit at our Paddy and me before shooting us both in the head with an engraved bullet. Minor detail. The Dusters could survive that short-term inconvenience if they had to. The preference would be for that situation to be avoided, but it's preferable to the other that could arise. That somehow Sophia finds out her fiancé and the man who currently won't put his dick anywhere near her has been messaging the love of his life all this time. Naturally, that revelation would not sit very well with the Sicilian mafia. Heads would roll. Our Paddy's being one of them.

As for Jessie and me?

Well, it's obvious why I'm getting the silent treatment. Jessie saw Grace in my apartment wearing nothing but a dressing gown and me sporting my 'just got out of the shower' look. Is her huff deserved?

Maybe it is. Maybe it isn't.

I got her number from Eoin in the end as I'd never used it. I sent her a message, but I'd been blocked in advance. Probably from the moment she returned to her apartment after witnessing the condemning visual.

Sophia, meanwhile, is still trying to get Paddy to fuck her, while he's continuing to politely decline and coming up with every excuse under the sun.

Molly is still being fucked but now by a distracted Eoin. Was he ever really into her or was he just trying to lull our folks into a false sense of security? Pretend he would toe the Duster line when he never had any intention. Is the novelty starting to wear off?

The latter is the main reason our Eoin's never been in a serious relationship let alone contemplated marriage. Why he always reverts back to daily desk sex with good old faithful Candice. No woman can ever hold his attention long enough.

Apart from Jaine, that is.

As for me. I've tried to get out of my arranged marriage. I've sat down with my folks. I've begged. I've pleaded. I get the feeling it's my ma who's refusing to budge, that my da would be receptive to having Jessie as his daughter-in-law. I appreciate he has to weigh up his options, however. If he didn't side with my ma she would make his life a misery by making him sleep in the summer house and have him fend for himself.

It boils down to a simple case of every man for himself.

So, unless The Almighty grants me a miracle like he did our Cillian, then there's no way out for me. Or for Paddy. So, does it matter if the girls aren't speaking to us?

Yes. It does.

Because call me either a hopeless romantic like that Noah fella in *The Notebook* or call me an eejit, but it's not over. Not until I'm standing at that altar with a gun pointed at my head being forced to say I do by the fat lady herself as she hums the wedding march.

I think the odds of Paddy being able to extract himself from his upcoming nuptials are short. Sophia said yes to the dress some time ago, and the guest list will have been compiled. It's already earmarked to be *the* society event of the year. The ceremony itself will be for the very chosen few due to Paddy's insistence it takes place at St. Peter's. But if you've not got an invitation to the evening do at The Meeting Rooms, then you're not worth knowing by Manhattan's elite standards.

Eoin and I haven't even proposed, so no engagement party has been diarized for either of us.

Yet.

Given he got caught by the ear first, I'm hoping his will be announced before mine, but there's no guarantee. His event will be a bigger draw, as he's the future Irish King, whereas I'm the Duster no one can ever remember the name of.

"Have you tried messaging Jessie from another number, Dyl?"

I roll my eyes. "And what difference will that make, Paddy? As soon as she knows who it is, she'll just block it."

He nods. If she doesn't want to speak to me or listen to anything I have to say, I can't force her. Messaging from a plethora of numbers will make no difference. I can only be heard if the other person is willing to listen.

And Jessie's clearly not.

"When's Cill due back?"

I frown, wondering where Paddy's going with this.

"Tomorrow, why?" Eoin looks at him.

"Aren't we planning a trip to Nevada?"

"*We* aren't planning anything, Paddy. You're going nowhere. Cill and I are going."

"Can I go? In Cill's place. I mean, he'll only just have got back." I pipe up.

I'm met with two equally penetrating stares. I know why. I never volunteer to go anywhere. But Jessie's worth coming out of my comfort zone for. I always said if I met the right girl and they accepted me for who I am, then if I needed to, I would change my ways or I would at least try. Well, I will try. Because I've met the right person.

Jessie *is* my right person.

"Are you sure, Dyl? I'd probably feel more at ease having Cill at my back. No offense, but…."

I interject. "In the meantime, I'll do the wet work with Paddy."

They continue to stare likely thinking I've gone insane. And maybe I have. But to earn my spot on the trip to Nevada, I'm offering to kill for Jessie. Deserved people only, but still cold-blooded murder all the same.

If that's not a declaration of true mobster love, then I don't know what is.

CHAPTER FORTY-TWO

JESSIE

Jessie's Family Home, Colton, Nevada

"ONLY TWO MONTHS TO GO, GIVE OR TAKE, PARTNER?"

I'm lying on my four-poster bed in my childhood bedroom, feeling like a teenager and like I've never left home and adulted before. The pink and white space remains unchanged. A shrine to my childhood I come home to worship at from time to time. I just never expected to be stuck in little girl heaven for the foreseeable future.

"It's actually five weeks. And trust me, I'm counting down every goddamn day."

"How are you coping?" My hands fidget with an old set of cheerleading pom-poms.

"Some days are better than others."

"Well, at least now you have a diagnosis. Pre-natal depression is kind of a big deal."

"It's actually fairly common."

"Well, yes, it is, but you've had it for weeks. Probably even months, the doctor said. That's not common. And neither is it common to lose weight during pregnancy."

"No, you're right. That part isn't common."

"Remember, the offer stands if you want me to be your shrink. My rates are competitive, and my terms are extremely flexible."

"I want to get better, not worse."

We both snicker.

"And have you spoken to Razr?"

"Yup. He's suggested I keep a journal like he does so I can write down how I'm feeling. He says it will help me pinpoint and know what my triggers are. People, feelings, times of day. That sort of thing."

"Who'd have thought Razr being insane would have its uses? And is it working?"

"So, so."

"What does that mean?"

"Well, it's made my key trigger obvious."

"Care to expand on that?"

"My shrink thinks I need to lay the ghost of Irish to rest. Or at least the ghost of what Irish and I were to each other back then. More so as, apparently, in my head, that's how I still view our relationship."

"But haven't you already let him go?"

"Yes and no."

"Meaning?"

"I've replaced him with Dyl. I've been using him as a surrogate for Irish all this time because I've refused to let go."

"Well, it's easier said than done. I can vouch for that." I laugh dryly.

"But it's been the best part of two years for me, Jessie. And if I've changed in that time, then he will have too. He's not going to be the same person he was way back then."

"I mean, I don't know what he was like in the past, so I can't really offer any comparison."

"I'm about to have another baby. He'll be getting married. We can't ever go back to where we were. I'll be returning to Manhattan soon. Before I do, I need to close off that chapter of my life. That's if I'm ever to have any sort of relationship with him moving forward."

"And do you need to have a relationship with him? Would you even want that?"

"Need or want is irrelevant right now. I won't have a choice if I don't draw a line under the past. I need to move on. It's hindering my progress. It's stopping me from healing. It's clear he's moved on, even if it is reluctantly. It's time I did too."

"And why are they only suggesting this to you now? You've been seeing that shrink of yours for weeks."

"Because of what I'm writing in the journal, I guess, and the fact I did something foolish."

"Well, you and I are both guilty of behaving that way when it comes to these O'Connell boys. Go on. What did you do?"

"I messaged Dyl."

I pause. Whether it was as a show of solidarity or for her own reasons, she stopped all contact with him when I did. She's done something I've been tempted to do so many times, but each time I've managed to stop myself.

"Right."

"I'm sorry, Jessie."

"It's okay. You had a relationship with him long before I came along. And you should be able to continue right on with that. I'm a big girl. Just because I've fallen out with him doesn't mean you have to. Anyway, right now, your needs are far greater than mine."

There's a pause.

"I stupidly told him I miss Irish. That I can't even remember what he sounds like. I pretty much had a full-on melt-down. Ace was in Vegas at the time. I was home alone. I asked if I could give him a call. I just needed to talk to someone."

"You could have called me."

"I needed to speak about Padraig."

"I get it. Go on."

"It was the first time I'd messaged him in a while. It wasn't awkward or anything. We just sort of picked up where we left off like there hadn't been a long period of silence in between. He couldn't talk, though. It was the middle of the night, so I can understand why."

"Why couldn't he speak to you? It's not like he'd have much else going on."

There's a pause, and that hollow space in my chest where my heart used to be echoes loudly to remind me it's not there. Deep down, I already know the answer.

Perfectly lonely. Unlike him.

"He had someone with him. Didn't he?"

"Yes."

"Okay."

Rip that band-aid right off why don't you, Jaine? Another pause. This time to allow me to swallow the great big lump of self-pity that's formed in the back of my throat.

"What did he suggest you do in your time of need, then?"

"Call Irish."

"Jaine, you didn't?" If I sound shocked, it's because I am.

"I did."

"And?"

"He didn't pick up."

"THIS REALLY NEEDS TO GO," I'M HOME ALONE AGAIN, OR AT LEAST I think I'm alone. And for the nth time since I've been back, I curse as I bang my head on that big old chandelier that takes center stage in our front room.

It's tasteless. It's something you'd see in a casino. It was most likely some prize in a game of outlaw Russian roulette in Sin City. I wonder if my daddy won or lost. That if by losing, he had to swear to have this vulgar monstrosity on display from now until eternity as punishment. Then again, my daddy really does like to flaunt our wealth. Any opportunity to advertise the fact we have squillions in the bank. This piece showcases just that.

I've never relied on any of daddy's squillions. I've always earned my own.

I always knew I wanted to work with figures. Most people likely take one look at my physical appearance before concluding that The Almighty likely only bequeathed me with enough brain cells needed to breathe, eat, and shit. And that if I do actually possess the ability to speak, it's all about clothes, make-up, and what piece of jewelry the husband I rely on for everything has just rewarded me with for being his perfect little piece of arm candy.

I'm a straight-A student. I always have been. And my natural gift was in forensically analyzing and shrewdly manipulating figures. So, I left high school and headed straight to college, which I paid for with my own money by working in the accounts department of one of the city casinos.

I purchased my first apartment at twenty-five, which I still own to this day. And I'd be living there right now if it wasn't rented out. I'd definitely never choose to be living under the very watchful eye of my daddy.

Having started my own little business in Vegas helping professional gamblers manipulate their easily won millions, I then dabbled in money laundering.

It's an art form not many can master, but it came easy to me for some reason. Some might say too easy. Maybe because it involved doing something wrong. Let's face it. I'm a biker. Doing wrong's what I do right.

Jaine's correct about outlaw accountants. Apparently, my kind really are the walking-talking equivalent of rainbow-shitting unicorns.

Having initially been introduced by Rod as potential business acquaintances, she and I kept gravitating toward each other. Bikers are like pack animals. We like to be with our own kind. So, it was only ever a matter of time before we ended up working together.

"I'm going to see Ghost."

My moment of reflection is interrupted as I take in my lean, mean fighting-machine brother Tadgh who's lounging against the door frame with his arms folded across his chest. Tall, blonde, and perfectly formed with ink covering most of the visible parts of his thirty-two-year-old body and with a beard covering that handsome face of his. There's no hell for him. Nope. He's heading straight to Valhalla. That's how much of a Viking he looks.

"Will Ace be there?"

"Yup. He's heading back to California this morning if you want to meet him before he goes."

"I'd like that."

"Sure thing. You riding bitch?"

I roll my eyes exaggeratedly while shaking my head.

"There is not a chance I will ever ride bitch. My daddy's called Lucifer. He's the prez of an MC, don't you know? Spare hog?"

"There's a Sportster in the garage. You remember how to ride?"

"Isn't there an old saying? You never forget how to ride a bike."

He chuckles. "We leave in ten minutes."

"I hear you, VP." I salute my brother as I walk past to go change, and he shakes his head and laughs heartily in response.

CHAPTER FORTY-THREE

JESSIE

Jessie's Family Home, Colton, Nevada

I'VE NO IDEA HOW LONG IT'S BEEN SINCE I LAST RODE A HOG. Several years, I reckon. The roar when the engine sparks into life mixed with the smell of fuel and oil gives me a high I didn't even realize I was missing. And the vibrating hum from those straight metal pipes?

Sweet hog music to my biker ears.

Maybe I shouldn't have been so quick to turn my back on the life I was born into because, right now my blood is pounding in my veins. For the first time in weeks, I feel alive. I feel energized. Like my biker soul is somehow being soothed just by being sat astride this powerful, gleaming machine.

Tadgh grins at me and nods his head slowly as I sit wrapped head to toe in leather. He knows what I'm feeling. I'm wearing it right across my face. He's probably been waiting patiently for this moment for years. All of my family have. I've never denied what I was. I just never felt the need to embrace it. No one pushed me away. No one pulled me back either.

Everything had to be done in my own sweet time.

I walked away from the life to do my own thing. And now? Well, maybe now I'm finally letting those heavily inked arms of the one percent badge welcome me back home.

With the wind in my hair, we ride through the small town we grew up in.

Nothing's changed in Colton. Nothing ever does. There's still just the same little row of shops, including a filling station, a post office, and a diner.

Around town, it's the usual scene. It's like *Groundhog Day*. Teenagers hanging around the front of the diner. The boy pushing the girl he likes, trying to pretend he doesn't before they both sneak around back to make out. Old folks hanging around the church, leaning on their walking sticks and frames as they compare what's going to be inscribed on their headstones when their time finally comes to return home to The Lord.

I take in the familiar steeple that, as a little girl, I was sure reached all the way to heaven. You just had to climb right on up to find St. Peter waiting for you at the top. I've always loved the town church. The calm it affords. The peace. It feels like The Almighty is sitting right beside you.

And who knows? Maybe he is.

Father Murphy controls his flock from behind the raised pew inside those freshly painted walls, handing out penances as he sees fit. My daddy attends every Sunday to take the weighted one for his family's sins on his broad shoulders.

The only other building of any significance is the town school located right beside the church. Both Little Bee and Conor attended. Tadgh insisted he wanted to go to school in Vegas, where his friends were all headed. So, it meant I got to school in the city too.

I think I would have enjoyed my childhood years way more if I'd attended the town school here in Colton. But schooling in Vegas and going through the experiences I did is what made me, in part at least, the strong individual I am today.

I guess you can't have it both ways.

My eyes drift to the line of hogs parked up outside the diner. Colton has always been a biker town for as far back as I can remember. Home to the Undertakers MC and the Sons of Satan MC. My daddy, prez of the Sons. Reaper, prez of the Undertakers. Or at least, Reaper was. He was shot in the head last year by The Exterminator. Rumor has it the sniper doesn't tolerate trafficking or child abuse of any kind. Rumor also has it Reaper was heavily involved in both. That he had a fucked-up taste for underage, innocent flesh.

Like oil and water, they don't mix.

Click. Boom.

My daddy is now acting prez over both clubs. That may change in the future, but that's just the way it is for now.

My hog kicks dust into the desert air as I turn off the main drag and follow my brother. I smile to myself. I wonder if Ghost will remember me.

It's been a long time.

The Ghost Whisperers' Clubhouse, Colton, Nevada

We park up in front of the clubhouse. Well, at least they'll be keeping the local tradespeople busy as they finish constructing yet another grey eyesore in Colton. At present, it's just the building itself. Nothing has been fenced off, so there's no compound, and most likely no security.

These buildings are built in layers. Bombproof, bulletproof

layers. Throw on some security, a tequila-filled bar, some scantily clad eager-to-be-dicked women, and a bucketful or two of fresh cum, and it'll look and smell just like any other MC clubhouse.

I watch as my brother shakes hands and man hugs the prez of the Ghost Whisperers. He's still an arrogant asshole, pretty much naming this club after himself. I mean, who even does that?

Both of them look in my direction. I lean my ass against my hog and fold my arms.

Ghost smiles at my brother then pats him on the shoulder, and Tadgh grins, glancing at me once more before heading inside.

Yup. The topic of conversation is standing right here.

Ghost turns and walks towards me. He's filled out over the years. He's taller and broader. He's no longer a boy. He's all man. His skin is tanned from the sun and covered in ink. His black hair is tied back at the nape of his neck, so it's difficult to tell just how long it is these days. His eyes are as black as a demon's. Eyes that perfectly match his condemned soul and set on a face that's lost all traces of adolescence over the years. He's also grown a beard which does nothing to disguise those angular features he's got going on. He's one beautiful son of a bitch. And doesn't he just know it?

"Tyler."

"Jay."

I raise an eyebrow at the man I gave my virginity to when I was sweet sixteen.

"Oh, so you *do* remember my name from that conveyor belt of women you were fucking around the time you were eighteen. Well, holy shit. I *should* feel honored."

He smiles, rubbing one hand behind his neck.

"Aww. Have I made you feel awkward, Ty?"

"Not at all. I was just hoping you'd forgotten. Or at the very least that you'd managed to rein in that outspoken mouth of yours. Unfortunately for me, it's neither. I was eighteen years old, Jessie. I was wearing a prospect cut so damn new the smell of the leather was potent. I felt like I was king of the hill."

"Really?" I laugh exaggeratedly. "So, as usual, this is all about your conceited self. Did the potency of the leather drug your brain, leaving you with no consideration for others? Well, let me tell you, Mr. Biker Hotshot, I was a virgin. And no one ever forgets their first time. So, how can I ever forget the fact you used me and then tossed me aside like I was a cum slut?"

"I'm sorry about that."

"Not as sorry as I am, asshole."

"It was fifteen years ago."

"It still happened."

"Interrupting something?"

"Of course you're interrupting. Can't you see we're in the middle of a private…"

I swing my head towards the deep voice and immediately take in the tall, lean biker who's walking toward us. His blue eyes are searching my very soul with his penetrating gaze, and his hair hangs way down his back in inky waves. He has a short beard, which displays perfectly the chiseled features underneath. Damn, he is one mighty fine specimen.

He smiles at me, and I smile back.

"Has anyone ever told you you have really wolfish canines?"

His grin widens. "My wife tells me that most days."

"It's good to finally meet you, Ace."

"It's good to meet you too, Jessie."

I don't know whether to shake his hand or hug him, but he makes the call for both of us as he pulls me against him. He's a wall of steeled muscle. The yang to my business partner's yin. Or at least one of them. He and Paddy look so alike they could be brothers.

Shit, no wonder the poor girl's so confused she's depressed.

He releases me, and we turn our attention back to Ghost, who's stood looking on. He's probably hoping I'm done wiping the floor with him. I am. For now.

"You guys need another private moment?" Ace grins.

"Nope. I'm just about done reminding Ty of how he took my virginity and then dumped me the very next day. But then, you'd know all about that shit too, wouldn't you, Mr. Ace of Broken Hearts."

Ghost lets out a low whistle before snickering.

I walk away, leaving them both standing there in my dust. I'm pretending I'm pissed off, but I'm really wearing a wide smile.

Biker boys. You've got to love them. And let's be honest.

Most women do.

CHAPTER FORTY-FOUR

DYLAN

Play Gentlemen's Club, Manhattan, New York

We own several disused areas of the New York subway system. Each is sealed, completely soundproof, and easy to hose down. All have facilities to turn bodies into soup or wrap them in concrete, depending on how long we have to destroy any physical evidence.

The selected venue for my re-introduction into the cold-blooded murder Duster Hall of Fame is directly underneath Play. It's a concrete prison. It never sees the light of day, so as well as being dank and depressing, it's also bone-chilling cold. This must be what it feels like to be buried alive. The only sound is dripping water, no doubt caused by the rain currently pounding off the city streets above.

I stare at the nameless man who's been bound to a canteen-style chair and is currently unconscious. I've only just arrived. In his excitement, Paddy started without me. Today's deserved victim already has a few missing digits all of which have been neatly arranged on a small kidney tray sitting atop a wheelable trolley nearby.

"What's he done, Paddy?" I ask as I put on a pair of disposable coveralls that match his.

"Our brother Gavin here." Paddy throws a glass of water in his face, and I watch as the balding man wakes up with a start. "Has been grooming two young Irish girls. Both of them are only twelve years old."

Gavin was probably in the middle of a really good dream, and he's now been awakened into his worst possible nightmare. A nightmare you wouldn't wish on your worst enemy. From what I've heard from Cillian, our Paddy is a bloodthirsty fecker. I wouldn't know. I've never seen him in action. I guess there's a first time for everything.

"Haven't you, Gavin?" Paddy leans forward and slices a scalpel up the corner of his mouth. Gavin screams his agony as blood pisses everywhere. Gav now doesn't need to smile to show us his teeth.

"I didn't do it, Paddy."

"Don't lie to me, you fucking swine," Paddy hisses before slicing the other corner of his mouth. More screaming. More teeth on display. Gavin's top lip is now more of a flap that vibrates as he sits there sobbing away to himself.

"Cut his shirt open, Dyl."

Paddy's pacing now. He looks demented. Like he's got some great inner turmoil going on. Something must have happened, and this fucker here's going to pay the price whether he likes it or not. Because it would seem the only way to appease Paddy's demon is to offer a blood sacrifice.

I reckon it's best to just do as I'm told. Brother or not, I don't want our Paddy waving his blade in my direction. I might not be the best looking of our lot, but I still quite like my facial arrangement as it is. I pick a scalpel up off the trolley and do the honors. Gavin's pissed himself, and going by the stench, he's also emptied his bowels. I almost feel sorry for him.

Almost.

Because when I think of those two wee girls whose lives will never be the same again, any fleeting thoughts of sympathy vanish.

Just as I'm putting the scalpel back, Paddy comes to an abrupt standstill beside me. My own bowels almost turn to liquid.

"She called me, Dyl."

"Who did?"

"Jaine."

I nod. I saw the message exchange the morning after, but I've not seen him since to ask about it.

"So, she actually did it? And what did you say to her?"

Paddy holds up a hand to silence me before waving the blade at Gavin.

"Stop listening to us, you nosy fecker." He walks across to Gavin, slicing his ear off before shoving it in the man's mouth.

"Swallow it."

Gavin's crying, tears streaming down his blood-stained cheeks, his eyes bulging.

"I. SAID. SWALLOW. IT. YOU. DIRTY. PEDO. FUCKER."

In his defense, Gavin tries his best, but the slippery appendage falls out of the hole in his cheek.

Wearing a look of disgust on his face, Paddy stands there staring at it as it lays on the floor. His hands are slung low on his hips, his coveralls are splattered in blood, and his fist is clenching a scalpel dripping with the same. Today, I'm seeing my baby brother in a whole new light. This monster is a far cry from the happy-go-lucky lad that exists beyond these four walls. He looks at Gavin, shaking his head like a parent at a child that's come home with a bad school report.

"I ask one thing, and you couldn't even get that right. You useless fucker."

He slices off the other ear and shoves that in his mouth.

"Swallow it!" he hisses. He's right in his face now. "If you manage to get it right this time, you dirty fuck, then I'll let our Dyl here grant you a quick demise. If you fuck it up, then I'll torture you for hours before I let him end your suffering. It's your call, Gavin. What's it going to be? I'm sure you've heard all about my methods. Well, let me tell you, sonny boy, the rumors don't do them justice." Paddy runs the scalpel up Gavin's rotund stomach just as 'sonny boy' manages to successfully swallow his own ear.

Paddy doesn't cut into him. He's leaving that for me.

"Paddy, I…." I shake my head. I should never have been born into this life. This sort of thing has never come easy to me.

He passes me the blade. It's hot and sticky with blood.

"You've killed before." He says it like it's routine. Like it's the same as going to the store, buying a loaf of bread, and then successfully finding your way back home.

Same difference as far as he's concerned.

"That was with a gun. All I had to do was point, close my eyes, pull the trigger, and hope for the best. This is hands-on. It's not quite the same."

"Many of the life and death situations we face are hands-on, Dyl. We're not always going to be conveniently carrying a weapon. This isn't the movies. Sometimes you have to rely on what you can find or just use your own two hands. Now, do it. He's a dirty pedo fucker. He's asked for this ending. Do it for the girls' lives he's destroyed and do it for Jessie. Close your eyes if you must. In my opinion, that's disrespectful to the life you're ending. But either way, just get the job done."

Walking across to the trolley, I take in the tray of hacked off digits. Then I study the array of weapons sitting alongside. I put the scalpel down.

I glance at Paddy over my shoulder, and I can see the look of disappointment on his face.

I turn my attention back to the trolley, pick up the gutting knife, then walk back toward Gavin.

He's resigned to his fate. I can see it in his eyes. He wants quick. Fortunately for him, that's what he shall have as that's all I can offer at this stage in my apprenticeship.

With my eyes never leaving his, I plunge the knife into the bottom of his stomach. Then, with two hands and using all my might, I drag that fucker upwards.

His guts spill all over the floor.

"May God have mercy on your diseased soul." I maintain eye contact until the light goes out in his eyes. Then I grimace as I'm hit with the stench of fresh shite.

I'm only grateful I'm wearing coveralls.

I'm conscious Paddy's behind me, and I close my eyes when his hand squeezes my shoulder.

"I doubted you, brother. I'll admit it. For a second, I doubted you had it in you."

I turn to look at him.

"When it comes to Jessie, never doubt me or my intentions, Paddy."

He nods. He gets it.

We're almost nose to nose. I look deep into my brother's eyes. I see my da. I see our Eoin. I see our Cill. All four of them are wired up wrongly. I'm sure of it.

I wonder what Paddy sees as he stares into mine. Does he see the same?

One thing I do now know. Why he does what he does. Yes, of

course, he wants to make all these fuckers pay by ending their lives, and rightly so. But as they're dead men walking anyway, he gets to torture them beforehand. Why?

Because he wants them to feel pain. Because he feels pain. All day. Every day.

For them, there's light at the end of the tunnel. A way out. For him, there is no end. He and his pain are bed partners. It's a lifetime thing.

"She didn't say anything."

"Who?"

"Jaine"

"Why?"

"I didn't pick up."

"Why?"

"Eoin messaged me just as the call came in. Told me if I did, he'd tell Da everything."

Tears fill his eyes. My poor brother likely just wanted to hear her voice. The rest of us hear it all the time. Or at least we did. All this time we've taken for granted something he wants more than anything in the world.

More than anything, he just wants Jaine to say her name for him. Something no one else calls him.

Irish.

CHAPTER FORTY-FIVE

JESSIE

The Ghost Whisperers' Clubhouse, Colton, Nevada

"WHY CAN'T I SIT IN THE COUNCIL MEETING, TY?" THIS IS THE sixth, maybe seventh time I've asked. I sound like a child sitting in the back of a car asking repeatedly, 'are we there yet?' I'm grating on his last nerve. That's my intention. But the determined asshole's still refusing to budge.

"*I said* it's not for women."

"If it were an Angels' council meeting, Jaine would be allowed to sit in. Wouldn't she, Ace?"

He nods.

"Well, Jaine wouldn't be welcome in any Whisperers' council meeting either, Jay. So, as you can see, it's nothing personal, sweet thing."

"Are you bikers ever going to drop this chauvinistic approach? I mean, maybe I can add something to the mix. Suggestions? Ideas?

Women do have brains as well as pussies, you know? Who knows, maybe a mere woman can help you Neanderthalic men find a way out of this stalemate situation you keep finding yourselves in. You all must be dizzy by now going round in circles as often as you do."

"I doubt you'll be able to offer any help, Jay. Even if you could, you're still not invited."

I roll my eyes exaggeratedly, but I refuse to give up.

"So, call it a pre-council meeting. Just me, you, Tadgh, and Ace. I'll do all the talking. I'll also ask all the questions, and you can choose to answer only the ones you want to and deflect any others."

"Do you ever…"

"Nope. I never shut up. So, sue me. Bear in mind, I do have a damn good lawyer." I wink at Ace, and he smiles. "If you don't let me talk and say my piece, Tyler Grayson, then so help me God, I'm going to come a calling day in and day out to this little clubhouse of yours, and I'm going to talk your ears off."

"I'm sure I can think of ways to get you to stop talking, Jay."

I laugh out loud at the sheer arrogance of this man.

"That might have worked when I was sixteen, Ty, but these days, orgasms just make me even louder."

Ace snickers. Tadgh grimaces, shakes his head, and looks decidedly uncomfortable. I guess my brother doesn't want to hear his sister talking about orgasms.

"Why don't we just consider what she's asking, Ghost? Like my wife, Jessie's a business professional as well as a biker, so she's not going to breathe a word of what gets discussed outside of these four walls."

"Finally, a man with some common sense," I mutter.

"She can talk to me on my own."

I stare at him and frown.

"What? One on one? Just you and me?"

"That's if you want to hear what it is I've got to say, Jay."

I nod at Tadgh and Ace and watch as all then leave Tyler's office.

I STARE AROUND THE ROOM AND WAIT FOR HIM TO COME BACK. THE walls are new, crisp, and white. A direct contrast to the battered old wooden desk Ty sits at.

I inhale the smell of new paint.

Tears prick my eyes at the memories it evokes. Manhattan. My apartment.

Dylan O'Connell.

It's been two months since I left, and not a single word. Then again, he can't contact me as I blocked his number. Maybe I'll unblock it in time.

I'm not saying I won't return to Manhattan. In fact, I'll have to at some point. JAA has managed to use good old Candice as an intermediary, but matters requiring a person-to-person meeting are piling up. And if I'm going to have to talk to them, I'd rather it be in the same room as opposed to virtual.

I lean back in the beat-up old brown leather armchair and turn my attention to the window. It overlooks the front of the building, over the area where the compound will eventually be. Beyond that, it's just miles and miles of uninterrupted Nevada desert.

Tyler comes back into the room. He has to walk behind me to reach his side of the desk, and the smell of his leather cut and his spicy cologne washes over me. He smells good. He looks good.

Too good.

But then, he always did. That's why all the girls were chasing him. And why he no doubt serviced each and every one of them. I watch as he runs his hand through his jet-black hair. He's likely wearing it down so I'll admire its mid-back length.

"Earth to Jessie."

"Sorry?"

"You were staring."

"Was I?"

"You thinking back to when I fucked you?"

"Nope."

"Liar. You're drooling."

"Am not." I wipe my mouth just in case, and we both snicker immaturely. Truth is, I wouldn't have been surprised if I had been. Unlike most, my first time really deserved its own fireworks display, even if the next day, when I got dumped, it all just turned into a damp squib.

"Anyway, it was so underwhelming I can't even remember."

"Happy to jog that memory of yours, Jay. Just say the word, sweet thing."

Black eyes bore into mine. He's being serious.

I smirk at him. "In your dreams, Tyler."

He grins back. "Going by the wistful look you were just wearing, I'd say it was actually in yours."

Conceited asshole.

CHAPTER FORTY-SIX

JESSIE

The Ghost Whisperers' Clubhouse, Colton, Nevada

"So, WHAT IS IT YOU WANT, TY?"

I watch as he leans back in an armchair that matches my own. Like mine, it's seen way better days. There's something quite homely about these old pieces of furniture. You just sort of sink in, then they wrap themselves around you like a comforting hug.

"To be prez of my own club. I've been VP for eleven years. It's my time to shine."

I snicker. "It's not Hollywood, Ty. It's Colton."

He stares at me across the desk, and I immediately regret that throwaway remark. I'm making light of this situation and I shouldn't. This is his job. The brothers do this to earn a living, same as my own family. Just because they're not accountants, lawyers, or professionals, they're still businesspeople in their own right. They still play a vital part in the chain of what we do. Some might argue the most important part.

"It may not be Vegas or New York either, Jay, but I worked my ass off for the Undertakers over the years. I made VP at twenty-two. I stuck it out. I put up with all sorts of shit, including carrying that dead-weight Reaper most of the time. The prez position was meant to fall to me. You may not know this, but Reaper didn't have long left. He had acute liver disease."

"I didn't know that. I'm sorry."

"Nothing to be sorry for. His time was up. The Exterminator did the world a favor ridding it of that piece of shit. But him shooting Reaper in the head also moved things along quicker than any of us anticipated."

"So why didn't you step up at the time? Make it known you wanted and expected to be handed the prez cut?"

"I was out of town. On a run with a couple of the other brothers. By the time I got back, Lucifer had already swaggered on in and taken control just like he always does."

I exhale because I know he's right. "Well, my daddy does like power."

"Exactly. And there's nothing wrong with that. But he wants it all. So, in many ways, he's not so different from Reaper."

"Aside from the fact he treats his fellow brothers well, doesn't traffick, and doesn't piss off the Irish mob."

"Aside from that."

"So that's all you want? To be prez of your own club?"

"That's all I want. That's all I've ever wanted. We all have our dreams, Jay. And that there's mine."

"I wasn't trying to belittle yours, Ty. I'm sorry if it came across that way."

"I realize that."

"And have you been dealing with the Undertakers' previous backers like folks are accusing you of?"

"I have not. Reaper always dealt with them direct. Towards the end, the Undertakers never even called church. A few brothers worked with the prez, but they weren't even council. They were just doing his bidding because he was paying them. The rest of us didn't condone the direction he was taking the club, so we didn't actively get involved. But there was nothing we could do to stop him. He had the backing of this faceless faction. Our families and friends would have been at risk if we'd attempted any sort of club coup."

He pauses, obviously to consider what he's going to say next.

"I admit I have been contacted by their intermediary. A few Colombian fellas I met when Reaper first started his dealings with them. But I've already told them the Whisperers aren't interested in hearing anything they have to say, no matter how much they're offering. We're not interested in trafficking. We're an MC. We deal in weapons and sex. Drugs if we have to. But we don't trade or transport people. I've told your old man this repeatedly, but he either refuses to listen or doesn't want to. Likely the latter as it suits his own damn purposes."

I ignore the barb directed at my daddy. It's clear Ghost has no time for him, and it's my guess the feeling's mutual, hence why they're continually at loggerheads and resolving nothing.

"I also heard you've been threatening brothers' families to get them to jump ship? Any truth to that rumor?"

He runs his hand frustratedly through his hair. "Jessie, you know me. Now that knowledge may be from some time ago, but we spent time together. You know that's not what I do. Not who I am. I'd never threaten a brother's family."

"And what about you offering them more money?"

He shrugs. "Even if I was, which I'm not, there's nothing wrong with that. It's called headhunting. Brothers have old ladies to keep happy, kids to feed and clothe—money talks. Regardless of what your old man thinks, many of the men in this town respect me. They like the way I do business. They want to work with me. Not everyone is a fan of Lucifer. Same as not everyone was a fan of Reaper. Different folks, different strokes."

"So why is Ace here?"

"Because he listens and most of the time your old man and your older brother don't. We'd never have gotten this far without him acting as mediator."

"And now you want in on the alliance."

"Yup. We've offered to take care of all the transport areas that are currently unclaimed so the Irish can sell further afield."

I nod. "Makes business sense for them."

"It does."

"Listen, Ty. Now I know what's going on, let me speak to my daddy."

"You do that."

I stand to leave, turning to the door.

"Oh, and Jay?"

I glance back over my shoulder only to find his eyes fixed on my ass. I turn fully, and he takes his own sweet time dragging them slowly up my body until his gaze connects with mine.

"Ty?" I roll my eyes at him, but I can't stop a smile from playing on my lips.

"Mind if I take you out to dinner some time?"

"At the diner?"

"At the diner."

"Like you did all those years ago?"

"Yup."

"I won't be fucking you in your truck afterward."

"I can just about live with that."

"I'll think about it."

"You do that. Meanwhile, can I have your phone?"

"Why?" I pull the handset from my leather pants, unlock it, then pass it to him.

"So I can check up on how that thinking of yours is coming along." He keys in his number and then calls his own, so he now has mine. "Oh, and Jay?" He passes it back to me. "For the record, it meant something to me too."

"I never said it meant anything to me."

"If it didn't, you would know what I was referring to."

"Screw you, Ty,"

"Any time, sweet thing."

I close his office door with a grin on my face before making my way back through to the communal area.

Tyler Grayson is still one beautiful, arrogant asshole.

"Are you heading back to Rising now, Ace?" I take in the inked biker who's standing at the unfinished bar area.

"Sure am."

"Well, you make sure you pass this hug to that old lady of yours." I smile as I wrap my arms around him briefly before stepping back.

"You have my word on that, Jessie. I can't wait to see her."

"Hopefully things will start to quieten down this end. I've had a good chat with Ty and have an understanding of the situation now and of what it is he wants. Fingers crossed it'll help with me having a similar talk with my daddy."

"It can't do any harm." He nods then pauses. He's thinking about something, I can tell. I'm curious about what he's going to say.

"Rumor has it the Irish will be paying a visit before too long."

"Great." I roll my eyes exaggeratedly.

Not that I'm concerned. It's unlikely Dylan O'Connell will come a calling since he seldom leaves his apartment. He's even less likely to now he has a live-in girlfriend.

"Dylan's a good guy, Jessie."

"So, you've heard all about him and me, then?"

"From PJ. Only some. And not in any detail, obviously."

"Well, he's not a *good guy*, Ace." I use air quotes. "He's one half of an arranged marriage. Something he's been aware of for months, maybe even years. A known commitment that still didn't stop him from signing me up as his fuck buddy, even though his fiancée's supposedly the great love of his life."

Ace shrugs. "Maybe that's the case. Maybe it isn't, Jessie. From personal experience, I suggest you listen to what he has to say before you jump to conclusions. If he wants to speak, let him. He can only do that if you're prepared to hear him out remember. Your mind may remain unchanged. Or it may make you reconsider. Either way, you have nothing to lose apart from a little time."

I stare up at the big biker, and he looks down at me, his blue eyes scanning my face like he's seen me somewhere before.

"You have a wise head on those shoulders of yours, Ace."

"Not wise. I've just been there. I lost PJ for a decade because she and I were useless at talking and listening. We won't ever get those years back. Don't go making the same mistakes we did."

"I won't. I promise." I'm lying. I have no intention of ever listening to anything Deceitful Dylan has to say.

"Good girl. Now, I'm going to travel home to my very pregnant wife."

"I spoke to her today. She's sounding heaps better."

"She is. I'm grateful to you for suggesting she speak to Razr. He's helped her so much. And I think in some ways, it's helped him too. Having someone to talk to. Someone close to you who understands. I also think he's glad he's been able to finally give her something back."

"Aren't you jealous?" I grin.

"Of Razr?" He smiles widely. "Nope. He loved her for four years. And he took good care of her all that time. I'll always be grateful to him for that."

"And what about Paddy?"

His smile is replaced by a frown. "Padraig's a great guy. But he'll be married soon. PJ needs to let go of what they shared. They both do. What's happened to her recently is proof of that. To be part of each other's lives moving forward, they need to draw a line under the past or things will just be confusing as hell for both of them."

"It's a hard thing to do when you love someone."

"Don't I know it, but life moves on, Jessie. It has to."

I nod. I know he's right. But it's still easier said than done. "You back here anytime soon?"

"Not until after my son's born."

"Two boys under two. I don't envy you."

"You should. Best feeling in the world being a parent."

"It's probably not on the cards for me." I sigh.

"I never thought it was on the cards for me either. Listen, if there's no future with Dylan, there's always Ghost." He laughs.

I punch him playfully on the arm. "Been there. Done that. He dumped me the very next day, remember?"

He shrugs his shoulders once more. "As I said, Jessie. People change. You've changed. Tyler has too, I'm sure. Anyway, I'm going to get hit the road. It was good to finally meet you."

I watch him walk off before turning my attention in my brother's direction. It's no surprise to see he's chatting with Ghost. There's only a year separating them, so in a two-bit town like Colton, they've grown up together.

I run my eyes over Ty as he stands there in snug-fitting black jeans and a white Henley, his prez cut finishing off his look. His arms are folded across his chest, causing his biceps and pecs to bulge way too impressively. When my gaze reaches his eyes, he's smug smiling, no doubt at my blatant ogling. I smirk in response.

Well, he ogled me earlier. Fair's fair.

I look away, exhaling slowly as I do. Who knows? Just because my heart belongs to an Irishman doesn't mean I can't have me some hot biker boy fun.

I look around as I wait for them to finish their discussions. There's not much to see inside. A bar in the process of being built. White walls, one of which has the club insignia painted on. I smile as I take in the pair of katanas on the wall facing me. They're probably fake as they look way too pretty and decorative to be the real deal.

At my daddy's insistence, we were forced to take up one form or another of self-defense. Both the Power Rangers-loving Bee and I studied the art of ninjutsu and aikido for several years. She throws shuriken better than anyone I know and has even killed with her lethal stars.

By all accounts, it was her throwing that, in part, saved Razr's life last year.

Me being the ultimate Uma Thurman fan? I used katanas when I trained. I've never taken a head off with one, though. Or at least not yet.

I look at Ty once more, and he catches my eye and winks. They do say there's a first time for everything.

CHAPTER FORTY-SEVEN

JESSIE

Jessie's Family Home, Colton, Nevada

I ARRIVE HOME WEARING A SMILE. IT'S NOT FOR ANY SINGLE reason. I think it's more a culmination of several moments I've lived through today combined with a realization.

That Colton isn't a bad place. That it isn't an evil place. It's just a town where MC blood runs in varying stages through the veins of every single person who lives here. For me, Colton's simply a way of life I've forgotten how to live. Somehow and somewhere along the line, I lost track of who I am. Of what I am.

Of where I truly belong.

Maybe it's because I went to school in Vegas. I went to college in Vegas. I started my own company. I bought my first apartment.

Vegas. Vegas. Vegas.

I can't think of any other reason. Colton didn't push me away, and I didn't intentionally leave it behind. I guess I was so wrapped up in fulfilling my life ambitions I drifted farther and farther until I subconsciously felt like I no longer belonged. That I'd outgrown it somehow. That maybe I *was* different from my siblings. That perhaps I *had* been born in the wrong life. Born into the wrong family. Far-fetched maybe, but who knows?

In the end, it was just easier to avoid.

It was different for Bee and Conor. They schooled here. This town was their staple. And Tadgh? Well, he had no option but to return after Vegas. His destiny was mapped from the moment he drew his first breath. If he was fortunate enough to survive the years between being born and my daddy stepping down, he was always destined to become prez of the Sons. That was his future.

It's different for women in a biker town. There aren't many opportunities, and I had no intention of taking the easy way out and becoming an old lady.

I wanted a career. I wanted success. I didn't want to rely on a man. Not for anything. A woman doesn't have to. Not in this day and age. So, I worked hard and achieved what I set out to, but in doing so, I spent so long on the outside that, on the inside, I became more of a city girl.

I adapted. I changed. Maybe even in some ways, I compromised.

I mean, the thought of moving all the way to New York to start afresh was more welcoming than the thought of having to move back home to Colton. The first filled me with excitement, the latter with dread.

Now?

I realize I *am* a city girl. But I'm also a small-town girl.

I am a professional businesswoman. But I'm also a biker.

Me and Jaine Jones have more in common than we realize. There is one marked difference between us, though. There's only one man I'm in love with, and that's Dylan O'Connell. But who knows? Maybe I *can* have a future with someone else.

Maybe even with that beautiful asshole Tyler Grayson.

Today, for the first time in a long time, I've witnessed up close and personal the place I grew up. The familiar sights. The familiar faces. Will the novelty wear off after a while?

Maybe.

And if it does, then so be it. But, in the meantime, why can't I do what Jaine's planning? Why can't I have it all? The best of both worlds. Why can't I work between Manhattan and my hometown? Surely it has to be a consideration.

Today, for the first time in months, I feel happy. And it's not because of one thing or one person. It's because I fit in here. I belong. I'm no longer a square peg trying to squeeze into a round hole. I'm not the boyfriend-stealing beautiful girl I was always wrongly accused of being in Vegas. I'm not the business professional I am in New York.

In Colton, I'm just me. Jessie O'Brien.

Not judged. Just accepted. For who I am.

I'm still smiling an hour later when I answer the phone to my baby sister.

But it's always short-lived, isn't it? Happiness. Because there are always some ugly thunderclouds that sense your good mood, roll right on in, and then piss all over your parade.

"Little Bee," I singsong as I sit on the edge of my bed.

"Jay. I don't know how to tell you this."

"How are you, Jay? I'm fine, Bee. Thank you for asking."

"Jay. It's not funny. This is important."

"What is it? Surely it can't be that bad." My smile evaporates.

"Sarah's just left."

"Right."

There's a pregnant pause as my heart sinks in my chest. I

already know what she's going to say. It really is that bad. In fact, it's worse. It's the news I've been dreading hearing since I left New York.

"She's been visiting with Roisin and Fergal. Roisin told her Dylan's engagement party is being held in two months."

I can't speak. And for once, I don't need to pretend I can. I don't need to fill the silence with background noise or meaningless chatter to pretend I'm not affected by this news. This is my baby sister. I can be anything I want with her.

Even an emotional wreck.

Because he's done it. Dylan O'Connell has asked his cliché blonde to marry him.

"Jay."

"I'm sorry. Let me just catch my breath, Bee." I feel like I'm about to hyperventilate.

"Jay. I'm sorry but I didn't want you to hear it from anyone else. I thought it would be best coming from me."

"It sure is best. And I appreciate you thinking of me." My voice is a whisper. "Does Jaine know?"

"Sarah was going to call her on the way back to her apartment, so she's probably speaking to her now."

"Thank you. Um…do you mind if…?"

"Call me when you're ready, Jay. I love you."

"I love you too, Little Bee."

CHAPTER FORTY-EIGHT

JAINE

Jaine's House, Rising, California

"You Dusters really are the lowest of the low."

Maybe I should have started off with fake niceties. Asked after his health. Asked about the weather in Manhattan. Made small talk to pretend I give a damn when I don't.

But I'm way too pissed off.

It's been over two months since I spoke to this pompous asshole. I was warned by the future Ma Duster to stay away from her precious fiancé. Well, that gave me an excuse to do just that.

"Watch your mouth, Jaine."

"He could have told her. She deserved to hear it from him, and she deserved to find out before anyone else."

There's a pause.

"What on earth are you talking about?"

"Don't treat me like I'm an idiot by pretending like you don't know," I hiss. Standing up from the sofa, I grimace at the dull ache in my lower back.

"I still have no idea what you're talking about."

"The conversation Roisin had with Sarah."

"What conversation?"

"The one they had today at your family home."

"Do I have to drag this out of you one question at a time, Miss Jones?"

Miss Jones. I smile briefly. It's nice to know I haven't lost my knack for pissing him off.

"The conversation during which your ma told Sarah that Dyl's engagement party would be held in two months' time. I mean, Jesus Christ, I realize there's a lot of ill-feeling floating around, but Jessie shouldn't have had to hear that breaking news from her sister. The man of the moment should have had the balls to tell her himself."

"Dylan's been called to my parents' house. He's being told now." His voice is quiet.

I laugh dryly. "And you expect me to believe that?"

"It's the truth. Sarah shouldn't have said anything."

My back's instantly up. I'm constantly uncomfortable and in pain these days. I'm fully aware it's making me more reactive than normal.

"Now hold on a minute. Don't blame Sarah. Roisin never mentioned it was being said in confidence. On the contrary, Sarah said she was actively encouraged to spread the happy news."

I stop pacing as the reason why dawns on me. Roisin's done this on purpose. She knew Sarah would tell me and Bailey. It was to make sure Jessie found out. To let her know it was game over. Can this family stoop any lower?

"You mentioned Dylan didn't know. You did, I suppose?"

There's a pause. It speaks volumes. I'm right. Asshole.

"So, it didn't cross your mind to do the decent thing and let Jessie know?"

"It's not my place to tell Jessie."

"You could have told me. I could have told her."

"And how do you expect me to do that? You haven't taken my calls in months."

"Why don't you ask Molly why that is? Better still, why don't you ask your ma? And for the record, I called you once. Molly answered. You didn't return it, so I figured our communications were at an end and you'd received the same threatening memo from Ma Duster that I had."

There's a pause. He's digesting what I've said. I know him well enough to know what I'm saying is news to him.

So, Molly never told him. Then again, why would she when she thinks I want him for myself? She must have wiped all traces of the call from his phone. Figures. Still, that's between her and him and it was probably for the best.

"And what is it I've to ask my ma about?"

"I'm sure you'll figure it out."

Another pause.

"I called you several times recently, Jaine. You never answered. Does that seem like I wanted our conversations to be at an end?"

"By then, I had nothing to say to you."

"You called. You obviously had something you wanted to say. What was it?"

"It doesn't matter."

"What. Was. It."

I start pacing the floor once more, annoyed at his bossy tone. Who the hell does he think he is?

"I can't remember the reason."

"Don't lie, Miss Jones."

I close my eyes and exhale. "I wanted you to tell me what was going on because everyone else was keeping secrets from me."

There's a pause.

"Maybe they were trying to protect you."

I roll my eyes as I sit down on the old sofa, rubbing my hand across my lower back as I do. "From what? I don't need protecting. I'm pregnant. I'm not terminally ill."

"So, you called me thinking that I'm not hiding things from you."

"And are you?"

"Yes." There's no hesitation in his response.

I don't reply. For whatever reason, I wanted him to say that he was always brutally honest with me. Always had been. Always would be. Can he sense my disappointment?

"And are you, Jaine?"

"Am I what?"

"Hiding things from others?"

"That's none of your goddamn business."

He laughs. "You complain but you're doing exactly the same."

"What I'm hiding I'm doing for a very good reason."

"Aren't we all." he says dryly.

"Fuck you, asshole," I hiss. It's all his fault I'm having to keep things hidden.

"For heaven's sake, stop getting so agitated, Jaine."

"Stop telling me what to do."

"You're pregnant. You should be trying to keep calm."

"Oh, so you know all about pregnancy...."

I'm about to have another go when I'm suddenly conscious I'm sitting in a puddle of water. My heart sinks when I realize what's happened and that Ace isn't even home.

"Fuck." It's a whisper.

"Jaine, what's going on?"

"My waters have just broken."

"But you're not due to give birth for another month. Is your husband with you?" He sounds worried. I don't want his worry or his sympathy. I don't want this asshole's fucking anything.

"Ace is on his way back from Nevada. Listen, I need to go"

"Have you got anyone there with you?"

"I *said* I need to go."

An overwhelming wave of emotion threatens to drown me as I watch Ace cradle our newborn son in his arms.

My big, murderous biker stares down in awe at this little scrap of nothing like he can't believe he's real. That he's finally here. That he's finally ours.

It's past midnight. He's arrived on his big brother's birthday. Exactly twelve months separate them.

In some way, it feels like the blink of an eye since Finian was born, but so much has happened since.

Dr. Bruce's office in the center of Rising is a far cry from the state-of-the-art hospital in Nevada we were planning to have this little one in. A facility that catered for every eventuality should, God forbid, something go wrong. Thankfully, nothing did as little Jason Nathaniel Steele wasn't prepared to wait to make his entrance.

He was ready to be born. To fill his little lungs with the air of his hometown of Rising, California, and let it course through his blood where it will forever remain.

Ace arrived with only minutes to spare. Wearing a thick layer of road dust, he scrubbed up just in time to welcome our screaming little red-faced bundle of anger into this world of ours.

A little boy. With ten fingers and ten toes and hair as inky black as the midnight sky and eyes as blue as the bluest thing ever.

The mirror image of his biker daddy.

It seems only fitting that JJ was born in the same single-story nondescript grey building his daddy and granddaddy were born in before him. It also seemed only fitting that he be named after both of them.

As I did the first time around, I take a photo of my beautiful boy holding his baby son. This time, there's one difference. Not that anyone else knows that.

This time it's his own flesh and blood. This time it's not another man's child.

Not that any of that matters to Ace. I know he'll always love both boys equally.

My heart aches at the visual. At this precious snapshot captured forever in time.

Irreplaceable. Priceless. Perfect.

This image contains two of the four things I love most in the world. Who knows what this snapshot will capture in a year? Even in a month. There are no guarantees in anyone's life. There are even fewer in ours.

My heart aches for another reason.

I'm sorry, Irish.

When the truth comes out, which it will do soon, I hope he realizes what I did. The decisions I made were always for him.

I send the image to Dylan.

Why? Because it's time to move on. It's time to leave the past where it belongs. The birth of my son signifies a new start. A new beginning. A future I can no longer postpone or hold back. My life will change drastically from here on in, and there's nothing I can do to stop it.

I have no option but to embrace what comes next. I have no

choice but to deal with the fallout my revelation will bring. I have one son who is an O'Connell and one son who is a Steele.

And nothing will ever change that.

Different birthrights but still part of the same life. They will grow up side by side. I'll make sure of that.

Ace walks slowly across, cradling little JJ in his arms like he's the most precious thing in the world before placing the sleeping infant in the clear crib.

He sits on the edge of the bed, then leans over and kisses my forehead. I pat the spot beside me, and he positions himself until we're lying side by side, my head resting on his chest, his arm wrapped so tightly around me I can barely breathe.

"You did good, PJ."

"Oh, you think? Well, I can't take all the credit. It was a team effort, after all. *We* did good, Ace."

"I didn't have to do too much."

"I still couldn't have done it without you and that dick of yours." I chuckle as I nuzzle my nose into his neck, inhaling the scent of his familiar aromatic cologne, leather, and everything else that makes up Ace.

He presses a gentle kiss against my hair and exhales slowly. "You know, I'm not sure what I've done in life to deserve this level of happiness, PJ."

Tears immediately prick my eyes because I know they're pricking his too. For all his brawn and ink and all the dark, deadly, and dangerous he has going on, he really is a deep, sensitive, and kind soul, and always so conscious and aware of those around him. He lives day by day, never taking anything for granted, appreciating everything and everyone who takes the time to stop by his life. Like the situation in Nevada, Ace helps others where many would choose to turn a blind eye. And I know I'm so goddamn lucky to have him.

It's me who doesn't deserve him. I never have.

A sob escapes me, followed by another and another, and before I know it, my tears are soaking the front of his shirt. He pulls me tight against him. He doesn't question my moment of fragility. In fact, he doesn't speak at all. This is Ace just being Ace. He's leaving what I do or say next entirely up to me. It's my decision. In the meantime, he'll comfort me as best he can while giving me space emotionally at the same time. He's waiting until I'm ready. He will always wait until I'm ready.

Because for Ace, it's all about me. I'm his world. And I know that now. In all the years, he's never once asked anything of me except to marry him.

And I've asked and expected so fucking much of him in return.

"You know I've loved you since I was seven years old, right?" I'm repeating what he already knows, but somehow, it feels important to reiterate it. To cement it.

"The moment I met you, I knew, Ace. There was never any doubt in my mind that we were end game. Not then. Not now. Not ever. Even during those ten years I was gone, my feelings for you never lessened. It's why I never came home. I couldn't face what I thought I would find. That you'd moved on with your life without me in it when I'd struggled to do the same."

"Are you getting all reflective and emotional on me, PJ?" he whispers softly.

He asks, but I know deep down he appreciates it when I do. And I don't do it enough. Nowhere near enough.

We're each other's past. We're each other's future. But we're also each other's memories. Because Ace and I have made so many together. Just the two of us. No one else. And we need to build more. Way more. Because I will never have enough memories with Ace.

Not ever.

A man who loves so hard and feels so strongly. A man who likes to show his love as often as he can because he knows our lives can change in the blink of any eye and he wants to have no regrets.

And I know I don't do enough for him in return. I never have. I've taken too much and given way less.

I turn my face to look up at him and marvel as I always do. I've always said that Jason Steele was born to be stared at, and I stand by that. He truly was. Every day, my beautiful boy gets even more beautiful—both inside and out. And I'm so grateful that our new son is him in miniature form. I pray to God that he's got the same unselfish heart on the inside too.

Because our fucked-up outlaw world needs more people like Ace.

"I'm just being honest. And whether it's the hormones talking or something else, it really doesn't matter. I love you. I can't even explain how much. I don't even think there's a word invented that can adequately describe it. And I'm sorry for the past. And for the part I played in us losing all those years. All that precious time we can't ever get back. And I'm sorry for all the things I say that I don't mean. For acting like a hissy cat when there's no need. For having been so argumentative and childish these past few months. I'm sorry, Ace. I'm sorry for all of it. Because you deserve everything good in life. You deserve all the happiness and all the love and everything you have and more. And even if were times a million, it would still never be enough for you to have what you truly deserve."

He stares at me as I sit there, having just given birth to our son and with tears rolling down my face. Then he strokes his finger down my cheek.

"I love you too, PJ. Always have. Always will. And if all I ever deserve in life is you and our boys for today and tomorrow and the day after that? Then each day, I'll wake up knowing I'm the luckiest man alive."

CHAPTER FORTY-NINE

PADRAIG

Padraig's Apartment, Hudson Yards, New York

My hands are shaking as I stare at the image on my phone. Underneath, it says Jason Nathaniel Steele, or JJ for short, which I'm guessing stands for Jason Junior.

It's like déjà vu. History repeating. Proof paramount that life for others goes on, even though mine has all but stopped.

Ace is cradling his second newborn son twelve months to the day he did the first. The images are almost identical. The black-haired wee one is wrapped tightly in white swaddling. And he's being held ever so gently like he's the most precious gift in the world.

And he is. To his folks.

To his da.

Then again, a child would be the most prized possession to any da. He'd give anything. Do anything. Be anything for his child. For his daughter.

For his son.

It's a feeling I'll never experience because I'll never be a da.

I'll never know what it's like to witness my child enter the world. To see a first tooth. To be there to catch them as they stumble after their first step. Unfortunately, The Almighty decided that wasn't on the cards for me.

That, for some reason, I'm not deserving of any of that.

Ace has everything while I have nothing. I envy him, but I don't hate him. How can I? He deserves his happiness. He lost her for ten years. He pined for her. He loved her. For all the time she was gone. So, he's been where I am now—experienced the heartache. The desolation. The emptiness. He found light at the end of his tunnel, though. I won't be that fortunate.

Forever just existing in the darkness.

Alone. Unneeded. Unloved.

Every day just bleeds into the next now I don't even have her messages to look forward to. To anchor me. To keep me sane. To keep me company. To brighten my dark days. And in just over three months, I'll be married. My fate sealed. My bed made. My grave dug. My life over.

I love her. I will always love Jaine Jones. My heart doesn't have the capacity to love anyone else as she owns all of it. It's resident in my chest still. And it's beating just enough to keep me existing. But I'm not living. I can't do that without her.

She called. She said she would. She did.

But big brother was watching.

For a fleeting moment, I had hope. A small flicker of light. Then it was gone. Snuffed out. Foolish hope. Hope that took advantage of my gullibility. Hope that laughed at my dreams. At my wants. At my needs.

At my desperation.

Tears prick my eyes.

It's then I hear it. Singing its familiar siren song. Calling out to me. The intoxicating tendrils of the amber liquid reaching out to try to poison my receptive mind.

It's winning. Because all hope is lost. Foolish or otherwise.

It's so easy.

Pour. Drink. Repeat.

My shaky hand reaches out for the crystal decanter. See, I've always kept it in the house to prove my own willpower. Thou shall not give in to temptation. It was easy enough when I had her.

I hear a sob. It's me. There's no one else here. It echoes in my brain. Then I realize it's not an echo. It's just a new one each time.

Each its own cry for help.

But there's no one to help. There's no one who can save me from me.

Only her.

And she's gone.

Jaine: *I'm sorry.*

I stare at the screen, temporarily dazed. Two words. From her. Please, God, let there be more. I'm fucking begging you to let there be more.

My hand hovers over the crystal.

Do it. Do it. Do it. Drink. Drink. Drink.

She's typing.

Jaine: *I'd like to start again if we can, Dyl. Can we just go back to the way things were?*

I realize she doesn't know it's me. But she's missed the

exchanges all the same. Not his and hers. Mine and hers. *Our* exchanges. And I'll take that. I'll take fucking anything I can get. I wipe my face then sit on the sectional and lean back.

Padraig: *You mean where you message me a million times a day to complain with me responding with a hilarious joke each time to cheer you up?*
Jaine: *You mean they were meant to be funny? Shit. Sorry, I didn't realize. I clean forgot to laugh.*
Padraig: *I'm wounded. There's an old expression, Jaine.*
Jaine: *If you don't have anything nice to say, say nothing at all. I know. An extremely annoying Irishman used to say that to me most days. So, sue me. I forget that every time too.*
Padraig: *Not sure if suing you would be a good idea. Is that your unbiased professional opinion?*
Jaine: *Well, I can't really answer that due to the blatant conflict of interest.*
Padraig: *So, Jaine.*
Jaine: *So, Dyl. I'm sorry. I've missed you.*
Padraig: *I've missed you too.*
Jaine: *Moving forward, no more talk of the past. Can we agree on that? There's nothing there for any of us anymore. And we can't change what's happened. We can only move forward and try to heal. Focus on the future.*

I know she's been in a bad place. Sarah mentioned she'd suffered badly from pre-natal depression, and that's partially why she had to distance herself from everyone and everything.

Even me.

Jaine: *I'll be back in Manhattan soon. When I return, Irish is the first person I'm going to go see.*

Padraig: *You mean that, darlin'?*
Jaine: *Yes. It's time, Dyl.*
Padraig: *And what about my other brother?*
Jaine: *Has Cillian been missing me?*
Padraig: *You're hilarious.*
Jaine: *I'll call Eoin in the next day or so.*
Padraig: *And can I also ask... are you available for ALL duties moving forward?*
Jaine: *After nearly two years, most of which I've spent pregnant, my life is once more my own. So, yes. ALL services have now been resumed.*
Padraig: *It's good to have you back on board, Robin.*
Jaine: *Why, thank you, Batman. Because from this day forth, Jaine Jones is back in the goddamn building. And let me tell you, she means business.*

Whiskey? Who needs whiskey when you have Jaine Jones in your life?

CHAPTER FIFTY

JESSIE

The Ghost Whisperers' Clubhouse, Colton, Nevada

"Why don't you give the man a chance to speak, Daddy?"

I glare at my father. Ty's right. He doesn't listen, and neither does my brother. I can understand now why they need Ace's calming influence to mediate and diffuse these tense situations. I blame the Irish blood coursing through my family's veins. And I've dealt with enough of that recently to last me a lifetime. I watch as Ty and my daddy scowl at each other across the desk.

"Now, I suggest we all stop and count to ten because if we don't, we're going to go around in yet another circle, and I'm not keen on circles. They make you dizzy, and they're also misleading. They make you think you're getting somewhere when you're not."

There's a pause. We're in Ty's office. Another armchair's been dragged in for Tadgh. You know, because he's a man and has a penis. Meanwhile, little old Jessie, who only has a pussy to play with, has been relegated to a wooden stool.

Still, at least they're listening because they know I'm right. But is there a cat in hell's chance any of them will admit that out loud? Nope. A biker praising a woman for having any shred of intelligence or common sense. Are you insane?

"Okay. Now, Tyler. Please continue."

"As I was saying, the Whisperers will take on the areas the other MCs don't currently cover. Even though the costs will be higher, we'll agree to do it for the same percentage as everyone else and for a minimum of six months."

My daddy looks like he's about to interrupt once more, and I hold my hand up. I've had just about enough of him. He frowns at me but keeps that troublesome mouth of his closed. Now I know exactly where I get it from.

I motion my head at Ty to continue.

"If we agree things aren't working out after six months, then we take our cut for the duration we've fulfilled our end of the bargain, and we each go our separate ways. If things are working out, then we continue for another six months before renegotiating the percentage. I can't say fairer than that."

I motion my head at my daddy to tell him that the floor is now his.

"You haven't got enough men to satisfy that demand, Ghost. And that's the problem." He's hissing again. I roll my eyes at him.

"We're recruiting."

"Recruiting from where exactly?"

"There are men who want to leave the Undertakers and move to the Whisperers."

"You stealing brothers from me?"

"Nope."

I can almost smell the testosterone flooding the room. I hold my hand up once more.

"If numbers are the only issue Ty has, and brothers are queuing up to switch from one MC to another, then I'm not sure what the problem is. Last I heard, America is a free country. These men are allowed to do what they like. As far as I can see, it's a win-win for all parties concerned from a business point of view. If the Irish can sell farther afield, that means they can broaden their customer base along all their transport routes With more brothers, we could even consider handovers mid-route. You know, by using that expression neither of you seem to have heard of before. Teamwork." I use air quotes to make my point. "Word will soon spread the Irish are expanding to cater to the west, and orders will flood in. Win-win for everyone.

"From a business perspective and knowing those Irish boys as well as I do, I believe they'll be very receptive to the idea of adding another MC to the mix. Especially one that's prepared to cater to the harder-to-reach places that are ripe for the picking but just require that little more time and effort."

I can see my daddy is about to grumble once more, so I figure I'll say my final piece and then leave them to bicker between themselves like a group of retired old ladies who are no longer getting any big biker dick.

"It's six months, Daddy. If Ty can make the numbers, neither of you has anything to lose. It will also keep the townsfolk of Colton happy to see the MCs working in harmony just like they used to. This isn't all about you or Ty, or who can piss highest up the wall. This is business. It's nothing personal. Let's keep it that way.

"Anyway, you can let me know what you boys decide. I'm happy to deal with both the Irish and La eMe on behalf of the Whisperers if that's what's needed to progress matters."

I stand up from the hard stool and grimace as I rub my numb

backside. I notice Ty keeps his eyes very much to himself as a mark of respect. He knows my daddy wouldn't appreciate him ogling his daughter in front of him.

"Thank you, Jessie. Much appreciated."

"My pleasure, Tyler." I wink at him before leaving the room.

I TAKE A SEAT OUTSIDE AT AN OLD PICNIC-STYLE TABLE. IT'S SEEN way better days, and the paint is peeling off in places, but it's better than sitting my ass on the desert floor.

It's midday, and the sun is riding high in the sky. My skin's noticeably tanned these days, and my body's once more becoming accustomed to the Nevada heat. It probably helps that I've taken to wearing next to nothing as it's just so damn warm. Today it's a little pair of white Daisy Dukes and a matching halter top.

The only smell lingering on the desert air is fresh paint. I push aside the unwelcome thoughts it brings. I've gotten it out of my system. Gotten *him* out of my system. Well, as much as I ever can. The rest will just take healing time, and I've got all the time in the world. I've cried. I've had my conversation with The Almighty by asking my questions and receiving no answers.

Why would he speak to biker trash like me?

Life goes on. It has to. I fully appreciate now what Bailey went through. In the end, she got her happily ever after. I won't. Shit happens.

I look around. Things are swiftly progressing at the new MC clubhouse. Of course, there's still a way to go, but it's clear Ghost is a man on a mission.

When he wants something, he goes for it.

Looking around, I see maybe two dozen or so bikers now wearing a Whisperers' cut. All of them will be on their best behavior—all striving for a council position. From what I hear, no one's been selected yet. Not even a VP. Ghost is hand-picking each one personally. By all accounts, he's going to do it on a merit basis, which is unusual. Usually, the club prez simply chooses those closest to him. Everyone in Colton grew up together, so it's not likely any will be a stranger. Then again, I've seen a few faces I haven't recognized over the past couple of days, so news of a new MC forming is obviously gaining momentum farther afield.

I'm guessing they'll start recruiting cum sluts soon too. There's always a queue to fill those spots. Young girls desperate to become old ladies or just eager for lots of hot dirty biker boy action.

I have to admit, I'm missing intimacy. I went a long time without before I eventually hooked up with Dylan O'Connell. I'm not sure I want to go through another dry spell like that again.

"Anyone sitting here?"

I shield my eyes with my hand before glancing up at Tyler, and the coverage allows me the opportunity to discretely drag my gaze down his black wifebeater and dark blue jeans. In direct contrast to Dylan, Tyler's covered in black ink. I'm not sure which I prefer.

Maybe now I like both just as much.

"Well, it's your club, Prez. So, I guess you can sit wherever you like."

"You were here first, and you might not want company."

"Well, we don't need to talk."

"Fine by me, but you seem to always need to be talking."

"True." I chuckle. "Anyway, what's the outcome?"

"Lucifer's agreed to vouch for us in principle."

"And?"

"And so, if you could speak to the Irish to make sure they're receptive to the idea, I'd appreciate that."

"You need me to help produce a business plan. Those boys will expect to see one."

"That would also be appreciated. I'll pay for your time, of course."

"If you want access to my ongoing services, then yes, you will, unfortunately, have to pay. Even my poor, clearly destitute daddy has to pay, as much as he grumbles about it. And I don't come cheap. So, I'm warning you in advance. But for the business plan. Well, consider it my 'congratulations on your new club' gift to you."

"Well, thank you for your generosity, Jay, but I'd rather pay in full and have another kind of gift."

"Still the smooth talker I see, Mr. Grayson. The truth is, I'm not looking for anything right now."

"Me neither."

"So, are you asking me for a no-strings fuck in a truck behind Colton diner?"

"Might be."

I snort. "I think these days we'd probably get ourselves arrested."

"Only if we get caught."

"I'll take a hard pass. I'm not sweet sixteen, and you're an old-timer at thirty-two. I'm not sure either of us have got it in us anymore to run from the pigs."

"Less of the old. I'm a man in my prime." He closes his eyes and raises his face to the sun, a smile playing on his lips. He knows that comment will have me automatically giving him the once over. And I do. And I have to agree with him.

Prime. Indeed.

"Rumor has it you were seeing one of those Irish boys."

"Well, I sure as hell don't miss small-town gossip."

"Is it true?"

"It is."

"Can I ask what happened?"

"He was part of an arranged marriage. Apparently, it's quite common in influential families like his."

"So, will you be going back to Manhattan, or will you be sticking around Colton?"

I give it some thought before I answer. I know that same consideration's been playing on my mind a lot recently. Might as well make that decision right now.

"I'm going to work between both, Ty. Since I've been back, I realize Colton's in my blood. I spent so long away that I forgot what it was like to be home. I've missed it. I've missed that feeling of belonging somewhere."

"That's good to know."

"Well, I'm glad you agree. So anyway, do you want to go make a start on that business plan of yours."

"Right this minute?"

"Right this minute. If you want the Irish to consider your MC as part of their alliance, they'll want to see your proposals in writing. I know. It's awful. Having to do real work instead of just wiling away the hours drinking tequila, riding hogs, and fucking cum sluts."

I wait, and he eventually lowers his face. Opening his eyes slowly, he turns to face me.

"I haven't fucked a cum slut since I was eighteen."

I raise an eyebrow and grin widely. "That, Tyler Grayson, is only because you fucked *all* of them when you were eighteen."

He snickers back in response.

"True."

CHAPTER FIFTY-ONE

DYLAN

The Hudson Dusters' HQ, Manhattan, New York

It's the weekly meeting, and for the first time in I don't know how long, there are no women present.

It's a blessed relief.

Apparently, they're having a get-together with Ma at The Palace for brunch. Or at least Molly and Sophia are. Social gatherings aren't really Grace's thing. She's a loner like me.

Or at least like how I used to be.

"We've received an email this morning from Jessie O'Brien. A request to consider allowing another MC in on the alliance. All other parties have already agreed in principle, and Lucifer has also agreed to vouch for them. I've taken a look at the business plan attached, and it seems credible enough. Jessie's prepared it, of course, on behalf of this..." Eoin glances inside the front cover. "... Tyler Grayson. On the surface it has the potential to be extremely lucrative for the Dusters. It would allow us the opportunity to gain a foothold in those harder to reach areas on the west coast no one wants to venture into."

"How is she, Eoin?"

We all look at Da. He's ignored the commercial side of things, which isn't like him. It's clear he's missing her larger-than-life presence. We all are.

None more so than me.

"Her covering email mentions she'll be returning soon. She just needed some time away to regroup and gather her thoughts."

There's a pause as everyone looks at me like it's somehow my fault. I guess in part, it is. Not so long ago, the thought of anyone hurting her filled me with rage. What do I do when I'm the one responsible for that hurt?

There's no background noise these days as no one touches the Newton's Cradle. Not even Da. It doesn't seem right somehow. It would be like committing sacrilege.

"What? I can't help that I was entered into an arranged marriage."

"You knew it was coming. You shouldn't have gone anywhere near her," Da says.

"We've been through this before. The arranged marriage was mentioned once and then never again. How was I to know it was still on the cards? Maybe if you and Ma were overt instead of everything being cloak and dagger."

"Don't give me that, Dylan. You'd still have gone there. And in the end, what did it achieve?"

"Well, I got myself another wet work partner," Paddy pipes up, grinning at me. My da nods in reluctant agreement. Poor old Gavin was the first of many. It seems I'm as bloodthirsty a fecker as the rest of the family.

"Apart from that."

"Well, for the record, I wouldn't have gone there. But I'm glad I did as it made me realize how much I love her. That's what it achieved."

Everyone knows I do, so it's not that revelation that has all of us now sitting here in silent contemplation. Maybe it's the realization that out of four brothers, three are being forced into marriages against our will and when we're in love with other women. The fact that two are potentially in love with the same woman and she's already married is a minor detail.

"We have to think of the organization."

"The alternatives were as good if not a better fit for the Dusters, Da."

"Your ma…."

"Hates bikers. It's that simple." I butt in.

"LEAVE IT NOW, DYL."

He seldom raises his voice during these meetings. He usually just chucks the paperweight. But he knows I'm right, and his reaction is likely because he's as frustrated as the rest of us.

"Your engagement shindig is scheduled to be announced soon. So enough. Anyway, who is this Tyler Grayson fella? Which MC is he from?"

"The MC is the Ghost Whisperers. Newly formed. Same location as the Sons, so based in Colton, Nevada," Eoin continues.

"Were they not the ones suspected of being in cahoots with the traffickers?"

"They were, but it transpired not to be the case. They've admitted they were contacted by the trafficker's intermediary. The Colombians. We're already aware of their involvement given they were the face of the incident Sarah was caught up in."

"But we still don't know who the faction is behind this whole shebang."

Eoin shakes his head. "All we know is this time around it's not the Bratva. We've been keeping a close eye on them. For now, they're just dealing in drugs, crystal meth, prostitutes, and porn."

"Fucking assholes," Paddy mutters under his breath. We know he still holds them partially responsible for his own unfortunate situation. If he hadn't been kidnapped, there's every likelihood he would have been able to talk his way out of the arranged marriage with Sophia. It was agreed, and the contract signed in blood with the Luciano Ruocco when he was being held hostage by the Russians.

"And who is this Tyler Grayson fella?"

Eoin glances once more at the document. "It says he's the former VP with the Undertakers. Thirty-two years old and been in the life since he was eighteen. Reading between the lines, I think he's an old flame of Jessie's."

"And what makes you think that?" My back is immediately up. I've never been a possessive man, but Jesus Christ, regardless of who this Tyler Grayson is and whether he's guilty as charged or not, that comment makes me want to rip off his head and piss down his neck.

"She calls him Ty. No one would dare call a biker a name like that unless they know them extremely well."

"It doesn't mean they've fucked," I hiss.

"No, it doesn't. But it also doesn't mean they haven't." He smiles politely.

The weight of my da's eyes boring into the side of my skull has me turning to face him.

"What?"

He shakes his head and stares down at his blank pad, a small smile playing on his lips. "Well, I never thought I'd see the day Dylan O'Connell would welcome cold-blooded murder into his soul."

"Aye, well, there's a first time for everything. And a second."

"Seven, actually. And all in the space of a week," Paddy pipes up once more. "I've been keeping a tally."

"And if our Eoin doesn't shut his trap, he'll be number eight," I quip.

My eldest brother raises an eyebrow and smirks at me.

"And are we still planning a visit to Nevada? Because if we are, I'm happy for our Dyl to go in my place now he's finally able to fight his way out of a paper bag."

"Shut it, or you'll be number nine," I throw back at our Cill. He laughs and holds his hands up in mock surrender.

We all wait while big brother makes the final decision.

"Well, as it's been a year since we last visited, I think it would be in the Dusters' best interests to revisit old acquaintances and introduce ourselves to the potential newest member of the alliance."

"Dylan." He pauses and stares at me. It's reminiscent of what they do on a quiz show before they tell you if you've won or not. "You can come with me."

"When?" I immediately toss back.

"I need to clear my desk, so week after next?"

I nod my acceptance.

Jessie O'Brien, I'm coming to pay you a visit.

CHAPTER FIFTY-TWO

ROISIN

Private Dining Room, Palace Hotel, Manhattan

"So, ladies."

I watch as they glance across the table at each other. It's like pulling teeth. It's clear neither wants to go first, which can only mean one thing. That neither has a positive update to share. But then I already knew that. Because unlike them, I do my homework.

"Molly?"

I raise an eyebrow at her when she still doesn't respond. I had high hopes for this girl given her impressive background and track record, but they're being dashed more and more with every silent second that passes.

"Would you care to update us, please?" I prompt.

On the outside, she looks contained. Only a trained eye would notice, on the inside, she's ruffled. The problem is, when you operate at Ma Duster level, all enemy eyes observing you are trained. They miss nothing.

"There's been no change."

I nod. "And no philandering that you know about?" I take a sip of my Bloody Mary, knowing full well this question is a test.

"Not that I'm aware of, no."

Since our last girlie chat, I've tasked my driver, Liam, with keeping a watchful eye over Eoin and evidence suggests he's back to sleeping with his PA on a regular basis. But at her apartment now as he's no longer able to do so in his office. I'm sure Molly will be only too aware she's no longer got his undivided attention. Eoin's not exactly being discrete about it. He's also aware Liam's tailing him. I'm surprised he doesn't give him a wave on passing or stop to ask after his family.

Molly isn't stupid. Molly's a liar.

"That's good to know." I ignore the deceit for now. "And are there any signs of him asking to speak with your da privately?"

"I'm still working on that."

"Then you need to work harder, Molly. At any moment Eoin may declare you unsuitable as the future Ma Duster, more so if the novelty has already worn off. He knows given the importance of the role his Da and I would need to take any concerns raised by him extremely seriously. You need to coerce him into speaking to your da by whatever means necessary, and in the meantime, play the role to perfection."

"I'm trying my best, Roisin."

"You need to try harder. Because Jaine Jones has had her baby and her return to New York is imminent." My tone is clipped.

"I know she's had the baby. I overheard her and Eoin on the phone. It was during their heated exchange that Jaine went into labor."

My ears immediately prick up. Molly's never mentioned any of this before. I need to make a mental note that as well as being prone to lying, she's also an eavesdropper.

"You never said."

"I didn't think it relevant."

"What were they arguing about?"

"Dylan's engagement mostly."

"Anything else?"

"She told Eoin he needed to speak to you about something."

"And do you know what that something might have been?"

"He was complaining she hadn't been taking his calls. It's my guess she hasn't because I warned her off. She clearly took the threat seriously. She'll no doubt have mentioned that she had our call recorded. Apparently, she has all her calls recorded."

I take a sip of my drink as I digest this information that Molly's obviously been sitting on for quite some time.

"And you never thought that tidbit of information was something the Dusters should have been made aware of as soon as it was known given the frequency with which she speaks to my boys?"

"I didn't see the importance. She's not stupid. She'll never do anything with the recordings, hence why I never thought to mention it." Molly glances at Sophia for backup, but the Sicilian just stares at her.

"Jaine Jones is far from being stupid, Molly. That's the problem. She's as successful as she is for a reason," I hiss. "And tell me, how did you phrase this threat during this recorded telephone conversation?"

Molly frowns at me. "As we agreed beforehand. I said I had your blessing to tell her to back off from your sons. Which I did."

"So, you mentioned me by name."

"I did."

"And you mentioned the Dusters by name."

"I did."

"And did you add the 'or else' or did she?"

"Jaine did."

"All for the purposes of the recording," I say more to myself than anyone else.

My hands tighten around my glass. Molly should be grateful they're not wrapped around her foolish throat.

"Under no circumstances are you to speak to that manipulative woman again. Not without me or Eoin being party to the conversation."

"But…"

"No, buts. That biker woman has a recording containing a personal threat made against her by me and The Hudson Dusters. She's a legal professional. Do you have any idea what she could do with that? What that could do to our family, to our organization, if that recording ever got out? All threats should be veiled in this life and never blatant. I made myself perfectly clear on that at the time."

"But…"

"I said there are no buts. You do not speak to her again." My tone holds a warning, and one she'd best heed if she knows what's good for her.

"Of course, Roisin."

She sensibly backs down.

"Try to remember exactly what was said. Word for word. Write it down. I want to see it along with any other conversations you've ever had with her. I want to see the extent of them all."

"I'll do my best."

I take another sip of my Bloody Mary. At this rate, I'll finish the entire drink.

"Sophia." I smile at her.

"There's been no change, although I do now have a plan." She smiles saccharinely sweetly.

"Care to share it with the rest of us?"

She shakes her head. "When it's successful, I will let you know."

I smile and nod at her use of the word 'when' and not 'if'.

"Don't worry." She glances at Molly. "*I* will never let Jaine Jones win." She looks determined. I have every confidence she will succeed. At least one of them is on the right path.

Once our Paddy has taken that purity of Sophia's, he'll be lost to that biker woman forever.

CHAPTER FIFTY-THREE

JAINE

Jaine's House, Rising, California

"I'M SORRY."

I'm sat in the same spot I was last time we spoke, but this time I'm not pregnant.

There's no immediate response, which I can fully understand. I've been unbearable for months. Reactive. Argumentative. A complete and utter bitch.

Ace assures me my mood swings have been the stuff of nightmares. I guess I just have to take his word for that.

With Eoin, I wouldn't usually give a damn, but with the Duster big bang looming, I thought I'd best attempt to mend bridges in advance. He is Finian's uncle, after all. Whether I like it or not.

"For?"

"For being difficult to deal with."

He laughs aloud. It's a rare sound, and I find myself chuckling along, as much as I try not to.

"Difficult to deal with? That's something of an understatement, Jaine."

"Turns out I had pre-natal depression, and I didn't realize. Everyone bore the brunt of it. Well, men in the main given it was a dick that got me in that situation in the first place."

"You mean it wasn't the immaculate conception?"

I laugh. "Nope, and little JJ is not Christ reborn either, although he's an absolute angel compared to his big brother at the same age."

"Apology accepted."

"Thank you. Bear in mind it only relates to my short temper over the last few months. I apologize for nothing else."

"It's good to know you still hate me. No, wait. You don't hate me...." I can tell from his tone he's being light-hearted. Who knows, maybe we can get along if we both try.

"Because it takes way too much effort. I'm surprised you remember."

"You're somewhat unforgettable, Jaine."

There's a pause. See, it's comments like this from him that I'm never quite sure how to take.

"I'll be back in Manhattan in three months, give or take. So, not too long now."

"It will be good to see you."

"I can't say the same."

"Charming as ever."

"Nice to know I haven't lost my touch, Mr. O'Connell." There's a smile in my voice, which I'm sure he can hear.

"I've missed you, Jaine."

There's a pause. Yet another comment I'm not sure how to take. He can't mean anything by it, can he? I mean, he's with Molly now. I decide to answer just as truthfully.

"I guess I've sort of missed you too. Not in the traditional sense, but I have missed our exchanges in a fucked-up kind of way. You'll be pleased to know there isn't anyone who can make my blood boil quite like you can."

"Is that so?"

I can tell by his low tone where his mind's going.

"Not like that. You flatter yourself way too much, Eoin." I quickly steer the conversation in a safer direction. "Anyway, I thought you should know that when I return, I'll be making contact with Irish."

There's a pause.

"And do you think that's a good idea?"

"I'm not sure what harm it will do. He'll be married. I'm already married." *Plus, I have no choice.*

"And what will you tell him?"

"The truth."

"So, everything I said and everything I asked of you when I visited you that day."

"Are you suggesting I lie?"

"Not at all. I'm just not sure what good it will do dragging up the past."

"What good it will do you, you mean." I feel myself getting wound up as he shows his true colors once more. That it's always about him. It didn't take long.

"Partly that, yes. And are you going to tell him that you're still in love with him?"

"Not that it's any of your business, but no, I'm not." I snap, cursing myself inwardly for doing so. "It's clear he's moved on," I add much more calmly. I pause. Should I admit what I'm about to?

"I tried to call him."

"I know you did."

There's no delay in his response.

"He didn't pick up."

"I know that too. I told him not to."

"Right… and how did you know?"

I pause at the realization. I mean I knew they were monitored but surely not to that extent.

"You read my message exchanges with Dylan word for word, twenty-four seven, don't you?"

"Yes."

I pause.

"I guess it really is a case of big brother's watching, although I'm not sure I fully understand the need."

"It's for everyone's safety."

"Not for mine."

"It's how I found out about Nevada."

"You were still too late."

"I won't be too late this time around."

"Meaning?"

"Dylan and I are making plans to visit Nevada the week after next to meet with the new MC among other things."

"And is Jessie aware of this intended visit?"

"I haven't spoken to her yet, so it's unlikely. Dylan can't let her know as she has his number blocked apparently."

"I should let her know."

"He may want to see her."

"She may not want to see him."

"I thought we were all wiping the slate clean. He's getting wed."

"To his cliché blonde, Eoin. A woman he's been in love with for years. I'm not sure Jessie needs reminding of that fact, especially when he undertook a sexual relationship with her while already armed with this arranged marriage knowledge."

There's a lengthy pause. Something's going on, and I want to know what that something goddamn is.

"Then I'll leave it with you to let her know. Explain, please, that I'll email her the finer details closer to the time. And to you too, of course."

"Of course." I immediately disconnect the call.

I take it back.

Even if we do try, it's unlikely Eoin O'Connell and I will *ever* get along.

CHAPTER FIFTY-FOUR

DYLAN

Dylan's Apartment, Hudson Yards, New York

WHO KNEW TWO PEOPLE COULD FIND SO MUCH TO MESSAGE ABOUT? I trawl through their exchanges. Not to be nosey. Just to familiarize myself with what they've been discussing recently, so I don't drop the ball when I speak to our Paddy's cliché blonde.

I frown at the lengthy communications between Jaine and him. Exchanges she thinks have been taking place between her and me. I'm not sure why I agreed to be party to all these lies.

Then I remember I did it all for my baby brother.

"Hello, Jaine."

"Why, Dylan O'Connell. You have a voice."

"I do." I laugh.

"What's happened? You never call. Is it something you can't say in a message because big brother's watching?"

"Has he admitted as much now?"

"He has. He says it's for everyone's protection, but he means the Dusters. The asshole doesn't give a damn about me."

"I can assure you that's not the case, Jaine."

If only she knew how much of a damn he actually does give.

"Anyway, I don't want to spoil my good mood talking about him. What's up?"

"Shite. Your calls are recorded, aren't they?" I frown.

"Jesus Christ, news travels fast. Yes, they are, but not on this phone. This is my burner. Only five people have this number."

"But if Eoin can see our exchanges…."

"Good point. Six, then. I'll change it. Or maybe I won't. We don't say anything compromising in our messages, and it will no doubt mess with that big, conceited head of his that even though he knows I have two numbers, I've only given him one, whereas you have both."

"True." I laugh out loud. She knows him so well.

"So, Nevada."

"What about it."

"Are you going to be there?"

There's a pause.

"This is strictly between you and me, Dyl."

"You have my word on that, Jaine."

She exhales. "I was considering it."

"As who?"

"As Robin, of course."

"Very funny." I laugh again.

"I thought so too, Batman. I was thinking as my alter ego. Is that what you wanted me to say?"

"It is. Thank God we're on the same page." I breathe a sigh of relief.

"Well, I figured if the faction backing Reaper wanted to flex their trafficking muscles, then that would be the time to do it. When the Irish are in town."

"So, you'll definitely be there?"

"In the distance, yes. There's one thing I need you to do for me, though."

"Anything at all."

"You need to pick up the bullets."

"Why?" I frown.

"Because it took a long time to convince my clients that I work as a free agent. I say who. I say when. I say how much. I had to shake off the general assumption that I worked exclusively for the Scorpions and not just via them. The last Nevada incident I was able to get away with. It was, after all, the prez of the Scorpions himself who was at risk, so it wasn't entirely unexpected that The Exterminator was on standby to help out an old friend. But this situation isn't an out-and-out hit for hire. There's no price on a head. That's not possible when it's not known which head will receive the engraved bullet, if any. I don't need anyone misreading things and thinking the Scorpions are behind it. I refuse to have the finger of blame pointed at them."

"Won't that just be assumed anyway?"

"No one will act based purely on an assumption, Dyl. That's not how it works. No one will make an enemy and go to war with a top-tier faction without concrete evidence."

"So, you can't be seen to be linked with the Irish?"

"I don't want to be seen to be linked to anyone. It's bad for business. I'm independent. I need to remain so. Plus, if we're linked, that means every time I sink a bullet into some scumbag's head, the Dusters will be held responsible. Is that really what you want?"

She's right, of course.

"Point taken. But can't you just use bullets that aren't engraved?"

"That won't matter. The X is purely for show. Any gun expert would still know. They're unique to my rifle, and it's a one-off."

"Sounds expensive."

"Two million dollars' worth of expensive. Each part is handmade and by several different gunsmiths, so it's completely untraceable."

"What it if stops working?"

"I have three other rifles. All of them unique in their own way."

"So, you're prepared for any eventuality?"

"Always."

There's a pause.

"Thank you, Jaine."

"I would never let anything happen to you, Dyl. Your big brother, on the other hand…"

"Jaine," I warn.

"I'm joking. I would never let anything happen to that pompous asshole either." She chuckles.

"It's good to hear you sounding so chipper."

"That's a Jessie word."

"It is. How is she?"

There's a pause, no doubt as she considers whether to answer that question or not.

"She's doing okay. She'll be moving back to Manhattan when I do. Makes most sense. I'll be working between there and Rising, and she'll be working between there and Colton."

"She's asked the Dusters to consider repurchasing her apartment."

"And I hope you'll do just that. Either that or I will. Listen, Dyl, I'm not taking sides. What's happened has happened. I don't want to lose either of you from my life."

"I appreciate that, Jaine."

I pause once more to consider whether I should even pose the next question, but what have I got to lose?

"About this Tyler fella."

"What about him?"

"Can I ask one thing?"

"You can. What you ask will determine whether I answer or not. Go on."

"Was he important to her in the past?"

"Yes." Her reply is immediate.

"Good to know." Or not, as the case may be.

"I've told her you and Eoin will be paying a visit."

"Ah, well there's been a slight change of plan."

"And that is?"

"Molly will also be tagging along."

"At your ma's insistence?"

"Correct."

"That's fine with me. But let's just be clear on one thing. My alter ego won't be getting involved if she lands herself in any hot water. If your brother has agreed with your ma to bring her along then he can be the one in charge of her safekeeping. Understood?"

"Understood. So, is Jessie looking forward to our visit?"

"You don't want to know the answer to that question."

"I appreciate your honesty, Jaine."

CHAPTER FIFTY-FIVE

JESSIE

Jessie's Family Home, Colton, Nevada

IT'S JUST MY LUCK DYLAN'S STEPPED IN ON BEHALF OF CILLIAN. I mean, what are the chances? Still, it's been months. I can do this, right? It's all water under the bridge now.

How hard can it be to stand in front of the man you're in love with and ask him how he is? Or how he feels about the fact he broke your heart. Or about the fact he misled you and strung you along. Or about the fact he's about to marry that cliché blonde Disney princess of his. You know, the girl he's been in love with his entire life, but still went ahead and fucked you regardless.

And do I offer my congratulations, even if the words stick in my throat?

It's not like I can refuse to attend the meeting. Ty needs me. I can't abandon him in his hour of need, even though he abandoned me the moment he stole my virginity.

Two men. Both mislead me in their own unique way to get into my panties. I mean, they're both just as bad as each other.

Still, Ty needs someone on side to help answer questions on his business plan. This affects the alliance, so it's bigger than him or me.

Or Dylan O'Connell, for that matter.

Ty's an intelligent man but he's a biker. And while he's picking things up quickly, he's no match for the O'Connell brothers. At least not yet. So I have no option but to attend and be his tag-team mate.

But right now, I'd sooner get lost in the desert, be bitten by a scorpion, and then have my dead bones licked clean by a pack of wild coyotes.

I can't help Ty if I'm dead, though. Rock and a hard place? Story of my life.

And what do I wear to a business meeting at an MC clubhouse.

I glance at my leathers and my patched Sons jacket, then smile to myself. I know exactly what I'll wear.

This is a biker town.

And Jessie O'Brien? Well, that girl's a badass biker chick.

I ANSWER THE PHONE TO JAINE JUST AS I'M PUTTING ON MY JACKET.

"You about to set off?"

"Are you checking up on me, partner? I'll be leaving in around ten minutes. Are the Irish there already?"

"They are. They finished their meeting with Rod earlier than expected. I just spoke to him. Well, it was more a case of me listening while he ranted and threatened to back out of the alliance altogether."

"Why?"

"He's convinced Molly lied to him, and that she's trying to play him for a fool as a result."

"Dear Lordy Lou, and did she?"

"I have no way of knowing, Jessie, but to avoid the alliance collapsing in on itself I've had to reassure him that he won't have to deal with her moving forward and that I'll do so on his behalf."

"So, you've created an owing, but this time Eoin O'Connell owes you?"

"You could say that. The difference being, I won't ever call it in."

"Rod said something similar to me, you know but I never gave it much thought." I frown as I try to recall. "That Molly had to have Eoin hold her hand when she first spoke to him. She made an excuse that she'd tried to call previously but had been unsuccessful. I don't think Rod bought it."

"Maybe that's what he's referring to?"

"Who knows, but you and I both know the people in our life don't like being lied to, especially Rod. It's once a liar always a liar with him."

There's a pause.

"Be careful today, Jessie. I don't trust her."

I snort-laugh. "It's not like she'll be able to run rings around me professionally, Jaine."

"I'm being serious, Jessie. Don't under-estimate her. And that's not what I meant. This isn't an office-based meeting. She may well be carrying a weapon, so make sure you're doing the same. Any shit goes down, you call me straight away."

"Where are you anyway? Are you in a cage? Is that road noise I hear in the background."

"It is. I'm just pulling up at my destination now."

"Which is? And should you be out and about? I mean, what about little JJ?"

"I have no option. This is an appointment I need to attend. Ace is home with the kids, don't worry. He needs one-on-one bonding time with them, too. Fin's missed having him around."

"Aww, he must love having his daddy home. Anyway, I didn't make out where you said you were going."

"That's because I didn't."

"Confidential?"

"Extremely so."

I know best not to pry.

"Is everyone waiting for me?"

"Yup, including your daddy and Tadgh. Does your family know about your dalliance with Dyl?"

"They suspect, but I've never told anyone anything apart from Ty. Even then, I never went into any detail, and I never told him which brother it was."

"Well, they're not likely to think it's Eoin given Molly will be there."

"True."

"Are you fucking him?"

"Who, Eoin?"

We both laugh out loud.

"No, Ty."

"No."

"Dyl asked if Ty had been important to you in the past is all. I said yes. I didn't mention he was your first."

"You mean like I was his?"

"Who, Ty's?"

"No, Dyl's."

There's a pause.

"So, Dyl was a virgin?" She sounds surprised.

"Well, that's what he said. Not that anyone would have been able to tell. He pretty much earned that well-deserved title of Dirty

Dylan from the get-go. Why? Do you think he lied to me about that too?"

"No, of course not. I'm just a little shocked, is all, given his age and the fact that his siblings have fucked half of Manhattan."

She sounds distracted. I can almost hear her brain whirring. I'm not too sure I'm buying into this reply of hers.

"Anyway, I'd best go and not keep them waiting."

"Jessie."

"Yes, partner?"

"Any problem, you call me straight away."

"Yes, Mom! You've said that already. Are you expecting there to be any?"

"Nope, but that's typically when it comes calling. My phone's right beside me. You so much as sniff trouble, you let me know."

"Will do. Listen, I've really got to go, Jaine."

"Later."

The Ghost Whisperers' Clubhouse, Colton, Nevada

It's been just over twenty-four hours since I was last here and, in that time, the perimeter fencing has been fully erected with just a space left for where the entrance gates will hang. Like most other clubhouses, they'll be electric, connected to the security system and keypad entry so the numbers can be changed every other day. It's Saturday, so they probably won't be fitted now until next week.

Everyone's standing outside as I approach. When I say everyone, I mean the people I'm meeting. The clubhouse isn't ready for outlaw party time just yet. Give it a week or so, and I'm sure some biker will christen the place by fucking a cum slut over the pool table.

Most likely Ghost himself.

Swinging my hog through the gap in the fence it roars toward the front of the building kicking up a trail of dust into the air as it does.

Having acknowledged me with a single nod, Eoin continues his conversation with my daddy and brother.

Molly doesn't even glance in my direction. She's wearing a business suit and standing out like a sore thumb. I watch as she tries to inject herself into the menfolk's conversation. Does she not realize that bikers are chauvinist pigs? That they seldom, if ever, listen to a female?

I kick down the stand on my hog, switch off the purring engine and take in Dylan covertly through my closed visor.

It's been months. He looks different, somehow. More worldly-wise. Maybe he's started living life and stopped hiding away in that apartment of his. His hair's gotten too long again. It's curling over the neck of the white short-sleeved Henley that's gracing his toned torso. My eyes drift down to take in the dark blue denim caressing his slim hips before shifting to his face. Strong pale features, pouty lips that don't belong on any man, and familiar eyes of sapphire blue. He looks good. Too good.

Jaw-droppingly good.

And that tongue of his? That tongue that's licked every inch of my naked body. Well, it's almost hanging out of his mouth right now at the sight of me clothed head to toe in skintight black leather.

I step off the hog. My four-inch black stiletto boots making me the same height as both Ty and Dylan.

Removing my full helmet, I shake my long blonde hair free as they both watch on.

"Ty." I nod at him, and he nods back. I take in the man I've been spending a lot of time with lately. The jury's still out on whether I want to go back for seconds given what he plated up first time around. His hair is pulled back at the nape of his neck, and his black eyes pierce into my blue ones. He looks good in black jeans and a black Henley with his prez cut thrown over the top.

"Dyl."

I nod at him, and he nods back.

I walk across and stand in front of both, letting them have their fill before speaking further.

"I figure you two boys will have been introduced formally, so let me do the informal introductions."

I smirk at Dylan. "I gave Ty here my virginity when I was sweet sixteen. He dumped me the very next day, then proceeded to fuck his way through the rest of the girls in Colton that he'd also led on."

I then smirk at Ty. "I fucked Dyl for the last time three months ago, give or take. He then remembered he clean forgot to mention he'd been entered into an arranged marriage to take the vows with the love of his life. Convenient or not? I'll leave that up to you boys to decide. Me? Well, I've already reached my own conclusions. Oh, and feel free to compare notes. You both already know that I like to be the center of attention, and that my aim in life is never to be forgotten."

I smile widely, patting each on the shoulder as I walk past.

"I'll see you boys inside," I shout out as I enter the clubhouse, fully aware I have two sets of eyes trained on my ass.

CHAPTER FIFTY-SIX

DYLAN

The Ghost Whisperers' Clubhouse, Colton, Nevada

I HAVE NEVER SEEN ANYTHING SO PERFECT AS JESSIE O'BRIEN riding that hog of hers into the compound then parking up.

Actually. No. I take that back. What happened next topped that.

Knowing full well she was being admired, Ghost and I watched as she slowly dismounted, took off her helmet, shook her long blonde hair free, then walked over to us like she was on a Paris catwalk, all the while dressed head to toe in skintight black leather.

I'm not ashamed to say I was rocking a hard-on at having witnessed such a spectacle.

Now I get it.

Now I understand how my siblings feel. I've never seen Jaine or Sarah dressed in all their biker finery, but if they look anything like Jessie does, then it's no wonder my brothers are hook, line, and sinkered for these dominatrix-looking females.

If Jessie asked me to lick her boots right now, I'd be on my hands and knees in a flash.

I'm not sure what I want more. Her asking me to strip bollock naked so she can walk all over me in her stiletto heels or me stripping her of everything save those fucking boots, throwing her face down on my bed, tilting up her slim hips, and sinking my dick in to the hilt.

I'll take any of the above. Even better. All of it.

It had an almost dream-like quality about it until she opened that mouth of hers, reminding me that she thinks I'm a louse for not telling her about the arranged marriage. Then letting me know that the man standing beside me was her first ever fuck, and that he too was a louse for dumping her the very next day.

The only saving grace is we're each of us a louse in our own unique way. So, he's deemed no better than me.

Still, the easy camaraderie he and I instantly shared vanished. We immediately became each other's competition. But then I'm in no position to compete because the woman I love who may or may not love me back can't ever be mine. Why? Because my ma and da say so, that's why. Because all of us siblings have to toe the Duster line.

It still doesn't stop jealousy from coursing through me as I watch her walk away, staring at her perfect backside caressed in tight-fitting black leather and with a Glock shoved in the waistband, knowing that Ghost's doing the same thing.

He's been there. And first. Not that being her first matters. I'd much rather be her last. But I can't have that either.

I want to wrap my hands around his throat and choke the fucker, but that won't be good for business. And in his defense, I'm pretty sure the feeling's mutual. In fact, going by the look in his black eyes, I know it is.

He has one thing in his favor. He's currently unattached. So, I'd say may the best man win, but there's only one man in the running.

I want to punch something. That life can be so unfair it lets me have perfection such as her for all of five minutes, then steals her away again.

And just you wait. She'll become his old lady. And as part of the alliance and for the rest of my days, I'll have to put up with updates from him telling me how great it is to be married to her and telling me all about their adventurous sex life in glorious technicolor detail.

It's called rubbing it in.

It would have been far easier to deal with a nameless, faceless person. Now, I'll be living our Paddy's fucking nightmare all over again.

It's my own fault. It's shitty karma for getting involved in all the lies and deceit with Jaine.

I stare around the place, wondering where she is. There are only a few places out front where she could build her nest and not be seen. Hiding places are plentiful to the back, though, as we're not too far from where the ground starts to rise into the mountains.

Then again, I'm not sure about the range of that two-million-dollar rifle of hers. At that price and knowing Jaine's skill set, she could likely fire that thing from her front room in Rising and still hit a fucker square in the skull while sipping on a cup of tea.

I WATCH AS JESSIE COMMANDS THE FLOOR LIKE SHE USED TO IN OUR weekly meetings, co-coordinating everyone to a mutually beneficial agreement for all concerned.

"All in favor, raise your hand."

All hands are raised.

"Welcome aboard, Ghost Whisperers."

Lots of handshakes, back slaps, and smiles. But I'm not smiling.

Jealousy flows through me as I watch her congratulate Ghost. Opening her arms wide, she then throws them around his neck. In response, he wraps his inked ones around her slim waist. I watch as he deliberately drops one down slightly, so it's resting right at the top of her backside. The fucker's trying to cop a feel. If it goes any lower, so help me God, I'll hack the fucking thing off, alliance or not.

Let's see him grope her arse then.

"Grace is a better match."

I don't even look at Molly.

"And what makes you say that?"

"She's the same as you."

"I've changed, or haven't you noticed, Molly? I'm nothing like Grace. Not anymore."

"I don't mean that. What I mean is she's a mobster, not a biker."

I turn to look at her. "And what problem do you have with bikers? Are you saying you don't find Ghost or Lucifer or Tadgh agreeable?"

"I don't have an issue with them per se. It's Roisin who has an issue with them."

I nod. "You're right. Ma does have an issue with bikers, but she has more of a problem with Jaine, and we both know why. It's the only reason you're here. Given we're in her neck of the woods, it's to make sure she doesn't make a move on the elder of the two interested parties which is unlikely given she hates Eoin's guts."

"She needs to stay away from Eoin. From both of them."

"Good luck with trying to make Jaine Jones do anything she doesn't want to." I smirk.

"Trust me, I'm not the one who needs the luck." She smiles knowingly at me.

Is that a veiled threat towards Jaine? I stare at her retreating back as my phone vibrates in my pocket.

Speak of the devil.

Jaine: *What are you up to?*

Dylan: *I'm in Nevada. Are you at home?*

Jaine: *Yup. Sat on the front porch. I think some visitors just pulled up in a cage.*

She's trying to be discrete, so Eoin doesn't catch on that she's local and watching. We all spin around just as the doors to the clubhouse get flung open.

CHAPTER FIFTY-SEVEN

JESSIE

The Ghost Whisperers' Clubhouse, Colton, Nevada

"WELL, WHAT DO WE HAVE HERE? IS THIS A PRIVATE PARTY, OR CAN anyone join in?"

I take in the three dark-haired men who have stormed the clubhouse.

"Juan, Luis, Carlos. What the fuck are you guys doing here?" Ty glares at his uninvited guests.

"Now, Ghost, is that any way to greet old friends?" Juan or Luis or Carlos responds.

I suspect, given their overall appearance combined with the fact they're not Colton townsfolk, that these unwelcome visitors are the Colombians—friends, my eye.

Silence follows. No one speaks as everyone assesses the situation. This is not good. Not good at all.

What the hell are they doing here?

Thinking on my feet, I decide to use my stereotypical dumb blonde act as the opener before whatever main event it is that their planning.

Hopefully a headliner that won't see us all getting killed.

"Any friend of Ghost is a friend of mine, boys," I announce as I stroll over to them, adding a little sashay to my leather-clad hips as I do. "Allow me to introduce myself. My name's Jessie. And you must be…."

I look at the stocky one first. He's a whole head shorter than me with olive skin and a black buzzcut. He's forgettable-looking. I guess that's deliberate. That it's to make him less identifiable in a line-up.

"Juan." I take a stab at his name while adding a fake giggle.

"Good guess, beautiful lady."

I hold out my hand. He places a slimy kiss on the back as his eyes roam my figure, missing nothing. I almost feel violated. I force another fake giggle while making a mental note to bleach my hand. Given his unwelcome leer, I may do the same thing to my body.

"So, by process of elimination, that makes you Luis or Carlos. Well, eeny, meeny, miny, moe. I'm going to go with Luis." I do the same, but this time with the other hand. Luis doesn't speak. He simply nods as he shakes it. Again, the same overall appearance. Again, no doubt for the same reason. To blend in. He's tall and slim and around my height with my boots on.

"And that leaves Carlos."

This last goon is a combination of the other two. Tall but overweight and sporting the same regimented haircut. I don't bother offering my hand.

"Allow me to introduce you boys to everyone. You obviously know Ghost. Well, this here is Lucifer, Tadgh, Eoin, Dylan, and Molly."

I make eye contact with each of them, silently asking them to let me handle this for now. My main concern? I'm surrounded by Irish blood.

Reactive. Argumentative. Murderous when poked with a Colombian stick.

And I think we need to keep the peace for now. At least until we can figure out what the hell these guys want. Because it's my guessing they've dropped in knowing full well the Irish were going to be here.

"Now that the introductions are out of the way and we're all the best of friends, can I ask what we've done to be blessed with your presence this Saturday evening? Maybe you boys are looking for a little live entertainment."

I raise an eyebrow while running my finger down Juan's black wifebeater, only stopping when I reach his navel.

"Well, aren't you a feisty little one?" He laughs and I try not to grimace when his toxic breath reaches my nose.

"What, little old me? Feisty?" I fake giggle once more. "Not at all. I'm just the first cum slut the prez has taken on. I figured he wanted a little taste before anyone else got their hands on me, but I'm more than happy to work the room."

"Maybe later." Luis is firm with his friend as he eyes me up and down. He clearly likes what he sees, even though he's trying to play hard to get. Carlos remains motionless. He's obviously just a heavy with only enough brain cells to allow him to walk, stand, and breathe.

"Sure thing, lover boy."

My role is cemented. I'm now just a cum slut, so no one of any importance in their eyes, which means I'll be ignored from here on in. Goal achieved.

I turn around and wink at Ty and he immediately takes over. This really wasn't the tag teaming I had in mind, but needs must.

"What are you doing here, Juan?"

"We heard you had some friends visiting and thought we'd drop by to introduce ourselves. We figured it would be rude not to."

"Cut the bullshit and just get to the point of the visit."

Juan's smile vanishes at the unfriendliness in Ty's tone. Not that it was ever real in the first place.

"We heard the Irish were coming to town. So, our mutual friends asked us to drop by to personally deliver a message. They wanted to let you know that they won't take kindly to their toes being stepped on. They are, however, receptive to all of us working together as part of a new alliance."

Ty rolls his eyes. He's no doubt heard all of this before. "There's nothing mutual about them. I have no idea who your friends are, and you damn well know it. And I've already told you. I'm not interested in anything they have to offer. No one here is."

"They don't want competition on their turf, Ghost. They want to pick things back up where they left off. They're asking that you reconsider their offer. This is the last time they'll be making it."

"Are you deaf or something? *I said* I'm not interested."

My daddy steps forward. "Listen, son."

"I'm not your son."

Juan obviously doesn't appreciate that figure of speech.

My daddy ignores his response. "As the standing prez of the Undertakers, let me assure you there is no way on God's green earth that club will ever get involved in trafficking. Not now. Not ever."

Juan nods his head in the direction of Eoin before addressing him direct. "And what about the Irish? It's a very lucrative proposition. Will you join with us?"

What feels like an endless silence follows. I swear I can feel the temperature drop in the room. Given the heat in Nevada, normally, I'd be appreciative. But today?

I'd rather tolerate the heat and live to see another day.

Eoin walks slowly over to Juan as the rest of us look on. He then proceeds to circle him like a lion stalking its prey. After what feels like forever, he leans forward from behind the Colombian.

"If you so much as mention the word trafficking in my presence and in the same breath ask the Dusters to get involved, I'll rip you into tiny pieces with my bare fucking hands." The threat is a low whisper in Juan's ear.

There's a pause.

Yup. Eoin O'Connell is going to get us all killed here today.

The Colombian now looks like he's about to shit his pants. I guess he's heard all about the Irishman's bloodthirsty reputation.

Juan's eyes dart from side to side. He's thinking. It's clear he can't decide what to do next. Call Eoin's bluff or not. Meanwhile, Eoin is standing right behind him, exuding so much raw power and dark presence it's blanketing the entire room and making it difficult to breathe.

We're witnessing the future Irish king in all his mobster glory.

I look at Dylan. He's staring proudly at his big brother—the future leader of his family's organization. If he survives today, that is. If any of us do.

I'm not family, but I was allowed to be part of their inner sanctum, even if it was only temporary. Seeing Eoin 'at work' right now, I realize he's simply been born into a role.

Same as Tadgh.

They may dress differently, but both have the same duty to perform. And one they were given no choice but to undertake and fulfill.

I finally get it. Why their lives are dictated to in so many ways. It's because they have to produce heirs that can be as strong and as fearless as Eoin is being right now.

"Well." Eoin's threatening voice breaks my trance. I find myself still staring at Dylan, but now he's staring at me too.

"It's a very lucrative offer."

Juan is persistent, I'll give him that. Maybe he has a death wish.

"Are you asking me to get involved in trafficking?" Eoin emphasizes each word.

"Not me. The people I work for."

"Is that a yes?" he hisses.

The Colombian closes his eyes. Beads of sweat form on his upper lip even though it's relatively cool in here now. He's fully aware his next word could well be his last.

"Yes."

In the blink of an eye, Eoin grabs Carlos's head between his hands and forearms and snaps his neck. The heavy didn't stand a chance. He didn't even have time to react.

No one did.

He then turns, his expression loaded with deadly menace as he looks between the other two Colombians. "Who's next?" He smirks.

Luis, the one with no sense of humor, responds by sticking a gun in his ribs.

"You shouldn't have done that, *amigo*. We didn't come here to fight you." Juan starts pacing the floor.

"Bullshit. You did exactly that!" Eoin hisses back. "Who told you we'd be here? No one knew. Aside from the people present and a handful of trusted individuals, no one knew the Dusters would be here today."

Juan snickers as he wipes the sweat from his top lip with the back of his hand. "The people I work for are extremely powerful. They have eyes and ears everywhere. They see everything. They hear everything. They know everything."

Two at a time, Juan pulls the half dozen bar stools into the middle of the room. Luis shoves Eoin down onto one before binding his wrists with tape he's pulled from his pocket. Obviously, this is an everyday event for him.

"They wanted to make their presence felt. To make an example of you to others if you dared decline their offer of an alliance," Juan continues.

"An example of us."

"Yes. As a warning to those who would dare disrespect them or challenge their position."

"The other one." He motions to Luis, and I watch as he grabs Dylan's arm and pulls him across to sit beside his older brother. He doesn't put up a struggle. There's no point. It will only antagonize them, and he'll end up dead quicker.

"Bind the other men. Leave the slut. We may have a use for her later. We may even take her with us." Juan issues his instructions as he leers at me once more.

I can instantly feel the surge of testosterone fill the room, all ready to take offense on my behalf. To stop them from taking me anywhere. To prevent them from passing me around like a fuck toy before trafficking me. But they remain silent. They're not stupid. They realize I may be their only hope.

"Leave the other female too. She's just a secretary. She's no threat."

Under other circumstances, I would have laughed aloud. I don't. Because at least I won't be the only one not bound.

While Luis is binding the menfolk, I glance at Molly. She looks like a rabbit caught in the headlights. I thought this shit came naturally to her. That it was in her mobster blood. That she had killed. Then again, her victims were likely led to her like lambs to the slaughter. All she had to do was pull the trigger.

Given how hard she's shaking in her stiletto heels, I'm not sure she'll be of much use this evening. Then again, I'm not sure what good I'll be either. I mean, I have a weapon, but I'm a shit shot. I immediately regret not being more invested in target practice growing up. By all accounts, my mom was a great shot, but neither Tadgh nor I inherited her natural talent.

I walk across to Molly.

"Pretend to cry," I murmur She looks at me like I've finally gone insane. Her expression then changes as realization dawns. That beggars can't be choosers. That we're all each other's got right now. That we're all the others have too. She then does as I've asked and starts to fake sob quietly. I put my arms around her as a show of comfort. At the same time, I pull the Glock from beneath my jacket and pass it to her behind my back. She grabs hold.

I'm hoping she's a better shot than me, and that the gun's better off in her hands. I glance around, looking for any other weapon.

It's then I remember them. The katanas. Are they still hanging on the wall? I don't look. If they are, I don't want to draw attention to them.

Silence. The men are seated and bound, and Molly and I are sitting on the sidelines watching.

The two Colombians are now talking in hushed whispers. While they're distracted, Dylan deliberately catches my attention. I look at him.

Does he want me to go over?

"I think my friend has an itch, and I'm just going to scratch that for him." I smile and look at our captors while trying to portray the dizziest blonde God ever put breath in. They're bound. I can't release them, so what threat can I possibly pose? My dumb blonde act works.

Juan nods reluctantly.

I walk over to Dyl, leaning forward so my ear is close to his mouth. His lips touch my skin. His breath is hot.

It may be precisely the wrong place. It may be precisely the wrong time. But I want that fucking mouth of his on me. He chuckles in my ear. He knows exactly where my thoughts are going.

"We can fuck when we get out of here," he whispers.

My insides instantly turn molten. Well, we're getting out of here, that's for sure. Because Jessie O'Brien?

She's on a promise.

CHAPTER FIFTY-EIGHT

JESSIE

The Ghost Whisperers' Clubhouse, Colton, Nevada

"Pick up any bullets."

I frown at him.

"If any shots get fired, I need you to find the bullets and pick them up."

I nod slowly. It seems a bit of a strange request. But if I can, I will. I'm not sure of the importance. Maybe he has a collection going on. Maybe he's geekier than any of us realized.

Bullets. Stamps. Who knows what else?

Walking away, I retake my seat beside Molly. Having glanced at the wall on the way back, I know the katanas are still hanging there. Hopefully not fake and hopefully very sharp.

More silence follows. More hushed whispers. Juan takes a call. A hushed conversation follows. He nods several times before he disconnects.

"We may proceed." It's directed at Luis.

Proceed with what exactly? I watch as the two Colombians drag the other men away from Eoin and Dylan. What the fuck is going on? Then it dawns on me. They're singling the Irishmen out.

We watch as Juan switches his phone back on.

"Good evening, amigos, amigas."

Is he going to live stream whatever it is they're about to do to the faction behind all of this? Are there women involved too?

"As you can see, we have successfully secured both Irishmen. Unfortunately, they have declined your very generous offer to ally. As such, we will now be proceeding with Plan B."

"Luis? Juan? What the fuck are you going to do?" Ty struggles against his bindings, but there's no point. He'll never be able to free himself. His MC isn't even fully operational, and the grim reaper's already paid one visit to his door. It looks like he's about to knock again.

Twice.

It's the story of the outlaw life.

"What do you think we're going to do, Mr. Grayson?"

"You're going to slaughter them in cold blood?"

"Just as they did with Carlos. An eye for an eye. Our instructions are to end both their lives."

"Jesus Christ. Why?"

Juan shrugs. "It's simple. If they refuse to be part of our plans, they will get in the way of them."

My heart pounds in my chest as they approach Dylan. He gives no flicker of emotion. But then he's a Duster. He won't give the Colombians the satisfaction.

I watch as Juan points the phone in his direction and Luis walks towards him with the loaded gun.

He's not fucking dying. Not today. Not tomorrow. Not ever on my watch. I stand and pretend to smooth down my leathers, smiling innocently when both Colombians glance in the direction of the only-good-for-one-thing cum slut before continuing with what they're about to do.

Murder Dylan O'Connell in cold blood.

Turning to face the wall, I gently lift down one of the katanas, then, holding it behind my back, I walk slowly towards Dylan and Luis.

The Colombians pay me no mind. To them, I'm no threat. I'm just a fuck toy. A walking, talking trio of holes.

I unsheathe the blade as quietly as I can, swallowing thickly as I do.

Uma, I hope I make you proud.

All eyes are now on me. Well, I'll fucking take it. Even now. When I'm surely about to die for being a fool with a death wish brandishing what's likely a toy Samurai sword above my head.

The Colombians are so shocked they don't even react.

"DIE, YOU MOTHERFUCKER!"

I spin the blade, welcoming the familiar sound as it cuts through the air while silently praying to The Almighty that it's not a fake and that it won't immediately snap on contact. Which, let's face it, given my run of luck, is most likely.

The Lord answers my prayers for once as when it connects with the Colombian's neck, it slices clean through. It's followed by an almost slow-motion moment where his head topples to the floor, and his decapitated corpse starts spurting blood like a geyser.

All over me. All over Dylan.

The blood is quickly followed by bodily fluids and the resultant stench of shit fills the air. Adrenaline flows through me, and with the blade held back in position, I spin to take on the other goon. He's moved. Our friend Juan is now standing behind Eoin, one hand holding a gun to the Irishman's temple, the other clasping the recording device.

A shot rings out.

We all turn in the direction of where the sound came from to see Molly staring down at the Glock in her hand. Did she fire it? She must have as the Colombian is now flat on his back on the floor with a bullet hole in the center of his forehead, right between two very lifeless eyes.

Well, I'll be damned—credit where credit's due. I didn't think Molly had it in her, but it seems I was wrong.

"The bullet, Jessie."

Broken from my trance, I turn my attention back to Dylan and frown.

"The bullet," he hisses at me.

Well, thank you for saving my life, Jessie. You're more than welcome, Dylan.

Then I remembered what he asked. I nod. I can see it on the floor among the Colombian's liquified brains. While Molly starts unbinding everyone, I pick it up as discreetly as I can and put it in my pocket. I'm guessing now's not the time to be asking questions.

"Jessie." A New York accent with the perfect lilt of Irish.

I'm conscious of a pair of arms wrapping around my waist from behind, and I close my eyes and lean back into his embrace.

I've missed him.

He slowly turns me around, and my eyes drink in the man with eyes of sapphire blue who, like me, is covered from head to toe in the life blood of others.

"You saved my life, Jessie."

I shrug nonchalantly, a smile playing on my lips. "Well, you know. It's all in a day's work when you're an accountant."

He laughs out loud as he wraps his arms around me once more before pulling me tight against him.

Closing my eyes, I inhale the familiar citrus notes of his body wash mixed with the metallic stench of blood. When I open them, I take in the visual of Eoin looking down tenderly at Molly.

She's saved his life today. Well, good for her. Maybe I got her all wrong. I reckon after that display he'll commit now and marry her as soon as possible.

Result for her. None for me. My saving Dylan will make no difference to our fate.

I frown as I look from where Molly was standing to Juan's corpse. I don't know how she managed it from where she was standing, but aside from the deceased, she was the only person in the room with a gun in their hands, so it must have been her.

A miracle shot indeed.

"Let's go." I grab Dylan's hand and start pulling him towards the door. I figure the others can clean up the bloody mess—fair's fair.

"Where are we going?"

"Your hotel. You been on a hog before?"

"No."

"Well, you'd best prepare yourself, Dyl, as you're about to ride bitch."

Motel, Colton, Nevada

"Slumming it, I see."

A double bed and a unit holding up a TV. That's about it.

Still, it's clean if the overwhelming smell of Lysol is anything to go by, even if the wallpaper is peeling in places and the carpet is almost threadbare.

He slams the door closed behind us before kneeling, yanking off my boots, then standing back up. I'm struggling to breathe as his mouth instantly devours mine. I guess almost dying makes you flick the bird at everything.

Arranged marriages. Lies. Deceit. Morals. Principles.

You know, all the everyday stuff.

None of those matter. At least, not right now. All that matters is the adrenaline flavor of Dylan O'Connell exploding on the tip of my tongue.

"It's all they had. And at least it has a bed," he whispers hotly against my lips.

"The minimum requirement for it to be classed as a bedroom. Maybe you should build a Duster establishment here in Colton."

"And maybe you should hush your noise, Jessie O'Brien."

He picks me up, and I instinctively wrap my legs around his waist. We rode here on my hog using the back roads as we're both covered head to toe in Colombian blood.

Will the others wonder where we've gone? Maybe. Will they wonder what we're doing? Probably not.

"Where are we going?" I mumble against his lips.

"Shower."

It's a walk-in. And that's what we do. Fully clothed. He turns the water on full. It cascades down us both as we hurriedly strip, parting our hungry mouths as little as possible. I struggle with my leathers. In the end, he has to kneel under the steady stream of water and pull the clingy material down my legs, along with my panties.

He growls as he runs his fingers through my folds. I'm soaked. And it's not from the shower. Standing, he picks me up. I anchor my legs around him, and he thrusts deep. We stay there. Connected. As one. I can feel his dick pulsing inside me where it belongs.

The perfect fit.

He sucks on my neck bruising my skin before pulling out and pushing back in. Water pours down. Over us. Between us. Washing away the layer of blood as he fucks me hard against the shower wall. My back hurts, and my legs ache trying to stay anchored around him, but none of that matters either. All that matters is the feel of his huge cock inside me, the painful grip of his fingers as he holds me in place, and his tongue in my mouth. Filling it possessively. Tasting every inch. Claiming it as his.

And it *is* his. It will always be fucking his. Every part of me belongs to him.

He angles me so his groin bangs against my clit with every thrust. I feel dizzy. Delirious. Full. Fucked. And I am. Well and truly fucked.

In more ways than one.

"I'm going to come, Jessie."

He can't hold on. His thrusts are erratic as he loses all sense of control.

Pounding. Harder. Faster. Deeper.

He growls and curses as he embraces the first licks of his pleasure, and the animalistic sounds he makes as he does push me over the edge. I shatter around him, my walls clenching his dick so tight its veins and ridges will be forever imprinted.

Never forgotten.

His fingers dig in further. Bruising my skin as he fills me completely, and in return, I milk him dry.

We stand there under the steady flow of water until it turns cold. Then he lowers me to the floor, and we wash each other off using his citrus body wash.

We lie there in the lumpy bed, having only slept a few hours.

Dawn is breaking. The blinds are down, but the soft orange glow still manages to steal from the darkness that surrounds us, a reminder that it's the start of a new day. A reminder that it's time to move on. My head is on his chest, listening to his heartbeat. It's a sound I never thought I'd get to hear again.

"Jessie, I…."

I raise my head and press a finger to his lips. "I'll listen, but on one condition. We don't talk about the past. We don't talk about the future. Because whether we want one or not, we can't have one. We also don't talk about feelings. Because if we don't have a future then they're irrelevant. They won't change anything. Instead, we can talk about the here and the now. That's it."

He nods. It's followed by a deafening silence.

It's confirmation he was going to talk about one of the now-banned topics so I'm glad I got in there first because there really is no point.

It also speaks volumes. Because the silence is confirming what I already know. What we both already know. That we have no future

Our paths are mapped, or at least his is, which means mine is too.

As much as I want it more than anything in the world, Dylan O'Connell is not mine. Dylan O'Connell can never be mine. And this really is our last hurrah. A reaction to everything that happened. A physical release. Nothing more. Because it can't ever be anything more.

Because his silence is also proof paramount there's nothing more he's able to give.

CHAPTER FIFTY-NINE

DYLAN

Motel, Colton, Nevada

WHAT'S THERE TO SAY? NOTHING.

Because she's right. I could bring up the past. But all that will do is drag up things we can't change, so what's the point? I could pretend we have a future, but we both know we don't.

There is only the here and now. There is only the present. And my gift is Jessie O'Brien one last time.

I roll her over, pinning her down with my body weight, and she groans her appreciation.

Rubbing my nose against hers, I push my hips between her thighs. I can already feel her heat—her wetness. My dick rubs against her. It's already rock hard.

She positions herself so my cock's lined up.

She doesn't want to wait. I don't either. We spent a long time waiting. Too long. I rub the blunt head of my dick up and down, coating myself in her slickness as my mouth finds hers. She groans against my lips, and I answer by thrusting my tongue into her mouth, tasting her sweetness, never wanting to forget her. My tongue dances with hers as she fills my mouth back in her silent response.

We stop. Staring into each other's eyes, our souls connect one final time. Breathing against each other's lips, I sink into her willing flesh. She groans her pleasure, and I swallow it.

It's mine. Only mine. For now, at least.

I curse against her lips as her walls tighten around my shaft.

Tight. Hot. Wet.

I pause, relishing in the perfect fucking fit of her pussy around my thick dick as it welcomes me back home for the last time.

Because it is my home. *She* is my home. I know that. But I can't say that aloud because it won't change a thing.

I pull out and push back in. Her walls grip me possessively, and I growl my approval as she claims my cock as hers. My thrusts are slow and deep. Her skin moistens, and her breaths get shorter as she nears her release.

I pant against her neck as I fuck her, determined to take all the time in the world. To make this last as long as possible. Our last time. But Jessie has other ideas.

Her walls tighten around me like a vice, so my length is trapped. Then she rolls us over so she's straddling me.

Then I'm met with the perfect visual that is Jessie O'Brien riding my dick.

She grinds, and she rocks, and I struggle to hold back as I watch her chase her pleasure.

"I need you to come all over my cock, Jessie."

She leans over and presses her finger against my lips. She doesn't want words. She doesn't want me to say anything that will disturb this perfect moment. That will break this trance we're both captured in.

Her movements quicken. I know she's close. Holding on to her hips, I raise mine to meet hers.

Hard. Deep. Fast.

Her head is thrown back as she matches each thrust, flesh slaps against flesh, and the furniture in the room vibrates against the floor at our ruthless pace.

And then she shatters. And it's the most beautiful sight in the world as her lips part and her eyes dilate as she claims her release and her wetness coats my shaft.

She grinds those gripping walls of hers around me one final time, and I'm done for.

I can't breathe. I can't speak. I can only feel the intensity of my own pleasure. I growl my satisfaction as I bury myself so deep inside her there's surely no part that isn't coated with my cum.

She is mine. I am hers. Every inch of her smells of me. Every inch of me smells of her. It's how it was always meant to be

I want no other fucker to ever touch her. But it's not my choice. And it's not her choice either.

Because right now is merely a small snapshot in a far bigger picture. We both know that.

WHO NEEDS TO ENJOY THE AFTERGLOW ANYWAY?

Having just charged my phone, I sit bolt upright as I take in the timing of the last message on the exchange with Jaine last night.

Padraig: *Who was it, darlin'?*

There's nothing afterward. No more messages. No missed calls. Nothing. It's not a good sign. Not at all.

"Where's the bullet, Jessie?"

"It's in the pocket of my leather pants. Let me fetch it."

"Fuck. Fuck. Fuck." I grimace at the screen before squeezing my eyes tightly shut and throwing my head back against the pillow.

"What, again?" She chuckles, and I can't help but smile. "Give me a few minutes and I'll be good to go." I'm joking. Well, half-joking at least.

She passes me the bullet that went clean through the head of the short Colombian before crawling back into bed beside me.

"I have to say I was impressed by Molly. Your brother will be rushing her down the aisle after she saved his ass. I didn't think she had it in her."

"She didn't. She hasn't."

Jessie frowns at me. "What do you mean? I know everyone was carrying a weapon, but she was the only person with their hands not taped up."

I pass her the bullet, and she studies it.

"Yup. It's a bullet. A pretty one, but a bullet all the same. It's not one I'd use, but…."

She shrugs and passes it back to me.

"Whose gun did Molly have?"

"Mine."

"And what did you just say?"

"It's not one I would use… shit." She sits up and kneels beside me. "It wasn't fired from my Glock, was it? Let me see that." She snatches it back from my hand, a frown marring her forehead.

"Well, I'll be damned. It's got an X engraved on it."

"And what does that tell you, Jessie?"

"That he's real." She stares at me in shocked disbelief.

"The Exterminator is real. Yes."

"And he's the one who saved Eoin's life?"

"Yes."

"So, it wasn't Molly?"

"Correct. That girl can't shoot for shite. She discharged the weapon as we all heard the gun go off, but her bullet likely wound up in the floor or the ceiling. We should be grateful she didn't accidentally end one of our lives."

"But she took full credit?"

"You sound surprised. Of course she did. She was always going to, and she will continue to until someone proves otherwise."

"But how did The Exterminator know we'd be there? From the MC side, no one knew the meeting was taking place apart from those present and a few trusted others. Who knew your side?"

I shrug. "Family members only as far as I'm aware."

"Do you think The Exterminator was responsible for telling the traffickers the Dusters would be there?"

I shake my head. "Why would he do that then save Eoin's life?"

Her frown deepens. "Who was then?"

"That's something we'll have to figure out."

She pauses and studies my face. I can tell the moment she puts two and two together.

"You know him, don't you? The sniper? You know who he is. You told him where we would be. That's why you wanted me to pick up the bullet."

"I do. And I did." I smirk.

"Are you able to tell me who he is?"

"No can do. Their identity is a closely guarded secret. They would have to tell you themselves or let me know it was okay for me to. It's not my secret to spill. Not unless I want one of these in my own head." I toss the bullet in the air and catch it again.

"But Eoin and Molly?"

I frown. "That's the only fly in the ointment. I'm convinced

Eoin was planning on telling my parents she isn't cut out to be Ma Duster, but I reckon he'll be rethinking that given he'll think she saved his life."

"You need to do something."

"Like what? I can't break a promise, Jessie. The secret's not mine to share."

"But…"

"There are no buts. I've held onto this for a long time and from most of my family."

"Most? So, someone else knows?"

"Yes. One of my other brothers."

"Which one?"

"I can't tell you that either."

She gnaws on her lip. I can tell she has a host of questions but realizes I won't be able to answer any.

"But why the need to remove the bullet?"

"The sniper didn't want to be linked because it wasn't an out-and-out hit for hire. It would look like they were an ally of the Irish. We can't afford that, and neither can they. No bullet equals no proof."

"So, they're a friend of the family only two of you know about."

"Something like that."

"But can't you just tell Eoin it was the work of The Exterminator?"

"The marksman doesn't want anyone to know, Jessie, and Eoin would want to brag. You know what he's like. That the sniper had thought him so important he had gone out of his way to save his conceited arse, and without him even needing to ask. Nope. If The Exterminator chooses to tell him or wants me to, that's up to him Anyway, Molly will say I'm making it up. That I'm trying to discredit her even though she knows it wasn't her."

"So, she may already suspect it was the sniper?"

"Well, she'll know for sure it wasn't her. But as there's no proof, she'll happily take credit if it means securing her place at the head of our family by getting Eoin to propose."

"You sound like you don't like her."

I shrug. "It's not that. It's just Molly's priority is Molly, and to head our organization as Ma Duster, the company needs to be the priority."

"But surely Eoin must realize that."

"He does."

"But…"

I interject. "He thinks she saved his life, Jessie, and that changes everything."

We leave it there, both of us dressing quietly. We've shared a temporary respite from a permanent situation inflicted on us by others. Nothing more.

I wrap my arms around her, pulling her close to my chest and breathing her in. She smells of sex. She smells of me. I've never felt so possessive over anything or anyone in my life as I do right now.

But, in the absence of a miracle, this is the end of the road for us, and we both know it.

"Thank you," I mutter against her hair, my eyes closed.

"For?"

"For saving my life. And…"

"And?"

"For just being you, Jessie O'Brien."

CHAPTER SIXTY

JAINE

Jaine's House, Rising, California

I'M HOME ALONE.

Ace is at the clubhouse and Duke and Darla have taken the kids out. I needed time to come to terms with what I suspect has been going on. With what I know has been going on.

How fucking long have I been played for a fool?

How could I not see what was staring me in the face? All the signs were there.

The familiarity. The flirting.

Did I not see them, or did I choose not to? Did my subconscious know? Did that fucker let me down and betray me too?

All because it didn't want to let him go.

Because all those signs? Well, they're clear as day now.

Dylan.

I stare at the name as it lights up the screen on my phone for the first time since yesterday. It's a call, not a message.

It's my guess I won't receive any more messages from this number. Because I suspect the message sender now realizes how badly they dropped the goddamn ball. I suspect the caller now realizes the same.

Because they are not one in the same person. I know that now.

I ignore it. I'm not ready to face it.

Anger. Sadness. Disappointment.

Dis-fucking-belief.

I blink back tears because if I shed one, I'll drown in those useless fuckers.

The phone rings again and again. I ignore it again and again.

Not yet.

Lies. Deceit. Deception.

How could they fucking do this to me?

The phone rings for the nth time in a row. I'm tempted not to answer. That way I can pretend this shitshow isn't happening.

But it is happening.

I connect the call to a stranger. Because I realize now I don't even know this person. This man I thought a friend. My replacement confidant.

Turns out I never needed a replacement after all.

Now? I want confirmation of the lies straight from the horse's goddamn mouth. Or at least one of them. And I want to know why.

"You have five seconds to explain what the fuck's been going on."

There's a pause. He's surprised I answered. After spending so long trying to get through, he now has no clue what to say.

"Thank you for saving Eoin." He sounds cautious. He doesn't know how to react or behave. He no doubt thought I'd blow up his phone when I figured things out. I didn't.

My silence spoke more than my words ever could.

"I almost didn't." I'm trying to speak calmly but it's difficult to do when the bitter taste of betrayal laces your tongue.

"I'm sorry, Jaine." It's barely audible.

I laugh dryly. "You're sorry! You're sorry? Did you hear me, Dyl? I said, I almost didn't. I lost concentration! If I had missed that shot, he'd be fucking dead right now," I hiss.

"Calm down, Jaine."

"Calm down! CALM DOWN? I received a message from you. Dylan O'Connell. From you! Just when I was about to pull the goddamn trigger."

"I can explain."

"You can explain." I force a laugh. "Go on, then. You explain to me how the hell you can send a message while your hands are taped behind your back and I'm staring at you through the scope of my rifle. You explain that to me!"

I pause to catch my breath as I get tangled in their web of deceit and tossed in their ocean of goddamn lies.

I'm fucking drowning.

"How long?" My voice is quiet.

"Jaine."

"How long have I been messaging him, Dylan A few days? A few weeks? Months? The entire time I've been gone? How long have I been messaging Irish?"

Silence.

Reality dawns on me.

"Jesus Christ, Dyl. The whole time. The whole goddamn time!"

I drop to my knees, feeling so sick to my stomach that I heave. This cannot be happening. Why did they do this? I just don't understand any of it.

"You lied to me all this time." I wipe away the silent tears that have started to fall. I don't think I've ever felt so let down.

"I'm sorry, Jaine." His words are sincere, but it's too little too late. No amount of apologies will ever make up for this blatant act of betrayal.

"Who else knew?"

"Jaine."

"Who. Else. Fucking. Knew?"

There's a pause. He doesn't want to tell me, but he's got no goddamn choice.

"Me, Paddy, Eoin, and Cill."

I snort a forced laugh. "So, you all knew. Jesus Christ, you must have found it fucking hilarious discussing it in your Reservoir Dogs-style meetings."

"Jaine, Paddy wasn't coping. He turned to the drink. He was drowning himself in whiskey all day, every day. My baby brother was dying inside. It was the only way he could cope. It was the only way he could survive."

"What about me?" I say quietly.

"I don't know what you mean."

"You don't know what I mean." I snort-laugh. "I mean what about the fact that I wasn't coping either!"

"That's why I thought it would be a good idea, Jaine. That you could have each other back sort of."

"But I didn't get him back, Dyl, did I? Because I didn't fucking know it was him!"

"Jaine…"

I speak calmly. "All this time, I thought he didn't care. That was why he never made contact. Not once. In almost two years. I mean I know I asked him not to, but I still thought…. I still hoped." My voice breaks as a wave of self-pity washes over me. I breathe in and out before I continue. "In the end, it turns out he was messaging me every day like nothing had happened."

"Well, not for the first month or so."

"Oh, so that makes it all right, then!" I bite back.

I exhale slowly as I let every message exchange flash through my mind before it stops on one in particular.

"Jesus Christ, no. Please God, no." My voice is a whisper as I slowly piece two and two together.

"Jaine?"

"It was me, wasn't it?"

"What was you?" He knows. I can tell from his tone he knows exactly what's coming next.

"What Jessie said. What you… what *he* said!"

"What do you mean? You're talking in riddles."

"Jessie told me she was your first. I didn't ask. It came up in conversation."

The implications if this is true. The impact it will have had on Jessie. The impact on Dylan himself.

"I'm the cliché blonde. That's the reason everyone goes quiet whenever I bring her up. It was Irish all this time, and he was talking about me, wasn't he?"

There's a pause while he digests the fact that I've unearthed yet another dirty Duster secret.

"Yes." I can hear the guilt.

I frown. "But, Dylan…" He knows what I'm getting at. What this could have meant for him and Jessie had he not had to cover his brother's deceitful tracks. She only stayed away from him because she thought there was someone else. And there was.

Me.

"I couldn't do that to him, Jaine. Everything would have unfurled with that revelation. You would never have spoken to him again, and he would never have survived losing you from his life again. He's suffered enough. I wasn't going to add to his misery. He's my baby brother, Jaine. I love him."

Tears fill my eyes, but not for my benefit this time. For Dylan's. For what he's selflessly given up. For what he's fucking lost.

"I need to go."

"Jaine, what are you going to do now?"

"I *said* I need to go."

"JAINE!"

I disconnect the call, then stare at the phone in my hand. Or should I say weapon, as they've used it against me like one.

I understand Dylan's reasons. I do. Everything he did he did for Irish, even at the expense of his own happiness with Jessie. And for that reason, I will learn to forgive him, but I'll never forget.

Lessons have been well and truly learned.

Rage then barrels through me. No, this is all *his* fucking fault. The selfish asshole with the heart of stone.

Because what he did? He did it for no one but himself.

FIFTEEN MINUTES.

That's how long I took to mentally prepare myself before I dialed his number.

"Jaine."

He answers within three rings.

"You were right." There's a polite smile in my voice.

"Would you care to enlighten me?"

"You *were* hiding something from me."

There's a pause. He knows exactly what I'm referring to because this fucking asshole read every message exchange and now I know why.

"Who told you?" He tries not to act surprised, but he is.

"I worked it out. I received a message from Dylan at a time he wouldn't otherwise have been able to send one."

Another pause.

"Well, aren't you going to try to deny it?"

I'm pissed off that he's acting like it's no big fucking deal. It's more confirmation if ever I needed it that messing with my life is just in a day's work. My life means nothing to him. I mean nothing to him.

"I can't deny it, so I won't."

His nonchalant attitude has my blood boiling in my veins. I pause before continuing. I promised myself I wouldn't become reactive. I refuse to let him see the full effect this has had on me like I did with Dylan.

I want to verbally deliver what I have to say. Then deliver it in person when I return to New York. Because this asshole's not worth my rage. He's not worth my anything.

The only thing he's deserving of is my engraved bullet in his arrogant skull.

"So let me get this straight. You come to my apartment to warn me to stay away from your youngest brother. I do as you ask. Then you condone him messaging me the entire time while pretending to be Dylan?"

"I didn't know."

"I call bullshit."

"Not the entire time. I discovered it when you were in Nevada. He came to me, suggesting you needed help. He wanted to go to you himself, but I wouldn't let him. In the end, I went in his place."

"That was over a year ago."

"It was."

"And you've let it go on ever since."

"I apologize, Jaine."

I don't believe a word of his shitty apology. If Eoin O'Connell is apologizing for something, then it's to suit his own damn purpose.

It's not because he feels any sense of remorse. There's a reason behind it which I'm sure will come to light shortly.

"And do you think issuing me with an insincere apology fixes things?"

No response.

"So, the reason the message exchanges were being monitored was in case Irish said something he shouldn't and blew your Duster cover."

"Correct."

"Why did you tell him not to answer when I called?"

"It was inappropriate."

"So, you deemed it appropriate for us to message but not to speak."

"You didn't know it was him."

"That's right. I didn't. Although I'm not sure what difference it would have made given the messages were monitored. Why the need for all the deceit?"

There's a pause at his end.

"Sophia must never find out."

I laugh. "And there it is. The reason behind your goddamn apology."

It's my turn to pause because now the ball's in my court. My exposing their dirty Duster secret could start a war with the Ruoccos. More so because Sophia hates my guts over the comment I made at Leo's function. It was wrong. I should never have said it.

But I did.

"So, correct me if I'm wrong. But in this little outlaw game of chess of yours, I was merely the pawn used to stop Irish from drinking himself into an early grave, all so he could live long enough to fulfill his Duster duties."

I pause, but he makes no comment. He knows I'm right so he can't correct a goddamn word.

"And now I've got him safely to the starting line, you're telling me that Sophia must never know he's been messaging me covertly for almost two years?"

"He's engaged. He's due to be married in a couple of months." Is he worried? He doesn't sound it but I sure fucking hope he is.

"Then you should have thought about that twelve months ago, which is when you should have put an end to this fucked-up charade of yours. The things I've said. Jesus Christ. But then you know what I've said word for word. So, tell me, Eoin, just how long have you been reading our correspondence in minute detail?"

"Since Nevada."

"So, for the same duration."

I pause once more.

"Well, do you know what? I felt guilty about the bombshell I'm going to be dropping on the Dusters. But now? Not so much."

He responds immediately.

"I know about the recording of the telephone conversation with Molly if that's your earth-shattering news."

I laugh dryly. "Oh, your fiancée told you about that, did she? Well, that's good to know. But it's not that. Sorry to disappoint you."

I'm tempted to mention the silent owing I've created. That I'm having to play intermediary between Rod and Molly moving forward. Maybe he already knows, maybe he doesn't. I'm not going to lower myself to her level by bringing it up.

"She'll be my wife imminently."

"Is that so? And why the rush? A shotgun wedding, perhaps?"

"Not at all. She saved my life."

"Maybe she should have done the world a favor and not bothered. And when was this life-saving event exactly?"

"We had a situation in Nevada. I was at risk. Molly permanently ended the problem."

"Shoot someone in the head on your behalf, did she?"

So she's taken the credit for shooting the Colombian in the skull and he's rushing her down the aisle as a result. Well, I couldn't have wished for a better result. I've never known a couple more deserving of one another.

"How do you know they were shot in the head?"

"I know more than you realize."

"I'm sure Jessie will have told you."

"Maybe she did. Maybe she didn't. Anyway, more importantly, and the actual reason for my call. Do you remember what I said. That one day I would make your life as miserable as you made mine?"

"Vaguely."

"Well, I just wanted to forewarn you that your day of reckoning is coming."

"Is it indeed? And can I ask why all this vitriol is being directed at me? Why not at Paddy or Dylan?"

I laugh. "Because you ended our relationship without consideration or remorse. And then for the past year, you've allowed me to be used because it suited your selfish purposes. You should have put a end to this fiasco as soon as you found out. Either that or you should have come clean. You did neither. Now it's payback time and I hear karma can be a goddamn bitch when she wants to be."

"Are you threatening me, Miss Jones?"

"That's exactly what I am doing, Mr. O'Connell. Because I'm coming after you personally, and I will do everything in my power to make your life a living hell."

"Then bring it on. But mark my words, you will lose." His tone is filled with sheer arrogance.

This asshole's underestimating me. Again.

"Then I suggest you get prepared to eat those fuckers, Mr.

O'Connell. Because there's one thing Jaine Jones never does, and that's lose."

CHAPTER SIXTY-ONE

DYLAN

The Hudson Dusters' HQ, Manhattan, New York

"Don't say I didn't warn you. We allowed that biker woman to become too involved. Now look at the mess we're in, and all because she has intel on us. I mean, what was our Paddy thinking. What were you all thinking?"

Eoin, Da, and I sit around the circular table. Cill's away on business, and our Paddy is one of the main topics of conversation, so neither he nor the women have been invited to this extraordinary Duster meeting.

"He was drinking himself into a stupor every day, Da. I didn't see the harm in the beginning. In all honesty, I thought it would just fizzle out, but it never did."

"They spent the best part of ten years messaging each other, Dylan. It was their thing. It was never going to just fizzle bloody out."

I say nothing because I know he's right. I also keep my head down. It's safer. It's closer to the tabletop if I need to duck it below.

"And you say she threatened you, Eoin?"

"She did, Da. But I'm not sure what with exactly. I mean, we know she has a recording. But then she probably has several. I'm just not sure what else."

"Jesus Christ." Da shakes his head at the situation we've gotten ourselves in. Jaine Jones is a great ally when you're on the same side, but as an enemy? We're just not sure what to expect.

"She won't dob us in or anything like that, Da," I mutter.

"And you know that how?" Da's glare is fixed on me. I'm sure it is. But I don't make eye contact. I'm not brave enough. Not given the mood he's currently in. For once, he really is having to tolerate our combined incompetence.

"It's not Jaine's style. If she's going to seek revenge, it will be something noteworthy. Something she'll take pride in. It won't be anything sneaky or underhand. I know her well enough to know that."

"What could it be, then?" Da grumbles on.

We all stare at each other. None of us have any clue what this bombshell of hers is. Or indeed, what else over and above she has planned for Eoin. Because he's the one set to be on the receiving end of the plate of stone-cold revenge she's planning on dishing up. In truth, I can't say it's not deserved. Partially, at least.

I wouldn't want to be in his shoes.

"Should we consider using The Exterminator on her?"

Shite, here we go. If all else fails, shoot to kill. If only they knew. "No, Da. I'm hoping it will all calm down in due course. Jaine's just feeling let down, and rightly so."

"Maybe we should consider using Molly moving forward. She's an adept shot." I glance at our Eoin as he makes the flippant remark.

Da smiles proudly. "She is that. Stepping up to save your bacon when she needed to. It's not a bad shout. We'd save ourselves millions. I know there's been a lot of things said against the girl. We were all questioning if she was the right choice and so on. But I think she's earned her place at the head of this family and by your side."

Eoin nods. I can tell he feels indebted to her, which is understandable. Is it just that? Are his feelings towards her also changing as a result?

If only this pair knew who it was that really saved his pompous arse.

"Let's not forget Jessie saved my skin by decapitating the first Colombian with moves straight out of *Kill Bill*."

Da nods as he frowns and stares at his blank pad. He misses her. I should feel guilty for mentioning her, but I don't. Because if Molly is being praised for something she didn't do, Jessie deserves recognition for something she did.

Saving my life.

"Did you unearth anything from the Colombian's phone?"

Eoin shakes his head. "Nothing. It was burner to burner."

Da frowns and looks at me. "And how's our Paddy doing?"

It's my turn to frown. "He's not in a good place. He's disappointed with himself that he dropped the ball quite so blatantly. Jaine's not messaged him, or should I say she's not messaged me, since. In truth, she'd already made it clear she wanted her next communication with Paddy to be face-to-face. I also think, deep down, he knows it was time to draw a line under it. He can't continue this back-and-forth with Jaine after taking the vows with Sophia. That would be disrespectful. It doesn't make it any easier for him, though."

"And how is Jaine with you?"

I shrug. "I have to speak to her over the phone these days as she refuses to send messages. The temperature's still frigid. She'll take a long time to forgive any of us, that's if she ever does. She sure as hell won't ever forget."

"So, she speaks to you, but not to our Eoin?"

I nod. "Jaine holds him responsible for the whole shebang. For separating them in the first place. For allowing this web of deceit to continue after it came to light. It's my guess whatever she's going to dish up is something she wants to serve to Eoin personally. So, for that reason, it won't happen until she's back in Manhattan. She wants to witness both the fallout and his reaction first-hand."

Da nods. "And when is she back in New York?"

"She's scheduled to return the month after Paddy's wedding."

"After? Not before?"

"Definitely after. That was one of the key reasons she left Manhattan in the first place. To keep out of sight and mind until he was safely wed."

"And will she still honor that even after all this deceit has come to light? Or will she return earlier than planned to disrupt the proceedings and throw a spanner in the works?"

Eoin stares at him. "It's my opinion she'll stay away, Da. She may be upset with Paddy, but she would never harm a hair on his head. And she'd kill anyone else who dared try. She'd never put him at risk by making him a target for the Sicilians. At least, not intentionally."

Da nods. "Let's keep a close eye on this situation, boys. But this whole thing has gotten me thinking that maybe I should pay a visit to this Jaine Jones when she returns to the city. See what all the hoo-ha is over this girl."

"You definitely should, Da," I pipe up.

Because I know as soon as he meets her, he'll know exactly what all the fuss is about.

"And your engagement party, Dyl?"

"Next month, Da."

More's the pity.

"DYLAN, CAN I HAVE A QUIET WORD, PLEASE?"

Grace corners me as I'm leaving the meeting. I smile warmly at my future wife. This situation isn't her fault, and it's not of her choosing either. Grace is pleasant enough in her own way. Sadly, she's as dull as dishwater, but she's still like a breath of fresh air compared to Molly and Sophia.

At least for once, I didn't get the short straw. Still, I feel sorry for the girl. She'll be stuck in a marriage knowing full well her husband is in love with another woman.

She's dressed in a cream twinset and black pants. A pair of flat black shoes finish off her almost librarian look. Grace really is a recluse. It's hard to believe I was the same before I went into lockdown.

Before Jessie O'Brien infected my blood.

Did a new and improved Dylan O'Connell emerge? I like to think so. With Jessie's influence.

"Of course, Grace."

Taking my hand in hers, she leads me into my office.

Is it desk sex she's chasing?

I CLOSE MY EYES AND GRIMACE AS I DIAL JAINE'S NUMBER.

"Dylan."

"Have you calmed down any yet?"

"You don't deserve me to be calm. You should count your lucky stars I'm still speaking to you. You should also be grateful you're still alive."

"I am, on both counts, I assure you, Jaine. And I'm sorry. You do know that, don't you?"

"I know, and I also know you did what you did for Irish, unlike your big brother."

"My da's threatening to meet you, by the way."

"Is he now? And why is that? Is it to measure me up for some concrete shoes?"

I snicker. "No, not at all. I think he's just curious. He wants to know what all the fuss is about. Will you meet with him? And will you actually turn up this time?"

She chuckles. "So, Eoin told you about that, did he?"

"He did. During a very rare heart-to-heart moment. He's only told me, though. No one else."

"Heart-to-heart moment? You need to have one to be able to partake, surely. He doesn't. And if he did, it would be filled with adoration for his big, conceited self."

"He's not that bad."

"Let's agree to disagree on that. What Eoin has coming his way is deserved, and it's not a topic that's up for either discussion or negotiation."

"Jaine."

"Leave it, Dylan. He may be your brother, but he's an asshole. What he did, he didn't do for Irish. What he did, he did for his own selfish reasons. The rest of us were just collateral. A means to him fulfilling his own self-centered end. For that, he'll be made to pay."

There's a pause. She's waiting to see if I argue back or defend him. I do neither. I know better. But I can't say it doesn't worry me; Jaine's not the vengeful type, but she really is gunning for Eoin.

He's pushed her too far. I love my brother, but she's right. He's brought a lot of this on himself.

"I'll meet with your da when I return to Manhattan. In fact, I'll meet with you all. There's something I need to do. Something I need to say. And it needs to be done face to face."

"So, is it safe for me to tell my da you'll meet with us, then?"

"It is."

There's a pause. Jaine and I agreed we wouldn't discuss her business partner and everything that went on between me and her. Same as we agreed not to talk about Paddy or their situation. It's just easier that way. But I need some answers.

"How's Jessie keeping?"

There's a pause.

"She's okay." She sounds cagey.

"Can I ask a question?"

"Depends on what it is."

"Is she involved with Tyler Grayson?"

She exhales slowly. Is she going to tell me something I don't want to hear? Is she going to answer that question at all?

"They have a past, but things didn't end well for them as you know. I'm not sure Jessie's in the headspace right now to consider going back for seconds."

"So, they're not seeing each other?"

"I'm not saying that because I don't know for sure. But if they are, it will be slow burn."

"Can I ask another question, Jaine?"

"Depends on what it is."

"Is Jessie in love with me?"

There's another pause. "Well, that's not for me to say, Dyl. If you want that answer, you'll have to ask Jessie herself. But I think if you ask yourself that question, then you already know the answer."

"Jaine. I need a favor. Will you help me?"

"Depends on what it is."

"Is that going to be your stock answer to everything?"

She laughs out loud. "Depends on…."

"You're hilarious."

"I do try."

CHAPTER SIXTY-TWO

JESSIE

Jessie's Family Home, Colton, Nevada

"HAVE YOU BEEN HANGING OUT WITH TY, JESSIE?"

We've been talking JAA. Now that's over, she's changed the subject. I lie back on my bed and throw a pom pom in the air before catching it and tossing it to the side.

"Not like that, partner."

"You been thinking about it?"

"The thought crossed my mind, but it's way too soon."

"You still in love with Dyl?"

"Might be." Which she knows means yes.

"Good to know."

"From where you're sitting, maybe. Anyway, speaking of Ty. He suspects something's gone down and that everything's not what it seems."

"About?" I can tell I've immediately got her attention.

"The clubhouse shooting. He says there's no way Molly could have hit the Colombian in the middle of the forehead from where she was standing."

There's a pause.

"Right."

"Anyway, he took photographic evidence of that little tidbit of information before he handled the clean-up, just in case it was ever needed. And also…"

"Go on."

"I know it wasn't Molly."

Another pause.

"Really. And you know that how?"

"Because Ty also said she didn't aim and likely pulled the trigger by accident. Apparently, there's a bullet hole on the newly laid concrete floor right beside where she was standing. He reckons it hit the surface then ricocheted. It ties in with the fact that he found a stray bullet in the corner of the room afterward."

"And you know for sure the bullet was from the gun Molly was holding?"

"I do. Because she was holding my Glock. And I loaded it before I left home."

I frown when she exhales loudly. I thought she'd find all this interesting. Obviously not.

"And is there a point to all of this?"

"Yes. Because I also have it on good authority that The Exterminator shot the bad guy in the head."

Silence. Is Jaine surprised? Does she know who he is? She eventually responds.

"Really. And how do you know this?"

"I was asked to sneak the bullet from the puddle of brains because the sniper doesn't want anyone to know he was involved."

Another pause. What's with all these pauses.

"But you're telling me?"

"I trust you. You won't say anything."

"No, I won't, but I suggest you don't mention any of this to anyone else. Rumor has it The Exterminator has a way of finding these things out."

"Cross my heart and hope to die."

"I'm sure that could be arranged if you breathe a goddamn word, Jessie."

"Apparently, Dylan knows who he is."

"I know Dylan knows who he is."

"Do you know who he is?"

"You could say that, and before you ask for a name, the answer's no."

"Spoilsport." I huff.

I leave it there. I could pry until I'm blue in the face, but it won't get me anywhere.

"Speaking of Dylan. Have you spoken to him recently?"

"Earlier today."

"Anything I should be concerned about?"

"Nope. We were discussing a private matter."

"Was any of the conversation about me?" I don't know why I'm asking. Jaine never betrays a confidence.

"Curiosity killed the cat, don't you know."

"You can't tell me?"

"Nope."

"But I told you my gossip."

"I didn't realize it came with conditions attached, meaning I had to reciprocate."

"Nobody tells me anything." I huff once more and throw the pom pom back up in the air.

"Stop sulking."

I let out an exaggerated sigh.

"Anyway, to conclude, apparently Molly's taken the credit for killing the bad guy and because he thinks she saved his ass, Eoin's rushing her down the aisle."

"More fool him."

Again, she doesn't sound surprised so it's my guessing she was aware of that piece of gossip too.

"Anyway, now my news. I spoke to Leoluca Di Matteo before I called you. He wants me to meet with him and one of his colleagues in Manhattan. My dilemma is it's ear-marked for before my return date."

"Leoluca is?"

"One of my biggest clients. Leo has links with Cosa Nostra. The Sicilian mafia."

"Right. And does this have anything to do with Sophia by any chance?"

"He hasn't said as much, but as he doesn't want to discuss anything over the phone it's my guessing the answer's yes. That it may indeed have something to do with the Ruoccos."

"And are you going to meet up with him?"

"He's a client. I don't really have any choice."

"And when's this meeting taking place?"

"The day after Dyl's engagement party."

I DIAL HER NUMBER AS I STARE IN DISBELIEF AT MY LAPTOP SCREEN.

"Jaine."

"Jessie. I last spoke to you, what, half an hour ago?"

"I've had an email."

"That's a fairly common method of communication these days. And for that reason, I'm not sure it's worthy of its own telephone call."

I smile at her dry response. "It's an invitation to Dylan's engagement party."

"Right."

"Have you been invited?"

"Nope. It's unlikely I'll be featured on the guestlist with relations being a little, shall we say, strained between the O'Connells and me. Plus, Sophia and Irish will be there."

"You don't sound surprised that I've been invited. Did you know about it?"

"Might have."

"You think I should go?"

"You've been invited, haven't you?"

"But won't that be a bit weird?"

"Only if you make it so."

"But what if I cry? What if I shoot her in the head? What if I shoot him in the head?"

"I doubt they'll let anyone in who's carrying a weapon, Jessie."

"Good point. Well, what if I throttle her instead?"

"Then you'll get arrested. The positive? At least you've got yourself the best lawyer money can buy."

"You'd charge me?"

"It's a business I'm running, not a charity."

We both chuckle.

"All joking aside, partner."

"All joking aside, if you're invited, you put your big girl pants on and you show those O'Connells exactly what you're made of."

I pause before I ask.

"What happened, Jaine?"

"What do you mean?"

"I know you've had a falling out with them."

She pauses before she replies. I know she's wondering how much to reveal.

"Let's just say they did something they shouldn't have, more so Eoin. He crossed the line."

"So, is he going to be made to pay? Are you big girl pantying it when you return to Manhattan?"

"Yes, to the first question, and you bet your bottom dollar I am to the second."

I close my laptop screen. With a smile on my face, I throw the pom pom in the air once more. Decision made.

"Okay, then do you know what? I'll do it. I'll go to the damn engagement party, and I'll show delectable, despicable, dirty Dylan exactly what he's missing."

CHAPTER SIXTY-THREE

JESSIE

The Meeting Rooms, New York

I TAKE IN THE VENUE WITH ITS VULGAR CRYSTAL CHANDELIERS AND accents finished in marble and gilded gold. It's like Midas himself paid a visit in advance and touched everything just to make sure it had that over-the-top bling factor.

Only the best for The Hudson Dusters.

I'm expecting the actress from *Gone With The Wind* to make an entrance and glide herself down the sweeping staircase. Then again, it's more likely to be Grace Ryan. She's the woman of the hour. This is her night.

Just a small celebration of her engagement to Dylan O'Connell.

I glance at Little Bee, who's sitting across the table. In the absence of having anyone else, and much to Razr's delight as it got him off the hook, she agreed to be my plus one to this event. An event I'm still not sure I should have been invited to. An invitation I'm still not sure I should have accepted.

Bee looks stunning in a floor-length baby pink sequin number. She's just told me in the strictest confidence that she's two months pregnant. Razr's little swimmers have finally struck gold. Not that she's showing yet, but she's glowing all the same.

I'm pleased for her. Pleased for them. They deserve their happiness. Everyone does. Well, everyone apart from me it would seem.

Perfectly lonely.

She hasn't told anyone else yet. My daddy will be thrilled for sure. He's waited a long time to be a granddaddy. Let's face it, it's not like I'll be providing him with grandbabies any time soon.

If ever.

I gaze around the ostentatious establishment. By all accounts, it's the best Manhattan has to offer. My apologies New York but it's not a patch on the Vegas scene. It's my guess most of this evening's attendees will be mobsters, mafioso, politicians, and the rest of the upper echelons of New York's high society.

Or more aptly put, the people in this city who matter.

All the males are wearing tuxedos and only the most dazzling of partners decorate their arms. Outward appearances are everything.

Waiters strut around in their black and white uniforms, expertly balancing glasses of vintage champagne on silver serving trays.

Money is, of course, no object.

Given Bee's condition, she's on sparkling water. I've chosen the same. The last thing I need is to get tipsy and find myself crying tears of self-pity into an empty crystal flute as I witness the love of my life celebrate his engagement to the love of his.

"Did you know this venue is the one Jaine and Sarah were abducted from?"

I nod at Little Bee absentmindedly as I continue to people-watch. "Yes. Jaine filled me in on all the details."

"It's also where Sarah found out she was pregnant with Caoimhe."

I nod again then frown. "Where the hell is Sarah, anyway?"

"She's not here yet. None of the O'Connells are."

"Figures." I huff then roll my eyes exaggeratedly.

"What do you mean?" She frowns at me.

"Well, they're so full of their own self-importance they expect the rest of us to wait around like we've got nothing better to do."

My baby sister reaches across and squeezes my hand. She knows I'm just reacting.

"I really shouldn't be here, Bee." My voice is barely a whisper.

"You were invited, Jay." Her tone is firm.

"Yes, I was, although I'm still not sure why."

"Because the O'Connells respect you, and for that reason, they wanted you to be here."

"To rub my nose in it more like."

"Even if it were for that reason, we O'Briens walk away from nothing and no one. We hold our heads high, and we get through it. Our daddy didn't raise no yellow-bellied cowards."

I squeeze her hand back. She's right. Of course she is. I know what she went through with Paul Delaney. The humiliation. The hurt. The betrayal. She did exactly what she's expecting me to do in the same circumstances. She held her head high, and she kept right on. Well, if my baby sister can do it, then so the hell can I.

I answer my flashing phone.

"Jaine."

"Are you there yet?"

"We got here about half an hour ago. No sign of the O'Connells, though." I huff.

Bee rolls her eyes at me.

"They'll be there soon enough. You dressed to impress?"

"You know me, partner. When the opportunity arises, I *always* dress to impress."

"I heard Bailey's news."

I huff exaggeratedly. "Bee said I was the first to know. She never mentioned she told you too."

She laughs. "Delaney told me. He was crying like a baby down the phone. I could barely make out what he was saying at first. Congratulations, by the way."

"Why, thank you. Are you in Manhattan now?"

"I am."

"You'll keep me posted on what happens with Leo?"

"I will. Anyway, I should go."

"Why the rush?"

"Because the O'Connells are about to make their grand entrance."

"And you know that how?"

"That would be telling."

"Sounds ominous."

"Let me know how the evening goes. Three words, Jessie. You. Got. This."

I KNOW IT SOUNDS TWEE, BUT EVERYONE IN THE ROOM FADES INTO the background when Dylan's eyes connect with mine. For the briefest of seconds, time stands still, and we're the only two people in here. The only sound is my heart and his beating in that matching rhythm they find whenever they're in close proximity.

Fast. Furious. Erratic. Synchronized.

He's not wearing a tuxedo like everyone else. Instead, he's wearing a tailored black suit with a white shirt and a tie the same shade of blue as his sapphire eyes.

I could weep at the unfairness of it all. But I won't. Because I can't. At least not yet. I guess it's something to look forward to later when I'm back home and on my own.

Perfectly lonely.

He smiles at me, and my heart skips a beat. I feel like a teenage girl all over again, being noticed by the boy she has a crush on.

But my crush doesn't matter. My love doesn't matter. None of it matters. Because Fate was in a pissy mood when he decided our future. Or at least when he decided mine.

Still, I'll survive.

The gregarious Jessie will remain chipper until she's out of sight and mind. Then she'll go home and transform into the quiet and contained Jessie she wears like a comfy old pair of slippers and have a good old cry.

"Thank you for coming, Jessie."

The interruption has me dragging my gaze from his. I turn my head to see Grace Ryan standing beside me.

"Grace."

Her long blonde hair is in an updo, and her glasses are gone. She looks beautiful in an understated kind of way wearing an elegant long black dress.

I stand to greet her. In fairness, after the 'good riddance' remark, she never said anything untoward to me. In fact, she never said much of anything at all. Maybe she's not so bad.

"Congratulations." I hug her, and she smiles.

The lights dim slightly, and my heart plummets at what I'm about to witness.

I can't do this.

You can, Jessie. And you will. It's just another one of those short straws you keep right on pulling in life.

"Shouldn't you?" I motion my head to where the O'Connells are seated, but she shakes hers to decline and simply smiles once more.

I glance at her hand. She's not wearing her engagement ring. Maybe I should take back what I said. Maybe she is bad after all. A smiling assassin who wants to torture me by having me watch the whole thing up close and personal. Then just so we're all clear on who won, have him propose to her right in front of me.

I watch as he stands from the Duster table. I know they'll all be there, but I don't make eye contact with any of them. Not even dear old Fergal. I don't want to see their sympathetic looks when I'm already struggling holding it together.

The Dylan of old would never have had the confidence to do what he's about to. To speak in front of so many of Manhattan's influential people.

A group of complete strangers.

But that's exactly what he's going to do. In the end, he didn't change. He didn't have to. He just needed to embrace both sides of himself and, in turn, reach his full potential.

And he has. In every single way.

The now confident Duster phoenix is about to publicly rise from the ashes he's been content hiding under all this time.

He stands, and his very own captive audience falls into a hush.

"So, I met a girl."

There's a ripple of laughter at his opening line which is spoken in that beautiful New York accent of his. The one that's blessed with just the perfect amount of Irish lilt.

The cheeky smirk he gives in response reminds me so much of Paddy.

"And this girl. Well, she's so vibrant and alive she lights up any room. She's so beautiful all others pale in comparison."

The room fills with soft 'awws' mainly from women, of course, as Dylan wears his heart on his sleeve as he talks about Grace.

His Disney princess. His cliché blonde. The love of his life.

Tears fill my eyes.

"This girl makes me laugh. This girl makes me cry. This girl makes me want to be the best person I can be. A stronger person. A braver person. A better person. And I know I can be all of those things. But it's not because she expects it of me. Because I know she loves me just as I am."

How many times has Grace told him she loves him? How many times has he told her he loves her? Because they've obviously spoken the words aloud. Words he's now, as a result, confident uttering on her behalf.

"I want to be all of those things for her. Because when I'm with her, I feel like I can achieve anything. Be anything. Do anything. That I can take on everything and conquer the world."

My chest tightens. Each spoken word of adoration for her is like a rusty nail through my already broken heart. I'm conscious more silent tears are welling in my eyes. But I can't stop them forming. I've never been as strong as the rest of my family, likely because I spent so many years not living the life I was born into.

Maybe I need to find someone who can make me stronger. Make me braver. Make me better.

Because, right now, I'm not feeling any of those things.

I hoped that could have been him. That we could have grown together day by day. *Because whatever our souls are made of, his and mine are the same.*

But it's not.

He's not mine. He's never been mine. He will never be mine.

He walks towards Grace, who's still standing beside me. I'm conscious Bee has moved as her hand is now rubbing up and down my arm. She's trying to comfort me.

But nothing can comfort me. Witnessing this. Watching the man I love declare his love for someone else in front of the rest of the world.

In front of me.

How can I be comforted?

And then he's there. So close, I can smell the familiar citrus notes from his body wash.

"And this girl? Well, I need her by my side to complete me because, and I know it's an old cliché, but she really is my other half."

I close my eyes. I can't watch this.

Be brave. Be strong. Be an O'Brien.

"Jessie," Bee whispers.

I open them, hoping it's all over, but it's not. He's on one knee now. I can't breathe. I just want it to be over. But now I can't look away. It's like my brain wants me to witness this moment so it will be forever imprinted.

So I can play it on repeat and torture myself. So I can't ever forget the worst day of my life.

CHAPTER SIXTY-FOUR

DYLAN

One Month Earlier
The O'Connell Home, Darling, New York

WHEN GRACE RYAN ASKED TO SPEAK TO ME PRIVATELY IT WASN'T to ask for desk sex. And I have to say I was mighty relieved about that given I'd never so much as even kissed the girl.

Nope. It was to offer me a way out.

See, it turns out Grace has a secret. Nothing bad. Just that she's into women. She'd never told anyone that before. Not even her folks. I think, deep down, she was hoping I had a thing for men. I think she thought that might be the reason why, at the ripe old age of thirty, I'd never dated a female. She thought us marrying would see us both able to continue to live our lie.

It was a pretty big assumption on her part, but I get it. Desperate times call for desperate measures. And when you're faced with an unwanted arranged marriage, you'll clutch at any straw, no matter how flimsy.

She quickly realized she'd gotten it wrong. That I was in love with Jessie. It's why she quipped 'good riddance' when she did. Words she'd probably never uttered in her life before or indeed after. It was said to buy us some time. To buy her some time so she could break the news to me.

Grace didn't want to be the cause of us splitting up, and she'd seen enough of Jessie to know she wouldn't back down from the gauntlet being thrown. That her pride would get in the way and see her stay. Which she did.

Until dressing gown-gate.

That evening in my apartment, Grace was fumbling to find her words. I know now she was trying to tell me her secret, but she never quite managed. Instead, she knocked a café press of coffee all over herself and all over the wi-fi connection.

One quick shower later and wearing a dressing gown as her clothes dried, Jessie turned up at the door. Not knowing about Grace's secret, I didn't explain what had actually happened. There seemed little point. Was that the coward's way out? Maybe. But Jessie and I had both already been led into temptation earlier that day resulting in us having desk sex, thus proving we had zero willpower when it came to resisting each other.

It was the only way to nip it in the bud once and for all. To let Jessie move on and live a life without me in it. My future had been decided. No matter how much I loved her and how much I wanted her, it didn't lie with Jessie O'Brien.

Until that saving grace moment.

We're in the family room. I'm currently pacing the floor while my slacks and sheepskin-slipper-wearing folks and my casually dressed brothers are sitting on the large black leather sectionals, all likely wondering why I've called them here this evening.

"Grace came to see me today."

Ma immediately starts up. "Well, it's good to see you're finally accepting of her, Dylan. She's a good girl. She ticks all the boxes, and she's from the right background. She'll make a…"

I interrupt her because she's gloating and looks set to roll right into her 'a mother always knows best' speech.

"She's gay, Ma. Grace is gay."

A rare silence follows from her. Unlike the Dylan of old, I use the opportunity to continue.

"We've agreed between us that for that reason, the marriage can't go ahead."

Da nods. "And will she speak to her parents, son? As you know, it has to be her choice to walk away from this arrangement. It can't be seen that it's you who rejected her."

I nod. "She's speaking to her parents. We've both agreed to do so this evening, which is why I've asked you all here."

Ma shuffles on her seat. I can tell she's just about to find her second wind.

"Well, your da and I had drawn up a list, and many of the other choices were just as promising. Maybe even more so. We settled on Grace in the end because her parents were friends with your Uncle…"

"I will marry Jessie O'Brien," I interrupt my ma.

She glares at me. No doubt surprised her obedient little Dylan has finally grown a set.

"You will do no such thing! Fergal?" She looks at my da for backup. I repeat what I've said before he can add in his two cents worth.

"*I said*, I will marry Jessie O'Brien. That's if she will even have me."

There's a pause.

"Fergal?" Ma prompts him again. But he's staring at me now and I'm staring back.

Another silence. I'm sure I can hear his head whirring this time, though. Good sign or not? I guess I'm about to find out.

"Do you really love her, Dylan? Do you love Jessie?"

There's no hesitation with my response. "I do, Da. More than anything. But feelings aside, Jessie also makes me a better person. A stronger Duster. You must be able to see that. If I can't have her, I will accept no other."

What seems like an endless silence follows.

"Despite her being one of the most irritating people I have ever met in my life, her experience and work ethic is second to none. On that basis, I would be happy to welcome Jessie O'Brien into our family." Eoin breaks the silence, and for once, I'm grateful to hear the sound of his self-obsessed voice. I nod my thanks.

"From a business point of view, it makes obvious sense. Given how she handled the IRS matter, she would be an asset to have onboard permanently. Plus, Sarah thinks the world of her." I smile my thanks at Cillian.

"They're soul mates. They should never have been separated in the first place. Like Jaine and me should never have been separated." Paddy's slouched on the sectional. Since losing Jaine from his life completely, my baby brother is slowly falling apart.

"Oh, for heaven's sake, Padraig."

At not getting her own way, Ma's obviously decided to lash out. "Excuse my vulgarity, but you were fucking most of the females in Manhattan when the arranged marriage was agreed. No one knew about your dirty biker secret. About this Jaine Jones woman."

"I never mentioned her because we were just friends. I didn't know she was in love with me," Paddy bites back.

"And does she love you still? I would say not. She's a biker. She married one of her own. Their kind always chose each other in the end."

"Sarah didn't," Cillian quips.

"She was pregnant. Her bed was made."

"Sarah loves me," Cill argues.

"I'm not saying she doesn't, but her choices were limited once she was carrying a Duster in her belly. In fact, they were removed completely."

"ENOUGH!" Everyone is stunned into silence as my da raises his voice. No one dares speak. We all wait for him to continue.

"Paddy." Da runs his hands through his white hair in frustration. "We've been through this a hundred times now, son. It needs to stop. It's not helping anyone to keep dissecting it over and over. It won't change anything. Your marriage is a blood-written oath, and I also gave my word. If it doesn't go ahead, it will result in war. Now, your ma's right. You were working your way through all the single women in Manhattan for the umpteenth time, and most of the married ones too. And you showed no signs of ever stopping. It's like you were searching for the female equivalent of the Holy Grail.

"Sophia was deemed by us all, your eldest brother included, to be a good match for you. It was done to unite us with the Sicilian mafia. Making them lifetime allies rather than potential future foes. No one knew of your feelings for Jaine Jones when it was all agreed. I appreciate things changed for you both when the Bratva held you captive, son. That things came to light and evolved between you and her. But we weren't to know. We weren't even aware she existed. Not even our Dylan knew."

Paddy looks at me and all I can do is look back. Because Da's right. Even I didn't know about Jaine.

"Our decision was made with the best of intentions to secure you a high-ranking wife and the Dusters a strong ally."

"But I found my Holy Grail of women when I was nineteen, Da. I just didn't know she loved me back."

I blink back tears at how lost he sounds.

"By the time you did, it was already too late, son."

"I still should have had a say in my own future, Da"

"You would have turned the girl down the same as you would every other that was chosen for you. Sophia was given no choice in the matter either. And when push came to shove, she chose you over Cillian and Dylan."

"Lucky me," he mutters.

"Lucky or unlucky, the marriage must go ahead, or mark my words, Luciano will wage war against us. Your ma has been spending time with young Sophia. Trust me, she's as sharp as a tack, even more so than Molly. She will make you a good wife."

Paddy sinks lower on the sectional. He looks like a broken man, but then that's his default look these days.

Da turns his attention back to me. "Now, I've heard what everyone has to say on the matter. I know how your ma feels about bikers and their kind in general, but Jessie O'Brien is far more business than biker. I think we can all agree on that. So, as the head of this family and the head of the Duster organization, I'm giving my permission and my blessing for you to take her as your wife, Dylan."

"Thank you, Da." I whisper, closing my eyes as relief floods through me.

When I open them, Ma's glaring at him. She'll make him pay for going against her wishes. He'll be fending for himself for the foreseeable future that's for sure.

For reasons known only to her, Ma has a biased and disjointed view of bikers. She labels them all promiscuous heathens. And while I agree they do things differently. And while I also agree they may live a debaucherous lifestyle, it's also my view they share a camaraderie that's second to none. I know for a fact every one of those bikers I met for the first time in Nevada would have risked their life for mine.

That, as a biker, Jessie did just that.

I want my own children to grow up as part of that extended family. To always have people like that on their side. Of course, they will be Dusters first and foremost. But I know they will be all the stronger for embracing both worlds.

And for having Jessie as their ma.

CHAPTER SIXTY-FIVE

DYLAN

The Meeting Rooms, New York

On bended knee, I pull the black velvet box from my pocket as I stare up at the most beautiful woman in the world as she stands in a silver floor length gown that skims her slim figure. Then I say the words I pray to The Almighty she wants to hear.

"I love you, Jessie O'Brien. Will you marry me?"

I look up into tear-filled eyes of baby blue as I ask her to be my wife.

Because Jessie completes me. She's my everything. My reason. My life. My love. My soulmate.

I knew from the moment she entered the room on that very first day. When she made my cheeks burn with embarrassment then smirked at my discomfort. There has never been anyone for me. And now I know why. Because I was destined to be hers.

Just as she was destined to be mine.

And tonight, I want all of Manhattan to bear witness to my asking Jessie to take the vows with me. I want to prove just how much I love her by stepping out of my comfort zone and declaring so in a room filled with complete strangers.

But now I'm thinking maybe I've gone about this all the wrong way. Because she's now wearing a frown and she still hasn't answered the all-important question.

I get it. She doesn't know half of what's gone on.

"Do you trust me, Jessie?" Clutching at the only straw I can think of, I repeat what I said to her all those months ago and pray to God it works second time around. "Because I need you to trust me this one more time. I'll explain everything, I promise. But I just need you to do that for me. Will you put your trust in me once more, Jessie?"

The sound of prolonged silence echoes around the room.

"Jessie?" I prompt, suddenly nervous having declared my intentions in front of all of these people.

Shite.

What if she says no? What if I've gotten this all wrong? What if she's with Tyler Grayson now? What if she was only crying because of the emotion of the moment and not because she cares about me. Women do that, don't they? Weep at occasions such as these. And at sad, sentimental old movies like *The Notebook.*

What if she laughs in my face? What if she tells me to fuck right off because she thinks I led her on?

I never stopped to consider she might say no. Not until right at this moment. What an absolute eejit.

Well, if she does say no, then it serves me right for being a presumptuous fucker.

"Yes."

It's so faint I'm not sure if it was wishful thinking on my part that the word was actually spoken.

"Yes."

Louder this time.

Relief flows through me. Thank. Fuck.

Is it yes to the trust or yes to the marriage? I'm not sure, but I'm going to be greedy and I'm taking it as yes to both.

Because I'm taking her. She's mine. And I'm never giving her back.

My hands are shaky as I take the ring from the box. I couldn't find any as beautiful as her, but I'm hoping the oval-shaped diamond is seen as a suitable enough declaration of my love for my soon-to-be wife.

Slipping it on her finger, I stand. Then, resting my forehead against hers, I close my eyes and inhale her intoxicating springtime scent. Opening them once more, our gazes connect. Then, cupping her perfect face in my hand, I press my lips gently to hers to taste her unique sweetness.

A taste that's now all fucking mine. And if any other man ever tries to sample it, I'll kill the fucker with my bare hands. Let's face it. I've now had plenty of practice.

I hear cheering in the background, but nothing matters.

Just me. And her. And our future together.

En route to Nevada

We're heading to Vegas where we'll take another flight to a private airstrip in Nevada. A hired SUV awaits us there.

I've filled Jessie in on everything that's gone down. With Jaine's blessing I explained about the web of lies and deceit. That it's Jaine who is in fact the cliché blonde.

Paddy's Disney princess. Not mine.

And that I kept schtum about everything out of love for my baby brother.

I also explained that nothing untoward ever happened between me and Grace, and that after her revelation, Jaine was tasked with making sure Jessie turned up to her own engagement party.

So, Jessie's now my fiancée, and she'll be my wife within a matter of hours.

We left the party as soon as she said yes. After a day of back and forth, Lucifer reluctantly agreed to let me have her hand, but it was on the strict basis he be allowed to give her away. And that he be allowed to do so in the town church in Colton.

Unlike Paddy, I have no issue where I take the vows, although apparently, he's been asked to reconsider his own service venue at Luc's insistence due to how small St. Peter's is.

I think in a way Paddy's relieved. I reckon he realizes he made a hasty decision when he agreed to wed Sophia in our family church. I think he's now decided that, until he's dead and buried, there's still a chance he'll marry Jaine there one day.

And in this life of ours, who knows?

St. Peter's means a lot to me too. It's one of our family staples. But I'm not so bothered where I take the vows. Just so long as I'm taking them with Jessie and we're taking them soon. Knowing my ma and da, we'll have to relive the experience same as our Cill and Sarah had to. Then again, since I'm the Duster no one can ever remember the name of, maybe not.

I can live in hope.

So, we're on our way to Nevada to get wed. Unfortunately for Jessie, Bailey didn't want to risk flying since she's newly pregnant.

In the absence of her baby sister, Jessie asked Sarah to act as a bridesmaid. Sarah was delighted to accept.

My best man is and always will be our Paddy, but he's not able to step up. Ace will be in Nevada so he can live-stream the nuptials to Jaine.

Apparently, she's not able to attend as she's out of town on business. Something Jessie's been sworn to secrecy over, and her life threatened should she dare reveal who her business partner is meeting.

It's too much risk Paddy being there. Jaine's right. Their next communication needs to be verbal, and it needs to be face to face.

So, our Cillian is acting best man. As soon as we boarded, he and Sarah made straight for the bedroom because every opportunity is a baby-making one for them these days. I get it now. If I have my way, Jessie O'Brien will quickly be joining her sister in the pregnancy club.

The thought of her flat belly rounded with my offspring is now something I'm desperate to witness. I know I sound like a neanderthal, but I want to possess every part of her. I want the world to know she's mine, and what better way than for her to carry my seed?

"What an elaborate set-up."

She's got Jaine on handsfree and has been giving her the third degree.

"So, who was in on it?" Jessie's currently wriggling around on my lap. She could sit still if she wanted. She could even have a seat all of her own as there's plenty spare. She's doing it deliberately. This is payback for the part I played in this so-called set-up. My dick's rock hard, and she knows it. She also knows I won't touch her now until we're wed.

Abstinence.

Even if only for a few short hours. It's why I was so quick to give up the bedroom to our Cill. Remove the temptation that is Jessie O'Brien's perfect pussy for as long as I can. But if she keeps grinding that backside of hers on my dick, I'm going to flip her over and fuck her on this seat.

"Now that would be telling."

"I'll get it out of you eventually."

"You can try." Jaine laughs.

"Are you all set for tomorrow, partner?"

"As prepared as I'll ever be. And on that note, I need to go."

"Let me know how you get on."

"You'll be the second to know."

"And who takes priority over me?"

"Jason Steele."

Jessie snickers. "Ah, okay. I'll let him. But just this once."

"Well, that sure is kind of you. Now, I suggest you get some sleep."

"Dyl."

"Paddy." I'm in the same seat but it's reclined now. Jessie took pity on me. In the end, she gave up inflicting punishment on my dick and took a seat of her own. A seat on which she's currently fast asleep.

No snoring. No drooling. Even in her sleep, she's fucking perfect.

"I like how you get down on bended knee, and the moment she says yes, you and Cill are off like greyhounds out of a trap leaving the rest of us to hold the fort with your guests."

"Well, you know me, brother. I'm not one for mingling. Anyway, listen, Paddy, I'm sorry you couldn't come with us."

"Don't be. I understand. And for the record, I agree. My next contact with Jaine needs to be face to face. At least that way, I can apologize for being a lying, deceitful arse."

"I'm sure it will all be forgotten about by then."

"Then you don't know Jaine very well. She forgets nothing, although she's not typically one for holding a grudge."

Apart from against our Eoin.

"So, tomorrow I'm getting wed." I'm speaking my thoughts aloud more than anything. I still can't quite believe Jessie is going to be my wife.

"You are. And tomorrow I'm off out for dinner at the Palace with Eoin, Molly, and Sophia. A great evening that will be as they talk over themselves as part of this ongoing game of one-upmanship they insist on playing."

"You're just annoyed you won't get a word in edgeways given how much you love the sound of your own voice."

"Cheeky fecker." He laughs out loud.

"You know it's true, brother. Anyway, why the Palace? I know you're not a fan."

"It's Sophia and Eoin's choice. It's easier to agree than rock the boat. Anyway, I just wanted to call to wish you all the best. At least you're getting to marry the woman of your dreams."

I know he's happy for me, but I can still hear raw pain mixed with envy in his voice, and I instantly feel guilty. That all of us bar him will end up happy with our lot while he has to settle for—as he calls it—a fate worse than death.

CHAPTER SIXTY-SIX

JESSIE

Jessie's Family Home, Colton, Nevada

I'M EXHAUSTED. I'VE BARELY SLEPT. BUT I DON'T WANT TO because I don't want to miss a thing.

Dylan O'Connell is mine. Or at least he will be in around half an hour.

As soon as we arrived in Colton, Dyl went straight to the Sons' clubhouse with Ace, Tadgh, Conor, and Cill, and I went home with my daddy and Sarah.

In the absence of my own dress to wear, I'm wearing my mom's. It's something else she left behind when she skipped town and never looked back. It's like she didn't want to take any reminders of her past when she moved on to her future, including any of the day that should have been one of the happiest in her life.

The day she took the vows with my daddy.

I can't imagine marrying Dyl then running off with someone

else. But who am I to judge? I don't know her reasons. I'm guessing she had at least one. Maybe she had an armful. I'm the first to admit my daddy's not the easiest person in the world to live with.

So, is this dress my something borrowed? Or is it actually mine by default?

My mom was a little shorter than me, but it's still floor-length and perfect in delicate cream lace with long sleeves. My hair's up and decorated with a single crystal comb with a sapphire at the center so it's my something blue. It's also borrowed as it's Bee's and it's also new as I had to take the price tag off.

I'm sure my baby sister won't mind.

"You look stunning, Jessie." I smile at Sarah, my soon-to-be sister-in-law, who's wearing a simple skater-style dress in cream, her long strawberry blonde hair hanging down her back.

My phone vibrates, and I pick it up.

Tyler: *Best of luck for today, Jay.*

I smile at the message.

Jessie: *Thank you, Ty.*
Tyler: *Even though I'm jealous as hell, I wish Dylan the best of luck too.*
Jessie: *Me and you had our moment, Ty.*
Tyler: *It doesn't mean I didn't want a repeat. A do-over. A chance to do things right the second time around.*
Jessie: *Who knows what the future holds? Everyone's always telling me things can change in an instant in this life.*
Tyler: *That's because it's true, Jessie. I'm not saying they didn't deserve everything they had coming to them, but I'm sure those Colombian fellas had families waiting for them back home.*

Jessie: *Then I guess it makes you realize how precious every second is. And that we need to make sure each and every one of those seconds counts for something.*
Tyler: *Will you be heading back to New York after?*
Jessie: *Most likely. Dyl's a Duster. It's where they reign supreme. I meant what I said though. I'll be living between. I'm not giving up Colton. Not ever again.*
Tyler: *Good to know.*

We leave it there. What we shared is in the past. Did we have a future? I guess we'll never know.

My phone vibrates again.

Jaine: *Did your mom's dress fit okay?*
Jessie: *It did, and it's beautiful. Are you heading off soon?*
Jaine: *Yes, and I've chartered a flight for immediately after to get me out of Dodge pronto.*
Jessie: *Where are you meeting them again?*
Jaine: *At the Palace. I'm not a fan. It's a bit too extravagant for my tastes.*
Jessie: *Will you need to dress up all fancy-like?*
Jaine: *Something like that.*
Jessie: *Well, let me know how you get on. After you let Jason Steele know, that is, given I'm only ranked number two.*
Jaine: *I'm pretty sure Dylan will become your number one ranking as soon as he becomes your husband, that's if he isn't already. Anyway, what are the plans for after?*
Jessie: *I'm not sure, but we'll probably stick around for a few days before heading back to New York, so maybe we can catch up.*

Jaine: *I'd like that. You should come to Rising. Ace and I can show you around our hometown.*
Jessie: *Sounds like a plan.*

St. Jude's Church, Colton Nevada

I step out of the hired cage, and my gaze immediately drifts over the town church. The painted white building stands tall, its proud steeple reaching into the sky as though to part the heavens themselves.

A couple of new graves have been added since I was here last, the freshly turned soil a stark visual reminder that time marches on even in a sleepy little town like Colton.

Father Murphy shakes my daddy's hand. He's a short, portly man with rosacea cheeks likely caused by sampling too much communion wine. His appearance is finished off with a mop of untidy white hair. It's strange seeing my daddy wearing a suit, but I guess him displaying the grand title of prez on his leather cut wouldn't impress The Almighty all that much. It sure wouldn't grant him a pass through those Pearly Gates no matter how much he threatened poor old St. Peter.

Everyone is already inside. Trepidation butterflies flutter through me. In less than twenty-four hours, my life has gone a full one-eighty.

Yesterday, Dylan belonged to someone else. Today, he's mine. And shortly, we'll be husband and wife.

We step into the church entrance, and the peace and tranquility of the place immediately washes over me and calms me down.

Sarah fixes my dress, gives me a vicelike hug and a kiss on the cheek, then makes her way inside.

"You look beautiful, Jessie."

I look up at my tall, blonde, handsome daddy and tears prick my eyes. It saddens me that he's not had any luck when it comes to love. A first wife who ran off with another man. A second who left because he hadn't gotten over the first. Maybe one day he'll find his happily ever after. I do hope so. I don't like to think of him getting old and spending his life alone.

"Thank you for letting me wear Mom's dress today, Daddy."

His own eyes mist over. He nods because he can't speak. I know he's thinking about her. About their wedding day. One day, I'll ask him what happened. Why she left.

And why she never came back.

Father Murphy motions his head to let us know it's time.

The old church organ bursts into life. Even with the occasional bum note, it's still clear it's the wedding march that's being played.

Taking my daddy's arm, we enter the church. Tears fill my eyes as I take in Dylan standing at the altar, waiting for me in all his handsome glory.

My shy, reserved nerdy boy has embraced what he is and reached his true Duster potential. Not that it matters to me. I loved him then. I love him now. I love every single kaleidoscopic part of that beautiful soul of his.

I was born loving him.

He's still wearing his black suit but now with an open-necked white shirt. Cill is wearing the same.

My eyes never leave his, and I watch as my big tough Irish mobster wipes away a tear. When we reach him, my daddy takes my hand and places it in his.

He's given me away. I'm no longer his to protect. I don't have to look to know he'll now be wiping away tears of his own.

The rest is a blur. Dylan and I repeat what we have to as we stare at each other.

His face his solemn. Unlike my siblings and me, I know he embraces his religion. Moving forward, I'll have to change. For

Dylan as it's important to him, but also for our children, as it's important to both our families.

He kisses me almost chastely, most likely because we're under the watchful eye of my daddy. I know then we must have reached the 'you may kiss the bride' part which can only mean one thing. That I am now Mrs. Dylan O'Connell.

Jessie O'Connell.

I'm conscious my hand is being held firmly in his. He's looking after me. Guiding me. Caring for me. Loving me. As he will always.

Because I am his for life. And I know that Irishmen take that commitment extremely seriously. I know family means everything to them.

Ace pulls me in for a hug having live-streamed the whole thing to Jaine. He wipes away a tear, no doubt as today has reminded him of when Jaine and he took their own vows.

I squeeze his hand. "Thank you, Ace. Without you. Without Jaine…" I can't speak after that, and neither can he, so he just pulls me in for another crushing hug.

"Jessie, it's time to go," Dyl interrupts as he jangles the keys to the cage in my face.

I turn to look at him, and he smirks darkly.

Well, there's no need to ask what's on his mind.

CHAPTER SIXTY-SEVEN

DYLAN

Motel, Colton, Nevada

"What are you doing?"

"Carrying my wife over the threshold."

"It's a motel room."

"It has a door. It has a threshold. It's traditional."

"It's slumsville."

"Would you rather we spend our wedding night at your family home? That was the only other option available to us in this tiny little town. And would you really want your da hearing you scream like a scalded cat every time I fucked you? I reckon, even though we're now legally married, Lucifer would still try to see me off with a shotgun."

She snickers. She knows I'm right. Liam O'Brien could easily give old Fergal O'Connell a run for his money in the most insane Irishman stakes.

"Plus, this room holds memories, Mrs. O'Connell."

"True, Mr. O'Connell." She snickers again. No doubt, this time at being called by her new title.

Jessie O'Connell.

I place her feet on the floor. It's the same bedroom as before. The one where we washed off all the Colombian's blood in the shower. The one where we parted company thinking it would be for the last time. And now here we are. Man and wife.

"Strip."

She arches an eyebrow at me, watching as I quickly discard my own clothes.

"Unless you want me to rip that dress off to access those hidden delights underneath, I suggest you strip."

"You wouldn't dare! This is my mom's wedding dress." She pretends to look horrified but she's anything but.

"I don't care whose dress it is. Get it off. Now."

"Are you telling me what to do?" The small smile playing on her lips tells me Jessie O'Connell's enjoying being told exactly what to do by her new husband.

"That's precisely what I'm doing, wife. Clothes off, now."

Unlike her, I'm now naked, and my dick is hard as fuck and raring to go. I start stroking myself as I wait, rubbing the pre-cum around the tip. She watches and licks her lips.

I smirk. "You like watching me fuck my hand, Jessie?"

She nods as she slowly removes her dress. She's engrossed, her eyes never leaving the visual of me fisting my cock.

"Given that it's been so long I'd last all of five minutes, I'll give you a choice. Do you want me to fuck my hand or your mouth before I sink my cock into that little pussy of yours?"

"Your hand." No hesitation. She's clearly aroused watching me as her pink nipples are standing to attention, and it's far from cold in here.

Who am I to decline? Let's be honest, I'm a pro at jerking myself off.

"So, you want to watch me come, Jessie? Like this?" I stroke my length. She nods and parts her lips. It's also clear she wants my dick in her mouth.

Having stripped off, she walks across to stand in front of me before sinking to her knees on the threadbare carpet directly in front of my leaking cock.

I'm panting now, stroking harder and faster, my hand sliding effortlessly up and down my slick shaft.

I want to see my seed all over her face and all over those perky tits. I want to shoot my load all over her cupid bow lips, then watch as it drips down her chin. I want her to swallow my cum and then rub the rest into her skin.

I want her to smell of me.

"Open your mouth."

She does as she's told, and just the sight of that little pink tongue poking out to catch my seed seals the deal for me.

Hot ropes of cum hit her tongue, face, and tits, the intensity of my release causing my legs to almost give way.

"Fuck." I grunt as she leans forward and sucks my still pulsing, cum-covered dick into that hot vacuum of a mouth of hers while squeezing my balls and shaft at the same time.

When she's sure she's licked up every last drop, she proceeds to rub the rest into her skin. I pull her to her feet, my mouth instantly connecting with hers, my tongue thrusting deep to taste myself on hers.

Eventually, I let her up for air.

"Now, get on that bed and stick that little arse of yours in the air for your husband."

I grin as she does just that.

I've been awake for almost twenty-four hours. But fuck it. Who needs sleep anyway?

I SWEAR IT'S HER FAVORITE PLACE IN THE WORLD TO BE. PINNED underneath me so she can't move an inch. And now, as well as wearing my cum on her skin, her little pink pussy is filled with it.

It's mine. She's mine. A possessive fecker? Where she's concerned?

Always.

I lie there contentedly as she gently strokes her fingers up and down my bare back.

"You haven't told me you love me yet." I know she does, but I want to hear it.

"Haven't I?" She turns her face toward me, and I lift my head from the crook of her neck and smile down at her.

"Nope."

And then she does something I never thought I'd see. She blushes.

"I love you." She says it quietly.

"Sorry, I didn't quite hear that."

"I said, I love you, Dylan O'Connell."

"There's no need to shout."

She chuckles. "Asshole."

"An asshole who loves you."

Closing my eyes, I press my nose against her neck and inhale deeply. She smells of me. I like my smell mixed with hers. It's the best smell in the fucking world.

"Jaine's asked us to visit her in Rising while we're here." She yawns. It's clear she's struggling to stay awake now.

"I'd like that." Then my curiosity gets the better of me. "I know you can't tell me who she's meeting, but can you at least tell me where she was headed?"

"I'm not sure I'm allowed to tell you that either." She frowns.

I laugh softly. "What am I going to do? I'm in the middle of nowhere in Nevada."

"True."

There's a pause.

"She's in Manhattan."

My ears immediately prick up. "But she's not due back there yet."

"It was a client meeting. Apparently, she had no option but to attend. She's kept it very covert, so only me, Cherry, and Ace know about it. Well, aside from the people she's meeting, that is."

"And you can't tell me who they are?"

"Nope. I've been sworn to secrecy."

"Can you at least tell me where they're meeting?"

"The Palace."

My tiredness evaporates, and I immediately lift my head.

"Shite."

CHAPTER SIXTY-EIGHT

JAINE

Private Dining Room, Palace Hotel, Manhattan

THIS PLACE IS DRIPPING WITH MONEY.

Old money. New money. Legal money. Illegal money.

I'm not poor by any means. In fact, I'm probably wealthier than most of the clientele who frequent this establishment. But it's way too rich for my biker blood. It's one of those flashy places that pretentious people wine and dine each other in so they can flaunt whatever they've come here to flaunt while talking about themselves and talking over each other. It's no wonder Eoin wanted me to meet him and his folks here.

It's right up his self-absorbed street.

What's also clear is that this place is discrete. There's no waiting staff hanging around. You have to call for them if you need them. Money will buy everything and anything here, including silence. You could probably get away with murder within these four walls.

That's if you were willing to toss enough Benjamin Franklins into the mix to make it worth their while cleaning up the mess and keeping schtum.

I glance at the gold, cream, and crystal décor before placing my small bag on the gilded table that's been set at my side. It's a bit extreme, but I guess they have to make you feel like you're getting enough bang for your buck. Anything on the menu in this place will be three figures minimum.

Anything off it will be way more.

I lean back in my chair as I wait for Leo and his associate. Even though it's a fleeting visit, it still feels good to be back in Manhattan.

I've missed it. The city that forms part of who I am. The city that birthed The Exterminator and raised the sniper in its concrete arms. My phone vibrates, and I smile at the message.

Ace: *Have I told you lately that I love you?*

Jaine: *Have I told you there's no one else above you?*

Ace: *Maybe we can have it as our second song.*

Jaine: *What? So, I'm being promoted? I'm no longer a creep or a weirdo?*

Ace: *You'll always be my creep and my weirdo, same as you all always be my plain Jaine Jones.*

Jaine: *And you'll always be my beautiful poker-cheating Jason Steele. I love you too, Ace.*

Ace: *Does it feel good being back in Manhattan?*

Jaine: *It does. I want to share this city with you one day, Ace. I want you to see it for yourself. I want you to feel it in your soul like I do.*

Ace: *I'm a small-town boy, PJ. I always will be. You know that.*

Jaine: *I know.*

Ace: *But maybe next time I'll come with you. See those big city lights for myself. See what makes the other side of my wife tick.*

Tears prick my eyes. I know he'd be quite happy never to set foot in New York. It's just another selfless thing he's offering to do because he knows it will make me happy. I can't even visualize Ace here. When I think of him, all I see is Rising.

All I see is home.

Jaine: *I'd like that, Ace.*
Ace: *You paused. Have you gotten emotional?*
Jaine: *Story of my life these days.*
Ace: *You're starting to sound like Jessie. Speaking of the O'Briens, I should go. I'm holding up my poker game with Lucifer.*
Jaine: *Don't go removing those Aces from the pack now.*

I snicker to myself as my memories take me back to that day. The day he earned his road name.

Ace: *I won't. I love you, PJ.*
Jaine: *I love you too, Ace. I'll see you tomorrow.*
Ace: *I'll be waiting right here, sweetheart.*

Switching off my phone, I place it back in my bag.

"So, let me get this straight. The Ruoccos are parting company with the Sicilian mafia?"

We're speaking in Italian. It's safer that way and just as easy. I take in Leo as I wait for him to respond. He hasn't changed much in all the years we've worked together. A few more lines. A few grey hairs.

Still handsome. Still intelligent. Still charming.

And having done a comprehensive check on him only yesterday, something I've no doubt he's fully aware of, he's still quite the ladies' man. That's if the images captured of his recent movements are anything to go by.

It will definitely take a special sort of female to tame this bad boy and capture that Sicilian heart of his, that's for sure.

Piercing blue eyes sparkle against olive skin. His black hair is longer these days, and he's taken to wearing it tied back at the nape of his neck. I'm not sure I like it in that style as it's reminiscent of how Luciano wears his.

"Yes. But that is not common knowledge, so it goes no further than this room, please. It's also not something Gio and I can discuss with you in any great level of detail. At least, not yet. You understand, I'm sure, that our hands are tied for now. When it is announced to the outside world, their departure will be explained as being a mutual decision."

"But it's not?"

"Not exactly."

"And you can't tell me why?"

"Not yet."

"Okay. Well, I'm only willing to discuss this further, Leo, as you and I have known each other a long time."

"I appreciate that, Jaine."

"So, what do you want from me? You're already a private client. And why the need for me to come to New York when I'm due to return in a couple of months? Couldn't it have waited?" I raise an eyebrow at him

Leo makes eye contact with Gio, which causes me to also

glance at him. Giovanni Antico. Today's the first time I've met him. He's Leoluca's trusted right-hand man and has been for several years. Having run a search on him, he's clean, but I now know he's older than Leo. Forty-five to his thirty-six. That he's married to Isabella. And they have twin boys aged sixteen.

"I will be taking over the role of Don, Jaine. But, again, this is not something that is common knowledge at this time."

"So, Luciano and Sophia don't know?"

"It has not been formally announced although they suspect it is on the cards. That is the reason I wanted to explain all of this face to face. Due to the confidentiality of the situation."

"Thank you, Leo, but that still doesn't explain why I'm here."

"Because I wanted to ask if you would consider representing the Cosa Nostra once I am in position. You and I work well together. As importantly, we understand how each other works. But most importantly, I trust you implicitly."

It's what I half-expected him to ask. And after the recent spate of head-hunting, both JAL and JAA are more than equipped to cater to this request. I have one concern, which I decide to air out loud.

"As you know, there is some ill-feeling between the Ruoccos and me. It's my fault entirely. I said something to Sophia that she, quite understandably, took offense to at the time. It's something that should never have been said. In hindsight, I realized how disrespectful it was of me."

I'm referring to my saying I only hope Padraig grows to love her as much as he did me. From what I'm hearing on the Manhattan outlaw grapevine, she's still up in arms about it. It was an extremely foolish thing to say. I'm well aware I've stirred a Sicilian hornet's nest as a result, as Sophia and her elder brother have neither forgiven nor forgotten my comment.

"About her Duster fiancé? Yes, I am aware of what was said and, of course, of her and Luc's adverse reaction."

"With that in mind, I'm not sure how they would feel about me becoming involved with your organization."

"Their feelings are of no consequence, Jaine. They will be gone by the time I am in place, and by the time you are on board. We would expect their removal from the organization to take place over the next few months."

"That quickly?"

"That quickly."

My ears prick up. "And are they aware these changes are afoot?"

Leo smiles. "Yes and no."

"So, a coup in part?"

"Yes."

"What will they do?"

"We believe it's their intention to set up their own alternative mafia organization. That they may indeed have already done so."

My thoughts immediately drift to the Dusters. To Padraig. They think they're marrying him off to ally with the Sicilian mafia. They are, but it may well be the shortest alliance in history going by what's come to light during this conversation. They'll now also be allying with a new, and as yet unknown, organization.

We leave it there and make small talk while enjoying our meal. I'm fully aware Leo is affording me that time to digest what's been discussed. While not a snap decision, he'll expect an answer to his offer before we part company this evening. He'll want his inner circle in place before he assumes the position of Don.

Placing my cutlery down, I take a sip of water before I speak.

"Thank you for explaining your situation, Leo. I'm pleased to advise both JAL and JAA will be more than happy to represent the Cosa Nostra moving forward and once you are in place as the new Don."

Business discussions over, I take my phone from my bag. I've had six missed calls from Jessie. What the hell is going on?

"Please excuse me, Leo. I have to make a call."

He smiles at me like the cat who's got the cream. He's got what he wanted. That my working for him personally will now spill into our working side by side for his outlaw organization.

"Of course, Jaine. We will afford you some privacy and join you in a few moments."

I leave the room and stand in the foyer, taking in walls covered in gold flock paper adorned by ostentatious wall sconces. Vulgar and then some. Like most of the people who frequent this establishment.

I dial Jessie's number, but she doesn't answer.

It's then I hear voices, one of which I know extremely well.

My blood immediately starts to boil. Well, what are the chances?

Spinning around, I take in Eoin O'Connell as he stands there in a dark grey suit with a white open-necked shirt. He looks exactly the same as he did the last time I saw him in the flesh, which was when Sarah and Cill got married. Aside from a few more lines from living in the life, he's still GQ model-like handsome and still wearing that annoying, arrogant expression of his.

My nemesis. And the man whose life I will make a living hell at every possible opportunity when I return to New York.

"Jaine."

"Eoin."

I'm sure my expression shows my loathing. I make no attempt to disguise it. I frown inwardly. Isn't he surprised to see me in Manhattan? He doesn't look it. Did he know I'd be here?

My attention switches to the women on either side of him.

Sophia Ruocco, which seems a bit of a coincidence given who I'm meeting. I'm guessing the other is Molly McGrath. She even looks Irish with her pale skin, ice-blue eyes, and long black hair.

Both women scowl at me.

It's then I hear *him.*

"Eoin, our Dylan's been trying to contact you. He says it's urg…."

Time stands still as my gaze connects with eyes of piercing blue. Eyes that are identical to my son's.

I can't speak. I can't move. I can't breathe. I can't do anything but stare.

At him.

"Irish." It's a whisper on my lips as a thousand and one memories I thought I'd lost forever come rushing back all at once and hit me like a tsunami.

"Jaine." My trance is broken. I look up at Leo, who's come to join me in the foyer. He frowns when he sees Sophia, who's immediately gone on a call. As has Eoin.

"Your phone, Jaine."

I catch Molly's gaze. She smirks at me almost knowingly.

"Jessie?" I answer.

"Jaine, you need to get to Rising right now."

She's crying. Why is she crying?

"Jessie, what's going on?"

"It's Ace."

Author's Note

I hope you enjoyed Dylan's story.

DIRTY DYLAN is NOT standalone.
DIRTY DYLAN is BOOK 4 of a SERIES, which contains an ONGOING STORYLINE that CONCLUDES in BOOK 6, DIRTY PADRAIG.

These books contain MULTIPLE POVs from characters across the entire series.

Due to the nature of the CONTINUING STORYLINE, these books MUST be
READ IN ORDER.

The Outlaw Chess Reading Order

ACE

DIRTY CILLIAN

RAZR

DIRTY DYLAN

DIRTY EOIN

DIRTY PADRAIG

These books are NOT standalone.

Due to the nature of the CONTINUING STORYLINE

PLEASE READ IN ORDER.

Acknowledgements

For Bodhi.

About the Author

Harley Diamond is a writer of romance novels with plot twists that will leave you begging for more. In every dirty story, an angsty bad boy and a badass queen lead the cast.

When Harley's not reading, she's writing. When not doing either, she's plotting to unleash her next novel on you from her non-working farm in West Yorkshire, England, surrounded by her faithful but very needy companions. Her seven rescue dogs.

Facebook Group: Harley's Hangout
Facebook Group: Harley's Spoilers

www.harleydiamond.com

Printed in Great Britain
by Amazon

60266917R00258